PACIFICA

TOR BOOKS BY
KRISTEN SIMMONS

KRISTEN SIMMONS

PACIFICA

TOR TEEN

A TOM DOHERTY ASSOCIATES BOOK
NEW YORK

PACIFICA

Copyright © 2018 by Kristen Simmons

A Tor Teen Book
Published by Tom Doherty Associates
175 Fifth Avenue
New York, NY 10010

www.tor-forge.com

Tor® is a registered trademark of Macmillan Publishing Group, LLC.

The Library of Congress Cataloging-in-Publication Data is available upon request.

ISBN 978-0-7653-3663-7 (hardcover)
ISBN 978-1-4668-2880-3 (ebook)

Our books may be purchased in bulk for promotional, educational, or
business use. Please contact your local bookseller or the Macmillan
Corporate and Premium Sales Department at 1-800-221-7945, extension
5442, or by email at MacmillanSpecialMarkets@macmillan.com.

First Edition: March 2018

Printed in the United States of America

0 9 8 7 6 5 4 3 2 1

FOR THE WOMEN WHO TAUGHT ME TO BE STRONG:

MY GREAT-GRANDMA,
HARU,

MY GRANDMA,
MURIEL CHIYO,

AND MY MOM,
ANN KIYO

AUTHOR'S NOTE

This story is personal, not just because the characters have lived so long in my mind, but because their world is rooted in my history. Their adventures are framed by my interpretation of the stories passed down to me through the generations. In that way, *Pacifica* does not begin with an exiled pirate girl, a relocated Shoreling, and the son of the president, but with my great-grandmother.

This is a story that begins in World War II, and like Marin, Ross, and Adam's story, it's about relocation, only then it was called internment.

Its start is marked on December 7, 1941, when the Japanese bombed Pearl Harbor, killing over two thousand Americans. During that time, 160,000 people in Hawaii were Japanese—either born in Japan (*issei*) or the first generation born in the United States (*nisei*)—and made up 37 percent of the population. They worked for the sugar and pineapple industries, or as fishermen, in the lumber yards, or in restaurants or schools. Most lived a blended culture—Japanese and American drawn into one. Despite this, racial tension had existed for some time (exclusion acts had been passed since the 1800s attempting to stop the influx of Asian immigrants), and when World War II began, racial prejudice combined with the hysteria of war to create a dangerous situation.

A few months after the bombing of Pearl Harbor, in February 1942, President Franklin D. Roosevelt signed Executive Order 9066, declaring military zones in the United States where certain people could be excluded based on their perceived threat to security. These zones included much of the West Coast (California, Oregon, and Washington). It called for the forced removal and imprisonment of "all persons of Japanese ancestry both alien and non-alien," including both Japanese nationals and their children. Information on where Japanese could be found was given to the military by the U.S. Census Bureau, something that was not proven for almost sixty years. Those not interned fled, or were forced to observe curfews. Many lost their jobs, and were called "yellow japs" or "bananas" (yellow on the outside, white on the inside) by those they'd considered friends. The executive order came after hundreds of issei community leaders had already been incarcerated in Hawaii—my great-grandmother included.

Haru Tanaka had raised her American-born children in Hawaii, and was there on the Sunday morning when Pearl Harbor was bombed. She watched the planes painted with the Rising Sun fly overhead, thinking they were part of the American military's training exercises. It was not until one fell from the sky into a nearby house, and shouts of "*Senso* [war]!" rang out, that she knew it was real. She worried for her daughter—my grandma—going to an art college in Tokyo, and for her son in Honolulu. She didn't have a chance to tell them where she was going before the FBI showed up at her house that afternoon, moving her at gunpoint to an immigration station in Honolulu. Later, she would find out she had been watched by the government for years because she held a prominent position in the community—as principal of a school that taught Japanese language and martial arts to children. She'd taken over the position when her husband had died, years earlier.

She was held at that center for two months for her own "safety," without a change of clothes, before being moved to a camp on Sand Island in Hawaii, and then to a girls' reform school, converted to an internment center, in Dallas, Texas. She had no contact with the outside world or her children, and no idea what would come. For a year, she lived in that dusty climate, with scorpions and snakes, until she was finally moved to an internment camp in Crystal City, Texas. There, she lived on food rationing, seasoning rice with leftover coffee grounds and traded packets of sugar to make a kind of teriyaki. She received censored letters from her children, and bathed under supervision. She completed loyalty questionnaires, assessing her dedication to the United States. She began teaching art classes to teens, and Japanese to the nisei who had never learned it, so that they could be prepared when they were sent to Japan through a war exchange program.

She survived. And four months after the war ended, she returned home to find her house confiscated and the school where she'd worked sold, her son serving in the U.S. Army, and her daughter's citizenship revoked, making her unable to come home from Tokyo.

Nevertheless, she persisted.

She rebuilt her life in Hawaii, and was one of the first of the 120,313 internees from 1941 to 1946 to receive reparations from the government for her time in the camp (she donated it to charity). She returned to teaching. She practiced kendo and other martial arts. Haru lived alone until she was ninety-seven years old, and passed away surrounded by family at the age of 102. She lived the kind of life you write stories about.

In *Pacifica*, my great-grandma's experiences are reflected in the world Adam, Ross, and Marin live in. The relocation of the Shorelings was inspired by the internment of the Japanese, moved for their "safety" and others, to a new place, a Pacifica of sorts. A prison without any communication with the outside world. Adam, like the other Shorelings, lives with prejudice not unlike that my family faced. He was taken because of the way he looked and dressed, a product of the madness that comes from fear, and the dangers of racial profiling. The Shorelings line up outside the relocation centers, where certain eligible people are identified, just as those in our world were brought to internment and immigration centers. I have to think that some people, like Hiro in *Pacifica*, trusted the government, and believed they actually would be safer somewhere else. I imagine that trust was short-lived.

Like my grandma and great-uncle, Ross goes in search of his chosen family, Adam, finding the path more twisted and the obstacles more difficult to overcome with every step. Like Marin, my great-grandmother found herself exiled from her people, making "tar" the way the internees assembled traditional meals from scraps and traded spices like faux teriyaki as currency. Like my grandma, Marin finds herself without citizenship, or home, when she returns to the island, and faces a dilemma so many Japanese must have encountered: align themselves with their people—her own brother, in Marin's case—or turn against them, hope for something better in land that has already proven less than welcoming.

My great-grandmother once told a reporter, "Japanese do not show tears outwardly," when asked about her time in the camp. Though I have heard no accounts of riots like those in Lower Noram, those scenes became my outward expression of the grief she must have felt being forcibly removed from her home and family. The setting of this story—a world post–polar ice cap melt—is also meant to represent the world Haru faced. A world where people were thrown together, where cultures clashed, where leaders like Píero and Ross's father were ever prepared for war because of the inherent distrust that comes when so much is taken away. A world where the very ground beneath their feet had grown unsteady. It's also a pull to the future, though. A combined projection from professional research and interviews with the EPA (before 2017) describing a world profoundly affected by climate change. Had I been removed from everything I loved, I imagine I would see the world as Ross, Marin, and Adam do, shaken by quakes and storms, and physically falling to ruin.

It is my hope, however, that the world doesn't come to this, and that we learn from my great-grandmother's story. That we choose love when hate is the most accessible option. That when we lose everything, we still hold on to what we know, and teach it to others. That we survive together—an Alliance, not a division.

ADDITIONAL READING

Ishimoto-Morris, Mary. "Five Books on the Japanese American Internment." *Washington Post*, June 4, 2009.

Ishizuka, Karen. *Lost & Found: Reclaiming the Japanese American Incarceration.* Chicago: University of Illinois Press, 2006.

Kaizawa-Knaefler, Tomi. *Our House Divided: Seven Japanese American Families in World War II.* Honolulu: University of Hawaii Press, 1991.

Takemoto, Paul. *Nisei Memories.* Seattle: University of Washington Press, 2006.

PACIFICA

WHEN MARIN was twelve years old, her father told her two things. The first was that there were two kinds of people in this world: ones that stabbed you in the chest, and ones that stabbed you in the back. She'd thought this was some kind of riddle, and asked about the ones who stabbed you in the side, or even the leg. Surely there was a third category for people who aimed for your foot.

He'd laughed, a deep, proud sound she'd remember until the day she died, and told her the second thing—that there was no way around it. His little girl was a *corsario*. A pirate. Just like him.

She'd seen the truth in his blue eyes. Seen the open seas and the skies, built from the stories he'd whispered as she fell asleep at night. It was what she'd wanted all her life—to sail the ocean chasing adventure, a feather in his wing—and in that moment, her wish had been granted.

Then he'd placed a knife in her hand, a hooked silver blade with a gritty bone handle, turned, and pushed three men, bound and gagged, over the side of a boat.

CHAPTER 2

"Mr. Torres, how good to see you."

Ross returned a warm smile to the secretary of trade, a recent addition to his father's cabinet following the disastrous demise of the last one. Ross couldn't remember the details, but there was something about an only partially accounted for rail shipment from one of the farming districts and a mistress from some companionship service in Lower Noram. His mother had hugged the man's wife and told her it would blow over soon, and then spent the next four days on the comm telling anyone who would listen about the "scandal of the century."

"Likewise," said Ross. "I hope your family's settling into your new home."

"They are, thank you." The man ran a hand over his smooth, almost shiny jaw, clearly contemplating his next words. People often thought they needed to watch what they said in front of Ross. The truth was it didn't matter. His dad didn't listen to him anyway.

"So," said the secretary. "Only six days left until relocation. You must be so proud of your father's hard work."

George Torres' Relocation Act—a five-years-in-the-making *opportunity,* as his dad called it, for five hundred Noram citizens to start fresh on a man-made, secret island near the Alliance seaboard—was the point of tonight's gathering. The lottery for who would be chosen to go in the first wave was to take place within the hour.

"Absolutely," said Ross. He was used to this kind of small talk. Since his father had started in politics when Ross was five, he'd been coached on the right things to say. The Moderate Party lines his father touted—*Alliance citizens work hard to stand strong,* and *support self-sufficiency, individually and worldwide*—were all part of his vocabulary, though he maintained only a surface knowledge of their meaning.

His eyes roamed around the room. At ten stories, the Natural History Museum was one of the tallest buildings east of the jagged cliff that split the Alliance's capital city, Noram. It was a lightning rod for the superstorms that invaded the area for weeks at a time, a natural power generator whose electric ran on the energy it gathered from the clouds. The very idea of standing within it gave Ross the creeps.

He didn't like storms. Never had.

"It's unusual to find a leader so invested in the welfare of his people," said the secretary.

Ross thought he caught a hint of sarcasm in the man's voice, but it was hidden by a smile. Before he was forced to think of a shallow-but-clever answer, the lights dimmed. On the opposite side of the room, in front of a glass staircase leading to the second level, a screen lowered, drawing the attention of half the room.

"Ah, here it is now," said the secretary, grabbing a flute of champagne from a server passing by.

A woman's voice came through the speakers. "For too long our people have suffered, plagued by overcrowding, disease, and lack of work."

A view of the old hospital, recently converted to a relocation center, filled the screen. Men and women stood in a line that rounded the block, carrying application packets for the clerks sitting behind tables. It was a staged image, of course. The relocation center was the meeting point for those who objected to relocation, and rioted nightly in Lower Noram. This picture only really worked if the people in line were holding baseball bats and screaming at the police.

"We have only just survived for too long. Now we must take the next step and thrive."

The final image of the ad was of the island, oval in shape, blanketed by green, surrounded by blue. Not like Noram, where, unless it was storming, the skies were perpetually beige and hazy. The camera focused on a house with a cozy living area, already decorated with a two-seater couch and a painting hanging on the wall.

He didn't see what people were complaining about. Last he checked, a place like this was a step up from most of the slums below the cliffline.

"Pacifica," said the woman's voice. "A new beginning." A quick male voice followed up with, "Paid for by the Relocation Act. Relocation: a new beginning."

The lights came back on as a woman took the podium beside the screen, offering a welcome only acknowledged by half the people in the room.

"Excuse me," said Ross, waving at some invisible person in the corner before the secretary could ask him anything else. "It was good seeing you, sir."

Dressed in a new suit made of cool, synthetic material, he fitted his broad shoulders through the small clusters of men and women in formal attire, making his way toward the glass staircase in the center of the room. There, the buffet was fully stocked with bite-sized hors d'oeuvres, but he wasn't hungry. He'd been to three events this week alone to celebrate his father's Relocation Act. They were all starting to blend together.

There was a sameness here, as if everyone had been created by an identical mold. Men in black suits joking about politics, women in shiny dresses with too much makeup. Everyone made the same dull small talk and pried for the same gossip. It never changed.

"Try to contain your excitement," came a wry voice from beside him. "You're causing a scene." Ross turned to see Adam Baker, the vice president's son, reaching for a tomapple—a hearty apple-tomato hybrid, the newest creation from Noram's farming labs according to the overenthusiastic girl doing the serving.

Ross's mood lifted. He painted a painfully wide smile on his face. "Mr. Baker! Delightful to see you. Positively stellar suit, young man. What is it? Recycled plastic?" He brushed the non-existent dust off of Adam's shoulder, noticing the red flower above his chest pocket. Most people here tonight were wearing them—they must have been significant to the Relocation Act somehow.

"Pancake, actually," said Adam, bringing out the bass in his voice. "It's a bit crumbly, but completely biodegradable. And if you get hungry, you can just take a bite right off the arm."

Ross laughed overenthusiastically, then tilted his head forward.

"If we don't get out of here soon I'm going to bite off my own arm. I will literally chew it off."

The gleam faded from Adam's eyes. He turned his gaze to the plate of food, small samples balanced carefully one atop another. "Come on. It's not so bad."

Ross picked up a tomapple, eyeing it suspiciously. Next to Adam, he was tall, almost a head taller, and broader through the shoulders. Despite his family's Latino ancestry, his skin was paler than Adam's had ever been, like the others above the cliff who spent most of their time sheltered from the sun's harmful, cloud-piercing rays. He was built like his father: slim, but with enough presence to demand attention. His eyes were cobalt blue, his hair dark brown and forever sticking out sideways like he'd just rolled out of bed. It was a combination that made him adorable to grand-mothers, inappropriately intriguing to his mom's friends, and ir-resistible to the girls at Center Academy.

"You don't ever get tired of it?" he asked.

"Of what?"

"This," said Ross, motioning to the room. "All of it. The bene-fits, and the campaigning, and the stupid school assignments." He took a bite of the tomapple and cringed at the mushy texture. After forcing himself to swallow, he balanced the rest of the fruit on Adam's full plate. "It's exhausting. Can't we just do something *not* boring for once?"

"I guess," said Adam, in a way that seemed to mean, *you're intolerable.*

Ross turned slowly, surveying the room again, noting the security guards who stood like statues by the exits and windows, and Adam's parents, polished, but still noticeably different with their less formal attire and their tan skin. They seemed to be the only political pair not swamped by a circle of donors dying to have their voices heard, which could have had something to do with Adam's father's set scowl, and the way his mother kept shaking her head disapprovingly.

"At least your parents are having a good time," Ross said.

"Oh, they're thrilled," Adam grumbled.

Adam's dad was staunchly opposed to the Relocation Act and had been from its inception, five years prior. It was part of his *Progressive Party mentality,* according to Ross's father. Noah Baker thought it was unethical to uproot people from their homes when those people were poor and hungry—the desperate didn't make sound decisions. Ross supposed if the Shorelings, as they were sometimes called because of their proximity to the water, just got jobs like his dad sometimes let slip, they wouldn't be so desperate.

Noah supported what he called *revitalization,* not relocation—rebuilding the docks rather than sending away the occupants. It's what the protesters, who claimed relocation was just a way for the government to kick out the poor, yelled and screamed about each night at the old hospital below the cliffline. It was a huge point of contention between their fathers.

Adam, having finished his tomapple, picked up Ross's and took a bite. "This morning Dad said there were riots as far up as the Oregon Coast last night. They had to call in the Armament."

"Nobody that far north can even apply to go to Pacifica," said Ross.

Adam scoffed. "That doesn't mean they don't think it's wrong. People all over are protesting. Launch is only six days away. It's only going to get worse until then."

Ross hoped so. Maybe the Shorelings would light something else on fire tonight. *That* would be neat.

"We should go see it," he said.

"See what?"

"The riots," said Ross. Before the words were even out the idea had taken hold, rooting itself in his brain. He'd seen the people gathering at the old hospital on the news. The fights and fires. The chants they yelled at the cliff, hoping someone—his father maybe—would hear.

It would be a hell of a lot more exciting than this.

"No," said Adam, seeing the change on Ross's face. "No. Forget it. We'd be crazy to go down there. The place is practically a war zone. *Especially* after dark."

"Well, that's very dramatic." Ross rubbed his hands together, his wild eyes reflected in Adam's wary gaze. "You know the broadcasts make it seem worse than it is. That's how they get people watching." He ignored Adam, who was now shaking his head vehemently. "We'll keep a healthy distance from anything even remotely dangerous. I would go alone, but I've never been to the docks before. If I got lost . . . who knows what might happen to me."

"I know," said Adam. "I know exactly what might happen to you."

Ross slung an arm over his friend's narrow shoulders, causing Adam to almost lose his hold on the plate. "You know you want to see it."

Adam didn't look up at him as he shrugged out of his embrace. After a moment, he swore again.

Ross slapped him on the back. "That's the spirit."

He was caught in the gaze of a woman with silvery-white hair, cut in a straight line across her forehead. Her dress was black, conservative, and adorned with a semi-ridiculous bow on her right shoulder. At the sight of her, Ross felt a familiar mixture of warmth and dread.

She motioned him over.

"Coat closet, twenty minutes," said Ross quietly. "It has a street exit."

Adam nodded gravely and stuffed another appetizer in his mouth.

CHAPTER 3

MARIN PICKED her way through the debris and slush that lined the shore of Donner Cove's abandoned northeast rim. The night air was thick and heavy, and sweat soaked straight through her threadbare sleeveless shirt. One arm remained bent behind her, supporting the bottom of a canvas pack filled with six jars of sloshing black liquid.

With heavy steps, she climbed the sandy bank, wading through the heaps of *gomi*—plastic and metal trash that had washed up on land. It scraped the ankles of her taped-up boots, finally thinning as she reached the steep road that would take her above the cove. Boarded-up shops and small houses ran the length, some built straight into the alabaster rock, some sitting atop it, plaster fronts cracked from the pressure to not slide down into the water below. A few of the windows were dimly lit by flickering candle flames. Wariness of who might wait inside had Marin gripping the handle of her knife with her free hand and keeping out of the muted glow of the moon.

Her eyes turned to the sky, peering through the film of smog that clung to the harbor around Sacramento Bay. It was the final brink before the stormy season. She could almost feel the thunder gathering on the horizon, prickling the back of her neck with warning. The summer had been long and dry, but that time was ending. Soon the rain would start, just a sprinkling at first, but tinged with enough acid to scratch her skin. The growl of the clouds would follow, like the starving rumblings of a giant's stomach. Lightning would whip the skies, striking again and again, until one storm smashed into the next with no reprieve between them. By Christmas, even the night would be bright as day.

Her life used to depend on reading the sky's moods. Now, it was merely a habit.

Her thighs burned as she climbed the hill. The sounds of the slums grew louder as she approached the line where the electric started, and soon the haze grew brighter, and yellow, and gave way to blinking advertisements for drinks and dancers and gambling and every imaginable kind of kink.

Noram City, the great metropolis of the Western Seaboard. The capital of the Alliance.

Once, this had been a place she'd visited with her father, a trading port for supplies for her people. A dangerous place, divided in half by a jagged cliff that separated the poor Shorelings who lived on the waterline from the rich who lived above. Five years had passed since she'd come here to stay, and now her feet knew the steps by heart. Left turn at the bar. A right at the restaurant with the skinned cats in the front window. The way became crowded and hot, and it smelled like fry grease and rotten things. On every corner, people begged for food, more than a few of them kids, with empty cups stretched out before them. She passed a boy she recognized from the library playing some kind of electric fiddle, and watched while a little girl half his age made her way around the circle behind him, picking one pocket after another.

They stood in front of a tattered poster of a tropical island surrounded by blue water. In the corner of the screen a Shoreling family waved, looking happier than she'd ever seen anyone ever look. There was an electronic countdown over their heads that said "6 Days to Relocation," but someone had painted over the last word so that it said "revolution" instead.

Before she could pass by, there was a loud *clang*, and the power on the entire block shut off. The lights of the countdown went dim as the dingy streets were bathed in shadows. A collective groan rose from those around her.

"Not again," a woman said behind her. Despite the dark, Marin automatically combed her short, knotted curls behind her ear with her fingers to hide the black "86" tattoo on the side of her neck.

"How long you think *this* one's going to last?" came a sarcastic answer. "Think the kanshu are dark too?"

Marin smirked at the term. According to Gloria, the wealthy above the cliffline had been called *kanshu*, or jailers, since the malaria outbreak. It was an old joke. Something about the people who made the vaccine keeping it under lock and key.

"Course not," said the woman. "There's no erosion up there. It's just Lower Noram that's falling to shit."

Bitter laughter rose around her. The blackouts were becoming more frequent. The fuel shortages were taking their toll. The kanshu liked to blame this on the overpopulation beneath the lower part of the capital, that the land wasn't strong enough to hold everyone anymore, but most of the Shorelings she knew didn't buy that answer. More likely, the kanshu were just hogging all the power for themselves.

Keeping her head down, Marin made her way to an old stone library, and padded down the steps to where a guard stood outside, fiddling with a handheld electric game. The woman was as wide as the door, and at least a foot taller than Marin. A faint pink rash surrounded her mouth. Acid burns, from too much unfiltered water.

"You're back," the woman grunted, tucking the device in her pocket.

Marin adjusted the straps on her pack, and the heavy glass jars clinked together.

"Miss me, Frankie?" Her voice was rough. She hadn't spoken much since she'd left, two days ago, and it made her more aware of her own thirst. Gloria better have some clean water left upstairs.

The woman smiled, revealing several missing teeth. "Not really."

"You're a terrible liar," Marin said. "You cried yourself to sleep every night. I could hear it all the way on the beach."

"Keep telling yourself that," said Frankie.

"I will." Marin stepped through the door Frankie opened to let her pass. "You beat my score yet?"

Three months ago Marin had found the game in the heaps of garbage—gomi, her people called it—that lined the shore. With spare wires and a new computer chip she'd taken from an old e-reader someone had traded for canned food, she'd restored it to life. Fixing things was more a habit than a hobby, and it kept her busy on the days she wasn't cooking down in the cove.

"Twice over," said Frankie with a grin.

Marin snorted. "She upstairs?"

"For now."

That cleared some of Marin's fatigue. Two days poking at a

fire, stirring a pot, and dozing on a broken lawn chair had come with a decent payoff. Gloria would be pleased.

The door closed behind her, leaving her in a dim foyer. She climbed the stairs to the right, knowing Gloria always took the high ground, keeping an eye out from the top-floor window. A few guards played cards on the stairs, giving her nods and calling out their hellos as she passed by. One of them reached out a hand, which she gave a short squeeze. He'd been security for Gloria since Marin had first come with her father, when she'd been seven. He'd never asked why she'd come back without him five years later.

Hushed voices came from above, and when she reached the third floor she found the glass doors already open. Inside, a dozen kids curled up on blankets on the floor, ranging in age from thumb-sucking to knife-wielding. Orphaned Shorelings, whose parents had been arrested in the nightly riots outside the relocation center. Dim lantern light stretched a yellow glow over them, a gentle blanket on a hot night.

"Marin!" A girl about six jumped up from the floor and raced toward her, jolting her from her memories. Her shirt was too big and her pants were too short, but her smile could rival a pirate's. "What'd you bring back this time?"

"Nothing for you, Lila." From around the supply racks came a woman with corn-silk hair, thin arms loaded with clean towels. Sylvie, one of Gloria's friends. Her northern accent was slightly different than the rough tone of the other Shorelings. Longer, gentler, even in scolding. Marin's mother's mother had been from the far north, and whenever she heard it, she felt that absence like a blade in her chest.

Lila pouted.

"Sit down," Sylvie said, pointing to the blankets with the toe of her shoe. "I told you, it's bedtime."

Before Lila could turn, Marin dug into her pocket, and pulled out a plastic figurine she'd found near the water. Most of the paint was gone, leaving the doll wax white, and a little misshapen from the heat, but Lila didn't seem to care.

"Whoa," she said, turning the toy in her fingers. "Gracias."

Marin nodded as Sylvie ushered the girl back to the blankets.

"There's more of them." Marin nodded to the horde as Sylvie passed.

The woman hummed a quiet agreement, tilting her head toward two young boys with tearstained cheeks and black, clipped hair. "They came last night. Tim and Sun Lu's boys. Said *la limpieza* got their parents coming home from the store."

Marin's mouth formed a tight line. She'd seen the Lus around. They weren't trouble. The City Patrol didn't seem to care, though; they swept up everything and everyone in their way, claiming they looked like threats to Noram's security. That was how they'd earned their name, la limpieza. The clean-up crew.

Kids whose parents didn't come home generally ended up at the library, where they stayed until their parents came back or Sylvie could find them another place.

So far no one's parents had come back.

"Tell us a story," called Lila. Marin narrowed her eyes at the girl, the bag still heavy on her shoulders.

"I've got to see Gloria," she said. "Another time."

"Please," whined Lila. The others took up the charge, sitting up and begging. Sylvie tried to hush them, but it was useless.

"The one about the whale," Lila called, grasping the doll tight in her right hand.

"The whale!" called another boy.

One of the Lu boys—the older one, who had a neat scar running down the center of his chin—muttered something Marin couldn't make out.

"What's that?" she asked. The other kids went quiet.

"I said there's no such thing as a whale." His gaze stayed pinned on his lap, where he picked at his thumbnail. "No one's seen one in fifty years."

She scoffed. "No one you know, maybe."

The boy peered up at her through long, dark lashes. She wondered how long he'd waited before he realized his parents weren't coming back. How hungry he must have become. How scared.

He was not the only one who had watched a parent disappear.

"My dad saw one once," she said. "Outside the California Islands."

The sea called to her from her memory, the slap of the waves against the hull of a ship. It brought an ache to her chest, a quiet longing that made the walls seem too close, and the ceiling too low.

She swallowed the feeling down.

Sylvie had set the towels on a rack of boxes and blankets, and moved to a cabinet beside the window, where she retrieved a glass jug, a purification filter fixed around the mouth. She poured half a cup and handed it to Marin, who nearly groaned as the liquid touched her lips.

"What was he doing out there?" asked the boy. "Fishing?"

Nothing edible swam in those dirty waters; everyone knew that. You had to go deep, past Noram's nautical borders, to cast a net, and even then chances were it would come up empty.

"Sure. Fishing." When he snorted, she held up her hands. "Okay, okay, hiding. He'd had a misunderstanding with the

Armament over a crate of whisky." She stepped closer to the edge of the blanket, smirking down when Lila giggled. "See, they thought it cost something. He said it didn't. How was he supposed to know it belonged to the admiral?"

Now Lila wasn't the only one giggling. Several others joined in, but not the two new boys. They stayed somber, cheeks red, wary they were being taken, probably.

"How did he escape?" prompted Sylvie, taking the empty glass from Marin's hand.

"He plowed straight into a hurricane," said Marin, slicing her hand through the air before her. "Winds lifted his boat clear off the water and shattered it into a hundred pieces. How did he survive? Standing on a plank, holding his sail in one hand." She balanced on an imaginary board, lifting her arm overhead while the sea and sky swelled in her imagination. "But the worst of it . . ." She knelt down, bringing her voice to a whisper. "The worst of it he weathered in the belly of a whale."

Laughter erupted around the room. Even the boys in the back glanced at each other, cracking a smile.

"He lived?" asked one of the girls, a small thing with fire red hair. "It didn't eat him?"

"How you think I heard this story?" Marin asked.

"Where's your dad now?" asked Lila.

Instantly, Marin's gut tied in knots. It had been five years since she'd seen him and she missed him, like she missed the open sky and the sea, and the gentle rocking of her boat. Like she missed her home.

"Still fishing," she said, strong enough to convince herself.

Almost.

CHAPTER 4

PLASTERING ON his best smile, Ross cut his way across the floor, stopped only three times for a pat on the back on his way to his mother's side.

"There you are, sweetie," she said, as if she hadn't just waved for him to come. She held a flower in her hand, a red, frilly thing, and immediately began fastening it to his lapel. "A flower for each citizen Noram will help through relocation. They'll be announcing the first five hundred names soon. Exciting, isn't it?"

Although anyone could apply to go to Pacifica, those who lived in Lower Noram where the ground erosion problems had been the worst—who were running out of water and dealing with daily blackouts on account of the crushed pipes and broken power lines—would be considered first. Ross wasn't sure how a flower was supposed to help, but it didn't matter because in the next breath she said, "I'd like you to meet Ms. Roan Teller. She works with the public safety commission." Across from her stood a stocky woman whose chest was busting out of the neckline of her dress. Ross fixed his eyes on her face, and adjusted his shoulders to accommodate the weight of his mother's expectations.

"Pleased to meet you." He shook the woman's cold hand. "I suppose I should be thanking you for keeping our streets safe."

Cue irresistible smile.

Roan Teller gave him an amused grin, but the look seemed practiced, and didn't reach her hard, green eyes. "You can thank the City Patrol for that," she said, and Ross was surprised to find her voice familiar. "I deal more in project funding and management, I'm afraid. I represent some people who've made it their number one priority to invest in our continued safety." She waved her hand. "Uninteresting, I'm sure, to a young man your age."

Yes, thought Ross.

"Hardly," he said.

"Ms. Teller has had the extraordinary task of heading the relocation committee," explained his mother. "We have her to thank for Pacifica."

She smiled, and didn't disagree, which Ross found a little bold.

"Have you been there?" asked Ross, realizing he'd recognized her voice from the Relocation Act ad.

"Of course."

"Is it really that green?" He smiled.

The grin stayed fixed on her face. "The photos may have been touched up, but only a little. There are still beautiful places left in this world, I assure you."

Ross had the sudden desire to see it in person.

"My son has a keen interest in public welfare," bragged his mother. "I wouldn't be a bit surprised if he followed in his father's footsteps."

He wilted.

"Ah." Roan's brows raised, impressed. "Then I suppose one day we'll be discussing a great many things."

The way she said this made the smile fade completely from Ross's mouth. He wasn't sure what it was about the woman that gave him a bad feeling, but as she sipped her flute of champagne, he felt his teeth pressing together.

"Ms. Teller, I see you've met my bosses." The seas parted as the guest of honor approached. A man with Ross's dark, glossy hair and a suit that gleamed a little, as if he'd been standing out in the rain.

They all laughed. Because that was what they did when Ross's father made a joke.

"Mr. President," said Ms. Teller. "Your family is lovely."

"I'm a lucky man." He placed his arm over Ross's shoulders. They were nearly the same height now, but Ross hunched a little, to make his father seem taller.

"I was hoping I might get the chance to talk with you," Roan said, and though the president opened his mouth to object, she continued on. "With relocation happening next week, my investors see no need to delay phase two of the project. We could begin as early as next month with your approval."

Ross glanced toward his father, feeling the sudden tenseness in his grip. He was never included in business discussions, not at home, and especially not at public dinners.

"Ah, Ms. Teller," he said, a trademark, billboard smile lighting his face. "Keep up this pace and they'll be giving you my seat."

They all laughed again.

"There'd be no slowing progress then, would there?" Roan kept laughing. Ross choked, and then glanced to his father, whose chuckle ground to a painful halt.

"My dry humor." The woman waved a hand, as if to erase her

earlier comment. "There's no rush, is there?" Her pointed gaze said differently.

"Why don't we leave business at the office, yes?" Ross's mother said, touching her glittering necklace. "Have you tried the pastries, Ms. Teller? They're exquisite."

Roan leaned in, effectively cutting her out of the circle. "We could always bring phase two back into consideration after the next election."

At this, his mother inhaled sharply and looked over her shoulders to see if anyone was listening. Ross's thumb began to tap against his thigh. It was one thing for him not to take his mother seriously. It was entirely something else for a stranger to do so.

The president's arm fell from Ross's shoulder.

"Or, we could remain self-sufficient and begin next week," Roan said, sipping from her drink, impervious to the strain between them. "Campaign season begins again soon, doesn't it? I imagine my investors would be very interested in supporting the candidate who assured our continued independence." The words were sharp from her mouth, cutting through any remaining layers of social nicety.

Mention of campaign season made Ross's stomach sour. It was always an insanely busy time for his family, and since there was no term limit, and hadn't been since the Melt, they were always gearing up for the next run.

Ross's father hummed, then placed a hand on Roan's shoulder.

"Let's talk after dinner," he said after a moment, and even though Ross didn't know half of what was going on, or what his father might say, he somehow felt heavier than before.

Politics was a game. He'd been around it his entire life. His father knew what he was doing.

"Very good," said Roan. "Enjoy your night, Mr. President."

She nodded to Ross's mother. "I think I'll have a pastry. I hear they're *exquisite*."

"Relentless," his father said through his teeth as she turned away. Then he was gone, shaking hands with the next group and tilting back another drink.

"Well," said his mother, shifting her gaze away from his adoring fans. "I guess you'll want to spend time with your friends. Felipe and Jonas Gomez are here. Maybe Marcus is around somewhere too. I saw his mother earlier. So exciting that she made captain of the City Patrol."

A tightness formed in his jaw. Despite the fact that he'd quit running, his mother continued to ask about his teammates, almost too hopefully. He didn't tell her the truth, which was that there were few people he wanted to see less than the three of them.

"All right," he said. "We might go do something. See you at home later?"

"Take Tersley with you," she said, glancing toward the main entrance, where the security staff waited, Ross's bodyguard among them.

"Of course," he said. He kissed his mom on the cheek, and when he pulled away she smiled.

The antique clock at the top of the glass staircase showed 7:14 as Ross made his way down the hallway toward the coat closet. He meandered slowly so as not to arouse attention. Guests, likely needing a break from the main room, admired the exhibits in silence, and as Ross came upon the three-dimensional floor-to-ceiling images of Earth from space, he paused, reminded of school trips here as a child.

"Twenty fifty A.D." A woman's sweet, almost childlike voice came from above him as he stepped into the exhibit's sensor. "The

Earth's average temperature has risen by six degrees Fahrenheit over the last century. As a result, melting ice from the North and South Poles have caused the oceans to rise more than seven feet, changing the landscape of this ecosystem for the plant and animal life within." He looked at the shape of the continents, how different they all seemed then, how much bigger they were, while the voice went on to talk about the Midwest heat wave that destroyed the natural production of wheat, barley, and soybeans.

He moved to the next model of the planet. The shorelines here were tighter. There was a gap between North and South America, and much of the old U.K. was underwater.

"Twenty seventy-five," the woman's voice said as he stepped into the middle of the picture. "The elimination of the Winter Olympics due to the lack of snow- and ice-producing venues becomes one of the lead topics at the Global Climate Change summit, held in London. In the upper Northern Hemisphere, permafrost begins to melt, releasing carbon toxins into the air from trapped fossil fuels. This leads to an increase in methane gas, which expedites the greenhouse effect beyond scientific prediction."

Ross turned to a video clip of snow, something he'd never seen in real life, burning like paper.

"In the United States, Midwestern and Southern cities are evacuated due to continued heat waves and mega-storm cells which destroy the power grids and fresh water supplies. Despite this, humanity prevails. Scientists work to create artificial pollination systems as a result of the changing growing seasons brought on by the rise in worldwide temperatures and the extinction of honey bees." A buzzing filled Ross's ears, and he moved on, aware of how people looked at him and whispered to each other.

He passed pictures and glass-encased skeletons of animals he couldn't remember the names of—black-and-white snow birds that couldn't fly, large jungle cats, different species of whales, and hundreds of kinds of fish. Things from the past that no longer existed because they couldn't adapt, or migrate, or whatever. There was a picture of an old theme park with a cartoon mouse on the entrance, taken from underwater.

This place was so damn depressing.

He passed by the next two displays, stopping again when a group ahead blocked the entrance to the coat closet.

"Twenty-one hundred. Africa and Australia become entirely uninhabitable due to heat. Japan and the majority of Asia are abandoned as a result of radioactive contamination from two and a half centuries prior. The first outbreak of malaria VI is recorded in South America in 2102, with devastating consequences. The following outbreaks become impossible to halt. The Earth's human population, once projected at 11.5 billion people, drops to 6.2 billion in eight years." He cringed at the oversized photograph of a mosquito to his left. In the back of his mind he heard his grandfather's voice, saying the words he always used when describing the Shorelings—*survival of the fittest*. It was usually accompanied by words like "uncivilized," and "dangerous," and followed by Ross's mother telling him he could never say those kinds of things in public.

"Receding shorelines around the remainder of the world force residents to move inland, uniting with the common goal of survival." To his right, a picture lit up of the Lincoln Memorial, half submerged in water. "President Kiara Williams declares Washington, D.C., a national disaster area due to broken levees and floods, and the capitol is moved to higher elevation, in West Virginia. Two years later it is moved again, to the western seaboard in the Sierra Nevada, and named Noram, a title to celebrate the union of

Canada, the United States, and sections of Mexico as one, North American Alliance." Another photograph of the Lincoln Memorial, this one after its relocation to the Monument Park in the political district near his home.

The group moved on as he passed the last image of a watery world, giving it barely a look.

"Twenty-one twelve. The last of the polar glaciers melt. The re-created United Nations restarts the global clock . . ."

He passed out of the sensor for the exhibit, but knew what it would say. Every teacher he'd ever had made them stop there when they came on field trips. ". . . restarts the global clock at 0 post-Melt, and joins hand in hand, in celebrating a new future."

That was eighty-one years ago. And if they were celebrating, someone forgot to tell the Shorelings.

The coat closet finally came into view at the end of the hall. The room looked full through the open door—a sea of black and shades of gray, all fashionable and useless, considering it was still a hundred degrees outside. Standing at the front beside a wooden podium was an attendant, an elderly man with a dignified chin and bushy eyebrows.

Ross was nearly to him when he heard a man clear his throat behind him.

He turned, coming face-to-face with his bodyguard, a bald, bulky man in a beige suit, who was ignored by practically everyone despite the ferocious scar running down his jaw.

"Tersley," Ross said, failing to hide his annoyance. "Thought you were comparing chest measurements with the other security guards."

"I won. Where are you going?" He sighed, and Ross wondered, not for the first time, how much Tersley hated his job.

There were few people Ross encountered who were taller than

him, his father included, but Tersley had him by several inches. The shirt beneath his jacket was stretched to the point of button-popping over his chest, and his head was shining, as though he'd greased it up just for tonight.

"To the coat closet," Ross said honestly.

"You have an affinity for closets."

Ross huffed out a breath, recalling a certain brief, but enlightening, episode in the east wing storage closet three days ago involving Alia Bastet, the security advisor's daughter, and the smooth feel of her stomach beneath his hand. He'd been *this close* to figuring out the ridiculous fasteners on her bra when Tersley had wrenched open the supply room door.

"What can I say?" he grumbled. "Security's a pain in the ass. It's impossible to find a few minutes' privacy around here."

He hadn't really been alone since before his father's election, when he was ten. There were others before, but Tersley was the only security officer he'd ever talked to. It was impossible not to. For the last two years, he'd come to every track practice, wading through the locker room steam in his suit. He'd accompanied Ross every time he went out, which was rarely off the compound, and run background checks on all his dates. He was always lurking.

Tersley rolled his enormous shoulders back. "I know."

Ross paused.

"I was seventeen once too," Tersley said. "I'm not *that* old."

Ross side-eyed him, for some reason trying to picture his dad saying the same thing. He couldn't. His mother, either. They'd never have reason to. They only saw who they wanted him to be—a smart, athletic, younger version of his father—and he reflected that back because it was better to be something to somebody than no one to anybody.

"You're pretty old," he said.

An eruption of applause filled the main room.

"The first five hundred," said Tersley, as excited as he might have been over choosing a pair of socks.

The event was being televised. His father would make a speech—probably with that Roan woman. Pacifica, *blah blah blah*, relocation, *blah blah blah*, future, *blah blah blah*. His father's tie would spark just as much gossip as the names of those who'd won the random lottery.

"There's a lot going on out there," Ross said.

Tersley's brows flattened.

"I doubt anyone would notice if I disappeared for a little while."

Tersley sighed again.

"You do kind of owe me after the way things went down in the supply room."

Ross waited.

"Is she . . ." Tersley glanced toward the coat closet.

Ross nodded slowly, a hint of a smirk lifting his mouth. "I might be a while."

Tersley shook his head, but waved at the employee standing behind the wooden podium. They exchanged a few words, and while the old man was distracted, Ross slipped behind them into the rungs of coats. He raced to the back, impressed with himself and high on good luck.

It was going to be a good night.

"Adam?" he whispered when he got to the back. Near the left side of the wall was a lit EXIT sign, something he'd learned about from his track days when some of the guys used to brag about sneaking out this way to drink in the alley during events. He'd never done it, of course. Tersley had always been watching. But he'd quietly made sure it was legit two weeks ago when they'd come here for the Noram Healthcare banquet.

"Here."

Adam stood from beneath a row of coats. His hair was messed now, his tie askew.

"Were you hiding?" asked Ross, mouth cocked in a crooked smile.

"No." Adam straightened his tie. "Maybe. I thought it might be the old man running the coat check coming back. How'd you get back here? I heard Tersley."

"Doesn't matter. Anyone see you?" A slow drip of adrenaline warmed Ross's blood. He was already leading Adam to the far corner, where his coat had been hung beside his parents' in the VIP section.

"Are you kidding?" asked Adam. "I have the power of invisibility."

He said it like a joke, but Ross wasn't sure he'd meant it that way.

"All the guards are out front," Adam added. "There's no one in the alley."

Because they were more concerned about who was coming in than who was going out.

Ross removed the sleek silver comm from his wrist and stuck it in his suit jacket, which he hung up beside his father's overcoat. Then he loosened his black tie and untucked his shirt. They didn't want to look too formal and stick out.

"Well," said Adam. "So much for taking me out to dinner first."

Ross smirked, then led them out the door.

CHAPTER 5

"THIS DOES not sound like sleeping, *niños*."

Marin spun from the children seated on the blanket before her to face a woman with brown skin and short, dark hair tied up in a red scarf around her head. As always, Marin was surprised by the sharpness of her—the deep grooves of her collarbone, her bony wrists. Her age was difficult to place. She looked young enough to be Marin's mother, but there was a wisdom in her gaze that only came with time.

"They forced me to tell them stories," Marin said, thumbs hooking in the straps of her pack. "There were threats. I feared for my life."

"Undoubtedly," said Gloria. She leaned around Marin to face the children. "Eyes closed. The next one of you who makes a peep gives Frankie a foot rub tomorrow."

They groaned, and when Gloria snapped her fingers, went silent. Sylvie only chuckled, and turned out the lanterns one by one.

Gloria left the children's room, leading Marin down the hallway.

"You look like him, you know," Gloria said without looking back. "Your father. It's the hair. And the eyes, I think."

Absently, Marin's hand went to her dark curls, usually kept back in a tail the way her father had worn his. Sometimes she forgot that Gloria had known him before—that she'd been taking their contraband to trade for years before he'd disappeared. Even though Gloria was probably lying—her eyes were brown and her father's had been blue—she found herself longing for a mirror, just to see if she could find him in the reflection.

"Any trouble at the cove?" asked Gloria, using a key to unlock the glass door.

"All the trouble stays up here, doesn't it?" They entered another room, equal in size to the first, on the opposite side of the hall. A single lantern lit the space, placed atop a large crate beside a few tech items that were new since she'd been here last. A reader and a couple old comms people had brought in to trade. Marin set her bag beside them and opened it, revealing the first of the six jars of black liquid—a product that had come from nearly a month of gathering, blending, setting, *waiting*, and finally boiling over low heat for two straight days in an abandoned seafood restaurant in the cove. Gloria took it in her hands, examining it through the glass.

"It's darker than before."

"It's better," said Marin. "Cooked it longer."

The words came out harder than she'd intended. She had better skills than making tar, but it would fetch a good price, and that made it more valuable than pride.

She glanced back to the unmarked boxes on the shelves, knowing inside them were things like toothpaste, clothing, and blankets.

Cigarettes, contraband within the city limits because of the Clean Air Act, and empty gas cans for days when the kanshu loosened their grip on gas rations. Pots and pans and bowls, water purifiers and cooking grease. At least those things *had* been here. Most of the supplies were running dangerously low.

On the other side of the room were crates marked by the black bird, the symbol of the Oil Nation. Formal trade between the two countries had been stopped during the last war, but that didn't mean Gloria wasn't getting her hardware under the table from someone on the other side.

Most days Gloria could be counted on for a trade. All days she could be counted on to cause trouble.

"Finally, they're asleep." Sylvie entered the room, hands resting on her hips, back hunched like an old lady. Her brows quirked at the jar in Gloria's hand.

"What is that?" she asked.

"Marin calls it tar," said Gloria. "Last time she cooked it we got a hundred credits a dip."

She would have rather earned her keep fixing things, but times were thin. She would do what she'd always done: survive.

"A hundred . . ." Sylvie stepped closer, then pinched her nose. Even unopened, it reeked like cleaner and burnt sugar.

If only the things inside it were that nice.

"This'll get more," said Marin. "The kanshu will pay double when they get a taste of this."

"One in particular," said Gloria.

A line formed between Sylvie's delicate brows. "Who?"

"Teller," said Gloria with a smirk.

"The one from the ads?" Sylvie gave a shocked laugh. "This is *drogue*, yes? I suppose you never can tell about people."

Gloria's mouth turned up in the smallest inkling of amusement.

"She sends a guy to make her deals, but Marin found out her name for a bonus dip last time."

"What's so great about it?" asked Sylvie.

"Open it." Marin took a step back, and held her breath.

Gloria unscrewed the lid of the jar as Sylvie's eyes widened.

The second the tar hit the air, Marin felt the world go sideways. She held her breath, shoving Gloria's hand back down. Sylvie had been closer, though, and Marin caught her arm as she stumbled sideways. Gloria's cackle filled the warm room.

"Told you it was better," said Marin. "Kept it on the fire two whole days this time." She yawned. It had been a while since she'd slept more than an hour or two straight.

"How did . . ." Sylvie blinked, still trying to shake the effects of the tar. "How did you learn to make that?"

A knot formed in Marin's throat as she pictured a tiny shack at the edge of her hometown, and her small hand turning the handle of a great copper vat.

"Family business," she said.

"My mother taught me to flirt," said Sylvie, making a face. "This would have been more useful."

Gloria put an arm around Marin's shoulders. "What would I do without you?"

Marin grinned, but the truth was, she didn't know what she'd do without Gloria. When she'd come here, five years ago, she'd had little more than those kids in the other room did now. If she hadn't ended up at the library, or if Gloria hadn't taken her in, she'd be out on the streets.

Or back on open water, which meant she was as good as dead.

"How soon can you move it?" asked Gloria. There was a pressure in her voice Marin was unaccustomed to hearing, and she turned to face the other woman.

"How soon you need me to?" she asked.

Gloria sighed, then crossed her arms over her flat chest.

"We're down to the six rations, split between us all," she said. "We keep taking in these kids, we'll starve within the week."

A tense silence settled between them. It wasn't that she didn't believe Gloria, but she had to see it for herself. Striding to the crates marked "Food," she tipped them open, finding box after box empty.

"Thought you were farming the kids back out," said Marin to Sylvie. She didn't mean to be blunt about it, but that was the truth. This was a black-market trading post; most of what they dealt with was contraband. It wasn't meant to be a daycare.

"I try," said Sylvie. "But few families have the means to take in an extra child."

"Few? Try none." Gloria made a small sound of disgust. "I've turned away eight customers today alone looking for rations."

"What happened?" asked Marin. "I thought we were supposed to get more this week."

"La limpieza's cutting down on my business," said Gloria. "They're tightening security on the supply trains. My source wouldn't give up a single sack of flour unless I doubled his rate."

Marin felt the knife at her hip, thinking he might not have been so bold had she been negotiating.

"Want me to talk to him?" she asked.

Gloria snorted. "We can't burn him—he's the only in I have on that line."

"Let him hope he never finds his own plate empty," said Sylvie tightly. "He would find no generosity at my table."

Another sigh slipped between Gloria's teeth. "We don't get some income, we'll have to shut down."

Gloria had fed half the people of the docks at one point or

another. If she couldn't get the money to pay off her source—an Armament guard on Noram's supply routes—the food she traded would stop. It wasn't as if Marin could contribute with government-issued rations vouchers, either. As far as Noram was concerned, she didn't even exist.

Sylvie chewed her lip, anxious. "We can't turn the children out."

"No," said Gloria. She paced between the shelves, blending with the shadows the farther back she went. "This is our home," she finally said, an edge to her already hard voice. "These are our people. They can't send us away and they sure as hell are not going to starve us out."

Marin's dreams of a cot and a warm meal went up in smoke. Her own people back home on the island never would have stuck their necks out for others the way Gloria had. It made her homesick, in a twisted kind of way. Like missing something you never had.

"I'll go tonight," she said. "Sneak across the line while you're rioting."

She didn't have to ask if Gloria would be at the relocation center. She had been nearly every night since the paperwork had first come out to ship five hundred people to Pacifica, since she'd sent her errand runners out to rally the people and protest. Her husband had lived and died on this land, she said when anyone asked, and she wasn't moving. Now the masses gathered long before she showed, and fought long after she left.

"Be careful," Sylvie warned. "La limpieza will be out in force."

"Looking at her," Marin said, motioning to Gloria. But she felt a tension spread through her tired muscles. No one knew where the Shorelings charged with conspiring to riot were going—rumor was the mainland prisons were all full. Some said they were being taken to a jail out to sea or set to swim.

She'd seen that kind of justice. That was corsario justice.

After a moment, Gloria nodded.

"Be fast," she said. "Be safe."

Even if Marin didn't want to go, she didn't have a choice. Living here, *hiding* here from her own people, didn't come free. She would not starve, or let this crew starve, while she could still do something.

Marin took the jar and placed it gently back into her pack. She settled it on her shoulders. Without another word, she went down the stairs, ignoring the errand boys and security guards who joked about her just getting back. Ignoring that voice that whispered to her from the water to come home.

She couldn't go home. This was where she belonged now.

This was who she was now.

Into the black night she went, heading through the streets now vacant with the coming curfew. It was imposed each day at dusk by la limpieza on account of the riots, and when she heard the far-off wail of a siren, she ducked into an alley and waited until the sound had cleared.

Then she was off, nerves churning in her belly, eyes roaming, one hand in her pocket on her father's old knife. Another turn led her deeper into the city, and soon she saw it. A crowd bigger than all the corsarios on the island she'd once called home. A sea in which to lose a fish.

The riots.

Without wasting another second, she headed toward them, ready to make a deal.

CHAPTER 6

Two BLOCKS down from the Natural History Museum was the Plaza Centro, marked by a burst of old-fashioned Spanish tile and a fountain filled with stone trees, something that Ross had only seen live in nature preserves. There, beneath the sparkling gray limbs, he and Adam waited for the bus that would take them below the cliffline.

It was the first time in as long as he could remember that he was in the city without a bodyguard. He felt like jumping in the fountain. Yelling at the top of his lungs. He felt like doing something crazy.

Which was already in the works.

He bounced on his heels, then punched Adam in the ribs.

"Ouch," said Adam.

"What time is it?" Ross asked, looking for a clock on the shelter at the bus stop. The relocation event ended with a silent auction at midnight, but these things never really closed up before one in the morning. They had plenty of time to get to the riots and back without anyone noticing they were gone.

Adam retrieved his comm from his pocket.

"Seven fifty-two."

"What are you doing?" Ross hissed, slapping a hand over it. "You were supposed to leave that back at the museum." He looked around for a trash incinerator, ready to bake it. Their comms were a direct link to the security team, and bringing them with was a sure way to cut these festivities short.

"Relax," said Adam. "I turned off the tracking device."

Ross pulled back. "You can do that?"

"Sure," he said. "It's in the operating manual."

"You read the operating manual?" Ross shook his head. "Never mind. Of course you did."

How could he forget? This was the guy who turned in homework early and asked their teachers for supplemental reading when something was *interesting*.

He wasn't exactly sure how they were friends.

"Lose the coat," Ross told him, annoyed by how perfectly Adam had folded his suit jacket over one arm. Ross's was back in the museum, where Adam should have left his.

"Where would you like me to put it?"

"Toss it," said Ross. "Throw it in the fountain, I don't care."

Adam gave him a pointed look that said this wasn't going to happen. It didn't really matter what he did with it. Even without the accessories, every inch of Adam was clean and pressed. His dark hair was short and neat. Even his tan face was freshly shaven, though Ross doubted he'd had much to shave. He looked nothing like the kid who had moved up the cliffs with his family three years ago. No ragged edges. No sunburnt skin. No pants that sagged low on his hips just so the ends would cover his ankles.

It was difficult to remember sometimes that Adam was not like him in one of the most fundamental ways.

Adam was a Shoreling.

It wasn't that he looked so physically different; the same two seeds dropped in different countries would sprout the same sapling. But one would be watered, and pruned, and sheltered from the wind, while the other would face drought, and infestation, be broken down and cut up. Even if they both grew leaves in the spring, what existed beneath would be a different tree.

There were other Shoreling kids at the public schools above the cliffline—one of the schools, Ross had heard, had a busload sent up from the slums every morning—but Adam was the only one at Center. He was brought from the wrong side of town for a purpose, a fact Ross knew Adam was acutely aware of. It was why his shirt was perfectly pressed every morning, and why he consistently made the highest marks in every class.

He was their poster boy for integration.

As was his father, the vice president.

Cars whipped past—some white government vehicles like the one he was used to riding in, others privately owned. It would have been easier to flag down one of the blue taxis, but it seemed wiser to blend in with a crowd. Anyway, asking a driver to take them near the riots this time of night was sure to raise suspicions.

A bus came, a red line down its side, and they climbed aboard. It was the first time Ross had ever been on a city lift, and it surprised him that the seats were decently clean and the cabin air-conditioned.

"Ahem," said the driver, a woman with a short patch of yellow hair. She tapped the metal box beside the wheel.

When Ross hesitated, Adam stepped past him.

"I got it." He removed his comm from his pocket again, turned the dial on the side to the credit setting, and held it above the black scanning device. Ross moved quickly to a window seat, keeping his head down.

"You have to *pay* for public transportation?" It wasn't as if they were rolling around in a mansion on wheels. He felt like an idiot for not knowing this.

Adam glanced around the cabin. "We're in a fuel crisis. Welcome to the real world."

Shaking off the minor setback, Ross grinned. "Feeling nostalgic? This remind you of the good old days?"

Adam had been raised in the banks, a mixed section on the southern side of Lower Noram that was mostly residential. It was run-down, there was no question, but it wasn't nearly as poor as the docks or some of the other areas below the cliffline.

His father had been a store owner who'd gotten involved in local politics, and made a name for himself as a Progressive Party minority voice on the city council. When it was time for Ross's father's reelection, tension between those on either side of the cliffline had been high, so Ross's father picked a running mate that his advisors thought might buy the Shoreling vote: one of their own. He was the first elected officer since before the Melt not from an established political family, the first in over a hundred years from a different party. There had never been such a high voter turnout.

He couldn't stop the Shorelings from rioting, though.

"They weren't good old days," said Adam quietly.

"Of course not," said Ross. "I wasn't there."

Adam snorted.

The rest of the ride went slower than Ross had hoped. Each stop they took on people, and let a few more off. Both he and Adam kept their heads down and their gazes roaming. By the time they finally reached their stop, Diamond Peak, they were the last two on the bus.

The street outside was darker than the Plaza Centro, with only a few traffic lights to guide their steps. Around them, storefronts were empty, the glass cracked on half, boarded up on the rest. Apartment buildings, seemingly abandoned, stretched up into the night. This looked nothing like the brightly lit streets of the political district where he and Adam lived. This was a forgotten place. Nobody wanted to live this close to the cliffline.

"You sure about this?" asked Adam.

In truth, Ross wasn't. There was a flicker of doubt inside him, an awareness that he'd already gone too far. If they got in trouble, Tersley wasn't here to watch their backs.

"Of course," said Ross. He'd dragged Adam this far, he wasn't going back now. "But if you're scared, you can hold my hand."

Adam groaned.

Because the roads were blocked due to the riots, Adam suggested they take the pedestrian bridge off Sierra Street to the docks. As the streetlights spread farther apart, they walked quicker, the abandoned road drenched in long stretches of shadow. Ross's palms began to sweat. The darkness fueled his adrenaline.

"There's the visitor center," said Adam.

Ahead was a square, white building with a flat roof. An empty car lot waited to the right. The windows were dark. It felt like some sort of warning.

"The bridge should be behind it." Adam motioned to the left of the visitor center. They crossed through a parking lot, around the wreckage of a building that had been knocked down so long ago the rain had rusted away the metal beams. As they neared the bridge, a chain-link fence came into view. Large caution signs were attached at frequent intervals.

Despite the heat, a shiver worked through him as they reached the gate—an arching iron trellis that rose twenty feet in the air. At one time it might have been inspiring, but now it was eaten away by the weather and half covered by weeds.

"Not many people come this way, I guess," said Ross. He could see the bridge just beyond, though it looked more like a staircase, descending into the fog.

"Let this be a reminder of all those lost in the '07 post-Melt quake," read Adam from a tilted sign beside the gate. "And a tribute to those who followed in the landslide. We will never forget. We will rise again."

Oh-seven was nearly eighty years ago. He knew from school that prior to that, Noram had been on even ground, but once the ice melted, the quakes became more severe. There had been no way to predict this one. It had killed thousands of people, and become a permanent line drawn across the city.

"They say the next one is supposed to be twice as bad," said Adam. "All the erosion is happening because the tectonic plates under the city are shifting."

"This sounds suspiciously like paranoia," said Ross, pushing through the creaking gate. Before him stretched a thick, greenish haze, lit from beneath. "Maybe you should be on the other side of the riot line."

"Maybe you should be," Adam said under his breath.

Ross smirked.

Swallowing, he stepped onto the metal grate, gripping the rough, corroded bannister as he made his descent. At a rickety landing, the staircase flipped back the other way. The haze grew thicker, and with it came the pungent smell of garbage, too long baked in the heat. Soon he couldn't see more than a few steps in front of him.

"This used to be the good part of the city, you know," said Adam, voice tense. "Before the storms got bad they used the harbor for trade shipments. Most of the business took place down there."

Now trade between the nations was tense; Ross knew that much. Much of it was done by air, but that was expensive and unreliable. The storms had made the seas untrustworthy, but it was their fellow man that had ruined the skies. Planes that *were* able to take off through the storms often disappeared somewhere over the vast stretches of water.

His mind shifted for a moment to the woman who'd worked for the public safety commission—Roan Teller—and what she'd said at the dinner about supporting a candidate who assured continued independence. To him, independence sounded more like isolation.

"Did you learn that in Shoreling school?" asked Ross. It didn't sound as light as he'd intended.

"As a matter of fact, I did," said Adam. "I hope you know my dad will kill me if he ever finds out we did this."

Adam's parents were a little more protective than most.

"Or maybe he'll be thrilled," Ross offered. "He's all about the Shoreling pride."

They sometimes joked about Noah Baker's dedication to his home, but the truth was he defended his people more than Ross's father had ever defended his own family.

"I know . . ." Adam's voice had changed; it was quieter now. "I know all of that makes me sort of unpopular to be around."

Ross almost said something about his ugly face being the reason for that, but sensed they were being serious.

Their feet clanged on the metal steps.

"Popularity is overrated," he said.

"You say that because you have it." Adam gave a weak laugh. "You should go back to track. They'd probably still let you be captain."

Ross paused. Continued.

"And go back to waking up at dawn to run sprints? No thanks."

But even if he didn't miss practices, he did miss running. Not being harassed about his "Shoreling boyfriend." Not being told to choose between a *trawler* pet and his teammates by Marcus Pruitt. Just running.

Behind him came the slow draw of Adam's breath. "I know what happened."

Ross didn't know how Adam knew—he certainly hadn't told him. He hadn't told anybody, not even Coach.

"It's not a big deal," he said. But it was. Because by choosing Adam, he'd stopped doing the one thing he was actually really good at, and now he had no way to get away from the politics and drama of his own house. Some days he wanted to crawl out of his own skin.

"Okay," said Adam. "Thanks, though."

It felt strange for Adam to thank him for this. It was as if he'd said, *Thanks for not punching me in the face,* or *Thanks for not spitting in my food.*

Ross stopped. Ahead was the bottom of the bridge, just four flights down for the entrance to the walkway. The exit opened to a park, with outdated, rusted play equipment jutting up from the ground. Beyond it, on the sidewalk, a line of patrolmen in riot gear stood side by side, a menacing wall of black.

His pulse kicked up a notch.

He could hear something beyond them. A dull roar, drawing him forward. He couldn't make out anyone through the thick haze, but knew the relocation center had to be close.

"Hey," said Adam. "You said you wanted to find a place to watch."

"Just a little closer." Ross crept closer, toward the equipment. He ducked down behind a tilted plastic slide, hearing the noise more distinctly now.

Oh no, we won't go!

"We should leave," said Adam. Ross glanced over at him, seeing the line of sweat trickle down his friend's jaw. They were chanting about Pacifica, the achievement his father was currently celebrating by drinking old, expensive liquor in a suit that cost more than the property of this playground.

Oh no, we won't go!

"Just a little closer," Ross said again. He snuck forward.

"Hey!" A shout from their right. Ross, surprised, sidestepped into Adam, who bumped into the supporting beam of a swing set.

A patrolman had spotted them. He motioned to another. They strode quickly toward the center of the park.

"Shit," muttered Ross.

"We need to get out of here," said Adam.

"Let's see your hands!" called one of the officers. The other had a weapon drawn, pointed in their direction. Ross fought the urge to sprint back toward the stairs, like Adam had said. He didn't know if the officer held a gun or a stunner, but he didn't want to find out.

He lifted his hands.

"What do you got there, kid?"

"Nothing," said Adam, holding out his suit jacket. "It's my jacket. Look, this is a mistake. We just . . ."

Ross turned to face him, a sudden fear tightening between his shoulder blades.

His mind flew to his mom and dad, who probably thought he was still at the museum, or at least somewhere close with Tersley. This had seemed like a good idea before, but now he wasn't sure what he'd been thinking. *President's son caught in riots.* This kind of thing would not go over well in the morning briefing.

"Put the coat down and walk away," said the patrolman. "Now!"

Adam tossed his jacket on the ground as Ross took a quick step back. "We were just leaving. My father . . ."

"Shut up," said the other officer. A woman. It had been impossible to tell with her helmet and riot gear.

"Thought you'd sneak by, huh?" she asked, approaching the jacket with caution, like it might explode.

Behind the patrolmen, the rioters chanted: *Oh no, we won't go!*

"No," said Adam. "We live up there, not . . ."

"Shut up!" snapped the first patrolman.

The woman lifted Adam's jacket between her thumb and forefinger like a dead animal. "Where'd you get this? You steal it off some *kanshu* boy?" She spat the word like an angry curse.

Ross had never heard that term before. For a moment he thought she meant someone poor—a Shoreling, or a homeless person or something—but then he realized she thought *they* were the Shorelings.

"No," said Adam. "You don't understand. Let us explain."

"You planning your own little demonstration tonight?" asked the woman, shining the light in Adam's face. Adam threw up a hand to block his eyes, and the sudden movement had both officers on their feet, aiming their weapons.

The world froze, then snapped back into focus.

"Wait," said Ross. "Just listen, please. This was a huge misunderstanding."

"Listen to him talk," spat the male officer. "Huge *misunderstanding*. Where'd you learn that word, kid?"

Ross hesitated.

"We're taking you in," said the woman.

"We didn't do anything!" argued Ross. "Look at us. Do we look like Shorelings to you?"

"You're breaking curfew," she said. "You're carrying stolen items. Conspiring to harm. My guess, you have a weapon stashed somewhere."

"My father—"

"Should keep a better watch on his kid," snapped the woman.

Ross felt like something sharp had broken off inside him.

"Look at my face!" he shouted. "Do you know who I am? Your job is in serious jeopardy right now with the way you're—"

He was grabbed by the back of the shirt and hauled forward. His gaze shot behind him, frantically searching for Adam, who was knocked forward onto his hands and knees, and then jerked back to a stand by the woman.

He was going to have these patrolmen fired. Both of them. They had no idea who they were dealing with. Ross didn't care if they *were* just doing their jobs.

But the anger was thin, and Ross couldn't cling to it. It buckled under the pressure of something heavier. Colder.

Fear.

They were pushed to the side of the park, where a line of patrol cars waited.

I'm dead, thought Ross. *My dad is going to kill me.*

Just before they reached the cars, three men jumped from the shadows and leapt onto the guards. There was a crash of plastic and the scrape of metal against pavement, and then a grunt of pain.

Horror froze him in place.

"*¡Corre!*" shouted a man in a muddy shirt with wild hair. He jolted up and grabbed Ross's shirt. "Run! *Go!*"

Ross didn't wait. With Adam's shirtsleeve in his grasp, he ran away from the patrolmen, away from the park, straight toward the crowd.

CHAPTER 7

MARIN'S HEART pounded in time with her running feet. She needed to get to the park, and the stairs just past it that would take her above the cliffline. At the top was the old Shoreling visitor center, with the public comm system she could use to contact Teller's assistant. Tonight, though, the riot had spread from the old hospital, fanned out into the neighborhoods. People were everywhere, raging about the five hundred names that had been chosen to go to Pacifica. She'd seen the broadcast in a shop window on her way here, and the reporter's advice to stay close to your comm in case you were one of the lucky few.

The people she'd seen tonight weren't acting like they'd just won a lottery. They were ready for war. Maybe because they hadn't been chosen. Maybe because, like her, they wanted to know where the first five hundred were really going.

She'd sailed across that ocean dozens of times, and even if it had been five years, she'd never seen a place that looked like those Pacifica ads. The water south of the Alliance seaboard had been boiled in the harsh sun; the water north was coated with trash—floating gomi that got caught in the currents. Anything west of that dead mound of lava, Hawaii, was a cesspool of radiation from the reactor meltdown over a century before in Japan.

So where were the Shorelings being sent? The kanshu certainly weren't saying.

Soon, she was forced to walk, surrounded by rioters holding their signs and chanting to the army of soldiers in black helmets, lined up across the street from the relocation center.

Oh no, we won't go!

It hadn't been like this before. Not this big, and not this wild. She doubted even Gloria could have envisioned that her call to rebel six months ago when relocation had been announced would turn into this.

The streetlamps were still dark on account of the blackout. The only light left now was from the torches, the flickering flames that threw sinister shadows against the stone building where people were congregating.

Pushing through the crowd, she made her way in that direction, and with her knife tucked into her belt, she grabbed a vertical pipe and climbed onto the ledge of a first-story stone windowsill. The glass had been replaced by boards long ago, and painted across a sign stating RELOCATION CENTER were the words "Eviction Center."

Beyond this mass was the park, and to her right, the road that led up the cliffline onto higher land. But that road was empty, blocked by cars and flashing lights, and officers in black masks with shields. The park was surrounded.

There was no way she'd get past to the stairs. Not tonight.

"This is our home!" shouted a man, close enough beside her to make her ears ring.

Home. The word echoed through her, a reminder of all the things she'd left behind five years ago. Her cot, rolled up in the corner of the attic. The kitchen, where her father had taught her to read from the old sailing book called *Moby-Dick,* and her mom had taught her how to trim a fish and stab a man. The window outside the Blue Lady, where she had peeped through at Luc and the girl he'd had inside.

Luc. The memory of his face—sun-browned and framed by a dark curtain of hair—brought a twinge of pain to her jaw, like she'd bitten something sour. He was probably head of the captain's table now, raking in the tithes of rations and oil that kept their people afloat through the rainy season. Living the dream they'd once shared as children.

She didn't have a dream anymore.

She didn't even have a home anymore.

Across the street, three women had climbed atop the roof of a gas station. The windows below were knocked out, and a sign hung on the door that said OPEN TUESDAYS, 10 AM, ½ GALLON PER FAMILY.

"You can't get rid of all of us, Torres!" shouted one of them. "If Pacifica's so great, why don't you and your kanshu friends go there?"

Those on the ground below roared their approval. Their passion seeped through Marin's skin. You could feel the buzz in the air, the vibrations of hundreds of feet stomping on the verge of stampede. This wasn't a few dozen angry Shorelings; this was an army.

"THERE IS A CURFEW IN EFFECT." A voice boomed through the air, vibrating in her chest. "PLEASE RETURN TO YOUR RESIDENCES UNTIL SUNRISE."

The Shorelings shouted louder.

She squinted through the fog, suddenly torn between finding a way through and getting out of there. Ahead she focused on the line of officers in black. They pushed forward as one, tall, clear shields braced before them.

The Shorelings held their ground against the incoming tide. For a moment, neither side moved. Then there came a woman's high-pitched scream, a sound that zipped Marin's spine straight, and the guards advanced.

"DISPERSE," came the voice again. "THERE IS A CUR-FEW IN EFFECT. PLEASE RETURN TO YOUR RESI-DENCES UNTIL SUNRISE."

"We're not hurting anyone!" shouted a man near Marin. "You can't arrest us. This is a peaceful protest."

He sure didn't sound peaceful.

The Shorelings began falling back, filling in the empty spaces, pressing against her legs as she stood on the windowsill. The shouts were so deafening, they seemed to make her vision shake. Heat, more intense than that outside, traveled up her neck. She needed space.

She needed the sea.

She had to get out of here.

Taking a deep breath, she jumped into the crowd, squeezed and poked and stepped on by those around her. A wincing cry climbed up her throat as the sky above her disappeared, hidden behind swinging arms and paper signs. She wasn't short, but she was smaller than many of these people, and had to lower her weight to push through. Sweat rolled down her face and into her eyes. Bodies bumped against her and jostled the heavy jars in her pack. She was near the edge when the tide shifted and bore back hard against her.

"*Get up!*" someone shouted.

"*Move!*"

"*¡Corre!*"

Another scream, and then the haze seemed to take on a life of its own, expanding, growing thick and murky. One hand gripped her knife, the other cleared her path. Soon everyone was running the same direction, but they were bumping each other, throwing her off-balance. She clipped the heel of the woman in front of her and they both crashed to the pavement.

Then she inhaled, and the world tilted. A familiar smell, sticky sweet and rotten, filled her nostrils. She blinked down at the ground, where black liquid seeped across the pavement.

Blood, she thought slowly. No. That wasn't right.

Tar.

A hand closed around her biceps and heaved her up. She blinked, gaze locking on sharp blue eyes and a square jaw. He was about her age but tall, taller than most people around them. Wearing white in a sea of dark clothing. When he looked at her she went still; it felt like a spotlight had come down over her, like there was nowhere to hide. He looked at her like he saw *everything*.

There was a cut near the top of his forehead, and red smeared through the dark hair at his temple. He leaned forward and coughed, covering his mouth with the crook of his elbow.

"We have to go," he said. "Adam! Come on!"

She fought to keep her burning eyes open, but they stung fiercely. Her thoughts muddled, unable to keep up with her pounding heart. Somewhere in the back of her mind she knew it was the tar, that she'd breathed it in, that she had to get away from it to get right.

"Come on!" he shouted.

She looked at her pack, now lying on the ground. The canvas was stained black. Glass had sliced through the bottom.

The tar.

The money.

It was gone.

"Go," he shouted, eyes widening. "Go, go, go, go . . ."

She stumbled right, and nearly collided with a figure in black. A giant, carrying a shield and a stick and wearing a helmet that hid his eyes. One of the officers. La limpieza.

Her mind cleared in three blinks.

Throwing her weight backward, she collided with the two boys. The guard swung his black stick and she jumped out of the way, just in time to avoid a crushing blow to her side. He swung again, hiding like a coward behind his plastic shield. To her shock, Blue Eyes stood there, squaring off with him, yelling something no one could hear.

The guard raised the stick.

The boy Blue Eyes had called Adam was pulling him back, but not far enough.

Marin's next breath found her fingers tangled in the side of his shirt, jerking him out of the way.

She caught his gaze one more time. His eyes were crystal blue, just like her father's had been. Round with confusion and shock.

A screaming pain ricocheted from her wrist up through her shoulder. With a grunt she toppled sideways, hitting the pavement hard on her knees. Instinctively, she huddled in a ball, consumed by the fire in her arm. It stole her breath, dimmed the sound and the lights and the danger around her. Then the blood began to pound in her ears, and when she looked up, the shielded monster stood before her like a mountain, the club in his gloved hand rising to strike her again.

She tried to roll to the side, but was scooped up by strong arms, suddenly weightless and brimming with a panic beyond her control. She was caught. Trapped. Her legs hung over her captor's cradle hold, her shoulders twisted so that she was smashed against his chest. She gripped her bad arm against her chest with her good, and writhed hard enough to loosen his hold.

A jerk of his chin revealed his face.

"Hang on," Blue Eyes said between his teeth. "We're getting out of here."

And then they were running, and she had no choice but to wrap her arm around his neck and hold on, because if he put her down then, she would be trampled by the stampede.

"This way!" Adam shouted. He pointed ahead to the stairway, and they tumbled down the steps, coming to a stop against a boarded door. She hissed out a breath as an elbow jabbed her in the ribs, but he'd taken the brunt of the fall on his forearm, caging her between his chest and the ground.

Her lips brushed against his neck. Each time he breathed, his stomach pressed against hers. She became aware of every place they touched, and every place they didn't. Of the clean scent of his skin. Of his bent knee, pressed against the outside of her thigh.

Of her wrist, now throbbing harder with each beat of her heart.

She wiggled free.

He stayed on his knees and elbows for a long moment, back rising and falling, and she felt the sudden sinking sensation that he'd been hurt worse than she had.

"Hey. You all right?" she asked, quickly assessing the boy who'd pulled her from danger. Straight nose, broad shoulders, lips pulled into a tight grimace. His skin too pale to have spent time near the water, and there were no acid burns on his face like most of the other Shorelings. No weapons, from what she could tell.

Something was off about him. It didn't give her a good feeling.

He rocked back on his heels, brows scrunched together.

"Fine," he said, blinking and rubbing his eyes before looking up at her. "You?"

She nodded, but her breath came in shallow gasps, and she couldn't yet manage to peel her injured arm away from her chest. Every second that passed, it hurt worse.

"I'm great too, thanks," said Adam, who had stood and was wiping his hands down his pant legs. Though he was half shrouded in shadow, she could make out the dirt smudge on his cheek and the dust highlights in his short hair.

"Hey!" He banged on the door. "Anyone there?"

No one answered.

Above on the street, the smoky air glowed eerily with the blue flashing lights of the patrol cars. The crowd had thinned, but footsteps still slapped against the pavement, punctuated by the burst sirens. In unspoken agreement, they backed up against the door, hiding in the shadows.

"We have to get off the streets." The twist in her gut turned her mind to another problem. The tar she'd spent two full days making—that she'd spent weeks gathering supplies for—was gone. The credits Gloria could use to feed her people were gone.

Those kids may not have been her responsibility, but she felt the burden of their empty stomachs all the same. Where she came from, you gave everything you had to your people, and if you couldn't, or you didn't, you were sent out to face the storms. Even if she knew it was different here, the same desperation snaked through her. It left her raw, and unhinged, like a ship with no anchor.

La limpieza's siren wailed above them, kicking her pulse up

another notch. She could not be caught. The punishment for rioting would be different for her than for the other Shorelings. Worse.

Because she was not a Shoreling. She was a criminal.

The boys were arguing in hushed tones. Something about a comm, and how they could be out of here in ten minutes. Blue Eyes wasn't a fan of the idea, saying they'd be busted if their dads found out.

Their speech was wrong, the way their words flowed together, one leading seamlessly into the next. With his wary stare and hunched shoulders, Adam might have passed as one of the rioters, but Blue Eyes stood too tall, like the world had never bent his back. His skin was like polished marble, without even a hint of roughness.

He wasn't a Shoreling. Not just any land-born *terreno*, as her people called them. He was from Upper Noram. The type who dressed in suits and gowns, had more money than they knew how to spend, and *never* set foot below the cliffline.

He was from those who had betrayed her grandparents.

A kanshu.

Her body went rigid, strengthened by generations of distrust. She jerked away, putting a foot of space between them and bringing another sharp pang to her arm.

"What are you doing here?" she asked, teeth locked.

Blue Eyes faced her. "Same thing as you. Hiding."

"Why?" she pressed. "You in trouble or something?"

Adam gave a weak laugh. Shoreling or not, he was with Blue Eyes, and that made him just as dangerous.

"Are you?" asked Blue Eyes.

She was torn, unsure if she should run, or fight, or laugh because of course it was her luck that she'd found herself trapped in a stairwell with the most dangerous people in the country.

How had she not known who they were? She felt like a fool, and worse, a traitor to her own kind for helping them escape the riots. But they'd helped her too; they didn't seem like the kinds of pale, land-loving monsters her father had once talked about around the fire pit.

Blue Eyes looked more like a boy who'd tumbled down a hill, and Adam just seemed afraid.

It didn't make sense.

Her back scraped the wall as she pushed herself to a stand. Careful not to be seen, she extended her arm into a patch of blue light and looked down at her wrist.

"Your arm . . ." Blue Eyes stood, gaping down at her. She jerked away, and the movement brought another punch of pain. She squeezed her eyes shut, squeezed her teeth together, until it eased.

Her wrist wasn't lined up right. Her hand didn't make a straight line with her forearm. Her fingers were numb.

"You need to go to the hospital."

"She can't," Adam snapped. "Unless she wants to get picked up by the patrol. There's a curfew, didn't you hear them?"

She couldn't go to a hospital—hospitals asked questions about who she was, and where she'd come from. Questions she couldn't answer.

"Hiro," she muttered. "He's a doctor. He can hide us."

She didn't know why she said "us." These boys weren't Shorelings—their people were responsible for all of this. But in that moment she didn't care. They'd helped her, and all she could think about was that they needed to get off the streets.

"Come with me," she said.

But when she took the first step, she lost her swagger. Her stomach turned, the sweat on her brow turned ice cold. She blinked rapidly and braced herself against the wall.

When her vision cleared, Blue Eyes's face was before her.

"We'll stay together," he said. "Can you run?"

She inhaled, and when the world was steady again, nodded.

He peeked above the stairway and gave a quick nod. With both guys on her heels, she led the way up. Once they hit the street they were running, her wrist against her chest, making each stride uneven.

The noise steadily grew again, a wave of shouts and chants through the eerie yellow haze. Her nose crinkled with the sharp scent of burning plastic. The riots felt impossible to avoid, like water gushing from a broken dam through the streets of Lower Noram.

A turn, and then another. Blue lights cut across the cracked pavement in front of her, and she tore off to the side as they came to a dark shop front.

She banged on the door, feeling la limpieza getting closer, *closer*.

"Hiro!" she called. "It's Marin. Open up!"

No one answered.

Blue Eyes went to the shop window beside her and was banging on the glass through the metal grate.

"Hiro!" she tried again. "Hiro, Gloria sent me!"

Ahead, in the middle of a street, a bonfire stretched into the black sky, crackling and hissing as it burned through the furniture and clothes fed to it by the mob.

"Help! *¡Ayudame!*" She banged the knife's handle against a window, where inside candlelight flickered. Two eyes appeared behind the dark glass, and then the door cracked open.

"Hurry," came Hiro's low voice. "Hurry, get inside."

She shoved herself through the crack, tumbling forward as the two boys followed. A man old enough to be her father, with silver streaks in his oily hair and dewdrops of perspiration on his broad forehead, quickly slammed the door and turned the lock.

"Fools," he said at the crowd outside as he pulled down the ratty blinds. "They think just because they stand together, they won't all be arrested."

Marin tried to catch her breath. The pain in her arm extended up her shoulder. It made it hard to focus.

"What is this place?" asked Blue Eyes.

The slivers of firelight from the window revealed a small altar on the ground. A little stage, like the one she'd made from scraps when she was a child, only instead of pirate puppets made from threadbare socks, this held candles and a bowl half filled with water.

As her eyes adjusted, a dozen more artifacts became clear. Colors, feathers, small figures in clay. Bundles of weeds and bottles of amber liquid. A glass jar filled with bugs. An iron sculpture of a naked woman reaching for the moon. Like every time she was here, seeing it made her want to believe in something, and wanting to believe in something made her feel weak.

"Hiro's a healer," Marin said tightly.

Blue Eyes looked skeptical.

"There are many ways to be healed," Hiro told him.

"She's hurt," he told the old man. "Her arm. She was attacked by a patrolman."

She hadn't realized she'd braced her arm against her chest in her opposite fist.

"Patrolman, huh?" The word came from Hiro's mouth slowly, as if it were in another language. He glanced at Marin, as if looking for confirmation that they were indeed outsiders.

She nodded once.

He considered this only a moment, then waved for them to follow him behind the counter. "Come. We'll ride out the storm."

Pushing back the curtain on the wall, he revealed a narrow room running the length of the back wall, lit a moment later by the wave and flicker of candlelight. Just beyond the threshold was a cot, covered by a red-and-white quilted blanket. He bent to a square generator on the floor in the corner, wound the crank a couple times, and when it made a steady whirring sound, turned on a small lamp on the table beside the bed.

"Show me," he said, hands open.

Tentatively, she extended her arm before him, inhaling sharply as he gently attempted to move her hand from side to side. Her teeth locked together. Tears burned her eyes. She flinched as he felt his way to her elbow, unused to anyone but Gloria touching her kindly, even after five years on the mainland.

Blue Eyes watched her, an anxious kind of energy moving his hands from his pockets to wring in front of him. He didn't look away from her arm. Adam, shorter by several inches, was standing close to him, close enough their shoulders were pressed together. His gaze kept returning to the sleek, silver comm at his wrist. She'd seen plenty of rip-offs sold on the street corners in the docks, but that one looked real enough.

What were they doing here?

"Is our friend at the library okay?" Hiro asked, referring to her boss. Marin had run supplies here for Gloria a few times—medicine, and disinfectant, and bandages that she'd managed to smuggle off the supply train. Not everyone could afford to go to the hospital, and those who could not, came to Hiro. For that generosity, Gloria stocked his clinic with what she could, free of charge.

"As far as I know," she said.

Hiro did not seem upset that she had lied to get off the street.

He wove her numb fingers with his, and then offered a grim smile.

Then yanked.

She cursed, first in her mother's native tongue and again in hers, and then fell to her knees, gripping her arm against her chest.

"What'd you do?" Blue Eyes demanded. He forced himself between her and Hiro, just as he'd stood in front of la limpieza in the riots—as if nothing could knock him down.

She breathed in and out, forcing the air through the tight straw of her throat. Gradually, her fingers regained their feeling, though the pain lessened only a little. Blue Eyes reached down, helping her to the side of the cot, where she hunched over her knees.

"Ah, yes," said Hiro. "That will be sore for some time. Dislocated, is all. Not broken. Let me find something to wrap it."

A loud banging at the front door snapped their attention to the main room of the store. Jolted from his spell, she reached for her knife, but the weakness in her dominant wrist forced her to switch hands.

"Please," whispered Hiro, placing his pointer finger over his lips. "Quiet."

He made his way back through the curtain toward the front of the store, while they stayed behind the thin bed and the cluttered countertop.

"More people trying to get off the streets," she guessed.

"Think he'll let them in?" Adam's voice was strained.

"He let us in, didn't he?"

Another bang, and then a loud crack, like someone was trying to break down the door. Marin jumped, bracing her knife before her. In the main room, she could hear Hiro arguing, and then another thump against the door.

"Please! *Please* be calm!" Hiro begged. "There is nothing here to take!"

She searched for an exit, finding a door on the wall behind Adam lined with five locks down the seam. A tilt of her head, and Blue Eyes grabbed Adam's sleeve, dragging him toward it. But Hiro's cry stopped them, stunted by a crash in the front room, and she jolted toward the curtain without thinking.

Before she reached it, the thin fabric fluttered and began to draw back as if moved by a ghost. The room beyond was jarringly quiet; the roar of the riots outside muffled the space between.

A terrified curiosity froze in her chest, solid and heavy. The curtain opened, revealing a burly man in a suit. His head was shaved clean, and in his hand was a gun.

He took one look at the two guys, and then at Marin, and raised his weapon.

CHAPTER 8

"TERSLEY, WAIT . . ." Ross felt the world catch up to him in one hard lurch. Everything had happened so fast. The riots, those patrolmen, and then this Shoreling girl who looked a little too comfortable with a knife in her hand. Who was shielding him for the second time tonight.

"What's this?" his bodyguard demanded, gun aimed at the girl's chest. "What's going on here?" He kicked aside the small table, making them all jump, and took a quick glance under the bed.

"Nothing," the girl said quickly.

Ross saw everything. The droplet of sweat that cut a line down her dusty jaw. The number "86" branded below her ear. The holes in her paper-thin, sleeveless shirt and bulky pants, and the scuffs on the toes of her boots. He could feel her fear, hot and frantic, or maybe it was his own. Of all the things that had happened tonight, this was the worst. Because this girl had helped him. Because it was Tersley, and Tersley was his, and if Tersley hurt her, it was on *him*.

"We just wanted to look," he explained quickly. "Things got

out of hand." Questions slammed through his brain. *What are you doing? How did you find us? What took you so long?*

Adam had called him. Or activated the tracker in his comm. He must have done it before they'd arrived at the shop.

"We can't be here," Adam said quickly. "Do you know what this looks like? Us, here with her? Like *this*?"

Ross's heart pumped harder. He hadn't even considered it, but Adam was right. Four men—three of them kanshu, or whatever people kept calling them here—and a Shoreling girl with a gun aimed at her chest. If any of the protesters saw this, there wouldn't just be riots, there'd be a full-scale war.

"Tersley, stop," Ross said, voice unsteady. "Listen, this is a—"

"Hey! What's going on in there?" a man, not Hiro, called from the front of the shop. Tersley had attracted the attention of the people outside.

"Drop your weapon and lay facedown on the floor." His bodyguard's words were flat, low. Ross had never heard him talk like this. He spoke in sighs, and grunts, and suppressed eye rolls. It occurred to Ross he'd been given this job for a reason. Not everyone in the president's watch had the duty of guarding his only child.

"You first, *cabrón*," said the girl.

They may not have taught that word in his world language class, but he had a pretty good idea what it meant.

"Last chance," Tersley said. "I won't ask again."

She stared at Tersley, gaze like fire. *Don't do that*, Ross wanted to beg. *Back down*. But she didn't. She pulled back her shoulders, and lifted her chin. Her wild curls spread around her face, and her cheeks took on a hard, red glow.

Ross edged to her side. "Just do what he says. *Please*."

The girl bent her knees. Her eyes flicked to his. The knife clattered to the floor.

Okay, Ross thought. *Okay.*

There were more voices outside now, and another from the main room.

"Stop, both of you!" Hiro was somewhere behind Tersley, hidden by the man's giant frame.

Another crash came from the front room. Tersley, only five feet away, pressed the trigger.

The shot echoed through the room. Ross could feel the force of it in his teeth, in his skull. It shook through his whole body. It felt like something was tearing inside of him.

The girl was on the floor. Facedown. Unmoving.

Dead.

Tersley had killed her. *Ross* had killed her. *Adam* had killed her, because Adam had called for help.

"Come on." There was a hand in the back collar of his shirt, a voice in his head. He was jerked backward. He blinked, dazed, at Adam. He was saying something else. Ross saw his mouth moving. He couldn't think.

Dead. The Shoreling girl who'd taken a hit for him. Who had a number on her neck and a six-inch blade on her hip. She'd been light when he carried her, or maybe the rush of it all had made him twice as strong. He hadn't thought twice about it when he'd picked her up off the pavement and run.

"She had a weapon," Tersley said, looking down at the girl again. "You saw her." He swiped the sweat out of his eyes.

She was unarmed, Ross wanted to shout. *You disarmed her!* But he couldn't, because Tersley grabbed his shoulder, and pulled him into a crouch.

"Follow me. Keep moving," he said. "There's a car outside."

With a heave, Tersley kicked the door outward, and Ross caught sight of half a dozen faces whipping by as he was dragged through the front of the shop. Tersley roared and plowed past two, three bodies in the way. He was knocked back and forth between them before finally punching through. Another shot. A scream. Someone yelled, "*¡Corre!*" Just as they'd told him hours before at the riots.

And then, "In here! Hey! *Hey!*"

They'd found the girl.

Acid burned up Ross's throat.

They shoved through a door, into the chaos of the riots.

"Move, move, move!" Tersley ordered. Ross's feet couldn't keep up. He nearly fell into his bodyguard. He could hear Adam behind him—the clack of his shoes on the concrete sidewalk. And then suddenly, all he wanted to do was run. He wanted *out*. He hauled faster, and faster, bumping again into Tersley as he plowed onward. His breath came in shallow pulls. Dread gripped his spine.

The girl was dead.

Dead.

Dark shadows danced in a pulse of orange flames from the bonfire. There was a car parked ahead against the curb that he recognized. Shorelings surrounded it, wearing baggy, tattered clothes. A man with glasses held a bat, and as Ross watched, he swung back and knocked through the rear window. Glass shattered on the ground.

"What happened in there?" he called. "You hurt that girl?"

A dozen voices raised in question—about the girl, about what they'd done. They knew. They already knew.

"Back off!" shouted Tersley. The man saw the gun and jumped back, just far enough to clear a path. Against Ross's better judgment, they raced toward it, bumping into each other, stumbling. Reaching the back door of the car.

"Inside." Tersley hauled it open, pushing Adam, who was closer, inside, then Ross, and then jumping in himself. It was a tight fit. Adam wasn't huge, but Tersley was enormous, and Ross's knees were crammed against the console in front of him, pinning him in place.

The engine was already humming, and their driver, keeping low in his seat, inched forward.

"Drive!" Tersley snapped. "Get us out of here."

"I can't," said the driver. The front window was already cracked. One of the solar panels from the roof had come loose and slid forward, hanging at an angle in the center of their vision.

Before them, a dozen or more Shorelings blocked the street. They carried torches. Flames licked the night.

Those nearby closed in again, slapping their hands on the roof of the car, on the windows, trying the door handles. Adam's side was locked, but he still pushed away from the door like it might give. Ross was forced forward between them.

"Run them over," Tersley said.

"Shit," said Ross. "*Shit.*"

The tires squealed as the driver accelerated.

"Move out of the way!" Adam shouted.

Ross glanced over to the door, seeing now that it wasn't fully closed. Tersley tried to slam it, but it wouldn't hold. Something was wrong with it. Outside, the broken pavement crunched under the tires. Bodies bumped against the car—nothing under the tires, nothing that seemed hard enough to cause damage—but the very idea of it still made Ross sick.

"Get out of the car!" someone shouted.

They hit a corner and people outside jumped out of the way. Everyone slid into Adam, smashing him against the door.

"You stupid trawler bastard," Tersley growled, showing an

anger Ross had never seen in him before. "This was your idea, wasn't it?"

"What?" Adam balked. "*What?* No."

"I came as soon as your tracker came back online," said Tersley. "I should toss you out where you belong."

Adam squeezed closer to Ross's side.

Outside, the buildings whipped by. It suddenly occurred to Ross that there were no other patrolmen around. Tersley hadn't brought anyone. There wasn't a search, like he'd considered a dozen times throughout the night. Or if there was, they weren't here.

Up ahead was a blockade of some kind. The driver muttered something he couldn't make out. Ross squinted through the night, then shoved back against the seat when he realized what lay before them. His feet pressed against the floor of the car, hard, as if this might slow them down.

A mass of people, so close they seemed interconnected, spilled down the middle of the street, covering the sidewalks on either side. The lights here were out, and only the occasional torch and the beams of the car's headlights lit their way.

"Where are the patrolmen?" Adam asked. "They were shutting down the riots. Everyone was supposed to go home."

Tersley raised his wristband comm to his mouth.

"Calling in for backup. Seventh and Sierra. I've got the president's son. I—" He tapped the comm. Swore. Ross glanced at it. It wasn't even lighting up. He remembered the people in Hiro's shop. It must have broken when Tersley was pushing through them.

The crowd saw them. A few people splintered away, heading in their direction. Then a few more. They moved faster.

The driver slammed on the brakes. His arm reached over the passenger seat as he turned back to face them, throwing the car into reverse. Ross blinked at his face—his stern brows, and scruffy skin, cracked and wrinkled around his eyes, and the arcs at the corners of his mouth. He'd never looked at the man's face before. He didn't even know his name. And now Ross's life was in his hands.

People in the crowd were running toward the car. More were coming from a nearby brick building. They seemed to come from everywhere.

The car slowed. Tersley shouted at the driver to keep moving. The driver shouted back. Ross heard only a buzzing in his ears. Only his own fast, sharp breaths.

He looked at Adam. The whites of his eyes shone around the brown irises.

My fault. My fault. My fault.

Voices outside called to them. *What're they doing?* And *Hey, they've got kids in there!*

Then, *Get them out! Get those kids out!*

A crack on the front window. Ross's neck craned forward. Someone was hitting the glass—the bulletproof, UV-protected glass. It broke across the center, a long crack that veined like a lightning strike. Another crack and it bowed in, groaning, weakening around the edges.

"Back seat!" he heard someone yell.

They were coming for him. The fear swelled inside him and burst. He slammed his hand against the seat in front of him.

"Go!" he shouted at the driver.

"Get us back to the district!" Tersley roared over the shouts of the crowd.

An instant later Adam's window was hit. He yelled out, terror ripe in his voice, and blocked his face from the bowing glass. Again, it was hit, and this time the blunt end of a metal bat broke through. Glass shards exploded across the seat. Hands reached inside, blindly grabbing, reaching, clawing. Tersley's arm locked around Ross's chest.

The angry voices overlapped and blended together.

They're taking our kids now?

Where you think you're going?

Get them out of there!

Kanshu, they said. He heard it a dozen times or more. *Kanshu, kanshu, kanshu.*

Adam scrambled back against them, but it was too late. The door was yanked open, and then ripped back with a squeal of metal.

"Get them out!" someone yelled.

"No!" Ross reached for his friend, fingers slipping over his sweat-slicked arms.

Adam disappeared outside, swallowed by the crowd in a blur of hands and fire and ripped clothing.

"Adam!" Ross pulled free of Tersley's grip and dove after him, nearly spilling into the asphalt. Someone grabbed his shirt. His hair. Then Tersley was yanking him back across the seat.

"Adam!" Ross called again. He couldn't see him.

Something thunked against the back of the car. Hands slapped against the doors, the roof, the front hood. The crowd pressed inward, and as the car lurched forward, Adam's door slammed shut and locked with an audible click. Then they were driving, and the crowd was melting away, unable to keep up. Somehow they'd gotten through it. The quiet hum of the accelerator was accented by the high wail of a siren behind them.

"Wait," said Ross. "Adam. Where . . . What are you . . . We have to go back. What are you doing?" He slammed one hand against the back of the seat. It was numb. His whole arm was numb.

The driver didn't speak, didn't look back. Ross couldn't even see his face, just the sweaty hair that stuck out of the bottom of his cap. He turned the car around quickly in the middle of an abandoned street and sped on again.

"Listen to me!" Ross shouted. "He's back there! He fell out!" He worked at the lock on the door, but it wouldn't open. The driver must have controlled it.

"He knows," said Tersley. With one hand he held on to the passenger-side door, now bouncing against the side of the car, unable to close. Ross tried to climb over him, but Tersley shoved him back. He pointed a finger in Ross's face, but said nothing.

"We have to go back!" Ross stared through the back window in horror as the docks disappeared behind them. "We have to go back. We have to go back."

He said it as they careened up the twisted hill, past the old visitor center. As they sped through the Plaza Centro. As they entered the political district and finally, as they pulled in front of a massive white stone building, beside the thick pillars that ran the length of a circular overhang. Ross blinked at the wings that fanned out on either side, proud and solid, lined with glass windows. At this place of royalty that had for the last seven years been his home.

Then he spilled out the side door, and collapsed on the smooth black drive, sick, bleeding, and broken.

CHAPTER 9

ON THE morning of her ninth birthday, Marin woke up before dawn and plodded down the attic steps into the community kitchen, where the generator was already humming and the lights inside were bright. Her mother, a hard but handsome woman with a wiry frame and a nest of black curly hair, was behind a low trash-burning stove, apron spattered with oil, stirring a cauldron big enough for a grown man to hide in.

"Hungry?" she asked, without looking up.

Marin nodded, but it was nerves that gnawed at her stomach, not hunger.

Seema wiped her hands on her apron and crossed to one of her polished driftwood counters, where a small, dinged-up lantern waited. Picking it up, she carried it to Marin, who sat on a stool at the opposite end of the kitchen, away from the heat, and began to take it apart with the tools she'd brought in her pockets.

Her mother didn't return immediately to the stove like she

normally did. She stood over her daughter, watching, and as the moments passed, Marin's palms grew damp and her hands clumsy. She unscrewed the casing, cleaned it with her shirt, then squinted at the circuit and the rusty wires, trying to figure out how it worked.

After a while, Seema said, "You're getting faster. I'll have to choose something harder next time."

Marin deliberately slowed down. She despised these tests. At four, Seema had thrown her off a dock, forcing her to learn how to swim. When she was seven, Marin had been shut out of their home, made to build a shelter out of trash and face a storm alone. Six months ago, her mother had started bringing her machines— little things she picked up in the gomi fields—and told her she couldn't eat until she found a way to make them work. Sometimes they took hours. Sometimes days.

She'd started waking earlier just so there'd be some food left by the time she finished her mother's games.

Using wire cutters, Marin stripped, trimmed, and reattached the circuit. Despite her intent to take her time, she felt an over-whelming desire to fix this broken thing. To make it whole again.

"Next you'll build a boat, I think," Seema said.

Marin looked up at her, seeing the quick brown eyes, and the pointed nose they shared. Marin's lips were fuller, though, like her father's, and up until just then she'd always wished she'd resem-bled him more.

She said nothing, wondering if this, too, was a test. Her father was the sailor—as far as Marin knew, her mother had never been off the island, even for the day. It was her father who took her to the mainland, to the black-market trader named Gloria, and told her about the South American Federation freighters he'd hijacked alongside the coast of Chile. Her father who taught her to tie knots and trim sails. Her father who held her when the thunder shook their house and the wind lifted the roof.

Her father who said he loved her more than pineapple, and stars, and the open sea.

Her mother retuned to the cauldron, now steaming and smelling of rice.

"You don't like me," she said. "That's okay. You will not be stuck here forever, *mouette*. One day you'll fly away from this place; you just need to stretch your wings."

It was this Marin thought of while she was stuck in the in-between place, waiting to die.

CHAPTER 10

Ross FOUND himself standing in the foyer of his house, filthy and raw, unsure how he made the trip from the car through the front door. There had been something about the driver talking to the head of security, something about reporting what had happened. Ross didn't know if he'd responded.

He stared at the hall that led to the south wing of the compound, where the Baker family lived. Where Adam's parents might be right now, waiting for their son.

A hand on his arm made him jump. When he turned, Tersley was before him, his dirty suit jacket ripped through on one shoulder, revealing a wedge of white beneath.

"We have to go back," said Ross. His voice was so thin in this huge room, barely bouncing off the cold black tile and the stark white walls. He turned toward the stairs, intending to go to his bedroom to get something, but didn't even know what he'd need. A weapon of some sort? A comm?

"You're not going anywhere." Tersley was halfway turned

toward the front door, as if he was stuck between staying and leaving.

"You don't get to tell me shit anymore." Ross stalked toward his bodyguard, fury vibrating through every muscle. "You *shot* that girl."

Tersley didn't look away. He slowly faced Ross, a crumbling mountain, hunched against the weight of the night.

"I did my job." He inhaled. "I only stunned her."

"You . . ." She was alive. The breath tumbled out of his lungs, but relief did not come. "She'll be okay."

His face was grave. "It was a high setting. One I'm authorized to use for your protection."

"High setting?" Ross's stomach twisted. "What does that mean?"

Tersley didn't answer, which crushed all but a sliver of hope. A girl was injured somewhere, maybe in need of medical care, all because of him.

He fought the urge to punch his bodyguard in the throat.

"You let Adam go." Ross's voice broke over the name. Vivid scenes played in his head—Adam hurt, dead, beaten and bloody on the dirty pavement. Those people, wild and crazed, taking him. Taking the *kids* they'd seen in the car. They didn't understand. They were out of control, and dangerous.

"I made a choice," said Tersley.

Ross fell back a step. A choice. Him or Adam. The president's son, or the trawler bastard.

"It wasn't a very hard choice, was it?" he said.

Tersley flinched.

"Find me a new car," said Ross. "We're going back. And after we find them, I never want to see you again."

Lines arced around Tersley's mouth.

"You go back there, they'll tear you apart. You won't find either of them. You'll get yourself killed."

"I don't care."

"You should," Tersley shot back, and for a moment, Ross saw beyond that meaty exterior, to the man beneath. The Tersley who'd found him in the supply closet with Alia Bastet and not told anyone. Who'd loosened Ross's tie on his first day at Center so the other kids wouldn't tease him. Who'd been at every track meet, even once when he'd had the day off. *I was seventeen once too, you know.*

Ross hated him more for all of it.

But his bodyguard was right. If he went after Adam, there would be no way he'd get through the crowds undetected. He'd already had one run-in with the patrol, and to get through that wall again, he would have to be in a government car accompanied by bodyguards. Everyone would see him coming.

"Stay here," said Tersley. "I'll take care of it."

"You'll bring him back?"

"Go upstairs. Clean up. See your parents."

Never before had Ross felt so entirely useless, but he didn't have a choice. He nodded.

Tersley walked to the front door, pausing with one hand on the handle.

"It wasn't a hard choice, kid," he said. "I'd pick you every time."

Ross stared after him as the door shut, unsure if that meant looking out for Ross was more than a job, or if he really hated Shorelings like Adam that much. It didn't really matter. What mattered was his friend was gone, and it was his fault, and the only way to get him back was to trust a man he couldn't trust at all.

He had to tell his parents. The president. The first lady. He'd have to tell them before it got out, before Tersley and the driver made their reports. He couldn't even imagine what his dad might do. This could ruin him.

And then there were Adam's parents.

Cold pressed through his veins, weighing him down.

Adam's parents were different than Ross's. They ate dinner as a family every night. Adam and his dad walked every morning at dawn. They were close.

This wouldn't ruin Noah Baker; it would kill him.

It was still dark out, but dawn was coming. He turned away from the long rectangular windows that ran alongside the door, and forced himself to climb the stairs. A heavy fog had descended over him, so thick he had to work to breathe.

He could still feel Adam's hand in his, blunt nails scraping his palm. He could still see the girl's brown eyes, the round shape of them forever committed to his memory. Tersley said she was armed, that's why he'd shot her. But he'd seen her hands and they were empty. He couldn't *not* have seen them.

The breath shuddered from his lungs.

He stopped on the third step, gripping the bannister. As tightly as he closed his eyes he could not shake that look on the girl's face right before she'd fallen. The quake seemed to start in the center of his chest and work out, sending tremors through his limbs. He could barely catch his breath.

A cold sweat on his brow, he launched himself up the stairs, just making it to the bathroom in time to heave his guts out. When he could finally pick himself up off the floor, he peeled off his dirty clothes and got in the shower, watching the dirt and blood swirl down the drain.

Then he dressed and went to his parents' room.

His mother was sleeping calmly, her lips parted, a black light-reduction mask over her eyes that blocked the news always playing on the large screen on the opposite wall. Beside the four-poster bed, on an antique wooden nightstand, was a glass vial and dropper of sleep medication, and a clock saying it was almost two in the morning. He pressed the button that turned on the lights, but she didn't stir.

His dad wasn't home yet.

"Mom." Ross came close to the edge of the bed, looking at the plush gold comforter and thinking of the threadbare blanket on the cot in the clinic where the Shoreling girl had sat. "*Mom*," he said, louder.

She rolled onto her side, away from him.

The screen caught the corner of his eye, a familiar face drawing his attention. The man was in his late forties, with brown skin, short salt-and-pepper hair, and narrow shoulders. He had a trusting look about him, serious, the kind that made you pay attention when he spoke.

Noah Baker. Adam's father.

Ross's breath stuck in his throat—he had to be addressing the press about Adam's disappearance. Did he already know? Had Tersley told the Bakers what had happened? Ross scrambled for the volume button on the nightstand, and the vice president's voice filled the room.

". . . been skeptical about relocation. I, like many of you, have a history below the cliffline. I was born there, as were my parents, and their parents. Our family store sold the fish my cousins and aunts and uncles caught at sea." His smile was heavy with defeat. "The task force has announced the names of the first five hundred to be sent to Pacifica as part of the Relocation Act. It was decided that just like in the exploration of any new world, priority be given to the healthiest, which is why they claim no one over the age of forty, or under the age of fifteen, was included. I have been told that, due to high demand, additional spaces have opened for those interested, and for those not picked, a second wave considering all applicants will be sent in six months. Whatever your decision, I strongly urge you to consider what the loss of this middle block will do to the structure of the community they leave behind. If it will revitalize our culture, or further tear it apart."

Fury took Ross by storm. The people he spoke to considered him a leader. They were rioting because he said stuff like this. Because he couldn't let go of his stupid *revitalization*. If he just got on board with relocation, there wouldn't be riots. Adam wouldn't be down in the docks, missing.

The reporter pressed Noah, but the vice president had already turned to go. It was then that Ross noticed his suit—the same he'd worn to the dinner—and the backdrop of the museum. This had been filmed sometime tonight, maybe after he and Adam had left.

Ross collapsed onto the bed, a guilty kind of hope overriding his anger. Maybe Noah didn't know yet what had happened. Maybe he was still at the event. Tersley could have Adam back here before anyone caught on.

"Sweetheart?" His mother inhaled slowly, and pushed up her mask. "Everything all right?" Her eyes closed again.

Whatever temporary relief he'd felt plunged back into dread.

If Tersley couldn't find Adam, Ross had to do whatever he could to get him back.

"Where's Dad?" he asked.

"I dunno," she said sleepily. "Out? No, strategy session, I think . . ." She trailed off. "Big meeting with the SAF in the morning."

"I need to talk to him."

"He's busy, sweetheart."

Ross bit his lip. Hard. Harder. He wasn't a kid. He wasn't going to cry. He wasn't going to think about Adam's parents, who would have stopped everything to make their kid breakfast, and sing him lullabies, and rub his damn forehead.

He picked up his mother's comm off the nightstand and dialed his father's number. He didn't answer. He sent a message. Still no reply.

"I need to see him now," Ross said, staring down at the small screen, willing his dad to look. He could call Ms. Scholz, his dad's assistant, but that would mean involving more people. He wasn't sure how his dad would feel about that.

"Sorry," she said. "You can talk to him after the meeting."

No, Ross wanted to say. *No* and *now* and *I'm his goddamn son* and *please.* But none of it came out.

"I messed up." He choked on the words. "Adam's gone."

It was better to tell his mother first. She'd know he hadn't meant for any of it to happen.

But she was asleep again.

He wanted to shake her awake. He wanted to throw her medication against the wall. He wanted to rewind the last day of his life and not be so *stupid.*

Part of him knew he needed to go to the other wing and find Adam's parents, but Ross's needed to be the first to know. His dad didn't like being surprised. He maintained his cool exterior by careful preparation, and there was nothing more unforgivable than jeopardizing his office.

Adam's family would have to wait.

Ross rose and walked down the hallway to the stairs. He began to skip steps, the weight on his shoulders a physical thing, threatening to crush him if he didn't move faster.

He hit the stairs at a run, jumping the bottom three. The

kitchen was a blur as he passed it on his way to the east wing, where the business was done.

The décor changed. At a corner, the tile on the floor became white, the walls a dusty yellow. He reached a large glass door—fireproof, bulletproof, and locked by a fingerprint scan—and placed his hand on a black circular podium, then waited for the click of the locks. When the door slid back, he was off again, feet keeping pace with his galloping heart. Pictures lined the sides—paintings of great men and women, past leaders who'd probably never made stupid, impulsive mistakes that had gotten someone shot. Marble statues immortalized some of them as heroes, and Ross felt their eyes look down on him in shame.

There were people here—there always were, even in the middle of the night. Officials. Security. Aides and interns, laughing like the world wasn't upside down just miles down the road. Most of them ignored him, acting as if the sight of a guy sprinting down the corridor of a federal building was a regular occurrence.

But he knew he was watched. The cameras on the ceiling tracked his every move. If he was deemed a threat, the building would immediately go into lockdown. The doors would remain inoperable until someone manually provided a key code. The film on the windows would black out, along with the lights, disorienting him. Security would have him on his face in seconds.

No one stopped him.

He didn't slow until he came to a sitting room, adorned with more antique wooden furniture and sofas and small lamps atop circular tables. Sweat dripped down his temples. His lungs burned.

A security officer stood in front of the main meeting room, where he knew his father was currently doing business. He didn't know what was on the agenda. He didn't care.

"Everything all right, Mr. Torres?" asked the guard. His suit was the same kind Tersley usually wore—plain, dark fabric, straight lapels, buttoned down the center.

"How much longer?" asked Ross.

"I'm not sure."

"I'll wait." He sat down on one of the sofas. He stood. He stalked to a window and back.

Every second that passed felt like a lifetime. Right now Adam could be being tortured. Who knew what the Shorelings were capable of? If word got out that a girl had been hurt, maybe killed at the hands of law enforcement, things in Lower Noram would only get worse. Adam had been right when he'd said that hurting her would mean trouble. They should have left her at that clinic when they had the chance.

Minutes passed. The halls quieted. Still no one left that room.

"Mr. Torres, you know I can't let you in there."

He was standing in front of the door again, the security guard blocking his way.

"I can't wait any longer," said Ross. He tried to push through him, but the man was bigger and stronger, and hooked him around the chest.

"Mr. Torres, if you'd like . . ." He set him back. "If you'd like, I can call into the meeting and see when they're going to be done."

Ross followed his gaze to a black message pad on the wall. One press of the button, and a red light would flash in the meeting room, indicating someone was waiting outside. His father had shown him this once, long ago.

"Call him," said Ross. "Do it. This is an emergency."

The guard left him to reach for the wall unit. As soon as he was out of arm's reach, Ross grabbed the handle and entered the room.

The second he was inside he knew he'd made a mistake. A dozen faces whipped in his direction. They gathered around a sleek black table, his father in the center. The secretary of trade was there beside him. Despite the late hour, everyone was dressed professionally and looking fresh, though Ross had seen almost all of them drinking at the museum just hours before.

Adam's father was absent—something that made Ross equally grateful and anxious. Still, it was odd he wasn't here.

"Shut the door," hissed a woman behind him. Ms. Scholz, his father's birdlike assistant, appeared at his other side, and closed the door quickly, motioning the guard to step back.

His father, cheeks pale and mouth tight, held up a flat hand in his direction. The move seemed to shrink Ross. It was like when he was ten years old and his father had brought him to a session of Congress, and he'd ruined it by burping into a live microphone.

"Your silence is taken as agreement?" A female voice, eager and robotic, came from all around them. Ross backed against the door, shoulders drawing inward, hands in his pockets.

"My apologies, Píero. We had a brief interruption. Please continue."

Ross saw then that they all faced a wall of large screens, dark except the one in the center, where a red light glowed above the face of a man wearing a sheer white wrap over his shoulders. His skin was darker than most of those in Noram, his eyebrows like coal. A crinkled brown beard reached halfway down his neck, stopping just above a pendant, a black bird with outstretched wings, that hung on a gold chain. He began to speak, his words fast and foreign. Ross recognized some of them from his world language class, which taught a hybrid of English, Spanish, French, and Japanese, but it was too fast for him to keep up.

The translator's voice began in the common language, speaking over the man.

"You have no choice but to comply," said the interpreter program, and Ross was struck by the grim meaning of her words and the contrasting friendliness of her voice. "We have oil. Offshore. Onshore. We swim in it. We bathe in it. And if you want it, you'll pay for it."

"Píero," said Ross's father. "You'll understand if we're reluctant to make arrangements. Our nations have a tumultuous history, and the people of the Alliance have a long memory. Even if a trade *were* mutually beneficial, I can't drive my people into debt with the SAF. You understand why."

His father was talking to the leader of the Oil Nation—technically called the South American Federation. Ross pictured it as he'd seen it on a globe in one of his classes. Mountainous, snakelike in shape, twisting toward the bottom of the globe. The eastern side was mostly a dead zone. Desert. Too hot to be habitable, like the middle of his own country.

He may not have paid a lot of attention in his classes, but he knew the Alliance had been at war with the SAF after the Melt. A settlement had been reached forty years before he'd been born, but trade between them was tenuous. He'd heard his father mention it to the other officials more than once.

"You call me out of bed for this?" Píero threw his hands up.

"I wanted to get back in touch with you sooner," said the president. "My attention was needed elsewhere."

Like at a party, Ross thought.

"You wanted to catch me unprepared," said the translator cheerily.

Ross's father did not disagree.

Píero spoke to someone offscreen, and then turned back toward the camera.

"We can serve each other," said the translator. "You still have food. My people are starving. Your people need oil. I have it."

There was a rise of whispers in the room. Strained glances were shared across the table.

"You're making assumptions, Píero," said Ross's father. He was stoic, his expression unreadable.

Now it was Píero's turn to look uncomfortable.

"Your vice president seemed to think your nation was scraping the bottom of the barrel, so to speak," the interpreter said.

"That was speculation only," said his father with a wave of his hand. "Our offshore drilling sites continue to prosper. It's true, solar power is inconsistent due to the weather, and wind has proved unreliable because of the storms, but our people are researching new renewable energy opportunities. With our current level of independence, we have no reason to look outside our own nation for fuel."

He remembered something Roan Teller, the woman in charge of Pacifica, had said at the fund-raiser. *I imagine my investors would be very interested in supporting the candidate who assured our continued independence.* That seemed a long time ago now.

"Now," his father added, "if you were in need of an aid package . . ."

Píero's eyes narrowed. "Such a thing would indebt us to you. And then what? We can't pay for it, and then you would turn around and take our oil anyway. I am offering you a trade, President Torres, not looking for scraps."

"It's just an option," said Ross's father.

"Where is Noah Baker?" asked the translator. Píero had lowered his chin, his lips pulled into a tight line.

Ross flinched.

"Ill, I'm afraid," said Ross's father. "But the vice president and I stand together on this. There's a lot of repair work that needs to be done before we can negotiate terms."

"Stand together," repeated the translator. "Like you do with your relocation plans?"

George Torres gave a slow, dangerous smile. "Like we do with our growing concerns about the mobilization of your troops on your western border."

Silence followed, and in it, Ross was afraid to move, even if he was offscreen. The tension was thick enough to arc half the globe.

He had barged into the wrong meeting. His own concerns were stripped back, replaced with a sudden real and terrible fear that the SAF might be preparing for war, that his father might be the only thing protecting his country.

"A training exercise only," said Píero via the interpreter. "You understand the need to always be prepared."

"Of course," said his father. And after another strained moment: "I appreciate the late meeting, Píero. Sleep well. We'll talk again soon."

It sounded more like a threat than a polite goodbye.

Píero's lips muttered something that didn't come through on the translator. After a moment he gave a curt nod and the screen went black.

Around the room, voices raised, all in a jumble, each trying to speak over the other. Ross caught words like "soon enough," and "self-important," and "strategy." He shrunk farther into the shadows.

His father was meeting with foreign leaders, trying to resolve international conflict, while Ross was running through riots looking for fun. Shame didn't even cover it. He despised himself.

"Give me ten," his father said. He didn't get up. One by one, people filed out of the room. The trade secretary glanced at him in surprise, as if he'd forgotten Ross was there.

Soon, Ross was alone with the president.

"Are we going to war?" he blurted.

George Torres tapped his fingers on the table. "We're on the verge. Which makes this day no different than any other day since I took this office."

If this was supposed to make him feel better, it didn't.

"You always said that they were smaller than us, though, right?" More land, his father had once told him, but so little of it livable because of the inaccessibility of water. "They couldn't do any real damage."

"They're the largest arms manufacturers and distributors in the world. They could take out half the Alliance if they got through the Armament."

"But . . ."

"It's a stunt to get our attention, nothing more."

The way his father said it made Ross think he should have already known this.

"What about the riots in Lower Noram? Are they a stunt too?"

They weren't. This he knew with absolute certainty. What he'd seen had not been a game.

The president gave a small, annoyed sigh, and though Ross's head was screaming for answers, something to help him make sense of what had happened, he knew his father would not tell him more.

He became increasingly aware of the chill in the room; it stuck to every droplet of sweat on his brow and down his back. *Talk fast*, he willed himself. *Get this over with.* But he couldn't even bring himself to meet his father's gaze.

"What you did here was unacceptable," George finally said. "And it will never happen again, do you understand?"

"Yes, sir."

His father stood from his chair and turned to the back of the room, where a long table against the wall held a carafe of coffee, mugs, and a three-tiered serving plate of fresh fruit and breads and meats. Ross wasn't sure how he hadn't noticed it until now, and it occurred to him that the leader of the SAF must have seen it during their meeting, when he had talked about his people starving.

His father sat down. He placed a cloth napkin on his lap. His plate was piled high with thick breads and bite-sized pieces of fruit.

"What is it," his dad said flatly, without looking up.

Ross moved closer. He remained standing.

"Something bad happened." He gave a weak smile, though nothing about this was funny. "I . . . Adam and I . . . we thought . . ."

His father took a sip from his steaming coffee cup.

"We went to see the riots. We left from the museum last night. I don't know what I was thinking."

His father set down his coffee.

Ross cleared his throat. "The City Patrol thought we were Shorelings."

"Don't use that word," his father said, annoyed. "It's slang, and it has unfavorable connotations."

"Sorry," Ross mumbled. "The patrol thought we were part of the riots. Things got out of control, and this girl was hurt. We took her to this shop."

"You met a girl in Lower Noram?" His father shook his head, laughing bitterly. "I see. Who saw you? Were any pictures taken?"

Ross felt his brows draw together. "No. I mean, I don't think so."

"Which is it?"

Ross felt the pounding of his heart hit harder and harder, until his whole body was shaking from the reverberations. This wasn't about what anyone saw or who might think poorly of him.

"It wasn't like that." His hands had balled into fists. "Why can't you just listen? Just one time, *listen to me*." His voice cracked off the walls.

Ross's father lifted his brows. He set down his fork. His hand rose, as if to say, *go ahead*, while Ross took a breath to steady himself.

"I ditched Tersley at the museum. He tracked us down to the docks. He found where we were and came in, and then he shot the girl, okay? She didn't do anything to him, and he shot her, and I don't know if she's stunned, or injured, or dead. We ran and everyone was there." Ross pulled at the hair at the back of his skull. "Adam fell out of the car. I told the driver to stop, but he wouldn't. He's still there, I think. Or, I don't know. I *don't know*."

His father was still for a long time.

"Again," he said. "Did anyone get a good look at you?"

Ross nearly crumbled.

"I don't know," he said.

"Sit down."

Ross collapsed into the nearest chair.

George rose and turned to leave, but before he did he placed one hand on his son's shoulder. Ross sank as his father's grip tightened. There was a fierceness in his tone when he said, "Stay here."

His father left the room. Left Ross to his thoughts, to the shouts and screams of the riots, and the girl's face, and her wild hair, so unlike the polished look of the girls here. To the "86" on her slender neck, and the feel of her head against his shoulder while he ran, and to Adam.

Adam.

Soon his father was back. He sat in the chair next to Ross.

"We're going to get in front of it," his father said. "This is going to blow over."

He thought he should feel relieved, but he felt nothing.

"What does that mean?" His voice was ragged.

"It means I'm going to take care of it."

"I don't understand."

His father tilted his head, seeming to consider this. After a moment he said, "You were never there. You'll never talk about what happened. Not with your friends, not with anyone. Adam's had some trouble in the past. His family will address this quietly."

Ross's heel began to pound against the wooden floor.

"What do you mean trouble?" Adam freaked out if his homework assignments weren't finished the night before. He saved his leftover lunches for the next day and pointed out when Ross's socks didn't match. "Trouble" was not a word Ross associated with *Adam.*

"His parents knew their son's adjustment to this area wouldn't be easy. Children raised where Adam was face significant hardships. Drugs. Resistance to authority." He waved his hand as if to say, *and so on.*

Something had to be wrong with Ross's brain, because he wasn't following.

"So they know what happened? Someone told his parents."

"They'll be informed."

"And people are looking for him, right? That's the vice president's son." He couldn't believe he felt the need to clarify this.

"He'll be found soon enough."

The confidence in his father's voice didn't reassure him.

"What about the girl?"

His father sighed. "The girl is no longer your concern."

He understood then. His father was fabricating a lie. Like it was *nothing*.

"Dad, you can't . . ." But he couldn't finish, because his father *could*. The president was the most powerful man in Noram, in the whole North American Alliance, maybe even the world.

"It was a mistake, Ross. Don't beat yourself up for it."

A breath huffed from Ross's throat.

Once, in a track competition, he'd forgotten to pace himself and burned out before the last lap, coming in dead last. That had been a mistake. This was something else entirely.

Ross leaned over his knees, the guilt making it impossible to sit upright. "This isn't right. I need to go back. Or . . . report it to the City Patrol. Something."

"You need to grow up."

Ross lifted his chin.

"Do you know why we never got you a pet?" There was no disappointment in his father's tone; he was simply stating facts, and somehow that was worse.

"No."

"Because you couldn't see anything beyond yourself," he said. "Responsibility is about sacrifice. It's about seeing the bigger picture. If this information gets out, the violence below the cliffline will escalate. Relocation will fail. People will die—not just one or two—and those that survive won't blame you, they'll blame me. Then it won't matter that I've kept us out of a second war with the SAF, because a *civil* war will be the only thing on their minds. Every decision I've made that has fed and housed and provided protection for the seven million people left in the Alliance these last seven years will be forgotten, because they will only know that my son was involved in the attack of a *Shoreling* girl." He took a slow breath, sizing up his son with a tired, weighted gaze. "We are on the tipping point, Ross, and the things I do each day determine which way we fall."

Ross hung his head.

"Now," said his father, standing. "Eat something. Get some rest. Choose better friends and let this be the moment you became a man."

CHAPTER 11

"YOU'RE BACK."

Marin blinked. Her breath was a loud noise, screaming through her eardrums. With a groan, she extended her fingers from their tightly furled fists. A second later she could turn her head. She was not *stuck* as her mother had once said. She could move.

"Be slow," a man said. "You've been shot."

Hiro. She was in his shop. Cloudy memories came back to her of the last moments before she'd been hit. They were dreamlike, soft around the edges, and she couldn't quite tell what was real and not.

"I . . . know . . . that . . ." she managed.

"Just stunned," he said. "*Que suerte,* huh?"

Lucky? Oh, she was all luck tonight.

"They have a setting on their weapons," he explained. "It knocks you down and hurts awhile, but no permanent damage. Unless you have a heart problem, of course. Or epilepsy. Or . . ."

"I get it," said Marin. Things were loosening now, thawing.

She stretched her arms out to her sides, dragging her fingertips across the floor. She tried to push up, but couldn't. A few breaths, and she tried again.

Finally, she succeeded in making it to a crouch, gaze drawn to Hiro's tight frown. Apart from a bruise on the side of his head he looked all right.

"There," he said. "Better, yes?"

The initial freeze had worn off, but her nerves felt electric and twitchy. She blinked too much. Her shoulders jumped. But apart from the wrist she was pretty sure she'd rebent the wrong way when she'd fallen to the floor, she appeared to still be in one piece. The only evidence of what had happened was a purple bruise just under her collarbone—a small circle that stung a little as she pressed her fingertips to it.

"Better," she said. "How long was I out?"

"Some time. More than an hour."

More than an hour, defenseless. Anyone could have shoved a knife between her ribs in that time.

Gripping a corner of the checkered quilt on the cot, she heaved herself onto the creaky mattress, aided by Hiro's hand beneath her elbow. The bedside table was tipped over, the lamp shattered on the ground beside it. She remembered the crashes from the front room, and any relief she'd felt instantly ran dry.

"It's all right," he said when she tried to stand and staggered. "Sit for a moment. Rest." He acted as if the roar of the crowd outside were no more than a wind chime.

The riots had never been like this before.

"Those guys I came with . . ." she began.

"Gone," said Hiro. "They went with the man who shot you."

Of course they had. How easy it had been to believe they weren't a threat. They looked no older than her, talked to her like they were on the same side. She'd fallen right into their trap. The second she'd been cornered, he and his friend had called in the muscle, and the next thing she knew she was facedown on the floor.

She should have known better. They were kanshu, after all.

"How did you know them?" Hiro asked.

She peeked around him through a crack in the curtain at the front room. Clutter littered the floor near the entrance, now barricaded with boxes. The tiny stage was in pieces, shattered across the laminate store floor.

"I didn't know them at all." It had felt like she had when they'd been running from la limpieza together, but that kind of kinship wasn't real. It was just like it had been growing up on the island. They'd all work together when they had to, and then she'd go right back to being the muck on the bottom of everyone else's boots.

A crash came against the side of the building outside, making her jump. Then, in increments, it grew quiet, as if the mob were moving away. An eerie silence filled the night, putting her more on edge.

When she looked back at Hiro, she found him frowning at her.

"Well," he said. "Someone was looking for them, so either they were important, or in a lot of trouble."

Based on how fast they had run, she guessed the latter.

"Something about their faces," he mused, scratching his chin. "Familiar, yes?"

She pictured Blue Eyes—the flex of his jaw, and the smudges of dust on his pale skin. The way his hair stuck out sideways when he scratched his fingers through it. There was something vaguely familiar about him, though she knew for a fact she'd never seen him before. It was as if he looked like someone she knew, though she couldn't place who that might be.

"You have a lot of kanshu coming in to buy your junk?"

"Junk?" His chin pulled inward. "I take it you were not raised in a church."

Her eyes lifted above the stove on the opposite side of the narrow room, to the white wooden relic in the shape of a cross. At the bottom knelt a tiny gold figure, hands clasped together in prayer.

"Sure I was," she said. "The church of liars."

He laughed, and the warm sound of it relaxed the knots in her shoulders.

"My mother prayed to a friend of hers. *Mary, full of grace.*" Where Mary was when Marin had been forced to leave her home, she didn't know, but it didn't exactly make her a believer. "My father prayed to whoever put money in his pockets."

"And you?" he asked, eyes twinkling.

"I pray to the gods of canned corn and roasted chicken." Her knife was on the counter beside the sink. She reached for it with her good hand and tucked it into her belt. "Pretty sure they don't hear me, though."

"Then perhaps you are not loud enough." When she snorted, he only chuckled, then returned to the stove to light the burner. Atop it sat a covered pot, and he reached into a drawer for a ladle to stir the contents. She watched the slim window near the ceiling warily as shadows streaked by, stomach grumbling as the scent of spiced broth infused the stale air.

She hadn't eaten since yesterday morning.

How long would it be until the kids at the library had their next meal? Until Gloria took more than a few bites for herself?

They were all starving.

And now she didn't even have the tar to sell. It would be a month before the next batch was ready, and they couldn't last that long.

Her gaze landed on a blue suitcase in the corner she hadn't seen earlier. The zipper was stretched, making a weaving line across the middle.

"You going somewhere, Hiro?" she asked.

Hiro hesitated at the stove, then filled another bowl for himself. "You'll stay here until curfew is up. There are many dangers out tonight."

Firelight filled the main room, flickering across the floor. Then darkness again.

"You're not answering," she said. "Things getting rough?" Gloria wouldn't like hearing about that. Hiro was a healer, the only option many of them had. If he was in trouble, she could arrange for protection.

Hiro laughed weakly. "Rough? An innocent girl was just shot in my shop. No, not rough. Just another night in the docks." He laughed again, but it ended in a tense sigh. "It's getting worse, Marin. Surely you can see that."

"You think it will be better somewhere else?" she asked.

"Maybe. Maybe not." He rubbed his chin. "My name was chosen in the lottery."

The bowl of soup dropped to her lap, sloshing over her thumbs. "For Pacifica."

"I did not think they would take me. They seemed to like that I have a medical degree, even if I don't work for the hospital." His cheeks flared red, and he busied his hands with the dishes.

Maybe he didn't work there now, but he had in the past. Gloria had once told her he'd been let go for taking supplies for the people in the neighborhood who couldn't afford the clinics.

She couldn't believe he was leaving. They may not have been close, but even she knew that removing the corner post of a building would leave it unsteady. Hiro was important. She admired him, and what he did for his people.

"They've announced there was so much interest, they're opening more spots."

Given the riots outside, this seemed impossible. "How many?"

"They didn't say. I take it you did not apply."

She shook her head. Even if she'd wanted to, she couldn't. She wasn't eligible. She wasn't an Alliance citizen.

"A man who cleans the jail came to the library last week," she told him. "He said the cells are all full. That they're sending the rioters la limpieza is picking up to an offshore prison."

It wouldn't be the first time the kanshu had sent Shorelings out to sea, though she doubted many people here knew much about that.

"The jail on the oil rig." Hiro nodded. "I have heard those rumors too."

This part of the story was new to her, and came as a surprise. She'd seen the oil rigs that lined Noram's seaboard, twenty nautical miles off the coast. There was one just off the California Islands. A giant, rusting tabletop, emerging from the water. Five years ago it had been packed with workers; maybe now they were sending prisoners to do the jobs.

"Well, if you think Pacifica is anything more, you're a fool."

If there was a place out there like the one in the ads, she'd have seen it. Some time may have passed since she'd been past the California Islands, but they couldn't scrape enough floating gomi from the water to build a place as nice as they claimed.

Which made her wonder, not for the first time, where exactly the Shorelings were going.

"Then I am a fool," he said bitterly. "But a fool with faith. I am tired of treating hunger pains and mending broken bones with weak painkillers and scrap-wood splints. I must believe there's something better out there. My people deserve it. *You* deserve it."

She scoffed, because he wouldn't say this if he really knew her. If he knew what she'd done.

He sat beside her now, one hand on her shoulder. She flinched, but he didn't move.

"You should go too. Head north. Go to school. You're smart. Make something of your life."

"I like my life the way it is, thanks very much."

"Oh," he said knowingly. "Is that why you hide in Gloria's library? Why you peddle poison to the highest bidder?" The wrinkled cracks around his eyes and mouth seemed deeper in the dim light.

A jerk of her shoulder dislodged the gentle pressure of his hand. She pictured the broken jars of tar on the street again, though it wasn't regret that filled her now, but a hollow kind of shame. She wasn't meant to sell drugs; she was meant to sail the seas. To sit at the captain's table. To command a crew and lead the people of her island, like her father before her.

She was a corsario, proud and defiant. Not a measly drug runner who hid in the shadows.

And yet.

"I've got to eat, same as you, old man."

"Ah." He raised his hands in surrender. "I am not here to judge. We could all use a new start."

She glanced again at his suitcase, hoping, for a moment, that he was right. Because if there was something better for him out there, maybe there was something more for her too.

"Help!" The male shout was loud enough to make her jump. It came from the front of the store.

She crouched behind the foot of the cot. Soup sloshed from the bowl, dripping down to the floor.

A series of knocks, and then the voice came again.

"Please help!"

Hiro stared down at the knife she hadn't realized she'd drawn until just then. Her hand tightened on the grip.

"Be calm. I will take care of this." He motioned for her to lower the weapon.

She hoped he didn't plan on taking care of it the same way he'd taken care of the guy who'd shot her. Ducking out of sight at the foot of the bed, she kept one hand firmly on her weapon.

Another knock, followed by: "*Hurry!*"

She listened to the rustling of boxes, and when she peeked out from behind the bed she saw Hiro move aside the barricade he'd placed in front of the broken entry. Outside the shop, the crowd still hollered and roared, and the sound of glass shattering set her nerves on edge.

When he opened the door, a boy spilled inside. Thin. About her height. About her age. His eye was nearly swollen shut, and blood trickled from his nose.

Adam.

Marin jolted up.

His white shirt was ripped and stained with dirt, and his mouth was set in a hard grimace. One of his legs was bent at the knee, and he gripped a large stand-up cross, working hard not to let his foot touch the ground.

"What is this?" Hiro slammed the door shut behind them and quickly replaced the boxes.

"The patrol . . . they were pulling people in . . . I didn't know where to go . . ." He reached into his pocket and removed a small silver band. "My comm is broken. I need to call my family. *Please.*" He held up a bracelet with a sleek, rectangular box opposite the clasp. The tiny screen was cracked, and black, and it took her a second to recognize the communication device Adam had carried during the riots when they'd hidden in the stairwell.

His gaze swung wildly around the room, landing on Marin and growing wide with fear.

She hadn't realized the knife was in her fist, or that she'd entered the room, holding it braced before her. She was aware of the tattoo on her neck, prickling, just as it had when her father had marked her with the inky needle on her fifth birthday.

"Your friend shot me." She took a step closer.

Hiro stepped between them, as if she weren't holding a blade. "A kanshu boy dies on our streets and they're bringing in the Armament."

Mention of the military that roamed Noram's waters and land had her blood running cold. If people thought la limpieza was bad, they had no idea what awaited them with the Armament.

"Please." Adam's eyes were wide, his bottom lip trembling. "My dad's the vice president. Noah Baker. My friend and I were just being stupid. We didn't think. We didn't . . ." He swallowed a breath. "It's the truth, okay? Look it up on one of your tablets. If you hurt me, there will be consequences."

Hiro gaped at him, then quickly stepped back.

Part of her registered what he was saying—that he was important. The son of one of the most powerful men in Noram, in all of the Alliance.

The other part of her flew to rage, because where were the consequences for hurting *her*?

"Adam Baker," Hiro said under his breath, making her remember how he'd said they were "familiar" earlier. "And your friend. He's the president's son. Torres's son."

Marin glanced at Hiro, wondering if this was some kind of joke.

"It's not true," she said. There was no reason for someone like him to be down in the docks. "He's just saying it so I don't poke a hole in his gut."

But she was filled with doubt. She did recognize them now—she'd seen them at some point on the news with their families.

No. That was impossible. A Torres would never be caught dead in this neighborhood unless surrounded by a team of security.

Or one angry man, willing to shoot her just to get him out.

"He can't be harmed," said Hiro, suddenly urgent. "His people . . ."

He didn't need to finish for Marin to understand his intent. His people included the vice president and the president. If Adam were harmed, the bodyguard and his stunner would be nothing compared to the wrath they would face.

"Please," Adam whispered. "The men who pulled me from the car thought I'd been kidnapped or something. They were trying to save me. The patrol just took them up a block away."

She did turn toward the window then, ears perked for sirens. Any sign that la limpieza was nearing.

"Why don't you just tell the *patrol* who you are?" she asked.

"They won't believe me," he said. "They're not even looking at me. They just see my clothes and skin and think I'm something I'm not."

"A Shoreling?" she asked.

"A *criminal*," he said, and pressed his thumbs to his temples. "I *am* a Shoreling, okay? Please. Do you have a comm?"

Part of her wanted justice, wanted to throw him to la limpieza. The other part of her feared what Hiro did: that his pain would cause much more of her own.

Her knife lowered an inch. Then another. Her throat tightened.

"Step back." Hiro helped him into the other room and settled the vice president's son on the same cot Marin had sat on just minutes before. He removed supplies from the same cabinet he'd pulled her bandage from—clean cloth, needles, thread, and antiseptic. Peeling back the leg of Adam's pants revealed a long red gash, running from the inside of his knee halfway down his calf, and when he grimaced in pain, even Marin had to look away.

She sheathed her knife and snagged the comm he'd dropped on the floor. Gloria had scored a box of them a year or so back, then tossed them because they were too busted to use. But she'd gotten one to work. She'd tinkered with it, taking it apart, figuring out how it worked, then putting it back together.

She tucked it into her pocket. If it did start working again, she didn't want Adam to do something stupid, like call his bodyguard again.

His face contorted with pain as Hiro attempted to straighten his leg. He tossed his head back, gripping the covers on the bed with both fists. She felt a tiny bit of pity for him then. The gash was deep, the mouth of it opening wider than her finger.

From outside came another bang on the door, this one heavier and more insistent.

"This is the City Patrol; open up," came a male voice.

They all froze.

There were more voices outside. Closer now. All talking at once. A beam of light streamed through the front window of the shop.

"We saw people run this way," said the man outside. "Open up!"

She extinguished the candlelight between her thumb and forefinger as Hiro hurriedly tried to bandage Adam's leg, then ran for the back door, lined with locks. Pressing her ear against it, she heard the whir of the sirens, too close for comfort.

Her whole body pulsed with a singular need: escape.

She ripped open the locks, one by one, and cracked the door. A dark alley appeared before her, in full view of the street, just fifteen feet beyond. Blue light flashed from the patrol cars parked there, and in horror she watched as a shirtless man running past them crashed to the ground and began writhing like a worm left to bake on the asphalt. An officer came running to kneel beside him, still holding the weapon that delivered the shock. A few people had appeared outside, staying on the fringe, despite the earlier warnings of curfew violations, but they scrammed as three more cars appeared, two of them black vans.

The man was lifted and hauled through the sliding door of one of them.

She slammed the door, recalling with a jolt of dread her words with Hiro about an offshore prison.

He'd finished dressing the wound and was helping Adam to stand.

"Leave him!" Marin hissed at Hiro. Their best bet at making it out of here in one piece was for Adam to be found alone.

The old man gave one quick shake of his head, and then glanced toward the front of the shop. "I can hold them off."

"You're crazy," she hissed, grabbing his shoulder. "We need to get out of here."

She turned back toward the alley door, but the sirens on that side of the building were still screeching.

They were trapped.

She should have left when she had the chance.

"Go through the back," said Hiro. "Keep your heads down and move fast."

She didn't like it; leaving felt like turning him over to la limpieza. Like he would soon disappear just like the Lus, maybe to that offshore prison. He'd done nothing wrong.

"Be safe, Marin."

With that, he ran to the front of the shop.

Her eyes met Adam's, and the white-ringed horror in them was too familiar. They brought her to another place, another time. The moment where everything in her life had broken in an unfixable, irreplaceable way.

He looked to the side, then gave a small groan. "Help me get out of here and there will be money, I promise."

Her fingers moved to the bruise on her chest. This sounded like a trap if she'd ever heard one.

"Ayúdame." Adam's voice was a broken whisper. *Help me.*

If there was a reward, Gloria could use it to buy the food they needed.

If.

There was no time to weigh the options. She grabbed his arm and slung it over her shoulders, then plowed through the back door into the alley.

It was saving all of them, she told herself. If she was caught with him looking like this, they wouldn't believe she was innocent in a million years.

They snuck through the alley toward the main street, and the patrol cars, and the people who shouted their insults from the sidewalk. She stayed behind them, keeping her head down.

Not more than twenty paces and she knew they'd been spotted.

"Hey!" a woman shouted. "Stop!"

They had to get off the road. Frantically, they ran, a three-legged hobble as Marin supported half of Adam's weight. She searched for a place to hide, making the split-second decision to dive behind a trash compactor. Her knees skidded across the ground, the pavement scraping through her pants. Fumbling with Adam's shirt, she pulled him close. Their bodies smashed together, jammed against the dirty metal bin and the rough stone wall.

Footsteps ran in their direction. Voices: *They went this way. Did you see them?*

Adam folded closer against her, trying to pull his leg in. The knife was smashed between them, useless. She could feel his comm pressing into her hip, in the pocket where she'd shoved it. The sharp smell of his sweat brought on a fresh wave of fear, and she felt her body harden and brace for a fight.

The footsteps stopped.

They became statue-still, mouths open to keep their breaths as silent as possible. She could feel him shaking, and she wanted to scream at him to stop. To hold it together.

Shadows moved against the far alley wall, then blended with the darkness.

She slid one hand over Adam's face, over his parted lips, feeling his hot breaths on her hand. *Be quiet. Be quiet. Be quiet.*

"Got you," came a gruff voice from the side.

With a shout of surprise, he was sucked away from her, out from behind the trash compactor. Her fingers grasped his hair, the collar of his shirt, just as his dug into the floor, making an awful scraping sound that gripped the base of her spine. His next cry was that of pain, and a sob rose in her throat, silent and choking.

"Looks like someone just got himself a one-way ticket out to sea," said the man in the boots. "Where's your friend, huh?"

She stayed where she was, even when everything within her screamed to fight. Adam wasn't her problem. She needed to get herself out of here.

While he argued, she braced the knife before her. Another set of boots approached, and though she could hear the unmistakable sounds of fists striking flesh, Adam never gave her away. She could only see his feet around the corner. One hung loosely, the other kicked the bin.

"The other's got to be in there somewhere." The trash bin's metal lid clanged against the wall as it was flung open. In the street she could hear more sirens coming. They screamed with the blood pounding in her ears.

They dragged Adam away, laughing as he said his name, and his father's.

There was nothing she could do. As soon as they took him into the street, she ran.

She ran until the sirens were a faraway whisper, until her lungs felt like they would explode. She ran until she could hide, and then she huddled in the dark until the shaking passed.

CHAPTER 12

IN HIS room, where he'd been told to go to wait for information, Ross gripped his comm, delivered an hour earlier from the museum along with his coat. For the fiftieth time, he tapped the small screen until Adam's face appeared, then dialed his friend's device.

When he lifted it to his ear, he heard nothing but static.

"Hello?" His voice cracked.

Nothing.

He turned the comm off and on, over and over, feeling another punch of guilt each time Adam's face appeared. He opened the tracking screen to locate the other device, but the GPS map was blank. Questions streamed through his brain. *Where are you?* And *What is wrong with everyone below the cliffline?* He willed Tersley to return with news, but the only person who'd come by was Barrett, the head of housekeeping, offering him a sedative.

He'd declined.

Standing, he paced around his bedroom, unable to shake the image of Adam being pulled out of the car from his mind. Too much time had passed. Hours, Adam had been down there alone now. Anything could have happened.

From beneath his collarbones came a stabbing pain, making it hard to breathe.

Blankly, he stared at the black screen mounted above his desk. It was as wide as he was tall. A game console sat below it, untouched since it had started boring him a month ago. There was a plate of food on his desk that Barrett had brought, but he'd yet to take a bite. There was enough purified water in the attached bathroom to drown a horse.

He wanted none of these things. All he wanted was Adam back, and that girl alive. But he couldn't even help the security team find them, because his father had ordered him to go to school and pretend things were normal. If he didn't make *better decisions,* the president would be blamed. The entire nation would face consequences. *Civil war,* his father had said. They were on the tipping point.

The responsibility of it all threatened to crumble him. He collapsed into his desk chair, sick with himself. Sick that Adam hadn't pushed harder to stay at the museum.

Sick that the girl hadn't put her knife down faster.

Was she alive now? Was she hurt? He tried to think of something—anything—else, but his thoughts kept returning to her wild tangles of dark hair, and the number just below her ear— "86." To the sound she'd made when she'd been shot, and when she'd crashed to the ground.

After a moment, he turned on his computer and stared down at the keyboard, finding the microphone button Adam had shown him a long time ago.

He cleared his throat, but it didn't make it any easier to breathe.

"Number eighty-six," he said.

Instantly, the screen was filled with a barrage of images and words. The pictures drew his attention. Some of them were old, grainy scans—military pictures of submarines that could no longer be used because of debris in the water, restaurants and bars from the pre-Melt days. Most were just various scripts of the same number.

"Refine search," he said. "Tattoo number eighty-six. Photos only."

He looked at each of them but they were too big, or too fancy, or part of something else. He wanted to see *her* 86. The simple, small numbers in black ink.

He scrolled down through the pages until his eyes landed on a faded stamp on pale, bluish skin. Immediately he recoiled. The tattoo was clearly on someone's neck, just below their ear, and from the looks of it, they'd been dead awhile.

It wasn't her, he told himself. She had curly hair, and what was shown here was short and light—with stubble on the jaw. A man. Not a girl.

Ross's hand hovered above the clicker for a long moment before he pressed down.

The image expanded to fill the screen, and his chest constricted. Words popped up on the right side, a jumble of letters and numbers that swam in his mind like his memories from the night before last.

"Search result six hundred forty-seven," came an automated male voice. Ross jumped. He'd forgotten the computer was still in audio mode. He scrambled for the volume button, lowering it to a whisper. "Department of Justice archives, photograph of unidentified male found by Armament, tangled with ocean debris, ten nautical miles west of California Islands. Age: late twenties. Date: January, forty-one post-Melt."

The picture was forty years old.

"Tattoo," Ross said quietly, glancing at his door. The house was quiet.

"Unidentified body with seventeen black ink tattoos, in various states of decomposition due to water damage."

"Tattoo beneath his ear," Ross clarified.

"Tattoo number eighty-six, thought to be in gang affiliation with the Original Eighty-Six."

"What is the Original Eighty-Six?" asked Ross.

The screen flashed to a white screen with red letters.

"Access denied," said the computer.

"Refine search," said Ross. "Gangs, Original Eighty-Six."

"Access denied," repeated the computer. This wasn't unusual. The security restrictions on the internet were tight in the political districts. It was a way to protect sensitive information. Sometimes they were ridiculous, though. He could have been blocked because the numbers eight and six had been used in a legislative bill this week. It might have nothing to do with what he wanted.

He sat back, then tried other search terms. *Gangs, Noram City. Gangs, post-Melt. Criminals. California Islands. Armament. 86.*

Every time he got close, he was denied access.

The alarm beside his bed beeped. It was time to go to school.

For the first time since he'd entered high school, Ross was early to meet the car. A new security officer stood beside it, a man with a narrow nose and short, dark hair, clasped hands hanging below his belt like he was afraid someone might kick him between the legs. His eyes were hidden by sunglasses, and he wore Tersley's same plain, navy suit.

"Good morning." He held out a hand. "I'm Brighton. Your new security officer."

Ross did not shake his hand. The man's arm lowered. Beyond the overhang, a light drizzle had begun, making the air thicker. In the distance, Ross could already hear the grumble of thunder.

"Where's Tersley?"

"He was reassigned." The man's expression didn't change. "I've been briefed on your schedule. If there are any changes just let me know."

So it would be like this. Like everything was fine. Despite what he'd said the last time they'd spoken, Ross didn't want a new Tersley. He wanted things to go back to normal, the way they never could. Where Adam was beside him, giving him a synopsis of last night's history reading, and Tersley was motioning him to walk faster, and what existed below the cliffline was a curiosity, not a reality.

He said, "I want to know what's going on."

Brighton paused midway through opening the car door. "Your father wanted me to tell you to have a good day, and to remember what you talked about. A lot's riding on you."

The conversation with his father returned hard and fast, and disgusted him in so many ways. Because this new Tersley was probably his father's spy. Because Adam was missing, and yet still taking the fall. Because a girl's life was at stake and no one seemed to care. Because every day his father carried burdens that Ross couldn't possibly understand, and in one stupid night he'd jeopardized the president's ability to hold a whole country together.

He got in the car.

———

Center Academy's brightly lit main hall led into a dome-covered courtyard, filled with iron sculptures and benches where students sat and talked, awaiting class. Ross had managed to convince Brighton to stay outside, but now felt alone without Adam at his side. He hovered on the outskirts of the crowd, knowing that if he walked through, half a dozen people would want to say hello. Today, he couldn't even pretend to be social, so he detoured down the first hall on his left, a familiar path that cut through the athletic wing.

The walls were lined with banners and trophies for the school's various athletic teams—rowing and swimming, which were done in Center's pool; archery and shooting, which were so much like his console games at home he never bothered signing up; dance; wrestling and boxing, both noncontact and done in simulators, which couldn't be more boring or fake; and track.

His name was stamped into thirteen plaques on the wall for different length sprints, and as he continued on, he looked up at his father's name beneath a section marked "Worthy Alumni." George Torres had done distance running in his day. He'd tried to convince Ross endurance required more skill and dedication, but Ross had always preferred to run all out, full speed, until his legs shook and felt like they would buckle.

He stopped and stared at the plaque for several long moments, wondering how many times he'd wanted his own right next to it, just so one day his father might see.

Moving on, he passed the coaches' offices and found himself pushing through the door into a dark gym, notably cooler in temperature and smelling faintly of sweat. The lights rose slowly, revealing eight treadmills, all sleek black and spotless, all facing a giant wall screen.

He walked to one and climbed aboard, feeling the spongy padding beneath his uniform shoes. He pressed a button that activated the machine with a loud hum, and the screen before him burst into light. It had been a couple months, but his fingers remembered the moves. He turned the dial and the screen before him flashed from a stadium track, to an old red dirt road, to a mountain trail. In the keypad he could type his name, and it would bring up a log of his old stats: times, race dates, practice runs. He didn't, though. He stared at the dusty road leading up the hill toward a clear, blue sky, and thought of how he'd never run farther than the length of his own stride.

"Look who finally came around."

Ross turned to find Marcus Pruitt standing just inside the door. At under six feet, he was one of the shorter guys on the team, but what he lacked in height, he made up in muscle. He was flanked by the Gomez brothers—Felipe and Jonas—fraternal twins who shared the same broad forehead, but little else.

Ross rolled his shoulders back, aware of every muscle that refused to relax. They thought he'd rejoined the team. That he could, after what they'd done.

"Finally," Felipe said. He was thicker than his brother, generally less of a pain in the ass, though they hadn't spoken since the day Ross had quit the team. "We slipped to second without you."

Ross faltered. "Kasca?" The northern school was always their biggest competition.

Felipe nodded.

For an instant, he wanted back in the game. To put on his uniform, lace up his shoes. Leave Kasca in the dust. All he had to do was sign back up for the team.

"Don't see your shadow. You and your boyfriend have a fight?" Jonas, the taller, skinnier Gomez, asked, making a show of scanning the corners in the room.

Ross's hands clenched. He stepped off the treadmill.

"Don't be ridiculous," Felipe said, gaze landing somewhere on the far wall.

"Felipe is right," said Pruitt. "Ross doesn't let him out of his cage until nine o'clock." He took a bite of an apple in his hand, and juice sprayed into the air. Jonas chuckled. Even Felipe cracked a smile.

Before Ross knew it, he was standing inches away from Pruitt, staring at his ruddy face. Fury vibrated down his limbs as Pruitt took a slow look at the hand Ross had fisted in his collar.

"I told you before to leave him alone," Ross said. He wanted Pruitt to try to hit him. To test just how thin his control actually was.

"What's wrong with you?" Pruitt said, unimpressed, as he shoved Ross's hand away. "You don't have to play diplomat every second of the day. In case you forgot, his trawler friends are putting good people on stretchers every night."

Ross felt a slash of regret as he remembered that Pruitt's mother was the chief of the City Patrol, and that she could easily be one of those good people he mentioned.

But she also could have been the other kind, who'd forced him and Adam to run for safety.

"He didn't do anything to you," Ross said.

"Yet." The word hung between them like a threat.

"All right," said Felipe, though he didn't follow it up with anything.

Ross inched closer to Pruitt, ready to pound him into the floor. Maybe it would make him feel better, maybe not. He'd have to see.

"Is there a problem, gentlemen?"

Ross turned to see Professor Dorn, his English teacher, standing in the threshold, and the backs of the Gomez brothers as they made a quick escape down the hall.

"I don't know," said Pruitt. "Is there a problem?"

Ross took another step back. He pushed his hands in his pockets, fists clenched so hard they vibrated.

But it wasn't his fist vibrating. His comm was vibrating. Automatically, he looked down, and saw Adam's face on the small screen.

He felt a sudden sense of lightness, as if he'd tripped and had yet to hit the ground.

A message was typed beneath the picture.

"No," said Ross quickly. "We're good here. I just need to, uh . . . take a walk."

"Take your time," said the professor, as if class weren't starting in a few minutes.

No one at Center questioned the things Ross did or said. Last term, he'd passed math without turning in one piece of homework. Last week, Professor Atwal had given him perfect marks on an essay about the North American Culture Clash, and the two paragraphs he turned in were copied straight out of his sociology text.

He strode away without another word, head throbbing, feet moving in time with his racing pulse. His gaze lowered again to the message.

Plaza Centro. Need help. No security.

Adam was in trouble.

He didn't know why he'd said no security, except that maybe he was afraid of his dad finding out. Ross didn't blame him. Every fear he'd felt pushed against the ragged edges of his control. He needed to get to the Plaza Centro now.

The halls were empty; class had begun. At a jog, Ross tapped the screen, but the call was met with static. It didn't go through—something must have been wrong with his comm.

On my way, he messaged back. He hoped Adam got it. If not, he'd be there soon enough.

Because he didn't know how to turn off the tracker, he decided to turn the whole comm off. Adam didn't want security, fine. Adam got whatever Adam wanted for the rest of his life as far as Ross was concerned.

He ran back through the athletic wing, past the practice room, out the back doors into the now pelting rain. Maybe the camera outside the building caught him leaving, but if it did, no one came to stop him. He kept his head down and crossed the street, entering the back of Monument Park and passing an ancient, giant statue of Lincoln that had been moved from the old capital. Then he ran through the rain to the courthouse, where he waved down a taxi and told the driver to take him to the Plaza Centro.

CHAPTER 13

MARIN HID in the alley between a giant stone theater and a restaurant, eyes on the tiled fountain marking the middle of the
plaza, the bracelet comm she'd taken from Adam in her hand. Her
fingertips traced the cracked glass of its face and around to the
back, where earlier she'd popped off the slim battery pack with her
knife and found the chip dislodged from its holding place. Once
she'd realigned the parts, it had turned back on. Shortly after, it
began to vibrate, and a picture had flashed up on the small screen.

Blue Eyes. *Ross Torres.* The son of the president.

She was so shocked by the fact that he was there that she'd
nearly thrown the comm across the street and made a run for it. It
was like he was following her, and if he was, maybe his bodyguard
was too.

But then she'd remembered that this was Adam's comm, and
that if Ross was calling, he was looking for Adam. She'd held it
up to her face again, staring at his thumbnail-sized photo, still
unable to believe she'd met him—in a *riot*, no less. The whole thing

seemed half dream, half nightmare now. Too impossible to be true.

She thought about the way he'd picked her up off the pavement when they'd run, and how he'd tried to talk his man out of shooting her. There'd been genuine worry on his face when he'd told Hiro she'd been hurt.

Those things seemed most impossible of all. There were reasons the Shorelings hated the elder Torres, and none of them had to do with the kindness she'd seen in his son.

It didn't make sense.

So she'd kept the comm, huddled in her hiding place atop an old fire escape, and checked through Adam's messages as the sunrise finally released the docks from curfew.

Ross Torres had called twenty-seven times during the night.

He'd left messages too. *Where are you?* And *Tersley's coming to get you.* And *I'm sorry.*

He hadn't planned on being separated from his friend, which meant there was an even slimmer chance he'd expected Adam to be taken by la limpieza. The fact that he'd continued calling led her to believe that he still didn't know where Adam was, which meant that she possessed some potentially valuable information.

The kind someone with money might even pay for.

Adam had said if she helped him there'd be a reward. Maybe she'd lost him, but she knew where he'd gone at least. And if she could turn that into money for Gloria, she would.

They might not have to starve after all.

Because part of the comm was still damaged, she couldn't answer him, or call him back, but the messaging feature seemed to still work so before she chickened out she'd told him to meet her here, at the plaza. *No security,* she'd said. Last thing she needed was to get shot in the chest again.

Leaning against the theater, she rubbed her sore wrist, staying out of the way of the people who walked by. No one else was dressed like she was. No one else's skin was as browned by the sun. If she made herself too obvious, she'd make others suspicious, and she wouldn't put it past these rich kanshu to call la limpieza on her.

Besides, if Ross came, she wanted to see him first, to make sure he was alone.

Minutes passed, each one gnawing on the ends of her nerves.

"Come on, terreno," she said, using the word her people used to describe the mainland monsters. It reminded her of the past, of drunken words slung out around the firepit. Of her father, and stupid Luc, who was next in line to head the captain's table.

The thought made her cringe, like she'd just bitten into something too sour.

I am not the only one who wants a new start.

Hiro was wrong about that. She didn't want a new start, she needed one. Noram wasn't a destination for her, it was a hiding place.

Movement by the fountain caught her attention. A man, running from a car on the side of the road toward the fountain's cluster of stone trees. Despite his speed, he moved almost effortlessly, rocking as he came to a stop in the center of the pavilion. He was wearing a clean white shirt, made see-through on his shoulders and chest by the rain. His dark blue pants were streaked with water, but the way he held himself, shoulders back, chin high, brought on a punch of recognition before her gaze could rise to his face.

This was Ross Torres, son of the president. How she'd not seen that before, she didn't know. His dark hair was gleaming wet. Wariness had drawn in his black brows. His mouth was a thin line as he checked the comm on his wrist and then spun in a circle, looking all around.

He seemed to be alone, but it could be a trap. His bodyguard could be hiding somewhere—tons of them could have come with him. If they found out she'd tricked him into coming here, she'd surely be arrested, then they'd see her tattoo and know she was a corsario. They'd throw her in a box, and she'd never see the water or the open sky again.

She could set down the comm and run, and he'd be none the wiser.

It was her grumbling stomach that held her in place. She was hungry, and the people who'd helped her were hungry, and this could end all of it.

Her father's words whispered back to her from years earlier. *You are a corsario.*

It was time, once again, to think like a pirate.

Taking a deep breath, she stepped from the shadows, from the protection of the theater, into the rain.

He didn't see her at first, and she didn't go to him. She waited while he turned, and searched, and checked his comm. People moved around them, hiding beneath their umbrellas, wearing long sleeves and pants to protect their skin from the bite of the rain.

She could tell the moment he saw her. He grew very still and stared, mouth open, as if he were seeing something he couldn't make sense of.

He took a step forward, and then another, and she didn't move. Her heart pounded, but her feet stayed in place. Her head screamed to run, but she didn't falter.

She lifted her chin and tucked her strong hand behind her, around the handle of her knife, just in case.

His pace never went faster than that same cautious walk, though he still seemed to reach her too soon, before she was ready. An arm's length away, he stopped, gaze roaming over her face and falling lower, to the fist-sized bruise below her collarbone.

Rain slid down his temples, but he didn't seem to notice. He just kept staring until her skin began to flush, and she felt like he could see every secret she kept locked away inside.

With her sore hand, she tried to pull up the neck of her sleeveless shirt, to hide the bruise from where she'd been shot, but the shirt was too tight and sticky from the rain, and it clung to her narrow waist, unable to stretch.

"You're all right," he finally said.

Then, before she could answer, he closed the space between them and wrapped her up in his arms, smashing her against his chest, elbows at her sides. She wasn't immediately sure what he was doing—if he was trying to crush the life out of her, or just giving her a hug. He squeezed so tight she could barely manage to tell him to let her go, and it wasn't until her knee connected with his thigh that he finally set her down.

"Sorry," he said quickly. He raked a hand through his hair, blinking back the rain. "Sorry. I just . . . I didn't know . . ."

"You're glad to see me," she said. "I get it. Happens all the time."

But it didn't really. She spent most of her time lying low, or running errands for Gloria. It didn't leave a lot of time for hugging strangers.

He quirked a smile, then gave a quick shake of his head. "Have you seen the guy I was with last night? Adam?" He looked behind her, into the alley. "He's supposed to be meeting me here."

"What a coincidence," she said.

He gave her an odd look.

Lifting her hand, she unfurled her fist, showing the smudged silver band and the cracked face of Adam's comm.

Ross stared at it.

"I don't understand."

The space between her ribs felt liquid and cold as she straightened her back.

"He said there'd be money. A reward."

A beat passed, and then Ross's expression changed. Lines creased around his eyes. His jaw flexed beneath the smooth skin. A vein in his neck stood out.

It was nothing personal. She was doing this to help Gloria. To help herself. With the tar gone, she didn't have another way, not for another month at least.

"No security," he said slowly. "Is that because you have him?"

An old familiar rush filled her blood. It wasn't unusual for her dad or the other captains to ransom prisoners. The process was simple even. Board their boat. Steal their goods. Tell them to contact their families or employers and arrange an exchange.

If their people didn't pay, they swam. Simple.

But she had never taken a prisoner before. She didn't even have a prisoner *to* take.

It didn't matter. Selling information was the same as selling tar. When it came down to it, she had something he wanted.

"I don't have him," she said. "But I know who does, and for a price, I'll tell you what I know."

CHAPTER 14

Ross BLINKED. And then blinked again. For a moment, there was only silence in his head, and then the clashing of too many thoughts all at once. *Is he okay? What did you do to him? How did you find his comm? Is this some kind of joke?*

"Okay," he said. Because apparently that was what you said when your brain shorted out.

"Okay?" She gave a short laugh. "Well, that was easy, wasn't it?"

The rain grew heavier around them, cool enough to prickle his skin. Her shirt clung to her chest, and he looked again to the black-and-brown bruise that had to be from Tersley's shot.

Was she doing this because she was mad about what had happened? He couldn't blame her if that was the case, but still, this was his friend's life they were talking about. This was *Adam*.

"Where is he?" Ross asked.

Her brown eyes held his, steadier than anyone he'd ever faced before. She wasn't afraid of him. He got the sense she wasn't afraid of much.

"I need some money first," she said.

Whatever part of him had thought this might be a terrible plank dried up and blew away.

"You're serious," he said.

"As a fist to the face."

His chin lifted. "You want money in exchange for information."

She tapped the side of her head. "Now he's getting it."

She was trying to scam him, and even though he knew it, he had to let it happen. Without her, he had no idea where Adam might be.

"How much?" he asked.

Her gaze flicked to the side. Her hands and forearms were covered with small scars, he noticed—thin pink marks shades lighter than her skin.

"A hundred thousand credits," she said.

He choked.

Her cheeks darkened.

When they'd hidden together last night, he'd thought she was different from the other Shorelings. She'd taken a beating for him, pulled a knife in his defense. But now he could see she was the same as those maniacs who'd dragged Adam from the car.

"Let me check my pockets," he said, turning them out slowly to reveal their emptiness. "I guess I left my solid gold bars at home today."

"Make jokes, terreno," she said, using a word he'd never heard before. "But I know where they took your friend."

"Who took him?" He stepped closer. She moved into the shadow of the building, away from him, where the rain was lighter. He followed, giving her space, but checking over his shoulder to see if anyone watched them.

"Who took Adam?" he pressed.

"Uh-uh." She shook her head. "You help me, I help you."

"You could be lying."

"I could be," she said. And then she smiled, and it was equal parts dazzling and terrifying because of what she might be holding back.

"This isn't funny," he said.

"You're the one making jokes."

His thumbs drummed against his thighs.

"Is he all right?"

She held out an open hand. He swore and looked away.

"I don't have access to one hundred thousand credits," he said. "Do you have any idea how much that is?"

"I'm poor," she said. "Not stupid."

He wanted to yell. Kick something. Release some of the frustration trapped inside him.

"If you come with me to my house, I can get what you want," he said.

"If by *what you want*, you mean *shot again*, then I'm sure you can." She crossed her arms over her chest and cocked a hip. "Nice try, but I don't think so."

He pressed his thumbs to his temples. He could get a couple thousand transferred through his comm without question, but he needed her comm to complete the transaction. To get actual, old-fashioned cash—which he assumed she wanted if she didn't want to get caught blackmailing him—he'd need to go to a bank, and there was no way to do that without alerting his family and security team.

He had to be smart. His father negotiated with dangerous people every day. This wasn't that different.

He took a deep breath.

"Take me to Adam, and I'll double the amount."

She scoffed.

He held his ground, and held her gaze, remembering a time that Tersley had taught him to play poker, and how to bluff when he didn't have a good hand.

"Thought you didn't have access to that kind of money."

"I lied," he said. "I'll get it for you if you take me to Adam."

Now she balked, but she was considering it. He could tell in the way she tapped her teeth together.

"I don't have a tracker on him," she said. "I just know where they said they were going."

"So take me there."

"And if you don't find your friend?"

"I'll make sure you're compensated anyway," he said before he'd thought about it. "Half to get there, the rest if we find him. You win either way."

There were too many questions—who and where and how exactly she knew this information. Part of him was convinced it was all a lie. But he couldn't chance it.

She'd been with Adam last night. She'd seen him.

He needed her help.

"No *patrol*," she said. "No guards."

"Just me."

"What's to stop your friend from shooting me, soon as we get back?"

He cringed, the words washing back the memory of when he thought she'd been killed.

"That won't happen again," he said.

The arch of her brow said she wasn't convinced.

"Half to take me, the rest when we find him. Nobody knows I'll be with you. No one is going to follow us."

His father had been that bold with the leader of the Oil Nation. Hopefully that same boldness would pay off now.

After a moment, she nodded and thrust out a hand.

"You got yourself a deal, terreno."

He took her hand, but she didn't shake. She pulled him closer and whispered, "You don't make good on this, I'm telling everyone below the cliffline your friend shot me, unarmed, and left me for dead. You won't be able to buy yourself out of that."

Then she released his grip, and with a smile, told him they'd need a car.

Five minutes later, Ross sat beside the girl in the back seat of a taxi, heading toward Lower Noram. The rain grew heavier the closer they came to the cliffline, and Ross kept close to the window, keeping to his side of the seat.

She knew where Adam was.

She wanted money.

She'd threatened to tell everyone Tersley had shot her if he didn't deliver his end of the bargain.

It wouldn't work out, of course, not unless the Bakers coughed up the credits. His mom and dad certainly weren't going to agree to pay some random Shoreling girl that much to bring Adam home.

Maybe his father could take care of it, make this go away like he'd said he would last night. The thought made him a little sick to his stomach—he didn't even know what that would entail—but what other choice did Ross have? He needed to make sure his father was protected from his failures so that he could lead a country.

He'd worry about the details later. For now, he just needed to find Adam.

"Where is he?" Ross asked again. "Who took him?"

"You really have no idea?" She cocked a brow, and he was struck again by her voice. It was warm, and a little gritty, like sand blowing across the ground.

He shook his head.

"La limpieza," she said. "Your patrol."

That didn't relieve him as much as it might have two days ago. Now when he thought of the patrol, he didn't just think of Marcus Pruitt's mother in her shiny uniform at one of his father's events. He thought of soldiers in riot gear, crushing them with shields and sticks.

"They arrested him?"

"They took him."

He didn't understand the difference. "What's that mean?"

"It means he's not going to the jail," she said.

He looked her way, seeing how the rain tamed her dark hair and made it shine, and drip down her thin neck. She pulled at the ends, absently covering up the small tattoo beneath her ear—the "86" he'd looked up earlier.

"He came back to the shop after you ran off—la limpieza must have followed him. They rounded him up with the other rioters and threw him in a car. One of them mentioned a one-way ticket out to sea."

That didn't make sense. The suspicion that this was a setup, that she was lying to get paid, twisted his gut. The only boats he knew of that went to sea were the freighter ships that delivered food and supplies up and down the coastline. He'd never heard of a patrol boat.

"They wouldn't do that," he said. "Someone will figure out who he is and bring him home."

"If they had, don't you think they would have already done it?"

She fished Adam's comm out of her pocket again and showed a series of messages from his mom and dad.

Where are you?

Did you stay at Ross's?

You're in trouble.

Just talked to the principal. Not like you to ditch school. Come home.

Worried. Call your mom.

Bile turned in his stomach. He tried to think of where at sea the patrol would take prisoners, but came up blank. The Armament covered the Pacific. Their base was in Old San Francisco, across the bay, but the military would have recognized the vice president's son, and anyway, the jail and courts were on the mainland.

He and Adam had watched the riot footage most nights, but no one mentioned where the prisoners had been taken. Inland, he'd assumed, to the federal detention centers that were always petitioning his father for more funds. He'd never heard of a jail out at sea, not even a whisper of one from his father, or his father's cabinet.

He looked out his window, unable to gain his bearings surrounded by all these decrepit stone buildings and their neon signs. Groups of people gathered on the corners, looking up as they passed in mild curiosity. Automatically, he reached for the lock on the door, pressing the button and then wiping his damp palms on his wet pant legs. His heart was pounding. He wanted this over with as soon as possible.

On the seat behind the driver, a screen played images from the relocation center in the docks. Shorelings were lined up, smiling, holding their paperwork.

He turned it off.

"You know where this place is?" he asked.

"It's been a while since I've been out that way," she said, a little quieter.

It didn't exactly make him feel better about the whole thing.

"I didn't know that would happen," he said, realizing that if they were going to do this, he needed to clear some things up. "That Tersley would shoot you, I mean. He's my bodyguard. He was just trying to protect me. It's his job."

"Great job."

He scowled, and as she grew quiet, he wished he could tell what she was thinking, and that he could somehow tell her how Tersley had taught him to fight, and once even to drive a car. That for the last two years he'd been with Ross more than his parents, more than his teachers, even more than Adam.

But Tersley had shot her, and not just in defense. There were other reasons he'd done it that Ross didn't care to admit—that he didn't even have to, because as he looked at the girl, it was clear she already knew.

His gaze fell below her neck, to the wet, rust-colored shirt that clung to her like a second skin. He'd been so sure that a bullet had pierced her heart, but there was only a dark purple bruise below her collarbone. *I just stunned her,* Tersley had said. Ross had been so reluctant to believe anything the man said after what had happened.

"Donner Cove, you said?" called the driver from the front seat, as he took the winding road down into Lower Noram. Cars were stopped in a line trying to get above the cliffline, but those going down could pass right through.

"That's right," said the girl.

"You sure?" he asked. "There's no electric down there."

He thought the man might be talking about the erosion, but the girl only tapped the seat and said, "I know."

They took a road around the outside of the slums, leading toward the water. Even in the rain, the docks looked different.

In the dark it was hard to see how the buildings had been falling apart. The jagged cracks that split the stucco siding, the metal and stone debris that littered the road. A path had been cleared for cars, but it was thin, and the driver kept slowing in order not to scrape the side of the taxi. It was like the giant quake that had split the city had happened only yesterday.

"Here we are," announced the driver.

A terrible excitement shook through him as they reached the open gateway to the pier. The rain was a little lighter than before, the black clouds farther inland, leaving a rare breath of cool before the humidity returned. Mounted at the top of the gate, the blue, green, and red stripes of the Alliance's flag whipped in the wind, tailing east. Beyond it stretched the water, churning below a pale gray sky.

"Stop here," said the girl.

They pulled beside the overflowing trash bins a stone's throw away from a two-story stucco building. One side appeared condemned, and had been closed off by a chain-link fence. The other still had glass in the windows, though most of it was cracked. Light flickered in one of the rooms on the bottom floor.

"This is where they took him?" asked Ross, not even bothering to hide the disbelief.

She nodded toward the water, to the stone steps that descended to a rickety, boarded pier, where he saw a dozen or more boats. They weren't like the small speedboats he'd ridden on at the Green Energy Initiative in Ottawa last spring, or the freight ships he'd seen in pictures that Noram no longer used on account of the storms. These were actual boats, with actual sails.

"Down there," she said quietly.

Through the window in the boathouse, he could see shadows moving before a flickering flame. Someone was inside.

"You sure you want to get out here?" asked the driver.

Not really, Ross thought, but if these people knew where Adam was and he walked away, he'd hate himself. He knew this wasn't his job, that this was the sort of thing for patrolmen. That he wasn't any kind of hero and would probably end up just making things worse. But things couldn't get much worse. Adam was missing because of him. The security team for the president and vice president was searching for him. Patrolmen and Armament alike had to have him on their radar, and yet no one had picked up a trail. If he didn't go with her, his chance at finding Adam might disappear.

He turned on his comm just long enough to pay the driver, and then shut it off again. Brighton would track him here, but by then he'd hopefully have Adam back.

"Come on," said the girl. As soon as they left the car, the driver sped away.

He followed her at a jog toward the iron fence that separated the lot from the pier. A thick chain, fastened by a lock the size of his fist, crisscrossed over the gate. He mirrored her crouch, still mostly hidden from the boathouse by a pile of rubble in the parking lot.

"We need to get to my boat," she said.

He looked down at the lock, and then back at the lit window in the station behind them, thinking of how she seemed to be in quite a hurry.

"It is *your* boat, right?"

Her nostrils flared. "Course it's my boat. Who else's boat do you think it is?"

He held his hands up in surrender. "Just a question."

"It's mine," she said. "They shut the gates to keep thieves out."

"I imagine that's true." He swallowed down the growing sense that they were about to do something illegal.

"We'll take my boat to where they took your friend," she said. "Unless you changed your mind, of course."

His hand gripped the metal gate hard enough to make his knuckles turn white. He hadn't fully realized until now that she meant to sail him somewhere.

He thought of Adam's hand slipping from his. Of his father's advice to grow up, which really meant to shut up. Of a world where he ran on treadmills to nowhere, and nothing he did ever mattered, not even the potential murder of a Shoreling girl.

Maybe she was stealing this boat, maybe not, but she wasn't leaving without him.

"What's your name?" He swiped the rain out of his eyes. He watched the way it drenched her hair, formed points at the bottom of the curls and dripped from her chin. Her threadbare pants, which hadn't left much to the imagination before, now sagged on her hips and clung to her legs.

"What?" she asked.

"Your name," he said. "I don't know it."

She glanced at him, brows pinched. "Marin."

With that, she launched herself over the fence and was running, low and fast, down the concrete steps. He went after her, scrambling over the gate in an embarrassingly uncoordinated way that made him glad she wasn't watching, and then jogged down the stairs, shoes splashing in the puddles. By the time he reached the deck, the rain was coming down in sheets. He breathed in the thick, wet air, smelling salt and wet, rotten things, and felt his lungs work harder to keep up with his thundering heart.

He wasn't prepared for the unevenness of the dock; the way it bobbed and swayed between his steps and the waves below. The plastic planks were slippery, too, and as he skidded to the side and fell to one knee, he braced himself on his hands, like a runner at the starting gate.

She'd turned back for him, flying over the boards as if she weighed nothing.

"Let's go!" she shouted through the rain.

He gritted his teeth and shoved up, determined. While she ran past the strange boats, some covered with tarps, others taking water at an alarming rate, he teetered after her, breath catching every time he lost his balance. The brown-gray water below was flecked with floating trash, and who knew what kinds of things were festering beneath the oil-slicked surface. He trained his eyes on each boat, a feeling of being watched raising the tiny hairs on his arms.

Near the end of the longest dock, they came to the biggest heap of junk of them all. He was surprised it still managed to float, that the metal scraps that had been pounded into the sides actually kept out water. The sails, folded down, were mostly black, and tied by ten different kinds of twine—some blue, some green, some white. Cracked red clay pots, filled with what looked like dirt, and chipped crates were strapped to the circumference of the cockpit.

It was the kind of place you brought someone to murder them.

She hopped over the siding and peeled away the tarp that covered the front. Beneath, he caught sight of a wheel. At least that looked intact. Maybe this thing really sailed after all.

She bent beneath it, opening a wooden door to a compartment, and for a flash of a second he saw the curve of her back, and the taper of her thighs, and nearly slipped into the cove.

"Now or never, terreno," she called.

Gritting his teeth, he climbed over the siding, holding on tight to the edge as the water roiled beneath him. He was soaked to the bone, no part of him not wet. He'd never in his life been outside so long without an umbrella.

Lightning struck above the cliffline, and he ducked, an old remembered terror ricocheting out to his limbs.

He hated storms.

"Hey!" Someone was running down the steps—a man wearing yellow overalls. Ross squinted through the rain, holding his hand up to shield his eyes.

The man had a pole. Or a gun.

Definitely a gun. One of the old, long ones. A rifle.

"Someone's coming," Ross said. "Hey. *Hey!* Marin!"

"Where you think you're going?" The man's voice boomed through the rain. "You owe me docking fees!"

"He looks mad," said Ross. "How much do you owe him?"

"Close to what you're going to owe me," she said as she lunged by Ross to the engine. "I meant to pay him. I kind of meant to pay him. You understand."

"Not really," he said.

"*Mierda,*" she hissed. With more force than he would have thought wise, she swung back her leg and kicked the metal. The engine dropped, hitting the oily water with a splash. He looked over the edge, sure the debris beneath would catch in the propellers.

"Come on, girl." She grabbed the chain, then gave a small cry of pain and switched to the other hand. He remembered that her wrist had been dislocated only last night, and stepped forward to help, but she shoved him away.

She gave the chain a heave, and the motor sputtered.

"No, no, no," she chanted. "Not today."

He spared a quick glance up. The man in the yellow overalls

had made it onto their section of the pier and was coming fast, shotgun swinging with the motion of his arm.

Using both hands, Marin grabbed the chain and jerked back hard, teeth bared. The motor rumbled to life, and when she spun to grab the steering wheel, she tripped over Ross.

Falling on her hands and knees, she scrambled up, just before the boat cracked into one beside it. The mast gave a groan as they pitched sideways, and from within the cabinets came the rolling and thunking of objects tumbling out of place. Reaching the wheel, Marin gave it a hard yank, still on her knees. The ship rocked, groaned, and righted itself.

She steered for open waters, the man's curses ringing in Ross's ears. He didn't fire his gun; it was raised to the sky above him.

Marin gave a whoop and a final, victorious wave, then hoisted the sail, one-armed, and let the wind sweep them toward Sacramento Bay.

CHAPTER 15

A BLACK, terrifying thrill pulsed through Marin's body. Returning to the library with a fistful of money from tar would buy them a few weeks—only long enough to make some more. Returning with two hundred thousand credits would change their lives forever.

No more sleeping on a cot in the storage room. No more kids crying themselves to sleep with empty bellies. They'd be flush.

It might even be enough to buy her way home. To make the other captains on her island forget what she'd done.

The thought took her so by surprise that she laughed at it. And then promptly stopped laughing when she considered it might actually work.

Her people survived on tithing, contributions made to their supply hall through the summer to the start of the rainy season. From the time she'd been able to walk, she'd been sent into the gomi to find things they could use. Bottles. Plastic. Twine. The older she got, the more she was expected to bring to the table. She thought of those tithes now. Scrap metal from a dump up north. The log of all the motors she'd cleaned and fixed. Most of her ship work had involved thieving—supply runs to the mainland with her dad, raiding clinics south of Old San Fran for medicine. Twice, when she was eleven, she'd joined crews that had overtaken bigger, land-hugging freighters on the northern horn of the Oil Nation, but the people had all escaped in emergency speedboats before she'd set eyes on them.

Soft, Luc had called her when she'd returned to Careytown, the only town on the island where the people lived.

Absently her hand crossed her ribs, to touch the scar that would forever remind her otherwise. No, she wasn't soft. She was the worst of them all.

But with this much money, maybe they'd see past that. For the first time in five long years, she imagined herself striding into Careytown, imagined the shock on Luc's face when she took her seat at the captain's table.

You are a corsario, her father had said.

She just had to find the vice president's son first.

"So where are we going?"

Her head snapped in Ross's direction, but she avoided his bright, wary eyes. His hair was already curling a little. The rain had straightened it, but here, in the humid breeze, the waves were springing back. Her hair was doing the same, and the fact that they had this stupid thing in common annoyed her.

"Not far," she said, nerves tingling in her chest. In the five years she'd been on the mainland, she'd only taken her ship, the *Déchet,* out through the bay to hunt for supplies trapped in the gomi along the coast. She hadn't ventured past the California Islands for fear of tempting the Armament. But now she would take the risk. It was worth it for the payout.

More than she missed her home, more than she missed her own mother, she missed the open sea.

"To the islands?" He pulled up the lid of one of the side compartments, peering inside as though there might be a rotting animal within.

"Hey." She snapped her fingers. "Look, don't touch. Just because you think you own everything, doesn't mean you actually do."

He dropped the lid, holding his hands up in surrender.

"A little past the islands," she muttered.

"How much? Near Pacifica?" His voice thinned.

Her thoughts shot to Hiro and his packed suitcase. How he wanted a better life, and thought some made-up island would grant it. She focused on what he'd told her about the oil rig. That's where they would look for Adam.

One hundred thousand credits if he wasn't there.

Two if he was.

Either way, she could pay Gloria and take the rest to the captains. Just imagining Luc's face when she docked, rich enough to feed them all for years, was enough to make her giddy.

"Twenty miles off the coast. At an old oil rig." There were nine in total stretching down the coast, but this was the closest and as good a starting place as any. "Relax. I said I'd take you. I'll take you."

With one eye on the shoreline, she swiped the rain from her eyes and checked the provisions stowed behind the wheel in the bow's compartments. Three cans fruit compote. One can corn. One jug of water. It was enough to last her two days, and she kept it here for emergencies, in case the mainland was no longer a safe place to hide. She'd always felt guilty hiding it from Gloria, but now it wouldn't matter. They'd soon have enough food to feed the entire docks.

In the next compartment were extra lines and a small canvas sack holding twine, thick needles, a hunk of wax, matches, and a thinning roll of duct tape. They'd been tossed around when she'd launched, and she righted them now.

She became a machine, removing the tarps that covered the beams, attaching the halyard to the head of the main sail, winding the slack lines in a figure eight around her elbow and the heel of her hand. She climbed onto the bench along the side of the cockpit, hoisted the main sail up the mast, and unfurled the jib. Returning to the deck, she lifted the motor so it wouldn't catch any debris, but she could feel the larger pieces clatter against the front of the hull. She'd reinforced it with aluminum just for this reason, but that didn't make her less wary. If something sharp punched through, they'd be sunk.

Her eyes lifted to the black sails, a smudge against the gray sky. They needed to hurry. It wasn't just any passenger sitting on the back of her deck—it was the president's son, and if they were caught, no one would believe he'd asked a corsario to take him anywhere. It was just a matter of time before men like the one who'd shot her—like *Tersley*—would come for him.

"Come on, wind," she murmured, and, as if in answer, a light breeze picked up, carrying with it the salty mist of the open water. The sails above her luffed, then filled like a balloon, rounding away from the gentle pressure. The boat rocked and then steadied, and gave in to the pull that carried them away.

"Who taught you to sail?" he asked.

"My dad."

"Is he a freighter captain or something?"

She paused, just for a moment. "Or something."

He scowled.

Beside the compass she'd mounted on the wheel was a small GPS. Like the rest of the *Déchet*, she'd built it with her own hands, pieced it together with broken navigation equipment that had been cast aside. It took a couple shakes, but she was finally able to turn it on. She typed in the coordinates for the California Islands, remembering how her father told stories about the sailors of the old days who navigated by the stars.

The stars were shy these days. Most nights they stayed hidden beneath the clouds, lost in the fog.

They were only fifteen nautical miles out, but the persistent fog in this area was killing her visibility. She peered toward the horizon, but saw only gray.

"Did Adam say anything when you saw him? Did he look all right?"

Marin turned and eyed Ross curiously, struck by how worried he seemed to be. She wondered if Adam had something Ross needed, or owed him money. It seemed impossible that they were just friends.

Kanshu didn't have friends. They were like pirates; they just collected enemies.

"What is it about him?" she asked, training her eyes on the horizon. "Adam. You two . . ." She waggled her eyebrows at him.

"No." He blew out a tense breath. "Why does everyone think that?"

She planted a fist on her hip. "Because you're here. You don't do all this for someone who isn't important."

"Well, he is, just not like that."

He pulled at his hair, making it stick out to the side.

She turned away.

"He was hurt," she said. "He couldn't run."

Ross's chin snapped up. "How hurt?"

"A nasty slice on his leg from the riots. We were hiding when the patrol came; they roughed him up some more."

His back rounded, and for some stupid reason she found herself wishing she could tell him something to make him feel better.

"He could have given me up, but he didn't. Pretty stand-up thing to do, if you ask me."

A piece of debris clunked against the siding, making Ross jump to his feet.

"What is that?" he asked, gripping the seat as he stared down at the water.

"Iceberg."

He looked over his shoulder at her. "Ice?"

She sighed. "No."

Marin had never seen real ice. The last of it had melted eighty years before she was born. "It's trash that clings together and floats through the ocean." Icebergs were dangerous. Often, they dragged huge deposits of debris beneath them, some of it sharp as knives, some of it loose enough to tear up an engine. She glanced to hers now, to make sure it had been completely lifted from the water.

"Oh."

A wave caught the starboard side, so tiny she barely shifted her weight. It practically threw Ross overboard, and he lowered himself to a side compartment.

Terrenos.

He sat down again.

"My dad told me to look out for him," he said after a moment.

"Your dad." It was strange to hear anyone call the president *dad*. "What's he like?"

Ross was quiet for a while.

"Important."

She rolled her eyes. If he wasn't paying her so much, she would have told him she didn't need the reminder that he was so much better than her.

"I figured that one out myself," she said.

"He's . . . busy." Ross scratched his head impatiently. "He's got a lot of responsibility."

"Sure. Arresting Shorelings and tossing them out to sea is a lot of work."

He straightened. "He's not a bad guy."

"How do you know? He's the president. He can do whatever he wants."

"But that doesn't mean that he does." Ross groaned. "Look, if he's sending Shorelings out to sea, there has to be a reason for it."

Heat seared just under her skin. Was that what the terrenos who'd sent her grandfather out to sea had said? *Someone, somewhere, must have a reason.*

"So what *is* the reason then? Why's he letting la limpieza pack up the rioters? Most of them haven't done anything wrong." She thought of the Lu boys, sitting at the library with the other orphaned kids.

"I don't know," he said, staring off into the fog. "He never tells me anything. If he was doing something wrong, I'd probably hear it from the news, same as everybody else."

This she understood, more than she cared to admit. All her life she'd stood in the shadows of captains, waiting to be noticed, fighting to be treated as an equal. By the time she was eight, she could dress a ship quicker than Luc, but he still got picked for crews over her. It wasn't until she'd fled to the mainland that she'd finally been seen for what she was worth. But even then she wasn't a Shoreling. Not really.

She knew what it was like to be on the outside.

He ran his hands down the side of his face. "I shouldn't have said that."

She turned to find him standing, gripping the boom with both hands, and a little green, but upright. His cheeks and hands had never seen the rashes from bad water, or the burns from the sun, and looking at them made Marin aware of her own skin, red brown, like clay, and crossed with tiny scars. Where she was from, that was a measure of pride, because it meant she was strong, unsheltered, and unafraid. But she doubted he measured worth the same way.

Her eyes lowered down over his chest, pausing where his shirt had hiked up a little over his left hip. The gray sky highlighted a wedge of skin just above his belt, pebbled with goosebumps. She stared, just for a moment, before the curiosity turned to shame.

He would not make her soft. This was business only. A few hours on a boat together couldn't erase generations of betrayal.

Just as she was turning away, a foghorn blared through the mist. The deep sound vibrated the hull, shaking her all the way down to her bones. Beside her, Ross clapped his hands over his ears.

"THIS IS THE ALLIANCE ARMAMENT," boomed a disembodied voice. "ARE YOU IN DISTRESS?"

Marin's heart gripped in her chest. Had he done this? Were they tracking him? She looked to the comm at his wrist. No, this couldn't be happening. She'd expected things to get tricky outside the islands, but they hadn't even left the bay yet.

"Did you call them?" she asked.

"No!" He flashed the comm before her, showing the blank face. Just because it looked off didn't mean he didn't have something up his sleeve.

Moving fast, she climbed onto the raised siding, one hand steady on the line. The mist was thick, clinging to her skin and her eyelashes as she squinted behind her into the gloom.

"Where are you?" she muttered.

"Is this because of the docking fees?" Ross's face was horrified.

She silenced him with a wave of her hand, and for one long moment they listened, hearing nothing more than the lap of the water against the hull and the beat of their own hearts.

The white boat split the fog a mile downwind, boasting Noram's flag on the hull. Two rectangular sails, stacked one atop the other, carried it toward them. Neither was as large as her mainsail, telling her that this vessel relied mostly on a motor, one that couldn't be used with so much trash in the water. If they'd been on the open ocean, she had no doubt her boat could outrun the other.

But they weren't on the ocean.

Stupid her for taking her eyes off the horizon. Stupid her for wasting time talking to him when she should have been sailing hard for that oil rig.

She glanced behind her into the mist. If she'd lit her headlamp, she might have been able to see the chain of islands that separated the bay from the Pacific, but she hadn't, because she'd wanted to avoid drawing unneeded attention. Now it hardly mattered. The Armament had found her, and even if it was by dumb luck, she'd be lucky if they threw her in prison once they discovered who she had with her.

For a moment she considered making a trade. Telling them she had Ross, and if they wanted him, they could pay her handsomely. But who was she kidding? That wouldn't work. They had her in firepower, manpower, and every other kind of power that didn't involve a big sail. She had to make a break for it.

She checked her GPS, seeing the small outline of green islands four miles ahead of her blinking red dot. If she could reach them and navigate through, she might be able to lose the Armament on the open waterways.

Unless their friends were already waiting on the other side.

"THIS IS THE ALLIANCE ARMAMENT. THERE IS A WEATHER ADVISORY IN EFFECT. ARE YOU IN DISTRESS?"

It was possible they didn't know she had Ross. If she lowered sails, he might be able to talk them out of this, explain why she was here. Maybe they'd take him and let her go.

She didn't believe that for a second.

"Don't stop," Ross said, surprising her. "If they catch us, the deal's off."

She gaped at him for a full second.

"What are you running from?" she asked. The Armament worked for his father, which meant he shouldn't have been afraid of them.

"Take me to where they took Adam," he ordered.

Over Ross's shoulder, she saw the military boat, now just fifty yards away. The Armament worked for his father; they wouldn't hurt him. If she had to guess, he didn't care about that, though. He wanted to find his friend, and this ship threatened his ability to do that.

Panic welled inside her. She shouldn't have brought him in the first place. It was foolish to think she was like the other corsarios. She'd known she wasn't from the first night her father placed that bone-handled knife in her hand.

One hundred thousand to take him.

Double to find Adam.

There was no time for regret. If she was getting out of this alive, she had to move.

Swinging under the boom, she cranked the wheel to hoist the rest of the sail. It luffed in the wind, the clatter of rain against it so loud it made the rush in her ears seem like a gentle hush. The nose of her boat lifted with the extra push, and charged forward.

"Come on," she coaxed, looking back over her shoulder. She could see sailors onboard now wearing white hats and slickers, twenty yards back.

"Come on, come on, come on." She bounced on her heels, one hand on the wheel.

They started to pull away. Her sail was larger, faster, but she'd need to taper her speed before she crashed into an island. The fog thickened, swallowing her whole, hiding the other boat. She glanced down at the GPS. Half a mile and closing until she ran aground. Pulling hard to port, she set a course between two of the larger land masses, though from the fuzzy green shapes on the screen it was hard to tell what depths she faced.

If they were caught, she'd die in a cell. She'd never see the open water again. She'd never go back to Careytown or sit at the captain's table. Never repay Gloria for taking her in.

"Can you outrun them?" Ross asked, close behind her.

She nodded.

Another wave hit the side of the boat, and he was tossed onto a side compartment. She could see him out of the corner of her eye, pulling himself up the rail, staring behind them.

"They're coming," he said.

She gripped the wheel tighter and searched the water behind him, but saw nothing.

". . . TREACHEROUS WATER AHEAD. LOWER YOUR SAIL AND SURRENDER YOUR VESSEL."

Two quick shots cracked through the sky. Marin ducked automatically, just as a bullet ripped through the top corner of her sail.

"They're shooting at us?" he asked, voice suddenly frantic.

They were trying to slow her down.

She didn't look back.

Swells of land rose on either side of her, visible only in pieces through the mist. Broken buildings climbed to the very tops of them, though no lights drew her eye. The northern islands didn't get power. Farther south they were a little bigger, but only slightly more inhabited. This chain was the last wall protecting the mainland from the storms, and they suffered each time lightning lit the sky.

"LOWER YOUR SAIL AND SURRENDER."

Through the mist, great hunks of broken brick and concrete jutted up—remnants of a city, broken by quakes and buried by the sea long ago. Her hands were steady as she yanked the wheel hard to port. They avoided the ruins by a hair above the waterline, but below something scratched against the hull, like the teeth of a giant sea creature, dragging from bow to stern.

She winced, feeling the scratch as if it were nails down her own back. Cursing her hurt wrist, she let the sails down to half mast one-handed, the rope burning her left hand bloody as it ripped through her grasp. The waves and plastic bottles bouncing off the wreckage made a loud, threatening clatter. Just before crashing head-on into a wall of brick, she slowed, and squeezed between two buildings no wider than a city street. This had to have been easier in the old days, when the waters were low and people could drive cars on the ground below.

Another turn, and then another. A straight alley came into view. The rain increased, great buckets of it dumping from the sky, making puddles on the deck. She couldn't hear the boat behind her, and she didn't know who might be waiting past the break.

Quickly, she locked down the wheel to keep a straight course and dove beneath it to the cabinet holding her supplies. She pulled out the small canvas bag, ripped out the duct tape, and dropped the rest of it at her feet.

"What are you doing?" Ross asked.

She didn't answer.

Grabbing the tape in her teeth, she climbed the siding above the hatch and hooked one elbow around the mast. After a quick swipe of the water from her eyes, she felt her way over the half-folded sail, stretching higher, higher, finally standing on the boom itself to reach the place where the bullet had pierced the canvas.

She needed speed once she hit open water, and a hole in her sail wasn't going to give it to her. Balancing with the arches of her feet curving over the rounded pole, she pulled out a length of tape and tore it with her teeth. She tried to wipe the beads of water off the sail with her arm, but the rain kept coming.

The tape slid uselessly off the canvas.

"Stick!" she demanded. Below her, Ross was still crouched near the back of the boat, leaning over the edge. In the back of her mind she knew this was a bad idea—he'd go over if he wasn't careful. The water churned, frothy with white caps and trash, pummeling the sides of the channel. Even the strongest swimmer would be sucked under in seconds.

One more attempt with the tape, and it stuck. Not well, but enough to patch the canvas for now.

She swung down to the cockpit and hoisted the mainsail, watching the line of silver tape as it climbed higher and higher overhead. Every part of her worked—every part but her sore wrist. She used one hand to pull the line, then grabbed it in her teeth, tucking the rope's slack beneath her armpit. The lighter pieces of twine turned red from her bloody grasp, but she didn't stop.

Finally, the sail was up, and she tied it off in a hurry, running to unlatch the wheel. They hit open water a moment later, the islands drawing back on either side as the *Déchet* burst forward into the gloom.

From the south came yellow lights—two, then three. The Armament. She could hear the whine of their speakers, but couldn't make out the words over her own drumming heart.

There was a space between them. She could make it.

"Hold on!" she shouted. The sails billowed, round and full. Faster she went, faster. The wind stung her face, the rain pelted her body. Trash clunked against the bow of the *Déchet* as the lights disappeared in the gloom behind her. A dark thrill pounded through her veins. Not even the Armament could catch her. She had wings, just like her mother had said.

Ross didn't answer.

She looked back, but he was gone.

CHAPTER 16

Ross TUMBLED backward, knocked over the edge of the deck by a well-timed wave. The warm water embraced him, instantly dragging him under, and though he kicked his legs, the liquid clinging to his clothes made his movements slow and clumsy. With a burst of effort, he succeeded in lifting his head, just in time to grab a breath. The sting of his eyes was so harsh, he immediately closed them. In the back of his mind he remembered that the water was dirty and acidic, and that swimming in untreated pools of it was dangerous. Still, he didn't have much of a choice. He squinted as tightly as he could, seeing the back of Marin's boat through his compressed vision. Above, he could still hear the rain, tapping against the surface of the water.

He kicked on, heart thumping wildly. He knew how to swim. He'd done it before, in the pool at Center, and in the exercise lanes at his house. But this was the open ocean, and the enormity of it made the fear a loose, hot thing, sliding through his body.

Marin was gone, but he couldn't think about what that meant now. Land was behind him, and though it looked far, he could make it. He was going to make it.

Even now he felt torn, like Adam was slipping farther away.

His hands, stretched out before him, bumped into something. Automatically, he recoiled, blowing out half his held breath. He opened his eyes wider, fearing the slick, smooth thing was alive, some kind of monster from his dreams—a giant fish, or a shark, things in the moment he forgot didn't exist anymore in the wild.

But it wasn't an animal. Before him was trash, a pillar of it swaying in the waves, stretching down toward black, monstrous shadows. Roofs of buildings, just twenty feet below his feet, broken to ruins.

It was a dead place, filled with things long gone. It was a nightmare, stealing the breath from his lungs. He'd seen pictures of this in school, but they didn't prepare him for how small he would feel floating above it.

His eyes burned, and when he gritted his teeth, water flooded his mouth. He tried to spit it out, but there was too much. He needed air. He kicked toward the surface, but the light slid away, and everything went dim.

He kicked harder, stretching his fingers out, but they caught in something clothlike and slimy, which swirled around his hand as he pulled away. He tried to swim back, away from it, and bumped into the pillar again. When he turned, the trash surrounded him like a net and wrapped around his body.

His chest was on fire now. He tried to push through, but struggling just wound him tighter in the trap. Every movement made it worse. His comm was stuck in a tendril of cloth or soft plastic, and when he couldn't jerk it free, he undid the clasp and watched as it was swallowed by the trash.

Something squeezed around his right ankle. His arms were stuck out to the sides. A glint of light shone through the shadows—the sky was above him, only five feet or so, but he couldn't get there.

Air. He could hear himself screaming, even with his mouth closed. He twisted frantically, but couldn't break free.

His head started pounding.

Vaguely he registered a splash above him, and a new dose of terror spilled through his veins as a dark shape materialized before him. Marin. Her hair floated around her face. She was wearing something on her eyes—goggles of some sort. A knife was in her hand.

He struggled, but she shook her head, urging him to be still. Her hand felt down his arm, running over his bindings. After a second she seemed to give up and kicked toward the surface, and if he hadn't lost control before, he did then.

Don't leave. Every part of him seized with that one, singular thought. *Don't leave me.*

Another splash, and this time she had something else in her hand. A gray metal pot, upside down, that she was pushing toward him. When she was close enough, she hooked her leg around his immobile arm to anchor herself, then shoved the pot down over his head.

Suddenly, his hairline was no longer submerged, and he craned his neck back until his mouth found the pocket of air she'd brought from the surface. He gasped again, and again, taking small sips of dirty, salty water with each breath. Relief scored through him. His lungs expanded with every gulp.

She squeezed her leg around his arm, and he knew what she was going to do. He wasn't ready, but it didn't matter. One last breath, and she released the pot. It spun on its side before his face, a bubble of air escaping to the surface before the gray steel sunk like a rock.

Her hands were on him then. On his neck. Down his shoulders. She cut away the debris with her knife, and soon his arms were free. She swam back to the surface for a breath, and he tracked her through squinted eyes, never more thankful than when she returned.

She dove deeper, hands sliding down his waist, over his thighs, slicing away the plastic and cloth and rope. He didn't think about the placement of her shoulder when she braced it between his thighs, just of the knife in her hand as it cut him free. Finally, he was clear enough to kick out, and she fitted herself beneath his arm and guided him toward the surface.

They broke through together, both drawing in loud, deep breaths before paddling toward her boat. She led with the knife and kept her other hand knotted in the collar of his shirt until they reached the ladder mounted to the back. He didn't speak, just followed her lead and grabbed the bottom rung. His body felt like it weighed a thousand pounds. Water sloshed them back and forth, making it hard for his weak legs to find their footing.

"Next time . . . you want to . . . take a swim . . ." she said, breathing hard. "Try not to . . . jump into . . . an iceberg . . ."

He turned to face her, eyes still burning fiercely from the water. Her goggles were pulled up over her forehead, roughing her wet hair up around the strap. Water dripped from her nose and her chin. Her small body bumped against his as another wave hit. Her eyes, dark and angry, caught his for one suspended moment before she looked away.

She'd saved him.

He started to climb up the ladder, and when he'd reached the top, he flung himself over the ledge, landing chest down in the cockpit. She started to come up after him, but hesitated before she could swing over the side. Behind her, a round yellow light sliced through the gray. She must have seen the reflection on her boat because she froze, and her eyes went round.

Ross pushed himself to his knees. The light spread into a giant white hull with a broad, rectangular sail overtop it. The boat was twice the size of Marin's, with a glass-encased cabin above the main deck. People in rain slickers lined the outer railing. One held a gun. Another was placed behind a stationary weapon of some kind. As they drew closer, he could see the man swivel the metal nozzle in their direction.

"THIS IS THE ALLIANCE ARMAMENT," a voice boomed through the closing space between the two boats. "PRE-PARE TO BE BOARDED."

Before the voice had finished, a thick spray of water exploded from the metal contraption. It hit the back of Marin's boat with a roar, just seconds before it swung toward the girl. As it pelted her back, her mouth opened wide, but she didn't scream. Still, the pain and fear tightened every feature, and he reached for her without thinking.

Her hand, small and slick, slid free from his grip as she dropped into the water.

Ross sat on a padded bench in the air-conditioned cabin of the Armament ship, huddled beneath a thick wool blanket. A woman in a crisp white uniform with faint red rashes on her broad cheeks stood before him, scratching her furrowed brows.

"Tell me again how you got on that boat?" Captain Ingold had introduced herself just after Ross had been rescued. She was the shape of a brick, with rigid posture and the kind of fixed, stern expression that said she didn't waste a lot of time laughing.

That boat—Marin's boat—was currently being towed behind them as they made their way north. Apparently the weather was too bad behind them, near San Fran, where the base was located, so they were going to a sister station somewhere offshore in the Pacific.

Ross frowned as he glanced around the cabin. Half a dozen crewmembers attended to various jobs steering, pressing buttons, and turning dials, all of them stealing glances at him when they thought he wasn't looking. This didn't bother Ross as much as their weapons, hanging from their belts or strapped across their chests. In his visits to the Armament base with his father, Ross had never seen them dressed this way before. These sailors appeared combat-ready, and he couldn't help but wonder if this had something to do with Marin.

Sitting a little straighter, he squeezed the bottle of eye drops Captain Ingold had given him beneath the blanket. They did help relieve the sting from the seawater, but his skin still itched.

"I was looking for a friend of mine," said Ross. "Marin—the girl on the boat—said she'd seen him."

"And you believed her?" Captain Ingold's mouth made a small, straight line.

"If I hadn't, I wouldn't have gone with her." Ross recalled the way the soldier sailors had heaved Marin from the water with a net. How she'd fought to escape it when they'd hauled her to the deck, getting more tangled, just as he'd been tangled in the trash when she'd rescued him.

"Where is she, anyway?" Ross asked, his voice quieter.

She'd saved him in that water. He'd almost died. It wasn't like at the riots when for all she knew he was just another Shoreling. She'd made it clear she had no love for him or his father, and still, she'd jumped in after him.

Probably just for the money.

"She's in the brig," said Captain Ingold. "Detained."

Ross cringed. It had taken two men, one sitting on her back, smashing her face against the deck, to get her cuffed. He'd tried to stop them, but they'd cuffed him too.

Somehow they'd been a lot quicker to let him go. He couldn't help wondering if that had something to do with that fact that she was a Shoreling.

"She's all right, isn't she?" he asked.

"She won't be any more trouble to you, Mr. Torres."

In order to stop them from hurting Marin, he'd told them who he was. There wasn't much use hiding it. Once they'd done the retinal ID scan, they would have figured it out anyway.

"That's not what I asked," he said.

Captain Ingold gave a curt smile. "Tell me, did *Marin* mention anything about other people she might be meeting?"

He frowned. "No. Just that she knew where Adam was."

"And Adam is?"

"The vice president's son."

She gave a short hum. "Yes. I saw that he went missing. He's a Shoreling, isn't he?"

Of course he was a Shoreling. Everyone knew the vice president was a Shoreling, so obviously his son would be. Ross didn't understand why she felt it was necessary to point it out.

"He's the vice president's son," said Ross, slightly concerned that an alert had not been issued that *he* was missing. "Adam hasn't been found?"

"The alert was still active as of an hour ago."

Ross sunk in his seat. He'd had a feeling that would be her answer, but he still needed to ask, just in case.

The captain crossed her arms over her chest.

"So the girl who abducted you knew the vice president's son."

"Hold on," he said. "I didn't say she abducted me. I just said she knew where Adam was."

The way her gaze narrowed on him made him feel like he should probably consult his father's lawyer before he said too much more.

"But they knew each other," she said.

Ross scratched at his arms, the itch from the water growing more uncomfortable under her barrage of questions. "They'd met."

"How well did they know each other?"

"Not well."

"You're being intentionally vague, Mr. Torres," said the captain.

"I didn't realize this was an interrogation," he responded, both a little surprised that he hadn't been reported missing yet, and worried that whatever he said might be getting Marin in more trouble. Even if she was some kind of criminal, he didn't like the thought of her being hurt because of something he did.

"So you don't know where she was taking you?"

"Not exactly, no." Ross pinched the bridge of his nose. He was getting a headache.

"Where did she take Adam?"

"She didn't take him anywhere," he said. But his hand dropped into his lap, and he wondered if Marin might have been lying about everything. Maybe she didn't know where Adam was. Maybe this whole thing was just a hoax to get money.

The captain gave him a small, patronizing smile.

"Did that girl tell you who she is?" she asked.

"No. Why?" asked Ross. "Is she in trouble or something?"

The captain sighed in the way that older, wiser people sigh when they're confronted with younger, stupider people.

"Be glad we found you before she got too far," she said. "Why don't we get you settled below deck? If you need anything, one of the crewmen can get it for you."

Apparently she was done talking.

"Wait," he said. "What about the prisoners from the riots? Do you know where they're going? I heard something about a ticket out to sea."

A vein appeared on her forehead.

"Perhaps it would be better if you focused on yourself, Mr. Torres," she said. "The water is a dangerous place."

He couldn't tell if this was a threat, but regardless, Marin had been right about the prisoners. Whatever else she had lied about, she'd been telling the truth about that.

"Wait," he said again. "I need to call my father. He'll be looking for me. I'm surprised you haven't already received an alert that I'm missing."

His irritation had warped into an unsettling anxiety. The president's missing son would be frontline news. He could already imagine his mother's face in the interview, tears streaking down her cheeks as she made a plea to bring him home. His father standing beside her, one arm wrapped tightly around her shoulders. The photo op would be tremendous.

But the Armament hadn't heard he was missing yet, even though he'd left school hours before. His comm was gone, trapped in the grip of that murky water, but his security detail was part of the best in the world. Surely they would have followed his trail, or at least sent out an alert accessible by the taxi driver. He thought again of his father's vague agreement to fix what he'd done in the riots, and how he hadn't been able to find Adam, despite having more connections than anyone else in the country. He wondered if his father had even put forth an effort to look for Adam, and then immediately felt like a terrible person. Of course his father was looking for the vice president's son.

So why wasn't he looking for his *own* son?

"Steward," Captain Ingold said sharply. A uniformed crewman who didn't look much older than Ross broke from his statuelike position at the door and trotted toward them. He was thinner than most, with big eyes and patchy, tan skin. He looked like Adam when he'd first moved above the cliffline: neat, hungry, and eager to make a good impression.

"Get Mr. Torres a line to the mainland."

"Lines are out, Captain."

Ingold sighed, as if this wasn't entirely unexpected. "My apologies," she told Ross. "This happens during storms. You'll have to wait until we can get to the station."

"Fine," Ross said, though it wasn't. Despite everything, he wanted to hear his dad's voice. To hear him say it would be all right, the way he used to when Ross was young and thought he ruled the world.

But nothing was all right.

Ross looked out the window into the dark sky, seeing yellow lightning flash in the clouds behind them.

"Shouldn't we be getting off the water?" His voice sounded detached, as if another person had spoken.

"We will soon enough," she said, then turned to the crewmember who'd said the line was out. "Take Mr. Torres to a cabin and post guard. In case he needs something."

Ross didn't argue.

The steward led the way down a narrow stairway into an even narrower hallway, where Ross's shoulders bumped against the walls with each rock of the ship. He was immediately sorry he'd come down here. If he'd been a little queasy before, he was nauseated now. His stomach was rolling, and the pressure in his head increased tenfold.

He took a deep breath. He needed to find Marin, and even though Captain Ingold was with the Armament, and the Armament worked for his father, he wanted out of here. The people who were supposed to be good didn't feel so good at the moment.

"So you're really the president's son," said the steward.

"That's right," said Ross, keeping his eyes on his feet. The boat tilted again as they rounded a corner, and he placed one hand on the wall to steady himself against the smooth siding as they made their way to an oval-shaped door. The steward turned the metal wheel in the center and led Ross into a bare white room no wider than the span of his arms. There were two bunk beds attached to the right side, leaving barely enough room on the left to slide past them. On the far wall was a circular window, though there wasn't much of a view beyond the gray haze.

"Saw him speak once," said the steward. "He came down to the docks and went on about how we all needed to pitch in and pull ourselves out of the hole. My dad and mom lost their jobs when the marine shop closed, and we had nothing. These guys from the Armament were with him recruiting, and I signed up that day. Best thing I ever did, all 'cause of your dad."

Ross nodded, but he couldn't muster the usual enthusiasm he saved for when people complimented his father. Not while Adam was missing. Not when his dad had told him they'd blame his absence on drugs and a failure to adjust to life above the cliffline.

"Where's the brig?" asked Ross.

The sailor's eyes darted away. "Lower level. But like the captain said, she's not going anywhere."

"I need to talk to her."

"I can't let you do that."

"Why not?"

"Because she's a prisoner, sir. It's not safe."

Ross held on to the top bunk and the wall while the room rocked from side to side. It was like being shaken in slow motion. "I thought you said she wasn't going anywhere."

The steward chewed on the corner of his lip. "We'll be at the station soon. It's just twenty or so nautical miles off the coast."

Twenty miles off the coast was where Marin had said they were going. Another swell, and he felt the bile crawl up his throat.

"What kind of station is in the ocean?" he muttered, blowing out a tight breath.

"It was an oil rig," said the steward, snapping Ross to full attention. That was exactly where Marin had been taking him. "They converted it to an Armament base a couple months ago when the fuel tapped out."

Our offshore drilling sites continue to prosper. We have no reason to look outside our own nation for fuel. Ross's father had said that in his meeting with the leader of the SAF.

"The oil ran dry?" asked Ross.

The steward nodded, seemingly relieved at the change in subject. "They're all running dry. We're generally posted on the perimeter of number six, off the lower Californias, but pretty soon they'll be dry too."

"How soon is pretty soon?" asked Ross.

"Couple weeks, I heard." The steward looked over Ross's shoulder, out the window.

"A couple weeks?" Ross shook his head, now hearing the leader of the SAF whisper in his ear. *Your people need oil. Your vice president seemed to think your nation was scraping the bottom of the barrel.*

The steward shrugged, and in that small, careless motion, Ross was reminded of how his father had accused him of being careless about the burdens he faced, the weighty decisions he made.

"So I guess you have a lot of prisoners at the station," Ross said, trying to sound casual. "My dad said they've been shipping a ton out this way."

"Oh, they don't stay." He laughed weakly. "We'd be overrun. A special detail takes them to the gyre."

"The gyre? Is that a jail or something?"

"No. It's where the currents meet." The steward's chin pulled in, a frown tugging at his mouth. From the looks of it, he was regretting speaking so freely.

"What's out there?" Ross asked.

"I'm sorry, sir," he said. "I don't have permission to say any more. Anyway, we're here." He raised his hand to point behind Ross to the small, circular window.

Ross turned to see a great, looming metal island, spiderlike with its six legs and thick platform that hovered above the water. Part of it was still hidden in fog, making the angular metal arms that stretched into the sky look like they were floating, and might drop at any time.

They were already close, the clouds parting at the last second to reveal their arrival, and as Ross squinted through the splashes of water on the window, he made out a white shape directly beneath the main platform. It bobbed in the waves and cracked against one of the supporting beams.

"I think one of your boats tipped over," said Ross.

The steward pushed past him, and Ross fell back on the bottom bunk. His mouth fell open. "Where are the other—"

A horn blared from the hallway, loud enough to make them both jump. Red lights began flashing in through the door, streaking across Ross's wet clothes, painting the sailor's white uniform the color of blood.

The captain's voice came over the speakers. "All hands report to deck. All hands man battle stations."

The steward pushed back toward the door, tripping on Ross's knees in the small space. Ross sprung back to his feet, and a quick glance out the window didn't just show one boat on its side, but two. One white hull was completely upside down, its own island beneath the spider's belly. Above, fire burst from one of the middle floors of the compound, spouting out the window and painting the gray sky black.

"Were those the prisoner boats?" he asked, pointing to the overturned vessels, picturing Adam stuck underwater as he had been. Drowning.

The steward didn't answer.

On one of the other supporting legs, three small metal speedboats were tied to the landing dock. A person wearing gray, shabby clothes stood on the platform, but quickly dove beneath the stairway. From above deck, Ross could hear a shout of pain, and then the shatter of glass. He gritted his teeth.

"You have to stay here," said the steward. He was outside the door, but Ross was already pushing through after him. "You should hide. I'll lock you in."

Ross's pulse spiked. Without thinking, he grabbed the sleeve of his uniform. "Two boats are already sunk; I'm not staying here!"

The steward tried to wedge through, but Ross had braced his body in the door, and was stronger and larger than the sailor.

"They'll kill you."

"*Who?*"

"The Shorelings, who do you think?" The red lights in the hallway lit his face as he tried to shove Ross back in the room.

Civil war, his father had said. It was happening, just as he'd feared.

Ross pushed into the hallway. A volley of gunfire came from the upper deck, the distinctive *pop pop pop* that Ross had only ever heard on television.

A muffled sound came from overhead—not the captain's voice on the ship's speakers, but a male voice, amplified over some distance. Ross and the steward both froze and listened.

"*We want the prisoners.*"

The steward's breath caught. He looked young then, younger than Ross felt by a long shot.

"*Deliver the prisoners, and we'll let you go.*"

"Are the prisoners here?" Ross demanded.

The steward grimaced. "These guys have been out all week protesting the relocation. Captain thought that's what you were doing when we picked you up."

Ross thought back to Ingold's questions. Her suspicion didn't seem so unwarranted now.

"*Those people are innocent!*" called the man from outside. "*You can't force us to leave our homes!*"

Frustration had Ross grabbing the boy's collar and shoving him against the wall.

"The prisoners from last night's riots. Where are they?"

The steward looked down at Ross's hands, wide-eyed.

"My dad is your boss," he said. "I'll have you fired if you don't tell me."

"They . . . they left early to bypass the storm."

Ross released him. Adam was gone. Heading toward some gyre with a special detail of Armament.

He had to get off this boat.

He had to find Marin.

But if Marin knew this awaited them . . . if she'd planned to bring him here because she knew the Shorelings would be rioting . . .

Be glad we found you before she got too far.

Who *was* Marin? And what was she doing out here?

Captain Ingold's voice boomed around them, making loose metal pieces around the door rattle.

"*We do not negotiate with radicals. Surrender, and you will not be harmed.*"

One breathless moment passed, and then something slammed into the side of the boat. It rocked hard to the side, then fell back into place. Ross clung to the boy's shirt to stay upright.

The Shorelings had not liked Ingold's answer.

From overhead came a roar, and in the following impact, Ross and the steward were thrown down the hall. Ross hit his knees, scraping his hands on the metal grate that covered the floor. A siren sounded, wailing over the shouts and the burst of the horn. The boat rocked harder than it had in the waves, tossing the two of them from wall to wall.

The steward was the first to pop back up to his feet. He ran toward the exit, bouncing off the sides as the boat continued to thrash.

A cold sweat dewed on Ross's hairline as he followed toward the stairs. More gunfire came from above, where the light and rain slashed down over him through the swinging portal door. He gripped the metal bannister hard in his fists, feeling the muscles in his legs work to run.

Another impact against the side of the boat, this crash accompanied by a loud, metallic hiss. Ross's shoes skidded over the floor, his hands on the bannister the only anchor holding him upright. Fear took him then, overriding the panic, relaying a singular message throughout his entire body.

Get out.

The interior lights shut off, leaving only the red flashers. In the dark he heard his breath, rasping through his throat. His heartbeat, pounding in his ears. The shouts of those above, mixed with the volley of gunfire.

And then the roar of water, breaking through the hull somewhere below him.

CHAPTER 17

"Help!" Marin shouted. "Hey! I'm still down here!"

She was locked in a cell no wider than the span of her arms. The metal bars surrounding her on three sides were solid, the inner shell of the hull at her back. There was no chair or bench, nothing she could use as a tool to break out through the door. One of the crewmen had stolen her knife and her belt, even her shoelaces thinking she might hurt someone with them. He wasn't wrong.

She had nothing to help her.

"Is anyone there!" she called, but her voice bounced off the wall outside the cell. The room was windowless and dark, and though her eyes had adjusted, she could barely see the door ten feet away. There was a bench beside it. Until five minutes ago, a guard had sat there, feet kicked out, toying with a gun on his lap, while he'd asked her what one of the 86 was doing with a boy from above the cliffline, and what the Shorelings were up to, and told her that if she didn't start answering questions, they might just have to see how well she could swim with her hands tied to her ankles.

She'd didn't tell him anything, because the truth sounded too much like a lie, and he'd never believe her anyway.

He'd taken off as soon as the lights had gone out, and shut the door behind him. Now there was only the flash of red from beneath the doorframe. Just a sliver, every few seconds.

"Help!" Marin shouted again. Her arms reached through the spaces between the bars, her fingers working at the lock that held her captive. She needed something to pick it—a needle, a knife, something sharp. Even then, she wasn't sure if she could. This wasn't an old, rusted lock like the one Luc had on the shed in Careytown where he'd taught her to make tar. The front was smooth, polished. She could barely fit her fingernail into the keyhole.

She pulled her arms back into the cage.

"Okay," she said. "Okay, Marin. It'll be fine. Just think. *Think*."

The bench had to have a screw, something she might be able to loosen, but that was too far back as well. The wall behind her was a smooth, single piece of metal, without anything she could pry free. The siren wailed over a blasting horn, the only sounds she could hear. Her mind turned to Ross, but he couldn't help her. Wouldn't, even if he could. By now, they would have figured out he was a Torres. They'd be shipping him back to the mainland with a team of armed guards. They'd probably told him she was a corsario too. He was probably thanking his lucky stars he'd gotten away from her before she sunk a knife in his belly.

Closing her eyes, she tried to concentrate over the noise, but she couldn't even breathe without shaking.

"Stop it," she said aloud. She would not be weak now.

The boat rocked hard to the side, and she clung to the bars to stay upright. Over the blare of the horn, she heard the rending of metal, a high-pitched squeal, followed by a low groan. If Marin had had any doubt they were under attack, it evaporated now.

Fleetingly, she wondered if it might be corsarios. But even if it was one of the crews from the island, that didn't mean they knew she was here, or even that they'd rescue her if they saw her.

It was every person for themselves on a mission. This would be no different.

Her gaze was caught by a gleaming puddle on the floor, originating from beneath the door, and seeping across the room toward her. It glowed red, and for a sickening moment Marin thought it was blood.

Her heart tripped, stumbled, caught itself.

Not blood. *Water.* Glowing red with the reflection of the emergency lights in the hallway.

The hull had been breached. This ship was going to sink.

"Help! Someone's down here!" she yelled.

She jerked on the bars again, again, becoming more desperate with each unanswered plea. She wasn't going to drown here. She wouldn't meet her death locked in a cage.

"Help!"

"Marin!"

She stopped. Her hands tightened around the bars. She leaned closer, listening for the sound, but all she could hear was the siren. It was so long before she heard it again, she swore she'd made it up.

"Marin!"

"Here!" she shouted as loud as she could. "I'm here!" She didn't care who was coming, just as long as they got there quickly. Water was coming in faster now, sloshing over the toes of her shoes. The hull groaned again, and then tilted harder to the side, forcing her to cling to the bars of her cell to stay standing.

"Keep talking!" shouted the voice, this time closer.

"Here!" she cried. "Hurry up already!"

The door shoved inward, the way impeded by water.

Ross.

She saw only his silhouette first, bathed in a wash of red light coming from the hallway. It reminded her of the stories sailors told, about souls sent to a watery grave returning for vengeance, and in that instant she regretted every bad thing she'd ever done.

"Marin." Her name from his lips was no more than a whisper, but still she heard it, and it haunted her.

His gaze met hers. He held fast to the sides of the doorframe, making him appear too big for this narrow space, and strong, like he could tear the bars away with his bare hands.

Any small amount of relief that had come with his presence faded when she saw the hard look on his face. He must have forgotten how she'd saved him when his idiot self had nearly drowned.

He sloshed toward her.

"Hurry!" she said again. He was still soaked, his clothes sticking to his chest and legs. Red light slashed across the side of his face and his wild, wet hair.

"You need to find the key," she said. "The guard had it." No, who was she kidding? This guy wasn't going to take on a guard. "Okay, wait. Okay. There's got to be some kind of tool in the supply room. A lever, or maybe an axe." She was grasping. She didn't even know that this boat had a supply room.

The water was rising. She could feel it in her laceless boots, making her socks cling to her toes. From somewhere behind him, she could hear it rushing, like a faucet on full blast.

He reached the cage but did not even glance at the lock.

"Did you set me up?"

"We don't have time . . ."

"Did you set me up?" he shouted, and the hard gleam in his eyes had her spine drawing straight as a ship's mast. "Did you know the Shorelings would be here?"

"No," she said. "Shorelings are doing this?"

"Who are you?"

"Please, you gotta let me out of here."

He didn't move.

She swallowed. The water was coming faster now, climbing over her ankles.

"I'm Marin. I told you."

"Are you a criminal?"

"No more than your father!" she snapped, anger bursting over the fear.

Ross grew still, a strange, unsettling image with the gradual tilt of the room behind him. The water had reached the bottom of her calves now, and was still rising.

"Please." Panic squeezed her chest. "I didn't mean that. You get me out of here, I'll take you wherever you want to go."

"The gyre," he said.

"*What?*" Earlier, he'd lacked the sea legs to stay aboard a moving boat. How did he know about the gyre?

It didn't matter. She couldn't go there. Not yet. Not without money.

She didn't have a choice.

"Fine," she said. "Great. I love the gyre."

"Swear it. Swear you'll take me there."

She would have sworn to stand on her head for the next week if it meant he got her out of there.

"I swear," she said.

He lunged forward through the water and bent low to examine the lock. He shook the bars. They didn't budge.

"I'll be right back."

And then he was gone.

The door was pushed as far open as it would go, and as she waited, she watched the flashing lights and willed him to go faster. The dark and the lights and the sounds felt like they were inside her body, shocking her, making her quake. She couldn't escape them, even when she covered her ears with her hands and closed her eyes as tightly as she could.

Over it all came a voice, whispering from the past.

It'll be quick, Marin. One breath in, and it'll all be over.

I can't.

You have to.

Tears filled the corners of her eyes. She looked up, imagining she could see sky. *Please hurry, please hurry, please hurry.*

Ross crashed into the room, reaching above the threshold to keep himself upright. "There's nothing that will work."

His face was pale, his eyes round.

"Then find the key, the guard . . ."

"They're all on deck. We're being attacked. I can't go up there."

He took a step back.

"Wait," she said. "Don't leave. Help me."

"I'm sorry." His voice was low. She could see his throat working to swallow.

He disappeared out the door, leaving only a red pool of water in his wake.

"No!" she screamed.

The water hit her knees.

The bottoms of her thighs.

He wasn't coming back.

She shook the bars. She braced her feet against the hull, and pushed back against the gate, straining every muscle as one. It didn't budge.

The water reached her hips. Then her waist.

One breath in, and it'll all be over.

"Dad, help," she whispered, and it was as close to her mother's prayers as she had ever said.

Ross appeared back in the doorframe, gripping the handle as he trudged across the floor toward her. She choked down a sob.

"I found this in a glass case."

He held up a silver gun, not unlike the one his bodyguard had used. The handle was short, the barrel not more than an inch. The trigger was a button directly on the top for the thumb, beneath a fingernail-sized, auto-aiming screen.

She could barely speak; her throat was too tight. She motioned for him to give it over.

He handed the gun to her through the bars, but the second it was in her hand she realized this would do her no good. She couldn't shoot the lock from inside her cage; it was on the outside, and needed to be hit from there.

She shoved it back toward him. Swallowed. "You have to do it."

He took it, though he held it uncertainly in his open hand.

"I've never done this before."

"Thumb on top," she said quickly. "Make sure the center of the circle on the screen is on the lock. Don't let it autofocus on me, all right?"

He gave a curt nod.

"Then press the button."

He lifted the gun.

"Wait," she yelped. "Back up."

He was going to shoot her. At least it would be better than drowning.

He moved back, the water now just rising to his belt. The warm liquid climbed up her hips, a tempting comfort drawing her down while above her wet clothes twisted around her body and cut into her skin.

He squinted his eyes.

"Keep them open!" she said.

He did.

She scrambled to the far corner, making herself as small as she could. Her cheek and shoulder wedged against the bars. She was the one to close her eyes.

He fired.

The gun made only a hard *pop*, but the clang of the metal as it slammed back against the hinges made her good ear ring. A quick feel of her arms and neck told her she was still in one piece, and she rushed forward to push at the door. It moved an inch, then another. Ross, finally shaken from his freeze, moved toward her and pulled it the rest of the way open.

She nodded.

He tucked the gun in his hip pocket.

They made their way out of the room, him in the lead, her holding on to his forearm. His height made it easier for him to still walk, though each step was labored as he dragged his legs through the water. She was practically swimming behind him. Giving up on her boots, she kicked them off, and let him pull her into the hall.

"This way," he said.

The overhead lights were flashing as they reached a hard turn in their path. He peered around the corner, then trudged forward, pushing aside a packaged life jacket and some other floating debris.

"Where's the *Déchet*?" she asked. "My boat? Where is it?"

"I don't know."

If her ship had been sunk, they were trapped.

They reached another turn, this one marked by directions painted on the wall. To the right was the galley, to the left, the deck. Arrows pointed each way.

Ross stared at the sign. "I . . . I don't remember how to get out . . ."

Clearly not through the galley. Maybe he'd been underwater too long before she'd cut him free.

"Come on." She took the lead, pulling him toward the deck. His grip stayed firm on her wrist, and even though she was dragging him, he didn't feel like deadweight.

They came to the stairs, where she'd been hauled down before the attack. Up they climbed, out of the water. The metal grating dug into Marin's socked feet, but didn't slow her down. She continued on to the next level, where she heard the distinctive sound of gunfire.

Shorelings, Ross had said. She remembered the boxes of weapons in Gloria's storage room at the library, crates with the Oil Nation bird on them. Apparently the Shorelings were tired of fighting with their fists.

"We have to go up," she said. "Stay close."

He nodded.

Keeping low, they crept up the last stairs, clinging to the bannister so they didn't slide off to the port side, where the ship was sinking deeper into the water. When they reached the top, she kept close to the hatch, glancing quickly outside to find the side of the deck clear. Even with the shouts and bitter smell of smoke cutting through the rain, she felt infinitely better. Her blood began to buzz.

"Give me the gun," she said.

"Don't shoot me." He handed it over.

She grinned.

Keeping low, they ran the length of the deck through the sheets of rain, around the swell of the lower cabin. A gun wasn't her ideal weapon. She wanted her knife; she was more comfortable with it even in this fight, but the sailor who'd wanted to toss her overboard had stolen it.

Once they made it to the end of the upper deck, she glanced around the steps that led into the raised control room. The windows had been shot out, and shards of glass stuck up from the bottom sills like glowing teeth. Inside, she could hear a woman's voice shouting a message.

"We're under attack. The Shorelings have attacked Base Seven, I repeat, Base Seven is under attack . . ." There was a pause, and then, "I said *reverse*! Get us out of here!"

Looming behind the control room was the monstrous oil rig, smoking and smoldering from the attack. A black number "7" marked every support beam.

To her left was the cockpit and the front of the ship. A quick listen told her that that was where most of the action was happening. She glanced in that direction, seeing that the boom, cracked near the midpoint, had fallen, and dragged the mainsail into a triangular heap of canvas that half a dozen Armament crewmembers hid behind. Beyond it, she could see two Shoreling women with red scarves in their hair, hanging on the outer stairway that wrapped around one of the supporting beams of the oil rig.

Grabbing Ross's hand, she ran toward the back of the boat.

Soon she could see the *Déchet*'s white mast, stretching defiantly upward despite the sails that had been tacked down. Twin steel ropes had fastened her boat to two steel hooks on the back of the Armament ship. The *Déchet*'s cockpit appeared empty and the hull was in one piece.

She was still seaworthy.

Using the autofocus, Marin aimed the gun at the far line and fired. The rope broke apart with a snap, the smaller boat immediately drifting away from its holding. She aimed at the second line and waited for the auto-aim to focus.

Relief singing in her chest, she almost missed the Shoreling man charging from the far side of the stern. He collided with Ross, sending them both tumbling into the railing. Though he was smaller than Ross, he had the advantage of surprise and ended up on top of him.

Marin didn't wait to see if he was armed, or what he would do next. She kicked him square in the side and sent him sprawling over Ross's head. When he turned back, she raised the gun.

"He's with me," she said.

The man scoffed, like this was some kind of joke, but when Marin took a step closer, he scrambled backward, flipped over, and ran for the front of the ship.

She reached for Ross's hand and hauled him up. He gave her a breathless nod.

"Try not to drown yourself this time," she said.

He glanced down to the twenty-foot drop into the water, just as she shot through the line. Her boat was free now, and she wasn't about to let anyone else put their hands on it.

Bracing her weight on her forearm, she swung her legs over the railing. The fall was quick, and in the corner of her eye she saw Ross jump before her feet even hit the water. Gunfire, raised voices, the crash of metal against metal were all silenced as the warm water swallowed her whole. Pinching her eyes closed against the acid, she swam hard, the gun handle slippery in her fist. Faster she went, until finally her hands found the half-submerged ladder beside the motor.

Ross was right behind her.

"What do I do?" he asked as she launched herself toward the boom to untie the mainsail.

His words made something swell beneath her rib cage, but this wasn't the time for fear, or anger, or doubt. Each second mattered, and feeling anything at all risked both of their lives.

"Stay out of my way," she said.

She barely stopped to wipe the rain from her eyes. Soon, the sail was raised, and she was beating a path through the heavy curtain of fog to freedom.

CHAPTER 18

Ross SAT huddled beneath a tarp while the boat sliced through the low clouds, listening to Marin hum to herself. It wasn't quite a song, but more like a one-sided, wordless conversation with her boat, or maybe even the sea itself. He caught whispers of it on the wind, and when he moved, and the tarp crinkled, she would abruptly stop and glance back, as if surprised he was still sitting there.

He couldn't stop thinking of the Armament, and what had become of the ship. He imagined Captain Ingold and the other crewmen floating facedown in the water and fought off a chill that had nothing to do with the heavy, salted breeze.

He should have tried to do more. Something his father would have done. Tried to negotiate, or used the radio, maybe. Part of him felt compelled to call the mainland now and tell his dad what had happened, but when he asked for Marin's radio he found that she had none.

His comm was gone. He had no way to contact his family.

Maybe it was for the better. He wasn't sure what he'd say at this point anyway.

His thoughts slid from the captain's suspicion to the steward's words about the gyre and the special detail taking the prisoners. How many of them were innocent, like Adam? How many Shorelings thought Ross's father was a criminal, like Marin had alluded? He felt like he was looking at a picture from behind a veil; a complete image existed, but as much as he focused on it, it remained unclear.

"Hey," said Ross, his throat dry and voice rough. "Stop the boat."

She turned back, one hand still on the wheel. Her hair bobbed in tight, wet curls around her chin. It wasn't raining anymore, but misting, and the bare skin of her arms and chest glistened, even in this dim light.

"Can't stop."

He rose to his knees, shucked the tarp, and then stood, steadying himself with both hands on the least sharp-looking piece of the motor. The boat hit a swell and jostled him sideways. Her weight only shifted from one leg to the other, which didn't irritate him in the slightest.

"We need to talk."

Her mouth tilted up.

"So talk."

At the next wave he gave up trying to stand, and sat on a crate fastened to the siding. "I can't think like this. Just slow down for a minute."

"And risk the Armament throwing me back in a cell? I don't think so."

His neck grew uncomfortably hot. His hands too clammy. Anger took control of his words before he had a chance to think them through.

"I could have left you in that cell."

His stomach turned again, both from the steady *thunk, thunk, thunk* of the hull smashing down over the waves and the reminder of what they had just left behind.

"I could have left you in that iceberg," she said with a shrug. "But I didn't."

He recalled the feel of his lungs squeezing, of the panic contracting inside his body as he fought to swim to the surface.

"That's fair," he said.

One brow cocked beneath her wet curls. He was struck by the rightness of her, standing there at the helm of this small ship. On land she'd stuck out; there was something different about her. Her skin was a little darker than those who lived in Lower Noram, like she'd spent all her life beneath the sun. Lean muscles defined her arms and thin waist, and she displayed them proudly, unafraid to let the rain touch her. She moved with a grace here that he hadn't seen when they'd been running, or even sitting in the taxi.

She belonged here, in a way he wasn't certain he belonged anywhere.

After a moment, she moved to the tall pole rising from above the hatch that led below deck, and cranked a wheel that lowered the sail. Momentum carried his weight forward as the boat suddenly slowed, and he braced himself against the siding with straight arms. When he looked up she was struggling to tie off the rope, a grimace on her face.

He stood and wobbled toward her. "Tell me what to do."

She turned away, guarding her hurt wrist against her chest. "I've got it."

Instead of arguing, he simply reached around her and grabbed the rope in her hand. The move brought them close; her back was an inch away from his chest. She must have noticed, because she went absolutely still.

"It wouldn't kill you to ask for help," he muttered.

She slipped to the side, putting some space between them.

"I'm not used to anyone offering," she said. And then, after a long pause, she added, "Why were you running from the Armament anyway?"

He lifted a shoulder. "I knew where that road would take me."

Straight back home. Back to Center. Back to his armed security. But not to Adam.

"And I'll take you somewhere else, is that it?"

He nodded.

She cleared her throat. "Thanks for getting me out of that cell."

He couldn't quite look her way. "You shouldn't have been in there in the first place."

She told him how to tie the line in a figure-eight-shaped knot around a metal spool, making him do it again when he didn't get it right. When he'd finished, he returned to his seat on the crate.

If he'd thought slowing would ease his seasickness, he was wrong. The boat seemed to roll in a circular pattern—up, down, and around—and his stomach went right along with it. Saliva pooled in his mouth, mixing with the bitter taste of bile climbing up his throat. The only thing that stopped him from puking was the way she was staring at him, as if she expected him to do so.

"Well?" she asked.

He leaned forward, elbows on his knees. "Where's the gyre?"

Crossing her arms over her chest, she leaned back against the wheel.

"West, but we'll head northwest to stay out of the patrolled zones. The Armament will figure out soon enough that the boat they towed to their station isn't with the rest of the wreckage. They'll be looking for us."

It took a moment for her meaning to dig its claws into his gut. Even if he wanted to, he couldn't return to Noram. Not on this ship. They'd be gunned down before they even made it past the California Islands. There was nowhere to go but forward.

There were no landmarks visible through the clouds. Nothing to swim toward if this boat sunk like the other one. His heels began to bounce. When they were moving, the clouds had parted around them, but now they seemed to press in, leaving only twenty feet of water on all sides before fading to nothingness. He couldn't even tell what time of day it was. Near sunset, from his guess, but the gloom made it impossible to tell.

"How long until we get there?"

"It's not a specific place," she said. "The gyre covers thousands of miles."

His shoulders dropped. "You're kidding."

"You don't have any specific coordinates?"

"No." He doubted the steward would have known that information if a special detail was in charge of moving the prisoners.

"It's a day to the closest edge with strong wind. Longer without. It's halfway between Noram and Hawaii."

He nodded, the two points of reference providing him only a little comfort.

"We'll keep to the edge," she added. "Don't want to get dragged into the gyre's center."

"Why is that?"

Her gaze turned toward the water. "Might not get back out again."

That wasn't exactly reassuring.

"Have you been to the gyre before?" he asked.

She nodded.

He remembered what Captain Ingold had said about her being dangerous, and wondered if it was possible that she'd escaped from this prison, or base, or whatever it was. At the moment, nothing seemed impossible.

"There's a jail?" he prodded.

"Not that I've seen. It's been a few years, though."

So either it was new, or she wasn't an escaped convict. If the gyre covered thousands of miles there was a chance she just hadn't seen it.

At this rate, he was never going to catch up with Adam.

"What were you doing out there?" he asked.

She stared at her feet, then lifted one across her knee and pulled off the wet sock. He caught a glimpse of her slender ankle and looked away while she moved to the next.

"Sailing."

"In this thing?" He was still amazed it floated at all.

Her chin lifted, and he got a very strong feeling that she was about to dump him over the rails.

"This *thing*," she said, "is called the *Déchet,* and it's the only reason you're not sinking to the bottom of the Pacific back there with your dad's friends."

Her tone put him more on edge.

"I just didn't know boats this small went out that far, that's all."

"Small?" She huffed. "What do you know about it? It's not the size of the boat, but the wind in her sails, my friend. I built the *Déchet* with my bare hands, by myself, from the scraps your Armament left behind. I know how she works, and how fast she flies. You do your thing and leave the sailing to me."

"And what exactly is *my thing*?"

"Looking pretty," she said. "Fixing your hair." She ran a hand through her own, then gave it a dramatic shake. "Wearing those special goggles that make it so you can't see the rest of us."

"You don't know me," he said.

"You're the son of one of the richest men in the world," she said. "That's all I need to know."

"It's not that simple," he argued. "It's not like I'm eating money for breakfast and sleeping on the crushed dreams of poor people."

"Well, I know you're not sleeping on the ground with the rats or wondering when the last time you *had* breakfast was." She made a sound of disgust and stared out over the water.

Ross couldn't imagine what she'd described. Even in the worst case, if his father were ever impeached, they'd never be out on the streets.

A strained quiet settled between them, and in it, he watched her lean into the waves, her body absorbing the movement. Part of him wanted to deny that this could be real. This girl was his age. She could have gone to Center. They could have sat next to each other in environmental history, and met in the supply closet between classes.

Or maybe not.

Instead, she was sailing a boat, using the kind of skill he didn't possess for anything, and running from the Armament. She was tough, and sharp, and from a completely different world.

"For your information, I don't do anything to my hair," he said. "It's like this naturally."

In her profile, he caught a smirk.

His eyes drew again to the "86" tattoo below her ear. It was faded around the edges, making him wonder how long she'd had it.

"What's that number on your neck?" Her fingers lifted to cover the black ink.

"Definitely not a running tally of people I've kidnapped."

"Well, that's great news," he said.

The waves slapped against the side of the boat, adding to the throbbing at the base of his skull.

"My people all have this. You get it on your fifth birthday if you live that long."

He cringed.

"Who are your people?" He was starting to get the feeling they weren't Shorelings.

"The Original Eighty-Six."

He knew the name from his internet search at home, but still didn't know what it meant.

"You know how the Oil Nation attacked the Armament base and some warehouses in Noram all those years back?" She didn't look back at him, and he saw she'd moved her hair to cover the mark.

"Sure," he said, pleased that he actually remembered something from school that Adam hadn't had to reiterate to him. That small pride was another punch to the ribs. "That's what started the war with the SAF."

She side-eyed him. "That what they teach you in your fancy school?"

He nodded, thinking of just a few days ago, when he'd asked Adam about Shoreling school.

"Well, it was your people that started it," she said, "when they hoarded the malaria medicine. Kanshu, yeah? Guarding the vaccines like jailers."

He scowled. "What do you mean?"

Malaria was a frequent topic in history classes at Center. After the Melt, people had to move inland. They crowded together in the coastal cities, dying from storms and heat and starvation. The only things that had thrived were the mosquitoes, and in a matter of years they'd wiped out five billion people.

"Malaria made your medical companies a lot of money," she said. "When the first wave hit Noram, who do you think got their shots first?"

His grandparents had. Because they were educated, and responsible, and that's what educated, responsible people did.

"The people who could pay for it," she answered for him. "And when they ran out of medicine, the people who couldn't were turned away."

He hadn't considered that people had to pay for the medicine that kept them alive. Then again, he hadn't known you had to pay to ride the bus, either.

"That . . . seems unfair," he said.

"The people that survived had nothing," she said. "The fishing had all dried up. They had no money. No food."

After a moment, she moved to sit on a crate across the cockpit from him.

"So one day this fisherman went past the California Islands. He hadn't caught anything in a month, but his family was starving, so he pushed farther and farther out, past the Alliance's boundary lines, because he knew if he did, he'd find something."

She crossed her arms over her chest and leaned back.

"What did he find?" Ross asked.

"Another boat. An *Oiler* boat."

"From an oil rig?"

"From the Oil *Nation*," she said. "And do you know what the sailors onboard promised him? Bread. And honey. And fish, because they still had fish in the southern waters. In exchange for a ride back to the mainland."

Ross heaved a breath, caught up in the story. "Was the fisherman an idiot? Who brings an SAF national to the capital without wondering what he's up to?"

Her eyes turned to slits. "You'd do the same if you were starving."

He wouldn't know. He'd never been starving.

"Five Oilers came back with that fisherman," she said. "Five more the next week, and the next. For a while, things were good. His family had food in their bellies, enough to share with their friends and neighbors." She took a slow breath, exhaled. "The attacks came from the mainland side—just a handful of men with bombs the Armament never saw coming."

Ross's forehead crinkled. He'd just assumed the SAF had attacked from the sea, but she was right, the Armament would have been prepared for that. They regularly patrolled the Alliance's seaboards.

"Afterward, the patrol found out and rounded up the ones who helped them. Didn't take them to jail. Oh, no. Jail was too good for them. Your people found their families, even their children, and had them all sent to an island on the stormy seas. A very special place, where there was nothing to eat or drink, where nothing could survive." She shook her head. "Whatever they had done, it was not worth that death."

This felt off to Ross. Even terrorists were given a trial, weren't they? Exile seemed barbaric.

"But they did survive," Ross said.

"Yes," she said. "The prisoners fought back. They drowned the men who'd brought them there. They burned their bodies in a fire pit." Her stare was filled with bitter challenge. "The revolution of the Eighty-Six."

Tattoo number 86, thought to be in gang affiliation with the Original 86.

"How did Noram not know their men had been overrun? Didn't they send supplies? Or wonder what happened to them?"

"My grandfather—Finn Carey—his first ship was an Armament skiff Noram sent from the mainland. After that, they didn't send many more. Guess we weren't worth the loss." Her grin was sharp as the knife at her hip.

We.

His grandparents argued over wines. Hers had fought in wars.

"You've been to this island," he said slowly.

"I was born there."

His insides felt hollow and cold as the warmth drained from his body.

"The Eighty-Six are pirates," he realized. "*You* are a pirate."

A slow smile tilted her lips.

"We prefer the term 'corsarios,'" she said. "But yes. I am."

When she picked up speed, Ross retreated into the cabin, and maybe the greenish tint of his skin was enough for her not to ask why. Inside, things were only worse. He was tossed around the tiny space like a pebble in a bowl, smacking his head on the low ceiling, his shoulders on the side compartments, his knees everywhere else.

A pirate. He'd hired a damn pirate to take him out to sea. And then, because he was the world's smartest man, he'd broken her out of a cell, given her back her boat, and handed her a gun.

A *pirate.* If it wasn't for everything that had happened today, he wasn't sure he'd even believe in them. But the way she'd said it, the fierceness and pride in that smirk, had held more truth than anything she'd ever told him.

His mind fit together the accounts he'd heard over the years from Tersley and his father's cabinet members. Pirates attacked freighters and commercial boats, running drugs and ransoming crews, and then sinking the stolen ships to destroy the evidence.

His stomach was still churning from the motion of the boat as he searched through the below-deck compartments. He couldn't believe the *Déchet* didn't have some kind of radio, despite how it looked. The thought crossed his mind that he should find a weapon of some sort, just in case she decided to go back on her word and he needed something to defend himself.

The light was fading, making it hard to see what he was doing. There were some matches beside the stove, and some strange tools in the cabinet beneath. The tomblike chute reaching toward the front of the boat was covered with a thin, hand-sewn pillow top, and when he searched beneath it, he found a storage compartment. A few buckets were inside, along with a large plastic jug of water.

His mouth dried just at the sight of it, his tongue suddenly thick behind his teeth. After giving a brief listen above deck for any sign of movement, he retrieved the water, and twisted off the top. He could already taste the liquid relief as he brought it to his lips.

"What are you doing?"

She was crouching in the hatch, a few steps above him. There was something elegant and dangerous about her, and he found himself questioning if the things he knew about this girl were as frightening as the things people had told him about people *like* her.

He didn't think they were.

"Shoreling," and "pirate," and "corsario" all jumbled in his head. Labels he'd heard used with words like "vicious," and "predatory," and "animal."

Labels given by people who withheld medicine and food from the poor, when they had more than enough to go around.

"I'm thirsty," he said, but immediately set the water down on the trunk.

"You'd be better off drinking seawater," she said, brows drawing inward. "That's for cleaning the deck."

He looked down at the white sticker and the large black print, and groaned internally as she turned to go.

"I'm catching rain," she said over her shoulder. "Not much cleaner, but it won't kill you."

He'd never had unfiltered water before. He'd never given much thought to where it came from other than the tap from his home.

He didn't follow her above deck.

His moves became more frantic as the last of the sky through the small overhead window turned black, and he could feel the sickness mingle with something more potent. The situation had seemed manageable in the daytime, but now, with the arrival of night, he felt the full weight of it, dragging him down into the water.

He was with a girl he barely knew, on a boat in the middle of the ocean. His family, his friends, everything he'd ever known had slipped out of his reach. He was heading toward the unknown, after running from the Armament.

He had lost his mind.

He climbed the steps and gulped the night air. It was worse out here. He could see nothing. No sky, no clouds, nothing before or behind them.

Sweat dripped between his shoulder blades. He stumbled forward to the edge and tipped forward for one dizzying moment.

"Hey!" Marin grabbed the back of his shirt and pulled him back.

"Let go," he managed.

He spun and tried to walk, stretch his legs, but there was nowhere to run. The cockpit of this stupid boat was only a few feet across, and he kept bumping into the siding or the pole that supported the sail.

"Sit down," she said.

His remaining strength slipped away. The sky seemed to press harder from all around them, weighting down this boat into the murky, trash-filled sea.

"Where are we?" He was breathing hard. "How much farther?"

"I had to arc northwest to stay out of Alliance waters," she said. "It'll take another day at least."

"Another day?" He hugged his arms across his body. His throat burned.

"You should really sit down."

His insides felt liquid, and scalding hot. His hands found the side of the boat, knees knocking against the crates as he fell onto them. If he'd had something in his stomach, he might have vomited. As it was, his stomach twisted and flexed, not relaxing long enough for him to inhale.

"It's too dark." He could hear the water, but there was no reflection off of it. He couldn't even see her. "Don't you have some kind of light?"

"I do," she said. "But it makes it worse. Shows you everything you can't see. Just breathe. It'll pass."

He'd never seen darkness like this. It seeped into his skin, filled his body. He felt the need to touch his arms and legs just to make sure they were still there.

Marin's hand settled between his shoulder blades. He struggled to push her back, but either he was too weak, or he didn't really want her gone. Every quaking muscle flexed as he gripped the siding and kneeled on the bench, but she didn't pull away.

Wrung out, he rested his head on the cool plastic rim between his hands. She spread her fingers, just a tiny bit, but enough that Ross could feel.

It was too quiet.

"Say something," he said.

"I can tie twenty-seven kinds of knots, eyes closed," she said. "Honest truth, right there."

He inhaled roughly.

"My dad taught me," she added.

Something clunked against the side of the boat. He squeezed his eyes shut.

"He said I had my sea legs before I had my land legs." She laughed quietly. "Once, he sailed straight into a hurricane just to outrun the Armament."

He squinted into the black, looking for any sign of civilization. He wouldn't even be upset to see the Armament now, just so they wouldn't be alone.

She moved the heel of her hand a little, and he became more aware of heat from her skin, and her warm puffs of breath near his biceps. She was kneeling on the bench beside him.

"Wind smashed his boat to pieces. They found him a hundred miles away on a piece of driftwood. He said a whale carried him there in its mouth."

He didn't tell her this couldn't be real. The sound of her voice was gritty and real and maybe he was the biggest idiot in the world, but when she talked, he wanted to hear more.

"He sailed to all nine nations," she continued. "Even Australia. Said it was so hot it burned a hole in the bottom of his boat."

Ross coughed, then laughed, then coughed again. He didn't want to imagine holes in the bottom of anyone's boat.

"He saw ice once too," she said. "Real ice. A chunk of it floating off the northern boundary of the Alliance."

He wondered what it would be like to see real ice, not in a glass or made into a sculpture at one of his father's functions. Snow. Like in the old days.

"What'd he do with it?" His voice sounded strange in the dark, or maybe he'd never really heard it without the distraction of sight. It was deeper than he'd thought, and so much more even and dull than hers.

"Fished it out of the water," she said. "Wrapped it in a blanket and brought it home to show me."

The pressure in Ross's chest eased.

"You saw it?"

"I saw a sopping wet blanket," she said with a snort. It was easy to picture for some reason. Easier than his own real memories of his father's assistant delivering some special fruit or token from one of his trips.

"Is he a pirate too?"

Her hand slipped down his back, but he caught her wrist before she pulled away. He didn't mean to say something wrong. He didn't want her to go away.

Her wrist turned in his loose grasp, and then he sat, and their fingers aligned on his thigh. Hers were small and slender, smooth calluses that gave way to the fragile bones of her knuckles.

"He's *the* pirate, terreno," she said, her voice a little softer. "He's the son of Finn Carey. Head of captain's table. He makes the rules. He takes the tithes."

"What are those?" Her thumb trailed along the outside of his index finger, back and forth, like the motion of the waves. Her pinky hooked around his. It may have been only a small movement, but it anchored him, and slowed his thoughts.

"What each person pays in order to stay on the island. Food, or metal, or fuel. Weapons. Whatever you can find. Like the rent money terrenos pay for their apartments."

"And if you don't find anything to tithe?"

"You're sent away." Her thumb went still, so he moved his, taking over where she had stopped, gently tracing the shape of her hand.

"Forever?"

"That's right."

He thought of her again when he'd first seen her in the docks. She'd known her way around, known where to take them to find the healer. He'd assumed she was a Shoreling because she acted like she lived there.

He might not have been wrong. If she'd been banished, she could have come to the docks for refuge.

Resentment surged through him on her behalf. He couldn't imagine a world where you got kicked out of your own home for not contributing.

The boat was rocking steadily now, but the breeze was soft. He held his other hand in front of his face, but saw nothing.

"So your father's still on the island?"

"Japanese recruited him to captain a big crew in Asian waters. Pretty dangerous stuff. Not exactly legal."

"Oh."

The boat tilted and rolled, in the same way it had earlier.

She must have slowed down again, or maybe they had finally stopped.

"Stupid guard back on that Armament ship stole the knife he gave me," she said quietly.

He wasn't sure why, but he said, "I'm sorry," and meant it.

"I'm sorry about your friend," she said, and he could tell she meant it too.

For a while they were both still, part of the silence, woven into the darkness. Was Adam out here in this same stretch of water? It seemed impossible he'd been gone a full day already.

"He didn't ask for this," Ross said. "He didn't ask to go to the riots that night. He didn't ask to come to Central. He didn't ask to get stuck with me, but he did. He's the only real friend I've ever had, and now he's gone, and it's my fault."

Ross hadn't said it out loud until that moment, and doing so felt like blowing out a breath he'd been holding too long. His shoulders sagged as he reheard every time someone at school had called Adam *trawler*. He remembered how Pruitt and the others had harassed him. How people had refused to sit by him after the riots had started, and how he'd taken speech lessons, and changed the way he'd dressed, just to blend in.

He'd never blended in. And he shouldn't have had to try.

"We'll find him," she said.

"I'll get you the money," he told her.

He was squeezing her hand—he hadn't even noticed until right then. She squeezed back, though, so maybe it was okay.

For a long time they sat in silence, barely moving. Both clinging to promises he wasn't sure they could keep.

"Look," she said. He wasn't sure where she'd meant until she grabbed his face, and tilted his chin back.

There, straight above them, was a patch of clear sky no bigger than his fist. Contained within it were stars, shockingly white and pulsing with life. They were more brilliant than anything he'd ever seen in photographs, or in the rare glimpses of the sky from the brightly lit city.

It was only a small piece of a bigger picture, but it felt like a promise. He didn't have to see the rest to know it was there.

Her hand had fallen to his shoulder, and rested there, and for a short time he cleared his mind of everything but the stars in the sky and the warmth of her fingertips.

CHAPTER 19

MARIN TOLD herself the reason she was so handsy with the president's son had everything to do with keeping him from going overboard again and nothing to do with the lightness she felt in her chest whenever they touched.

Nothing about him made sense to her. This crazy quest for his friend. The way he'd busted her out of the cell on the Armament ship. She respected that kind of reckless bravery more than she cared to admit, but she didn't expect it from someone like him.

Maybe she should have.

"Are you hungry?" she asked.

"What do you have?"

"If you're asking that, you're not all that hungry." She felt her way toward the red blinking light of the GPS, to the cabinet beneath the steering console. There, she pulled on the magnetic latch until it released, and felt through the compartment for a folded net. She'd made it herself—knotted twine and rope and plastic strips she'd pulled from the waves just like her father had taught her.

"It doesn't bother you?" His voice floated through the darkness. "Being out here at night, I mean."

Net in hand, she crossed back in his direction, reaching out to find his knee. His muscles stiffened beneath her touch.

"Sometimes it does," she admitted. "Look over there. In the water."

Over the siding was a school of fish, none larger than her hand, and all glowing a pale green.

"What are those?" he asked, as if they might jump aboard and strangle him.

"Moonfish," she said. "They only come to the surface on clear nights."

"Why are they that color?" he asked. "They look radioactive."

"Maybe that's why I have webbed toes."

He was silent.

"That was a joke, terreno."

The noise he made was disbelieving at best.

"What does that mean?" he asked as she pulled back the net. "*Terreno.*"

She felt her lips perk up in a smile. "Dirt-born. Land-loving. Fat and rich and scared of the water." Not born in the trash, like her.

"I'm not fat," he said, and she laughed before she caught herself.

It was easy enough netting them; she pulled up five on her first swipe. What came after was harder. Without a knife to clean them, she ended up killing them with the heel of her boot, skewering them on a clean oil rod, and then broiling them on the Bunsen burner in the galley.

"Hold out your hand," she said. He bumped into her forearm, and she passed him a flaky chunk of warm fish. "They're better with salt."

He didn't complain.

Her eyes roamed the horizon for lights, any sign of an Armament ship on their tail. When she saw only blackness, she rose, and got him some rainwater she'd caught in a cup. It tasted faintly acidic, but it wouldn't kill them.

She could hear him crunching, and told him to watch out for the bones.

"My dad brought me out on a night like this once," she said. "We spent hours looking for that space shuttle Asia sent up." She remembered how excited he'd been when he'd come back from the mainland with the news. The way he kept telling her he'd spotted it. How she'd strained her eyes and searched the clouds until she'd convinced herself she could see that tiny bright speck in the sky too.

"They lost contact with it," said Ross. "It was supposed to set up a colony on Mars, but they didn't hear back after the first month. No one had the funds to send up a rescue mission."

She stared at where she thought he was. "Are you always so cheerful?"

"Only when I'm on the verge of certain death," he said.

She thought maybe he was the one joking now. Whatever the case, she peered into the distance again for any unwanted visitors—not just the Armament. They were entering corsario waters. The closer they got to the gyre, the closer they came to Careytown, and without the money she'd get from this job, she had nothing to barter her own life—or his—with.

They would search the outskirts of the gyre for this place, but they would not enter those swirling currents. If they were pulled in too far, they'd find themselves at the center, at her island, and certain death might be more accurate than he thought.

"I'd like to see the stars," he said, pulling her back. "I wanted to be an astronaut when I was a kid."

It was kind of a disappointment to think that colony had never started. That night with her dad, they'd talked about what it would have been like to move to another planet. He'd told her there were lakes on Mars where she could sail. She'd liked the thought of that. Sailing on another world.

Their knees were touching. Neither of them backed away. Even if it wasn't true, right then they felt like the only two people in the whole ocean.

"I'd like to see snow," she said. "Or a peacock. I've never seen a peacock."

"A peacock? Like the bird?"

"Yeah, *like the bird*. I saw a picture of one once." She'd wanted to make a sail as beautiful as the tail feathers. Stupid. She'd probably be laughed off the water.

He gave a short hum. "I saw one once. In a preservation near Calgary."

"What's a preservation?" she asked.

He crunched for another moment. "A place where they keep animals that are almost extinct."

"They don't eat each other?"

"They're in separate cages."

"Do you eat them?"

"No," he said. "No, you just . . . look at them."

"So it's jail for animals?"

"Sort of," he said. "It's for their protection."

"Is that why you're getting rid of the Shorelings?" she asked. "For their protection?"

He was quiet for another long while. So quiet she could practically hear him thinking.

He shifted. "No one's forcing anyone to go. Anyway, it's supposed to be nice there."

"Then why aren't people on your side of the cliffline lining up to get a ticket?"

"We don't have the same problems." When she groaned, he added, "The power blackouts and broken pipes, I mean. They're being moved so they can have a better life."

In the light she would have laughed—people only got exiled when someone was trying to get rid of them—but the dark had stripped away her rough edges, and all she could think of was Hiro telling her they deserved better.

"Do the peacocks have a better life?"

She doubted it if they were stuck in cages.

"I'm not sure anyone asked them," he answered.

She crossed her arms, leaning back against the siding and feeling proud of herself.

"Well, I never heard of a *preservation* before," she said, thinking about all the things he'd probably done and seen that she had only dreamed about. Hating that she sort of wanted to see his stupid preservation, even if the peacock was in a cage.

"I've never been on a sailboat before," he said.

"You don't say."

He snorted.

The water lapped against the side of the boat. Five years since she'd been out this far, and it felt like she'd never been gone.

Her shoulders relaxed. "I've never eaten a real orange. Just the canned stuff."

"I've never eaten a radioactive moonfish."

"You're already glowing a little." She smirked when he choked. "I've never been busted from an Armament brig before."

Her cheeks warmed.

"I've never rescued anyone before," he said. "I guess we're both amateurs. Maybe we should consult a handbook."

"Like that would help," she said, giving him a light shove. "I could sail us halfway across the world before you got through the first page."

He fell quiet. Maybe it was dark and she couldn't see him looking, but he was, and that stare burned hot as coals.

"What does that mean?" He laughed, the way people did when something wasn't even a little funny. "I can read, if that's what you're saying."

"It's not that big a deal," she said. "I know lots of guys who can't." Most of the corsarios, actually. Even her mom could only recognize a dozen or so words, and they all pertained to stolen crates hauled into her kitchen.

"Yeah, but they're . . ."

"They're what?"

She felt the air fill her chest and hold. Whatever game they'd been playing was over.

"I go to Center Academy," he said. "It's the best in the nation."

"Well, look at you," she said. "*I go to Center.*" She mimicked his voice again, and he groaned. "Tell me, Mr. President's son, is it hard having everything?"

"A little," he admitted.

"Is that why you went to the riots? To feel better about yourself? Play poor for a night?"

That shut him up. But for some reason, she regretted saying it.

"I just wanted to be someone else for a little while, you know?" he finally said. "Being Roosevelt Torres gets old."

She snorted. "Your name is *Roosevelt*?"

Now he chuckled.

"After this old president my dad idolized."

One hand covered her mouth, but the laughter slipped through. "If that was my name, I'd want to be somebody else too."

"Thanks."

Their laughter built, swelled, ebbed.

Normally she didn't mind the quiet, but now a strange longing pulled at her to keep talking. She wanted to hear more about the things he'd never done, and maybe the things he had done too. It felt like she was a child again, staring up at the night sky, imagining a world beyond the stars.

He passed her the cup. She took a sip.

"It's not that I can't read." His voice was quieter, like he was facing the other way. "I just mix up the letters. It's not like you have to read now anyway. Everything has audio adaptation."

"Except for the directions on the wall of the Armament ship. And the label on the dirty water below deck." Her father had spent hours teaching her each letter, and the sounds they made when they fit together. How much she had practiced when he went away, just so she could show him her progress when he came back.

"Except for those." He cleared his throat. "I've never told anybody that before. I guess Adam probably knows, but he's never said anything."

She was glad it was dark then, because she never would have been able to live down the look on her face. No one had ever trusted her with something like that before. It felt like she was glowing from the inside. Like she was holding something worth defending, and it made her fierce, and sad, and proud, that her corsario father gave her something even the richest man in the Alliance couldn't give his son.

"So what's your secret?" he asked.

And just like that, she almost told him.

Her mouth was open, the truth lying on her tongue. It frightened her how close it was to the surface, as if she'd just been waiting for this exact moment for him to pull them from her.

"We should get some sleep," she said.

He didn't move.

Beneath her seat within the crate was a cone-shaped sea anchor made of waxed cloth. She tossed it overboard so they didn't drift. Then she lowered herself to the floor of the cockpit, where she'd spent countless nights in the Sacramento Bay, staring up at a black sky and dreaming of home.

"Marin?" he asked. "If you're a pirate, how come you're not with other pirates?"

Her eyes burned, either from the salty spray of the waves or the acid in the earlier rain, but definitely not from tears. She didn't cry, not in front of anyone, not even alone.

She turned on her side away from him, feeling him watching her. She needed to get back to where she belonged, somewhere where dreams of stars, and schools, and boys who wanted to know her secrets didn't exist.

Only right then, she didn't know where that was. The docks were going up in flames, and her island . . . she didn't even know if the captains would let her come back, even with all the money in the world.

"I'm better on my own," she said.

A long beat passed.

"Goodnight, Marin," he said.

"Goodnight, terreno."

She closed her eyes and dreamed of a boat with sails like the feathers of a peacock, and when she woke, the sky was red as flames.

"I don't understand why we're sailing into a storm," Ross yelled over the wind and surf.

Marin had just cut the wheel hard to the leeward side, attempting to beat a zigzag line south toward the clouds that gathered like a bruise on the southern horizon.

The wind was picking up, straining against her sails and making each turn more difficult. Had it been at their backs they would have flown to the outskirts of the gyre, but instead the clouds had regrouped, forcing her to sail into the wind in choppy, indirect strides back and forth.

"It'll move faster than we can," she shouted, using her teeth to secure a knot when her wrist sparked with pain. "We turn back, and it follows us. We make a drive now, we'll pass through before it gets any worse."

But it would throw off her navigation. Send her closer to the center of the gyre, to Careytown.

She couldn't go there yet. She wasn't ready.

She should have gotten the money first.

If they saw Ross, a descendant of the men who'd exiled them to the island, they wouldn't waste their breath negotiating. They would kill him. They would kill both of them.

He clung to the mouth of the hatch beside the wheel, hair tossed in wild streaks around his angular face. He squinted against the spray of water, and even in the gray shadowed light she could see the rise in color on his cheeks and forehead.

"What do you mean, *any worse?*" he called, knuckles white where they gripped the boat.

A cold brick lodged beneath her breastbone. It was impossible to tell how bad this storm would be. Last night's break could have been only a breath before the real show.

She didn't answer him. Wind gusted, throwing them hard to the leeward side. She scrambled to the other side of the cockpit, using her weight as a counterbalance.

He muttered something she couldn't hear. When she glanced over her shoulder at him, the pink tint of his skin had turned ashen.

The rain began suddenly, an angry chorus of wind-whipped drops sprayed against plastic and metal. It peppered her bare shoulders and face, harsh enough to make her shield her eyes. She was just about to go below to search for another pair of goggles when the low clouds drew back, a sudden reveal of the path that lay ahead.

Her mouth fell open, her heart stuttered. Before them, the sky darkened in shades of gray, blending with the churning, white-capped water. It looked as if they were sailing toward a giant hole, a direct route to night.

It was too late to turn back, even if she'd wanted to.

"Marin," said Ross. "Do you see the jail?"

They were still at least fifty miles off from the edge of the gyre. It was hard to tell exactly, because her GPS was only registering the storm.

"You should sit down," she said unsteadily.

"We need to turn around."

"We can't." He didn't hear her whisper.

Coming this way had been a bad call. She should have sailed farther north, hit the gyre from the top, and worked her way down the edge. Now the sea would get them before the pirates ever could. The rain pelted her nerves, reminding her of every wrong decision she'd made since she'd left the mainland.

They would not outrun this squall. It was going to tear them apart.

Unless they went to the one place that meant their own death. Careytown.

Ross's hand was on her face, turning her toward him. He'd been saying something, but she hadn't heard him. Her fingers grasped his, shaking, or maybe he was shaking. Maybe the ocean itself was roaring up around them, ready to swallow them whole.

"What do we do?" He stared at her, eyes bright and sharp, holding her in place just as they had the first time she'd seen him in the riots. "I'm not some worthless terreno," he said. "Tell me what to do."

She saw him then, the real him. The whole of him, that she hadn't allowed herself to see until fear had stripped away the last of her pride. He stood before her, leaning down so that they were on the same level, his gaze sharp with fear, his mouth set with determination. This boy, who she'd thought had everything, who she'd *relied* on having everything. Right now he had even less than her and was still strong enough to fight.

The fire in him shamed and ignited her.

She would not surrender to the sea. Her father had trained her to be smart, her mother, to be strong. If this storm wanted the *Déchet*, it would have to pry her from Marin's cold, wet fists.

CHAPTER 20

MARIN NODDED.

His hand was still on her cheek. He hadn't even thought of touching her that way, but the tremble in her lower lip when she'd seen the weather had taken him off guard. She'd been fearless as long as he'd known her, but her silence cut straight through him, and the decision to pull her back from wherever she'd gone had been automatic.

"All right," she finally said.

Moving in the strong, deliberate way she always did, she showed him how to move the pole that secured the base of the sail across the cockpit by lengthening and shortening the ropes on either side. He was a quick study with knots this time, and when he met her approval, she rewarded him with a curt nod and a tight smile.

They worked their way into the storm, going against his every instinct to turn the opposite way. The clouds embraced them once again, dark and heavy, seeping a bitter moisture that burned his eyes and needled at his skin. Soon, they could see nothing, but Marin lowered her head, gripped the wheel, and drove them on.

The deck became so slick he fell, smashing his shoulder on the crates that lined the sides, knocking her pots free from their ties with his knees and feet. The black mud that filled them spilled across his pant legs. With one elbow hooked around the wheel, she helped him up, her hand small inside his, her grip firm and unyielding. His mind swam with old fears of rattling windows and white bolts across gray skies. Nights he'd shivered in bed, covering his ears against the raging weather. His father's voice telling his mother not to coddle him or he'd never grow out of it.

He wasn't here with his father, though. He was here with a pirate girl with a tattoo beneath her ear, and he needed her more than he had ever needed anything in his life.

The boat rocked drunkenly, each time making his heart trip and slam against his ribs. They kept their weight on the rising side of the *Déchet* as the waves and wind threatened to throw them over, then switched as they turned the other way. The crates slid across the cockpit floor, bursting open, their contents lost to the sea. Marin lifted her arm straight up to the sky, seeming to measure the angle the mainsail bowed away, and when it went too far, she grabbed his shirt and pulled him toward the center ratchet.

"Reef the sail," she yelled, her voice whipped away by the wind just as soon as the words had left her lips.

"There's a reef?"

She shook her head, black hair sticking to her cheeks. "Lower the sail halfway!"

He followed where she pointed, then turned the crank until she grabbed his shoulder. The triangular sail was now a third of its previous size, but still filled with wind to the point of bursting. Their sudden decrease in speed launched him forward into her, chest to back. He could feel the tightness in her shoulders as she tried to pull the wheel and helped, hands beside hers, groaning as every muscle in both their bodies flexed as one.

It went on endlessly. A terrible, magnificent nightmare that spoke in roars and fought with whips of electricity. Ross was terrified, and it was within that cold, sharp terror that every other fear he'd ever had was finally realized. Fear of his father finding out he was weak and stupid. Fear of never mattering to anyone. Fear of losing the only friend he'd ever had.

Fear of letting Marin down and killing them both.

Lightning split the sky, shattering into a hundred branching roots that sizzled and crackled in the electric air. He knew the moment it struck the mast—sparks rained down around them, and his whole body vibrated like the pluck of a string that had been pulled too tight.

He searched for Marin. She was on her knees, still clinging to the wheel with one hand. Her feet were still bare, and one was bleeding, soaking the boards with red.

He made his way over and wrapped his arms around her, clinging to the wheel with both hands as the mast tilted, and tilted, and fell with a snap into the angry water beside them.

She looked back at him over her shoulder, eyes red with salt and tears.

"I'm sorry, terreno," she said.

He held her as tightly as he could as the top of the sail was sucked into the churning sea, dragged down by some invisible hand. The *Déchet* groaned and cracked, like the hull of the Armament ship when the Shorelings had attacked. The opposite side of the boat lifted higher, higher, the leftover crates and pots sliding across the cockpit, cracking as they glanced off his side and back and splashed into the ocean.

Ross buried his face in Marin's neck, accepting this final truth. Her boat would sink, and they would go with it.

Their feet slipped out from beneath them. And then there was only shadow, and water, and the last scream of the *Déchet* as the wind tore her to pieces.

They clung to a rounded piece of the hull, half submerged in warm water for what felt like hours. His legs turned to jelly, unable to kick even to stay afloat. Sharp plastic poked him in the ribs. A tired numbness took his arms and fingers, but every time his grip slid away, she was there to pull him back up.

"Don't give up on me, Ross," she said once, barely louder than a breath.

He didn't.

The storm passed the way it had come, fading out in rain and wind, and finally giving way to the same thick clouds that had surrounded them before.

Through half-closed eyes he watched her rest, her cheek on her folded arm, a lock of her hair swishing in the puddle atop the wreckage. Fatigue pulled at him, but he knew if either of them fell asleep, they'd slip into the water and wouldn't come back up. He reached for her, fingers fumbling over the back of her shirt and working to make a fist in her skintight top.

"Wha . . ." Her eyes barely opened.

He heaved her up, kicking hard with the last bit of energy he had. She crawled atop the hull and collapsed in a trembling mess, and he slid backward, head submerging beneath the water.

Her fingers, tangled in his hair, pulled him back. It took some time to get him aboard, but between the two of them, they managed. The piece was small enough they had to lie nearly on top of each other, and even then water lapped over their sides. But it was a welcome relief from swimming.

Her head found a resting place on his chest. Their legs tangled together. The water lifted them up and down, up and down, and with her fingers spread across his chest, and her soft whispered prayers, "Hail Mary, full of grace . . . ," he fell asleep.

Ross didn't know how long he slept, but he woke with a start to a loud *clunk* in the water nearby. When he pushed up to his elbows, Marin jerked up, nearly falling backward into the ocean. He caught her forearm and heaved her close, so that they were nose to nose.

She was breathing hard, and in that moment he saw nothing but her dark lashes and her round, brown eyes.

"We made it," he rasped, voice raw from seawater and thirst.

She laughed. And cried. And he held her, because he didn't know what else to do.

After a while, she steadied herself on her knees and turned to survey the scene around them, one hand anchored on his shoulder. Pieces of debris bobbed in the water in all directions. Hunks of plastic and shards of siding. It looked like the ship had been blown apart, with barely any recognizable pieces remaining.

Her lips parted, brows drawing together, and she didn't need to say anything for him to know how she felt.

He held her again, not just because of the boat, but because they had survived, and if he looked too long at the pieces of the *Déchet* he would realize that their survival didn't matter, because now they had even less than they'd started with. They were floating in the ocean on a hunk of plastic with no sail, no motor, and no sign of land.

She squeezed him back.

"If only we had a whale," he said, and she laughed weakly.

It felt like the kind of thing you said before you died.

Another loud *thunk* drew them apart, and they both strained their eyes into the gloom over her right shoulder, where a sleek silver shape appeared through the clouds.

His mouth dropped open. He rubbed his eyes. It *was* a whale.

But as it drew closer, he saw that it wasn't an animal, but a speedboat, manned by two sailors—men in tattered clothes. Ross's chest constricted. He was dreaming. He had to be dreaming. His pulse pounded harder and harder, and soon he was waving the boat closer.

They were going to make it out of this.

The man at the front had sun-browned skin and thin hair that stood on end. When he smiled, it became obvious dental hygiene wasn't high on his list of priorities. Marin's grip tightened on Ross's shoulder, hard enough to pause his relief.

"Don't say a word," she said. "Leave this to me."

He nodded.

"Well, I'll be damned," the man called as he pulled closer. "Look what the sea spat out."

"Picker," she said, grinning like the pirate she was. "What took you so long?"

CHAPTER 21

SHE DIDN'T like speedboats and never had. She especially didn't like speedboats where she had to sit an arm's length away from a guy who used to fill her boots with roaches and now ogled her like he'd never seen a girl before.

"Keep looking and I'll toss you over," she said, hunching forward.

He laughed, and this time made a real show of staring.

"Someone grew up," he said. "How long's it been, Marin?"

"Long enough for you to lose half your teeth and most of your hair," she answered.

He howled. "Still got that fire."

Right now it was all she *did* have.

Marin glanced over her shoulder to find Ross watching them beneath furrowed brows. He sat on the back bench beside an old man they called Japan, who'd gunned down more than twenty Oil Nation ships in his day, despite the fact that the radiation from his home nation had left him with a missing arm and one eye sealed closed. He worked the motor, shuttling them toward the island.

The *Déchet* had foundered less than a mile away. Had the sky been clear they could have kicked ashore and snuck somewhere where she could hide Ross from the others until she figured out a plan. She didn't want to face the captains this way, dragged in by Picker, who'd only been born with half a brain and fried out the rest on the tar he got from Luc. She was supposed to have money, enough to tithe and earn her father's spot at the table. Enough to help Gloria with the supply train. Instead she had no boat, no credits, and a terreno she didn't have a clue how to save.

Guilt coated her insides, like the thin, white layer of salt that covered her skin. She was a Carey, born to fight and scrap and sail, but right now all she could think about was Ross.

The dock peeked through the heavy clouds, half a dozen ships coming into view. Most of them were locked down for the weather, their masts dropped, sails tied. Others looked a little worse for wear. She spotted one skiff near the end of the pier that was already half sunk, the cockpit knee-deep in water. It reminded her of the *Déchet*, which made her stomach clench.

Japan reduced their speed, directing them into the cove. Another glance at Ross revealed wide eyes and high brows. Her neck heated as she realized this wasn't what he'd been expecting. He'd probably thought her island looked more like the Pacifica ads she'd seen on the mainland.

"Who's head of the table?" she asked, because that's undoubtedly who he would bring her to first. Panic whispered across her every nerve as she considered the options she knew.

"Who do you think?" Picker asked.

Luc. She'd known it would be. Even before she'd left, Luc

had captained the second biggest boat, and had the second largest crew, a feat topped only by her father. He'd started young. At fifteen, he'd been trading favors for loyalty. By eighteen he was coveted for the drug he called tar that he cooked up in the trash pits. By twenty, he'd surrounded himself with a bunch of meat-heads, Picker among them, who'd do anything he asked so long as he gave them a fix of the stuff.

When she'd left, he'd been twenty-one, and well on his way to the head of the table.

Picker leaned closer. "He's going to rip those brass balls you think you have right off, you know that." He laughed, a high, un-stable kind of giggle that made her think he'd already taken a dip in Luc's tar supply today. His fingertips hovered a breath above her exposed shoulder.

"Maybe we'll get lucky and he'll offer you up as a reward to his crew," he said. "His tithe for the rainy season."

She lunged across the bench, reaching for his throat, but stopped cold at the feel of a gun nestled against her ribs. She hadn't even seen him draw.

"Who is he, anyway?" asked Picker, looking down to where Ross had sprung forward and grabbed Marin's forearm. She quickly shook him free.

"Get your hands off me," she snapped at him. He blinked, surprised, then sat back. She willed him to keep his mouth shut. If anyone knew she cared, he'd be in even more trouble. They'd hurt him, just to hurt her.

She would have to make them see they couldn't. That he was too important.

And then, all at once, she knew what she had to do.

You are a corsario.

Marin turned away. "Found him on the mainland."

"Never knew you to keep a crew," Picker said.

"Never knew me much at all, did you?" He was always Luc's friend, not hers. Always chasing power, not loyalty.

Picker chuckled and finally put down his weapon, laying it across his lap still pointed in her direction. The flimsy metal boat wobbled and swayed, the smallest swell tossing it off course. It reminded her of the *Déchet* in her last moments, only those waves had been mountains, and these were barely a ripple.

"We've been in need of some fresh meat at the Blue Lady," he said. "Pretty face like that? He'll do just fine."

Over her dead body.

Through the fog materialized a great, looming shadow, a monster of a ship, twice the size the *Déchet* had been. The side was smooth and stained black—a single sheet of fiberglass, not the mismatched pieces that she'd pulled together for her poor boat. The deck was lined with six shielded posts, drilled with a hole in the center only large enough to stick the barrel of a gun in.

Above, the black canvas sails were tied down for the storm, but she guessed if they were stretched open the number "86" would be illuminated in white chalk, an omen of impending doom for any who saw it.

Two words were painted on the side. *Señora Muerte.*

She was without a doubt the fiercest ship Marin had ever seen.

"That Luc's?" Marin couldn't help gaping. Salvaging alone wouldn't get you a hull that big or sails that nice. This beast rivaled an Armament boat.

Maybe it had been an Armament boat.

Picker laughed. "You've been gone a long time."

Japan cut the engine in the shadowed water on the opposite side of the *Señora*. There, they were greeted by two more men from Luc's crew—both of them starved and bruised beneath the eyes.

They heaved Marin and Ross from the boat, and when she said she could walk fine on her own, they held her down and bound her wrists before her with thin, skin-chafing twine.

Ross objected enough to get a punch to the gut and a dirty gag shoved in his mouth.

"What's this about?" she demanded. "I haven't done anything to any of you."

"New rules," said Picker. "Luc's rules. He doesn't like deserters."

"Who said I deserted?" she volleyed back. "I'm here, aren't I? Deserters don't look back."

Picker only smiled.

They were hauled up the pier and onto a red mud path that led over a hill toward town. Her feet were still bare, and every rocky step bruised and bit into the flesh. Dread festered beneath her ribs, cold and sharp as knives. It cut away the exhaustion, leaving a twitchy kind of energy behind. Did they know what she'd done? They must. That's why they were treating her like an enemy.

She worked her wrists together, trying to break them free.

From behind her came the rough laughter of the men, and she turned to find Ross being shoved back and forth between them. He'd been bound too, and when he stumbled it was easy to see why they laughed. He could barely hold himself upright. He wove like a drunkard, blinking his eyes and shaking his head. His cheeks were pale again, and she suddenly feared he would puke, and that they would beat him for this show of weakness.

"Look at him," said a guy she'd known as a kid. They'd called him Greenhorn, due to three lost fingers from a poorly tied knot. "Can't even stand."

They all knew what it was. The adjustment from the water to the island was tricky—even now Marin could feel the tilt from side to side—but Ross felt it more, just as he'd felt the waves more his first hours on the *Déchet*.

She bit down on the inside of her cheek when Greenhorn kicked him behind the knees, sending him to the ground. Next chance she got, that pirate was going overboard. Picker right behind him. Japan laughed in a low voice, which meant he'd have to go too. Too bad. He'd been friends with her father.

Stopping them would only make it worse. They would hurt Ross just to get her riled up.

"Get up," she said harshly.

Ross's gaze flashed to hers, his jaw flexing around the dirty glove someone had shoved in his mouth.

She made herself turn away.

By the time they reached the swell, her heart was pounding. The wind shifted, bringing with it the sharp scent of smoke and rot and the salty sea. Her eyes strained for the first glimpse as she climbed higher, higher, pushing past Picker's lead, until finally Careytown appeared below them, a riot of color and sound, of metal and plastic, of every memory that had made who she was. This ruined city had pulled her back from exile. It had taken her beloved *Déchet* as payment, but she'd always known the price would be high.

She'd longed for this moment a thousand times since she left, but it was tainted by the twine around her wrists, and the innocent guy behind her, and the pirates who treated her the way Gloria and Sylvie and Hiro never had.

She suddenly missed the mainland, even with its violence and blackouts and hunger, so much it hurt.

Picker shoved her forward. Their path cut between two rows of shacks, built from plastic sheets and crates and mud and rope. Some were bigger, anchored by tile and composite bricks made from melted and resolidified plastic, and roofed with unfurled aluminum cans that had been nailed together. Some were smaller, barely large enough to fit two grown people standing.

People milled about, tossing insults the way terrenos traded pleasantries. Those nearby gathered beside the road as they walked by, and Marin lifted her chin, even while she was shaking inside. She knew they were staring at her.

She scanned the crowd for her mother, but didn't see her.

They passed shack after shack—mostly residences—until they came to an open-air bar. The tables were made of giant wooden spools, most of them half disintegrated, and the chairs were old crates. Things they'd found here, things they'd brought on their ships. Men and women drank whisky and rum and rainwater from an ivory bathtub, purified by iodine tablets, and at the sight of it, her throat burned with thirst.

"Keep moving, pretty boy," she heard Greenhorn say.

Glancing back, she saw that Ross had stopped short. His eyes were wide, his nose crinkled from the harsh scents. She followed his gaze over the main street of Careytown—not even a real street, but more a bumpy mud path, not even wide enough for one of the mainland cars to drive down. And instead of seeing the home of her memories, she saw only the rats, and the dirty rain barrels, and the garbage that filled every crevice, every pothole, every inch of this entire island.

She'd been born in a city of trash.

Her shoulders hunched. She led now, carving through the gathering crowd so that Picker had to chase after her.

"That Marin?" someone yelled. "Marin!"

"Does Luc know?" said another.

Her stomach was filled with razor blades.

They passed the Blue Lady, where the men and women who

sold their bodies catcalled from the open window. Passed the piti-
ful food storage, surrounded by armed guards in tattered clothes.
Passed the kitchen she'd once called home, where her mother was
probably cooking inside. Marin's bruised, dirty feet grew heavy
then, and she wanted nothing more than to turn and run there,
crawl up into the room upstairs, and will her father to come home.

But she kept going all the way to the fire pit.

It was the place where business was done, where stories were
told, and where her people had gathered since before she was born.
The large, open circle marked the center of the four quadrants. The
wet ground within it was always pearled with grease, the center
always filled with trash for burning. To her left was a field of rain
barrels where they gathered unfiltered water. To the right was
the corral where an old man called Farmer kept a herd of goats,
chickens, and roosters that were always escaping and crowing at
the crack of dawn. Behind the fire pit, the road continued on to the
gomi fields.

She remembered it all as if not a single day had passed.

As Marin drew closer, she saw that a chair had been dragged
in front of the blackened ashes. In it, a man slouched to the side,
leaning heavily on one arm as though he'd grown bored waiting
for her arrival. He was built like the snake he was: thin and long,
with straight, charcoal-colored hair that fell to his shoulders and
dark, peering eyes. Dressed in a loose black shirt and gray pants
tucked into open boots, he looked fearsome and untrustable, and
if there was any question he was a corsario, one needed only to
look to the guns on his belt or the broad, inked "86" tattoo across
his throat.

He sat up as she approached, and the scantily clad woman
who had been sitting on his lap shot an annoyed gaze over her
shoulder.

"Well, look what the tide brought in," he said, pushing aside his entertainment as he leaned forward. The girl fell on her backside in the mud, muttering curses as she rose and tromped away.

Marin was aware that a crowd had arced behind her, that half of them had followed her from the first step on the road from the docks. Subtly, she edged toward Ross, keeping him close. Even here she could still feel the ground moving beneath her feet.

The island was always moving, always changing. Luc's seat here proved that.

"Luc." She tried to sound unaffected, but fear was eating away every muscle in her body.

"Found them floating in the wreckage," said Picker, puffing his chest out. "Had this fancy boy with her. Says he's her crew now."

"That right?" asked Luc, voice darker, harsher than Marin remembered.

"Course, Captain." Picker's eyes lowered.

Marin tried to steady her breath, but her lungs seemed unable to hold air. Her eyes moved from his cold, curious stare to the weapons at his hips. If he intended to end it now, or make her suffer, she couldn't tell.

"You're back," he said.

"It's my home—"

He raised a hand. She held her tongue, though once, a long time ago when they were children, she would have punched him for even thinking that would silence her. He acted like a king now, but she wouldn't forget that he was only four years older. That they'd both been raised on this island, and had equal right to it.

The crowd to Marin's left side broke open, and a small, feisty woman shoved through. Seema's wild mess of curls was tacked down by a black scarf, and she wore an oil-splattered tunic and boots laced up to her knees over fitted pants. She didn't move any closer, but hovered on the edge of the crowd, glancing from Luc to Marin.

Marin felt her knees weaken, even as her mother's features twisted in anger. A fine welcome home, all the way around.

"Where is he?"

Luc didn't have to say who. She knew. Everyone knew. Her father's absence would not go unnoticed.

"He isn't here?"

Luc made a show of looking around. "I don't see him anywhere, do you?"

"Then how should I know? He . . ." She cleared her throat. "He dumped me on the mainland five years ago and disappeared."

Her chin stayed high.

"And it took you this long to come back," said Luc with a disbelieving smile.

She held his gaze.

"Had to build me a boat, didn't I? Took some time."

Luc chuckled. "Come on, where is he?" He rose, though he lingered beside his throne. "Where's that old rat hiding?"

Her hands were shaking.

"Don't ask me," she said. "Always said he had work with the Japanese. Check with them."

Luc tilted his head, as if to say, *I'm not stupid.* His gaze narrowed, and she felt trapped, like he already knew the truth but was waiting for her to admit it.

It was now or never.

"I'm here to offer a tithe," Marin said, as was the custom. "You should call the other captains."

His bark of laughter made her grit her teeth.

"Why would I do that? You haven't tithed for years. What makes you think we'll accept anything you offer now?"

Her fingers wove together, squeezed.

"This is worth the wait, I promise," she said as he moved closer.

"And I'm supposed to believe you, is that it?" Luc laughed, and taking his cue, the others laughed with him. His gaze flicked to Ross, then back, unimpressed. "I'm to trust the girl who deserted, just like her useless father."

Marin became excruciatingly aware of Ross standing behind her left shoulder.

"Coming back here, groveling with this pet of yours. It turns my gut," Luc said.

The others laughed again. She felt as though she were shrinking. Getting smaller and smaller with each burst of laughter, each step Luc took closer. Each second Ross and her mother stared.

Ross was trying to say something through the gag, but she couldn't make it out.

"Wait," she said as Luc stalked closer. "Wait. You have to listen."

She scrambled back a step, shoved forward by those behind her.

Luc snagged her bound hands, jerking her down to her knees. She struggled, trying to twist away, but her feet found no bearing on the slick mud, and her hands grasped only air. Filthy water splashed onto her chest and arms and face as her elbows hit the ground.

He was close enough now that she could see the fury in his eyes when she looked up. It wasn't just that she'd broken the code, but that she'd humiliated him. And now she would pay for it.

"Take the terreno to the post," said Luc, motioning to Ross, now restrained by Picker and Greenhorn. She pictured the place. The post was just outside the gomi fields, where they tied up the drunks who caused too much trouble.

Luc lifted his arm, and her heart stopped. She saw only the gleam of his rusty knife. *This is it*, she thought. *This is it.*

A shadow covered her, and when she lifted her chin, she saw Ross's back. He was standing between Luc and her.

"Leave her alone," he said, voice no longer muffled by the gag.

The crowd laughed around them. *Shut up*, she wanted to say to him, *you'll only make this worse.* But the world was still sideways.

"I take it you're the man in charge," Ross said.

Luc's low laughter cut through the sudden quiet. "You're right."

Marin stumbled up, trying to stop Ross from getting himself in more trouble, but when she opened her mouth to speak, nothing came out. Sweat dewed on her hairline. The more she tried to talk, the tighter her throat grew.

"We don't want any trouble," Ross said. "There seems to be some confusion. If you give us a chance to discuss this, I'm sure we can come to an agreement."

"Pretty boy sure has a pretty way of talking!" Picker hollered.

"My friend and I are in need of a boat," Ross continued. "You'll be well compensated once we get where we need to go."

"And where might that be?" asked Luc, crossing his arms over his chest.

Ross considered this for a moment. "Pacifica."

Several snickers rose from the crowd. Marin made it to her feet, but her ears were still ringing.

"Pacifica?" Luc spread his arms wide, the knife still gleaming in his hand. "*Que suerte*. You're in luck. You've found it."

Marin looked to him, thinking that maybe this was one of his tricks. He would embarrass Ross, and then hurt him for his defiance.

"That's impossible," said Ross after a moment. "Pacifica is—"

"A new beginning!" Luc called, striding up to Ross. As if he suddenly realized he was a good half foot shorter, he took a quick step back, though he didn't look any less smug. "A chance for those poor land lovers to get out before the shore they live on falls right off into the sea. Relocation begins in just a few short days, am I right? Four, if I recall."

Marin stared at him, wondering how he knew this and, more important, how everyone else did. Because as she looked around, she saw no surprise in the faces of the others.

"There must be a misunderstanding," said Ross, in a tone that suggested not even he believed it.

"I don't think so," Luc said. "It's time, once again, for a Noram president to ship all his bad seeds here to rot."

Marin went still, every muscle frozen in place by the clarity in Luc's words. The island paradise she'd never heard of, the Shore-lings, rounded up in the riots only to be sent out to sea—it was just as she'd feared. But as much as she didn't want to believe they'd been coming *here*, she knew he was telling the truth.

It was happening again. Exactly as it had before.

"That's impossible," said Ross weakly. "The Shorelings are going to Pacifica."

"Yes," said Luc. "That's what I'm telling you. The pretty ones are never too smart, are they?"

"No." Ross sagged, his voice now heavy. "*Pacifica.* The island . . . it's green. There's grass, and a compound. Houses. A lot of money was—"

"Put in my pockets," said Luc softly. "To rent space on *my* island. I hear there's going to be at least five hundred of them coming. I hope they like the gomi fields. No blackouts there. No power, either." Luc didn't even glance her way.

She tried to picture people living in the miles of trash that stretched behind Careytown. Yes, they took what they could from it, they'd built their lives in it, but resources were thin; that's why they had the code. That's why they tithed. Hundreds of terrenos wading through the muck and plastic, unaware of the sinkholes that plunged into the ocean below, was a death sentence.

"They'll never make it." But Luc's cold, twisting smile told Marin that this had been the plan all along. The people she'd seen in the riots, who'd been hauled into the vans—they had been shoved out of the picture, sent away to disappear.

"No," said Ross again. He'd grown pale. "You're wrong. The president would never allow this." He was shaking his head, but seemed to have accepted this just as Marin had.

As she looked at the faces around her, she knew the wheels had already been set in motion. Luc had bought the other captains by taking money from the mainland, and now the Shorelings were coming here. To Careytown. To the home she'd done everything to return to.

She had to do something. Unless she quickly made Ross important, Luc would kill them both.

"He's the president's son," she said. "He's Ross Torres, and I stole him so we could sell him back for a big payout."

Luc lifted his chin. Whispers rose around her, like the hush of a breeze.

"Whatever Noram's president paid you for the Shorelings, he'll pay twice for his son, I promise you that."

"What are you doing?" Ross hissed.

She ignored him.

"You snared the president's son?" asked Luc. She couldn't tell if he was impressed, or infuriated that she'd blown his big plan.

"That's right," she said. "If you would've just listened, I would have told you that when I first got here. I want back in, Luc. I think this more than covers my tithe."

He scratched his chin.

"How do I know it's really him?" asked Luc.

"Talk to him. Send someone out to check the Armament frequencies," she said. "I'm sure they're reporting him missing by now."

"Marin . . ." Ross faltered when she faced him. It was the disbelief in his eyes that nearly broke her. "You said—"

"I know what I said," she interrupted. "I lied."

Silence settled over the fire pit. After a moment, Luc tapped the flat side of his knife against his thigh.

"Take him to the post," he said. "Bring him water. I need to think."

Picker and Greenhorn grabbed Ross, and when he shook free, Japan and another pirate called Red joined in. She forced herself to look pleased as Luc moved forward and cut her hands free with his knife, but didn't breathe easier until he tucked it back into its sheath.

"Marin," Ross said one final time. "You're selling me to this *tyrant*?"

She rubbed her wrists, feeling her fingertips prickle as the blood flowed back to them.

"He may be a tyrant," she said, "but he's also my brother, so watch your mouth."

CHAPTER 22

THE METAL cuffs scraped Ross's wrists as he tried to work his hands free. He'd been fastened to a pole ten feet high that stuck out of the ground at an angle. It was rusted from the acid in the rain, but the ring where the old handcuffs were attached was still strong.

He pressed his teeth together and pulled, leaning the weight of his body back against his bindings. The men who'd brought him here—the corsarios—had disappeared. The one with the missing arm, who'd been in the boat that had found him, had brought a mug of yellow-tinged water and set it in the dirt at Ross's feet. He couldn't reach it with the cuffs on, and had stopped trying, because every time he looked at it his throat felt even dryer.

Behind him, a group of townspeople leered. For the first hour, he'd faced them, gaze darting between each sneering face. It was only Marin's brother's orders that he not be harmed that kept them from coming closer. For that, at least, he was thankful, because he felt certain they would beat him to a pulp if given the chance.

They called him "cabrón," and "son of the devil," and talked, with a little too much detail, about cutting off certain body parts.

After a while, he'd turned away and tried to shut them out.

He pressed his forehead against the post, breathing in, every inch of his damp clothes chafing against his itchy, salt-covered skin. Each breath made his stomach twist in hunger. The ground seemed to move beneath his feet. He felt like he'd never stop swaying.

Even now he couldn't believe Marin had betrayed him. Maybe he'd been suspicious before the storm, but after, things had changed. You didn't survive something like that together and just walk away. This had to be part of her plan.

But this place was like nothing he'd ever known. It made the docks look like a dream. And these people were *her* people. Their leader was her *brother*. She'd called this place home.

It was somehow worst of all that he hadn't found Adam.

The breeze changed, and with it came a rotten stench that made him gag and cover his nose in the crook of his arm. His gaze lifted to the gomi fields—at least he thought he'd heard someone call them that. Miles and miles of trash, stretching as far as the eye could see. Hills and meadows and valleys of shiny metal shards and plastic bottles and clothes and cans and nets. It was like looking into a garbage incinerator before pressing the button that made what was inside disappear. His ears were filled with the buzzing of insects. His stomach turned.

Movement pulled his gaze to his right, where a shack a hundred yards away sat just inside the border of the trash field. It looked to be made mostly of rubber tires, and from the roof spiraled delicate tendrils of white smoke. A man was walking from it in Ross's direction, his black shirt sticking to his narrow chest. A matching scarf covered half his face, and as he drew closer, he pulled it up over his dark hair.

Luc walked to him, stopping so close that Ross could see the beads of sweat dripping down his brow and smell the sickening burnt-sugar stench on his clothes.

"I see you're all settled in," he said, as if Ross had just been taken to a room at a fancy hotel.

"Let me go," said Ross, squaring his shoulders as best he could. "And this will turn out better for you."

He couldn't look at the pirate without seeing him shoving Marin to the ground, and it made his blood boil.

Luc grinned, and it felt like a dare. "Is that a threat, young Mr. Torres?"

Ross didn't care to be called "young" by someone who couldn't be more than a few years older than him.

"Just the truth," he said.

Luc looked mildly impressed. He rested his wrists on the guns on his hips. He seemed to be alone, but a few men had pulled from the group behind and were lurking in the shadows of the last building on the road. It felt reminiscent of the locker room, a million miles away, where Marcus Pruitt and the Gomez brothers had waited to teach him a lesson.

"Where's Marin?" Ross asked.

"Miss her already?"

If she was working an angle, he didn't want to appear too eager.

"Not exactly."

Luc's mouth formed a small *o*. "Broke your heart, did she? How'd she get you out here, anyway?"

Ross remembered jumping aboard her ship, eager to find Adam. Shooting the lock on the Armament brig door. He'd done this. She hadn't pushed him into anything.

"I see," said Luc, taking his silence as an answer. "Tell me, did you think she loved you?"

It took a moment for his intent to sink in.

"No." Ross shook his head. "I mean . . . It wasn't like that."

Luc chuckled, a low, disbelieving sound. "Don't take it too hard. She's soft that way. Always been desperate for a little warmth. You should have seen her with our dad, following on his heels like a hungry mouse." He sighed. "*Pathetic.*"

Ross's shoulders bunched on her behalf. He'd call Marin a lot of things, but pathetic was not one of them.

"Surprised she came back before him, even after all this time. But he'll turn up. He always does."

"Thought he was doing a job for the Japanese," said Ross, looking away.

He broke into laughter. "She really worked you, didn't she? I've got to say, I'm kind of impressed."

Ross's face heated.

"Aww." Luc squeezed his shoulder, and when he jerked away Luc didn't seem to notice. "Don't take it so personal. She lies. That's what she does. She learned from the best, you know." He chuckled. "Once, our dear old dad took Marin to the mainland for supplies and forgot about her. Two weeks later he came back and there she was, in the same spot on the dock. Told her something about the Armament chasing him, and being swallowed by a shark. Or maybe it was a whale." He laughed. "I forget."

Ross's fists were clenched. He could still hear the smile in Marin's voice when she'd told him that story. The man who'd done what Luc described could not be the same person who brought home ice wrapped in a blanket.

"Doesn't look like much," Luc said wistfully, staring off into the trash fields. "But growing up, this was my playground. Mind the *bocas,* though. Thin spots in the island. Hungry little mouths. When I was six, I fell straight through, all the way to the water below. Had I not been strong, I never would have made it through the night."

Ross shuddered, thinking of being trapped underwater in what Marin had called an iceberg. He couldn't imagine spending the night even half submerged.

"There's water below?" he asked, trying to sound curious, even while his hands continued to work at the cuffs.

"Of course," said Luc. "What did you think? We were built on a mountain?"

Ross supposed he had. That's what islands were, weren't they?

"I hadn't thought much about it," he admitted. "I guess I'd heard that Pacifica was man-made."

"Oh, it was man-made, all right."

Luc turned to face him, and Ross's eyes fell on his "86" tattoo, in bold black script across his throat. It was huge compared to Marin's small marking.

"What do you think happens to the trash you throw away?" Luc asked.

"It's burned," said Ross, feeling his face heat.

"*It's burned*, he says." Luc laughed again, clearly enjoying being the one with all the information. "It can't all be burned. It comes out to sea. Your people love having things for a little while, and when they tire of them, they become mine." He opened his arms to the field of trash.

Ross had seen the trash in the Sacramento Bay, and Donner Cove, but he couldn't imagine standing atop one of Marin's icebergs, much less building a town on it.

"How is this possible?" asked Ross.

Luc crouched low, hands spread inches above the red mud. Not mud, now that Ross was looking, but tiny pieces of plastic sand.

"Do you feel it moving?" asked Luc.

Ross nodded.

"Some call it the gyre. The cesspool, more like it. Right here is where the warm water from the south dances with the cool water from the north. They spin and spin and spin, catching all the trash the currents drag away from the mainland."

"This island is made of trash," Ross said.

"And it's trash that lives aboard it," said Luc, coming close enough that Ross could smell his foul breath. "Ever since the Original Eighty-Six were named traitors and sent here to suffer."

The other man's cold truths blended with the story of the Original 86 Marin had told him on her boat. Noram knew the 86 were here and had done nothing. Ross was a prisoner of the 86 because they'd done nothing. And now Noram was about do the same thing they'd done before: dump their trash in the ocean and pretend it didn't exist.

"How many people live here?" Ross asked weakly.

"A hundred and eleven souls. Well, soon to be *six* hundred and eleven, give or take a few dozen rioters."

It felt too impossible to be a reality, even as he stood here on a floating island of garbage. An overwhelming need to tell someone, to expose Pacifica for what it was, clawed up within him, but who could he tell? The media? Adam's father? People needed to know what was happening, to stay away from the transports coming here. He thought of the blackouts Adam had mentioned before they'd gone to the riots. The crushed pipes and broken water mains. Were those real problems? Was erosion even an issue?

But Ross could do nothing. He was a prisoner, chained to a pole. His father had worked on this bill for years, had supported it publicly nearly every day since it was announced. It made Ross sick to think that his dad had known the Shorelings were facing this fate. The president's job was to protect the citizens of the

Alliance. That he could send them to exile, under the watch of pirates, made him more of a tyrant than Luc.

"The prisoners from Noram's riots, the ones being sent out to sea—are they coming here as well?" It felt wrong to hope for such a thing, but he did.

"Of course," said Luc. "The new generation of Noram's traitors. They should already be here. I suppose the storm may have got them."

Ross's hands jerked against his chains. Adam was in the same storm he and Marin had been in. For the first time he considered that Adam might not make it through this. The storm had already shown him that he might not.

For some time Luc said nothing, then he gave a contented sigh.

"All the coin in the world won't make up for what your people have done to mine," he said quietly. "I'd see your head on a stake before I'd see you sent back home."

At these words, Ross felt an icy breath blow across every nerve.

"What happens now?" he asked.

"Now I tell your father I have you, and I kill you where he can watch."

With that, Luc turned and made his way toward the shed, where the smoke twisted into the sky.

CHAPTER 23

MARIN STOOD at the waxed curtain that led to her home, one trembling hand an inch away from pushing it aside. She'd been given food and drink, even new boots, which Greenhorn had taken off his own feet as they'd gathered in the tavern. They were a little big and clunky, but better than walking barefoot.

She was a hero. She'd captured the son of the empire they'd been raised to hate. Soon she would be rich, and respected. She'd have a boat, bigger and better than the *Déchet*—maybe even better than the *Señora*—and a crew loyal to her. Some had already asked to be on it.

They'd all wanted to hear a story, something as wild and dangerous as the truth itself had been, but she couldn't bring herself to tell it.

When she'd been little, she'd dreamed of this moment, but now that it was here, she just felt empty. Ross was tied to the pole on the gomi fields—a prisoner. Gloria and the others were running out of food. Soon the docks would find themselves without a doctor, because Hiro was packing his bags to come here.

Needing a break from the others, she brushed aside the curtain and stepped into her mother's house, aware of the man loitering outside that Luc had sent to follow her. The bottom floor was composed entirely of a kitchen, a small, dark space, buzzing with flies. Sticking out from the far wall was a smooth, clean countertop that took up so much room she had to sidestep to get around it. At the other end was a stone hearth, and atop it, a cauldron big enough to fit a full-grown man. A window had been cut into the plastic wall above the chopping block, but the breeze was blocked by the house behind.

Her father had read to her at this counter. Her mother had made her mend small machines there. Yet as she ran her fingertips over the smooth plastic she felt nothing. The room seemed smaller than it ever had in her childhood.

"Hello?" Marin called.

Seema emerged from the pantry, shadowed in the far corner, cradling cans in her arms. She must have heard the soles of Marin's damp boots squeak across the floor, but she hadn't shown herself until now.

"*Maman.*" The word came out like a croak. Her mother was angry, that much was obvious. But as accustomed as she'd been to the woman's hard moods, she didn't understand why.

After five years, she at least deserved a hello.

"So," Seema said. "You bagged yourself the president's son. Congratulations."

Her mother didn't look up as she began stacking cans of corn mash on the countertop in preparation for dinnertime.

"You don't sound too excited," said Marin carefully. She couldn't help wondering if her mother was disappointed that she'd returned, and not her father. If she'd prayed for him all these years to come back. If she'd ever prayed for Marin.

Seema snorted and turned away. "Is it a scam?"

She wished it were a scam. That Ross wasn't anybody important. Of course, it was that importance that was keeping him alive right now—that prevented him from being tossed out to the gomi fields or thrown off the edge of a dock. She drummed her fingers on her thighs.

"No." She cleared her throat. "A lot's changed around here."

The cans slammed on the counter.

A lot hadn't changed too. Her mother had never been particularly warm.

"Luc didn't even call the other captains when I offered my tithe," she continued.

"The council's done," Seema said. "The other captains follow his orders."

Marin chewed on her bottom lip. It wasn't supposed to be that way. Her grandfather and the Original 86 had set up the council for a reason, so that they could make decisions together, as a group. That way one person wouldn't get out of control and do something stupid, like repeat history by bringing a bunch of unwilling Shorelings to an island in the middle of nowhere.

"Why did he do it?" Marin asked. "He hates the terrenos. We all do."

Seema looked at her now, one brow cocked.

"We all *used* to," she said, in a way that made Marin think of Ross, made her heart squeeze as she thought of him chained to that post. She had to get him out of here, but she couldn't even approach him with Luc's man on her heels. If she did find a way to sneak past him, she didn't even have a boat for them to make a decent run for it.

"Now we're all friends," Seema said bitterly. "All it took was a little coin."

Marin snorted. She doubted it was a little money. Her people had always hated terrenos—Luc had learned how from their father, and their father from his, the great Finn Carey. That kind of hate couldn't be washed away without a significant payout.

"Who made the deal?" she asked, thinking of Ross's father. It would have to be someone high up the mainland food chain.

If it was the president, turning Ross in as her prisoner may have been a very bad idea.

"I don't know." Seema returned to stacking cans. "Someone at oil rig four. That's all he said."

Marin's thoughts shifted to the military boat where she'd been thrown in the brig, and the attack on the converted station, number seven. The oil rigs ran along the length of the coast, numbered from one to nine, south to north, twenty miles off land. When she'd been young, her father had ransacked number five, somewhere near San Fran. Four must have been just south of that.

"Why are they paying him?" She tucked her hair behind her ears. "They didn't pay anyone when they dumped the Eighty-Six here."

"No one was here to stop them before."

It didn't make sense to Marin. If Noram wanted to, they could destroy this entire island and everyone on it. Why make payments to Luc if they could bring him down in seconds with a fleet of Armament soldiers? No, Noram wasn't afraid of Luc, or anyone else in Careytown. Something else was going on.

"What's he doing with that money anyway?" asked Marin. "Buying a lifetime supply of new boots? A new boiler to make his precious tar? I sure haven't seen anything around here fixed up."

Seema returned to the pantry for more cans. "Paying off the Oilers, I guess."

"The *Oilers*?" The only deal they'd ever made with the Oil Nation was for their sailors to keep quiet while they were being robbed.

"That's right," said Seema, sounding tired. "He's got more than one deal in the works. His crew's been to the SAF six times since last summer."

"For what?"

"Hardware maybe. I don't know, ask Picker. They move all the crates to the armory, and then he stays in there for three days doing inventory after they return."

Hardware. Luc was using the money from the mainland to buy guns from the Oil Nation. They'd never engaged in this sort of business before—at least, not that she'd known of. These were big, broad sweeps across half the world. The kinds of things that didn't leave you hiding in the fog on an island of trash, but exposed to anyone and everyone.

"He's worried the Shorelings are going to fight back," she said. It wouldn't have been the first time it had happened.

She pictured it then, a bloody war in the gomi fields. The Shorelings rising to the edge of Careytown and getting slaughtered by a line of armed corsarios. Maybe it was the heat, but the kitchen seemed to be growing smaller by the second.

Seema flattened her hands on the counter. "If you're done with the questions, get out of my kitchen. I have things to do."

For a flash, Marin remembered the last moments on the *Déchet*, when it was clear they would capsize. Ross had wrapped his arms so tightly around her, smashing her between his chest and the steering wheel. She could hardly breathe then, just as she could hardly breathe now remembering it. After all she'd been through, she wanted her own mother to hold her like that. Just once.

Even if she didn't deserve it.

Guilt settled in Marin's stomach, old and remembered. She had never been enough for her mother. She *would* never be enough. In that moment she didn't care what Luc was planning. She wanted to board the first boat and get as far away as possible.

"I'm sorry I couldn't bring him home," she said.

Seema went still. She turned to face Marin, her brown eyes hard and the lines around her mouth deeply etched.

"Your father was a *menteur*."

"He never lied to me."

"Yes, he did," she said. "He lied to you when he told you scrapping and killing and digging through the gomi was the best it ever got."

Marin shook her head, tried to push past, but now Seema moved closer, blocking her path to the door.

"He left you because he couldn't live with that lie," she said. "He knew one day you'd see through it. Through *him*. And he wouldn't survive it when you did."

"You don't know."

"It's the truth. Wherever he is, let him rot there."

"How can you say that?" Marin snapped, feeling her guilt and shame finally burst free. "He was all I had. He made me who I am." She pressed a hand against her chest, feeling the sting of a lingering bruise where she'd been shot. "And now they'll give me a boat, and a crew. He would have been proud."

"And what will that pride get you?" Seema's voice broke. Her eyes had changed. She was smaller now, thin and fragile and pleading. Her hands were open, her lips trembling. "Marin, you don't want a ship and a crew. You want a home and a family. It's what you've always wanted."

Marin took a step back, her own chest quaking.

"I lied to you too," her mother said. "Because I never told you that you were better than him. Better than all of this. Maybe if I had, you would have stayed away."

Marin could hardly breathe. She needed to get out of this tiny space. She and Seema didn't do this. They *couldn't*. What little relationship they had would crumble under the pressure of these kinds of words.

"I guess I'm not," she whispered.

She pushed outside, wondering, as she shoved her way through the crowds toward the water, where she belonged if she didn't belong here, and who she was if not a corsario.

As the night turned black, she found herself outside a mud building triple the size of her mother's kitchen, staring at an armed guard who was too busy sharpening his knives to see her lurking in the shadows.

In town, people were starting to get rowdy. She could hear their voices from the tavern and the Blue Lady, brash and wild from drinking, and ached to be closer to the one person she couldn't.

Ross.

She could still feel eyes on her back; someone had been tracking her every move since she'd left the tavern. Luc didn't trust her, and she didn't blame him.

She wasn't so sure she trusted herself anymore.

Her thoughts returned to Ross, as they seemed to more and more with each hour that passed. The color on his face from the sun. The way he'd moved on her ship, clumsy but determined. How he'd fought beside her in the storm, and stayed with her until the end.

The way his heart had sounded beneath her ear when they'd held on to each other in the *Déchet*'s wreckage.

The feel of his fingertips on the small of her back.

Somehow he had become the safest place on this entire island.

Her mother had been right, and it felt like someone had stuck a knife straight into her heart. A ship and a crew wouldn't fill the space between her ribs. What she wanted was a father who came home. A mother who smiled when she walked into the room. A brother who cared if she drowned.

A boy who trusted her enough to let her take him into the middle of a storm.

She walked past the armory down the road, toward the hill that would lead to the docks. Instead of continuing on to the water, she doubled back into an alley, and scaled the support beam of the Salt Room, where extra moonfish were stored in barrels for the rainy season. Swiftly, and as quietly as she could, she hopped across the slippery, slanted roofs to the armory.

Crawling on her hands and knees, she made her way to the vent and peered into the slots. The room was dark as the bottom of the sea. She hissed in frustration.

A light shined from over her shoulder, and with a squeak, she flipped onto her back, the hard grates of the roof digging into her spine. Her hand flew to the knife handle that stuck out from her pocket, something she'd taken off one of the sailors at the tavern.

"Take a look, *soeur*," said Luc, standing over her.

Sister. As if they were ever more than competition, fighting for crews, and rations, and tithes.

She said nothing, and didn't move, so he lowered the small lantern toward the vent. Unable to stop herself, she turned and peered through the slanted hole into the room below.

Her mother had been right. The room was filled with hardware. Not just a few guns, as she'd seen when she'd snuck a peek from time to time over the years, but enough for every person in Careytown to have their own arsenal. Stacks of rifles leaning against the walls, knives in a box by the corner, crates marked "ammunition," and plastic tubs of handheld firearms. There were so many weapons in that room, there was hardly enough space to walk. It slowed the blood in Marin's veins, until it felt like sludge was pumping through her heart.

Luc sat beside her on the rooftop, his feet hanging over the edge. The ground was ten feet below. The guard below looked up and gave Luc a small wave.

Marin's body went stiff. Sitting this close, relaxed as he was, suggested a comfort with each other that didn't exist.

"What is all this?" she asked, still trying to process the weapons below them, and the deal with the Oilers, and just what he was planning.

"Power," he said.

"To fight the Shorelings?"

He smiled, and it was clear that any more questions would be met with the same answer.

"Tech found a signal," he said, referring to the gangly redhead who manned the island's only radio. It was ancient, and in Marin's youth it had only worked about a quarter of the time.

"Armament is broadcasting a missing person report for a Ross Torres, though they suspect Shorelings killed him in some kind of battle."

He raised a brow in Marin's direction, but she didn't explain. He leaned back on straight arms, and Marin's gaze shifted from the twin guns tucked in his ratty belt to the ring of keys that peeked out from his hip pocket. One of them must have been to the shack where he made the tar, though it was hardly necessary with the armed guard he kept posted there.

Another might be for Ross's handcuffs.

From this height, they could see the water, and both stared out over the rooftops to where the black sky and sea merged at the horizon.

"You did good," he said.

There was a time she would have given anything for him to notice her, but now the compliment felt misplaced. It shamed her that she'd done something worthy of his praise.

"I didn't do it for you."

He chuckled.

Her brother preyed on weakness, and revealing her anger would have shown Luc another point in which to stick his knife.

"Tell me about your adventures," he said. "Where have you been all this time?"

"The mainland," she said. "I told you."

"Is it as bad as they say? Riots and soldiers and all the rest?"

She gave a reluctant nod, remembering the fire, and the shouts, and Ross picking her up off the pavement.

For a while neither of them spoke.

"This deal with the terrenos is going to destroy us," she said. "The island can't support five hundred more hungry bellies. There aren't enough jobs for them, not enough scrap metal to build ships. They won't all be corsarios."

He twisted his hair into a scraggly knot.

"You're wrong," he said. "This deal changes everything. It *fixes* everything."

"For who? You?"

He picked at his teeth. "When you left, I was glad. You were always too noble for this place."

Anger swirled inside her, black and angry as storm clouds and thunder.

"But I underestimated you," he said. "You're more corsario than I thought."

She felt sick. When she stood, she slipped on the rooftop and fell against his side, braced against his hip. Their shoulders bumped, their knees cracked together. Fumbling, she righted herself while he only laughed.

"Been too long since you felt the ground move," he said. "Welcome home, Marin."

Her shoulder twitched. She shoved away, sickened by the sweet smell of tar in his greasy hair, and his rotting teeth, and every inch of his charred soul.

He patted her shoulder. "You get it in your head to do the right thing with Torres, I'll cut his throat. I'll leave him there until the gulls peck out his eyes. This deal with the mainland is too important. If you ruin it, he'll pay."

There was no further discussion. He swung down from the rooftop, leaving her to face the coming night, and she stood trembling in his wake, his ring of keys tucked tightly in her fist.

CHAPTER 24

THE THIRST made Ross crazy. As each moment passed, it grew more unbearable, an unscratchable itch that tickled his throat to the point of torture. It tore away his thoughts of Marin and Luc, of this island of trash, until all that remained were his aching veins, and his cramping muscles, and his dry, swollen throat. The people watching only laughed, and then gradually disappeared, because leaving him alone seemed to be a greater punishment than any insult they could throw his way. Soon, the only one left was Japan, sitting on a bench in the shadows thirty feet away, staring at him with one creepy eye.

After too long the thirst took control of his brain, and wild splashes of color appeared before his eyes. A ship tossed around by a sea. A cliff between himself and his home. Marin, her arms wrapped around his neck, her mouth against his ear.

"Hold on," she whispered.

He dreamed she held a dirty cup to his peeling lips, and when he drank he coughed and sputtered and shook with relief.

Hold on.

When he opened his eyes, he was hunched over his knees, his hands numb, his wrists still fastened in the cuffs above his shoulders.

The cup beside him was empty.

Marin was nowhere to be seen.

At sunrise he was woken by the metallic hum of a nearby generator. The sound cracked through his pounding headache, making him wince, and long for water and a soft bed. He was quickly distracted by the crunching sound of footsteps, emanating from the trash field beyond the wall of mist. Immediately he went back to work on the cuffs; the previous day's struggle had done a number on his wrists. They were scabbed and tender, and the skin that peeked out was purple and bruised. He tried to pull his hands through the metal rings, but as the seconds wore on he became more frantic.

People were coming; Ross could hear their voices now. As he watched, Luc appeared from the fog, leading half a dozen other corsarios down the red mud street from town. He searched for Marin, but she wasn't there.

In the back of his brain a voice whispered that she had done this to him. That he was only ever a payout.

He shoved it away. He'd trusted her this far. He had to believe she still had a plan.

But if she didn't, or if it fell through, he had to be ready.

The guard who had replaced Japan fell off the bench and startled himself awake. He rubbed his eyes with the heels of his hands, and then jolted up when he saw Luc.

"Here we go," Ross muttered to himself. Using the dead weight of his arms within the cuffs, he pulled himself upright, wavering a little as the world spun. Though his lungs seemed unable to pull in a full breath, he grasped the post to steady himself and lifted his chin.

He would make himself indispensable. He had to figure out what they wanted, and then offer it to them. That was the only way he was going to keep himself alive.

But Luc and the others passed as if Ross were invisible. They followed the line of the trash fields in the opposite direction of the shack where Luc had gone yesterday, and waited beside a tower of rubber tires.

Through the mist came a long dark shape, snaking between the hills. A cold terror rose in Ross's chest—the kind of fear that belongs to the things you can't name, like the memories from nightmares. As it moved closer, Ross backed away, as far as his arms would stretch, until he could go no farther. Behind him, the townspeople had gathered again, though they too had forgotten him. They were all looking at that great, dark shape.

"This all of them?" he heard a woman ask.

"Nah," said another. "Just the troublemakers."

Ross realized then what he was looking at. Squinting, he could make out more than just the shadows in the morning gloom now. They were people, moving in two parallel lines, toward where Luc and the others waited. There were a few others in the front, guiding them, but the rest of them appeared to be linked together. It took a moment to realize that they were bound that way.

It occurred to him that they might be the people he'd been chasing. The prisoners from the riots. *Adam.* Luc had said they'd come here too, though they might have been lost in the storm.

His throat, already thick, felt like it was swelling.

They drew closer. Men. Women. Teenagers, some his age. An old woman who could barely keep up. The girl beside her practically carried her with each step.

He wanted to look away, but couldn't. His father had taken part in this, and by association, he felt responsible. There had to be fifty of them. Fifty prisoners who'd been brought here from the mainland.

Relocation would bring at least five hundred more. He didn't know how many people had been added since the new spots had opened up.

He searched every face for Adam, but he wasn't there.

Luc motioned them forward to where he stood. He climbed to the top of the tires and waved his arms, and when he did, they stopped.

"My friends, you have come a long way," he called. "I know, because my people came here the same way. We mean you no harm, not like the kanshu who brought you here." With this, he pointed at Ross, who wilted under the weight of fifty gazes. "In the coming days there will be much to talk about, but for now, rest. Eat. What is ours, we share with you."

Fury boiled in his gut. The guy who'd threatened his life and dragged his own sister through the mud had now turned around to throw a welcome party for fifty fugitives.

"It's not true," Ross croaked as they drew closer. "*He* did this to you; *he's* the one who brought you here. Adam? Adam!" If Adam was there, he did not answer.

"Ignore this kanshu cabrón," said Luc as he brushed by. "On my island, this is what we do to traitors."

"No," Ross said. "I'm not . . ."

The Shorelings gave him wide berth as they passed. Some looked at him. Most kept their eyes down. The old woman was now carried by a man who told her quietly, "It's going to be all right."

"Please!" Ross tried to shout, though his voice was only a rasp. "Was there another guy with you, Adam Baker? He's my age. Dark . . . hair . . . *Wait*. Did anyone see him?"

"Some of the sick got left behind," mumbled a man near the back of the pack. When he looked up, Ross was taken aback. His skin was fair and, though dirty, barely touched by the sun. He wore a tattered suit, not unlike Ross's Center uniform.

The man was not a Shoreling. He had to have come from above the cliffline. Ross couldn't think of why he might be here now.

"Where?" Ross's voice cracked. Marin had told him Adam had been hurt. Something about his leg. And then an officer had beat him up.

"Out there," said the man.

"That guy's a pirate," said Ross, pointing to Luc. "You can't believe him. You can't—"

The punch came out of nowhere, a hard, solid hit to Ross's gut. All air was shoved out through his windpipe, and he sunk to his knees, mouth gaping. For one long moment Ross felt like he had when he'd been trapped in the iceberg underwater: desperate and frozen. And then the smallest breath slipped through.

When he looked up, one of the men who worked with Luc was laughing. Red, he'd heard someone say. Still laughing, he turned, and followed the rest of the Shorelings, who trailed Luc like a bunch of punished children.

Ross looked to the trash fields, but though he searched until his eyes watered, he could not see Adam.

The rain came, thick and heavy, drenching Ross's torn, dirty clothes. It didn't sting or itch as it had just a few days ago. He suspected the layers of salt and dirt coating his skin served as some kind of barrier, and tried to count the days since his last shower.

Four. He'd showered before he'd told his parents what had happened in the riots. And if that had been four days ago, that meant today was Saturday, and in two days half of Noram would be gathered in the park at the harbor, preparing to send off hundreds of people to Pacifica.

He had to get out of here. Warn them. Do *something*.

He could not die chained to a pole.

A figure appeared through the misty rain, coming his way. He recognized the swagger in Marin's walk before she was close enough to make out the details of her face. She walked with the kind of confidence he'd always pretended to have, and he would have given anything to borrow just a little bit of it now.

Her hair was covered by the hood of a soaked, long-sleeved shirt, which stuck to her chest and curved waist. At her hips, a thick belt held up loose, gray-green pants, rolled up just over the tops of her lace-up boots. She stuck out in this place like a flower growing in the crack of a sidewalk, and seeing her brought a punch to his chest.

"Don't be stupid, Marin!" called a guard who was watching from beneath the shelter of the nearest shack, thirty feet away. His voice was muffled by the ping of rain against the plastic and metal that covered this entire island.

Marin shot him what Ross guessed was a very rude gesture. "You want him to die before we get paid?"

The guard didn't move. Either he agreed with her, or his threat had been out of obligation only.

She was carrying a canteen in one hand and a wad of cloth in the other. When she came close, Ross stared at the water, unable to voice how much he wanted it.

Without a word, she lifted it to his lips. Liquid pooled in his mouth and poured out the sides, but he gulped and gulped, feeling the pounding in the base of his skull instantly lessen.

"Easy," she said. "It'll come back up if you go too fast."

"What took you so long?" he gasped.

She gave him another drink, narrowing her gaze. "Good to see you, Marin. So glad you came for a visit."

He kept drinking.

"They didn't trust me enough to trust you. I had to improvise," she said. "I came as soon as I could. Had to wait for the right kind of distraction."

She was still with him, still on his side.

"The prisoners . . ." He swallowed, and then cringed. She was right. His stomach turned, then settled. "They're here."

"Keep it down," she said. And then, after a quick look around, "I know. It's the ones they arrested in the riots. They're at the tavern now. Some of them have been sitting in cells for months." She gave him another sip, and when he tilted his head back, rain made tracks down his face.

"They said some might still be out there in the trash. Adam . . ."

"You can't worry about Adam now."

Ross blinked back the water in his eyes.

"You have to worry about you," she said. "Just you, got it?"

He didn't. He'd come here for Adam. If his friend was hurt, dying, because of his *father*, Ross would never forgive himself.

She was unrolling the fabric, sheltering it between their bodies from the sheets of rain. Inside was bread, something black and charred he didn't want to think about, and grayish rice.

He reached for it, but the chain didn't stretch. Instead of moving it closer to his hands, she pinched off a piece of bread and placed it in his open mouth. Her fingertips brushed his lips. Her round brown eyes stayed on his.

"Tougher than you look, terreno," she said.

She inched closer, so that his back took the brunt of the rain and his chest sheltered her from the guard's watchful gaze. As she fed him, he felt his strength returning, and with it came renewed determination.

He was going to get out of here, one way or another.

The cloth was empty now. He could feel it brush along his forearms. Marin's fingertips followed, the sensation so different than the cloth and the rain. She was warm, and soft, and though her body hid her hands, he still looked down, staring at the wild curls that escaped her hood.

A pinch on his wrist made him jump.

She hissed. "Don't move."

It was then that he realized she was working on freeing his metal cuffs. That she had *keys* in her hand.

His lips cracked as he grinned. He knew she had a plan.

"Behind you, out in the gomi fields, there's a shed with smoke coming out of a pipe in the window," she said quickly.

"I've seen it." Luc had come from that place yesterday to tell Ross he was on borrowed time.

"If you keep going in that direction, you'll hit a cove. It's quiet. No one ever leaves their ship there because of the storms."

"All right."

"You'll have to keep low. There's always a guy outside that shed keeping watch, and he's always got a lot of hardware. He sees you, you're done, got it?"

"I got it." He would make a wide arc through the trash field. If Adam was out here, hopefully he wouldn't be too hard to find.

"I'm working on a boat. I'll meet you there soon as I can."

Working on. Which meant stealing in Marin language. He found he didn't much care.

"What about the guard behind me?" asked Ross.

"After I get these off, I'll take care of him. You run. The others are all distracted with the new Shorelings, but they'll figure it out soon enough. I hope you're fast."

"I am."

She swore. "One of these has to work."

Tilting his head back, he saw that she had a whole handful of mismatched keys and was switching to the next one.

"That . . . doesn't look good," he said, forcing himself to be still even as he wanted to tear the pole out of the ground.

"Neither will I when Luc finds out I lifted his key ring," she said grimly.

He thought of what she'd risked, imagined her hurt. If his hands were free, he'd defend her if it came to that.

But he also could feel the guard behind him and hear raised voices less than a mile away. Luc struck him as the kind of man who didn't make foolish mistakes, and Marin seemed well aware of how lethal he was. Suddenly escaping in broad daylight felt like a very flimsy plan.

The doubt returned again, heavy and cold in his chest.

"Thought you might not be coming back," he said quietly.

She glanced up, measuring the truth in his face. There was disappointment in her eyes, and a huff of breath from her lips.

"Don't say you gave up on me."

The words were light, but they still stung.

"He told me your dad left you before. When you were a kid."

She went still. Her grip tightened on his wrist and then pulled back. It took only a moment for her to return to the task. "He doesn't know anything."

"It's okay."

It wasn't—nothing was—but right then he needed her to know that she could trust him just as much as he had trusted her. That it didn't matter who her family was, or what they'd done. She was better than this.

Because if she did, maybe he did too.

Her head bowed forward, her spine rounding. There was a brokenness inside her, and he felt it echo within his own rib cage.

"It's okay," he said again, softer now.

She moved to the next key.

"When I was twelve he took me out to see the space shuttle." She wiped the water from her eyes with the back of her wrist. "We stayed out all night looking for it. He told me he saw it, up in the sky, and that one day I could get a spot on one just like it and get out of here." She lifted a shoulder. "I knew he was lying, but I didn't care. His lies were better than the truth."

He'd sometimes thought the same about his own father, though he rarely talked about anything as nice as that.

"A boat showed up before dawn," she continued. "Traffickers from the Oil Nation. They'd gotten turned around in a storm. The crew had washed out. Just three men were left, and they were half dead."

The rain faded into the sounds of the water, lapping against a ghostly ship.

"They had fuel on board. A lot of it. Probably doesn't seem like a big deal to you, but it's gold out here. There was enough to power generators, charge our radios, and still gas up every motor on every boat. It was the biggest haul I'd ever seen."

When she took a breath, her shoulders shook, and without thinking, Ross took a step closer.

"I was poking around below deck when I saw them. These kids, hiding in the dark. They hadn't eaten for a week. They just . . . looked at me." She shook her head. "Like I was going to save them or something."

Ross's body felt like lead.

She switched to a new key.

"My dad wanted to push them over. The crew . . . all of them. Just take the haul and sink the boat." Her hands were shaking, and she made fists to steady them. "We brought the kids above deck. They didn't even fight when we tied them together."

Another key.

"My dad, he wanted me to sink them, but I couldn't. We fought about it. He tried to take over, but I blocked his way. He said, *Move, Marin,* and I said we could just take the fuel and leave and not tell anyone, but he said it'd be cruel to let them die that way. I wanted to bring them back to Careytown, tell the other captains, but he said they'd never, ever forget that I was soft. If I was a cor-sario, like him, then I needed to act like it. *It'll be quick,* he said. *One breath in, and it'll all be over.*"

She was talking faster and faster, the words almost blending together. It was as if he were watching water, spraying free from a broken pipe.

"He tried to shove by me, nicked me with his blade, this stupid knife with a bone handle. Got me right across the belly. I told him I'd tell everyone what he'd done, and he said he'd never taken me for the type to stab someone in the back. The chest maybe, but not the back."

She squared her shoulders.

"I pushed him, and he fell, and it was over. Just like that. He hit his head, and then went into the water, right after those crewmen he'd pushed overboard. By the time I jumped in to get him, he was already gone."

"What . . ." He swallowed. "What happened to the kids?"

"I sailed them to the mainland. Took them to the library and gave them to Gloria—she looks out for the people in the docks. She found a place for them and let me stay on."

Ross didn't know what to say. He could only think of how her brother had said Marin was pathetic, and that she'd followed her father around like a mouse.

"You wanted my secret, there it is. I killed my dad when I was twelve and let everyone think he ran like a coward."

The cuffs came free with a pop, and he jumped, having momentarily forgotten what she was doing.

"When I say," she said, her tone unchanged. "Run."

The crescendo of his heartbeat pounded in his chest, a reminder of every time he'd stood on a treadmill waiting for a race to begin. But those runs had been nothing compared to this. Every experience, every feeling he'd ever felt, they were just practice before he'd met Marin.

"Go," she said, as calmly as she might have said *goodbye*.

He made it three steps, and then slammed to a halt, finally seeing what she had seen.

Four men stood outside the shack. Japan and Greenhorn had

joined the guard, along with the pirate who'd found them in the wreckage—Luc's right-hand man. A half smile twisted Picker's lips, pulling at the rough skin of his cheeks. At the sight of the gun in his hand, anger seared through Ross's veins, overruling any fear, any sense of logic. His vision compressed. He returned to Marin's side, shoulders bunched.

"What are you doing?" she muttered. *"Go."*

She meant to fight them alone. That wasn't going to happen.

"Together again," said Picker. "Thought that might be the case."

"Luc wants to see him," said Marin. "I was bringing him in."

"Luc's been waiting for you to make a move since you stole the keys," said Picker.

Marin's breath whistled out between her teeth.

"Take the terreno to the *Señora*," said Picker. "Marin and me need to talk."

"No," said Ross.

"No?" asked Picker when he didn't follow it up with anything.

Marin glanced at Ross. "You're crazy."

"I'm fast," he said. "How about you?"

She gave a single nod. The trash fields. Running and hiding was their best chance, just as long as they didn't get shot on the way.

"Now," he said.

He grabbed her wrist, knowing before they took their first step it was hopeless.

They caught Marin first. And in the end, he surrendered, just so they'd stop kicking her.

CHAPTER 25

PICKER SHOVED the barrel of his gun between Marin's shoulder blades, urging her to pick up the pace.

"I don't have all day," he said.

She slowed down. If his plan was to kill her, she wasn't going to make it easy.

Their path was treacherous; the ground, uneven and slippery. Shredded plastic bags and pieces of rubber floated in the dirty puddles, and each step had to be considered. There were thin spots in the gomi, places where the water beneath had churned away the trash below, and left the top layer deceivably thin. Bocas, they'd called them when she was little. One wrong step, and the island would swallow you whole.

"Pretty stupid bringing me out here alone," she said. "Soon as I get my hands free I'm punching you right in the—"

He shoved her forward, and she tripped, catching herself just before she fell. Her wrists were bound behind her with twine so tight it made her fingers tingle with numbness. It threw off her balance, and reminded her with every pained breath of where he'd kicked her in the ribs.

"I'll remember you did that," she said.

"A little late to keep score," he said. "The game's over, Marin. You lost."

She shook her head. He was wrong. She was keeping a running tally of every stupid move he'd made. Every time he'd looked at Ross like he was weak, every time they'd shoved him and kicked him since she'd brought him to this cursed place. He would pay for it all, and so would Luc, because Ross was hers in a way that they never would be. She wasn't sure when it had happened, but sometime between the Armament and the storm, he'd been seared into the part of her that made her *her*. Not corsario, not Shoreling, but something more.

This was not over until she said it was over.

"He sent you to do his dirty work, huh? After all I did for him?"

"That's about right."

A small part of her had hoped Picker had just planned on delivering a message. The larger part had known the truth since she'd seen him come out from that shack with Japan and Tech. Luc wanted her dead, maybe because she was freeing Ross, maybe because he thought she'd pose a threat to him. Whatever the case, it didn't matter now. He was busy with the Shorelings, and Marin's time had run out.

As they trudged through the trash, Careytown disappearing behind the hills, she wondered grimly where they'd brought Ross. A potent fury shook through her when she thought of Luc laying into him, punishing him for what she'd done.

She had to find him, and steal a boat, and get as far away from this place as possible. Thinking about it loosened something inside of her, like a string tied too tightly. She felt untethered. Free.

Dangerous.

"What's he giving you for doing this?" she asked. "More tar? Listen, Picker. You let me out of this and I'll get you all the tar you want. I can make it, you know. Pulls a nice price on the mainland."

"That's far enough," said Picker. Her abrupt stop had landed her in a shallow puddle that soaked through the cracks in the toes of her boots. Rain slashed across her back as she hesitated. They couldn't be stopping so soon. She needed more time to think. For a moment, she considered running, but she wouldn't get far tied up like this.

Frantically, she looked for something sharp to cut her bindings loose, but the gray sky made it difficult to pick out anything sharp or metallic on the ground. There were plenty of places to hide, but each was only a temporary fix. She needed to get her hands on a weapon.

"Turn around," Picker ordered.

A cold sweat dripped down her brow.

She faced him, eyes locked on the gun he aimed low at her belly, and his thumb, resting on the trigger on top.

"Bang!"

She jumped, and stumbled backward, landing on her backside in a slushy puddle. The ground beneath her trembled, and then dropped an inch, like an empty box buckling under her weight. Scrambling away from the spot, she rolled to her knees, and then climbed to a stand, the roar of Picker's laughter cutting through the rain.

Her breath came in short gasps. A quick glance down at the puddle revealed what she had suspected. The water was lower than before she'd fallen. Not just because of the splash she'd made. Because it was draining.

She'd found a boca.

Her chin lowered in determination.

"Coward," she spat. "Why'd you bring me out here if you were just going to shoot me? Thought you would've done that in town where all your friends could watch."

He picked at a scab on his cheek, a symptom of the tar he loved so much.

"Maybe I wanted a chance to say goodbye."

Giggling a little, he stepped closer, and she rotated, just the slightest bit, so that when he faced her the weak spot in the ground was at his back.

The warm metal of his weapon came to rest against her collar. When she twisted away, he grabbed her by the hair, and snapped her head back.

Her eyelids fluttered in an attempt to block the driving rain, but she didn't cry out. She wouldn't give him that satisfaction, even as the gun barrel slid up, beside the pulsing vein of her neck. Her breath held, trapped in her lungs as she waited, waited, *waited*.

"Like my new hardware?" he said. "Look at it. *Look*, Marin."

With his fist knotted against her skull, he tried to turn her head, but though pain seared across her scalp, she refused to let herself bend to his will. The toe of her boot collided with his shin, forcing him back a step.

Just a little farther.

The short silver barrel of the gun pressed against her wet cheek with bruising pressure. Twisting his wrist, he turned it so that she could see the autofocus, and below it, the silhouette of a black bird.

"Fancy, right? I have three more just like it."

"I'm so impressed," she said between her teeth.

"You haven't seen the armory," he said. "There's enough fire-power to take over the world."

"It's not going to matter." She kicked him again, and was rewarded, again, with his slow retreat. "You'll be outnumbered five to one once the Shorelings get here."

Visions of them breaking from their prison ships and raiding Careytown filled her mind. Maybe it was a fool's hope—Hiro certainly wasn't a warrior—but they'd survived a lot in Lower Noram. They were fiercer than Luc was giving them credit for.

"Outnumbered?" mocked Picker. "Who says we're fighting *against* them?"

She hesitated.

"Luc's raising an army." A slow, manic smile lifted his scarred face. "We're going to take down the terrenos."

He turned her face so that their eyes could meet. He was too close for comfort, so close she could feel his warm breath on her lips.

"That's impossible."

"Oh, you've missed out, Marin. While you've been scavenging and fixing your little machines, Luc's been preparing the captains for war. We're about to get back everything that's been owed to us." His lips twisted into a pouting frown. "It's too bad you won't be able to see it."

Her mind couldn't wrap around this. "You've all been taking too many dips in the tar jar. Even with the Shorelings, we could never take the mainland. The terrenos have guards, not to mention the high ground. There are thousands of them above that cliff."

"We don't need to go ashore," he said. "We just need to take down the Armament. The Shorelings are already doing the rest."

Images of fire and bloodshed ripped through her mind. Luc was taking the refugees from the mainland and turning them against the Armament. She'd already seen the crates of weapons in the library—Gloria had been outfitting the Shoreling rioters for weeks.

"What about la limpieza?" Marin asked. "The City Patrol? Did you forget about them? I've seen them go at the Shorelings. They play hard, Picker."

Picker scoffed. "They're outnumbered by Shorelings ten to one. The only reason they play so hard is because they have the Armament backing them if the riots get out of control. We take out the Armament . . . you can figure out the rest."

Hiro had been in the shop when Adam had shown up there. *A kanshu boy dies on our streets and they're bringing in the Armament.* If they couldn't call in the Armament, the Shoreling rioters would overwhelm la limpieza in a matter of hours. It would be complete chaos.

Her brother was starting a war. One they would lose. The Shorelings brought here may be armed and angry, but they were not sailors or soldiers. They were no match for the enormity of the Alliance's military.

So many people were about to die. And the one person who could get the attention of those who could stop it was now in Luc's hands.

She had to find Ross.

"How will you even get them back to the mainland?" she asked. "You try to put that many people on the *Señora*, it's going to sink." Even all the captains' boats combined would not have enough room for an army.

"They'll go back the same way they came."

On the ocean liner. Would Luc's crew take it over? How? The thing would have to be crawling with Alliance soldiers to avoid a mutiny when the Shorelings realized what Pacifica actually was.

"Shh," said Picker. "Don't worry about that now. Worry about me."

He stroked her hair, still keeping the gun against her throat. Chills raced across her skin. It was now or never.

Jutting out her chest, she rammed into his body, causing him to fall back, then filling the distance, so that he had no room to move forward.

With a grunt, she kneed him in the groin, and this time he folded forward. Before she could kick him again, he'd spun her toward the weak spot. Lip twitching in a sneer, he shoved her back by the shoulders, until one foot broke through the thin barrier of trash.

She yelped in surprise, throwing her weight forward again. Her forehead collided with Picker's nose, sending a jolt of pain through her skull. With a growl, he gave her shoulders a firm shake.

"You think I'm stupid?" he crowed. "I'm trash-born, same as you. You think I don't know what you're trying to pull?"

The gun was still in his hand. She could feel it resting against her throat as he fisted the thin strap of her shirt. Her foot was stuck in the mouth of the boca; a twist of her ankle revealed nothing but air beneath. When she tried to pull it free, her other foot began to sink. She had no idea how deep the hole went before it collapsed into the sea below. It could have been a few feet, or close to forty. Either way, the water beneath was churning and hungry, and once it swallowed her, she'd be dragged into the base of this giant iceberg, and held there until she drowned.

"Oh, no!" Picker laughed. "The island has you now."

He let her go, and she crashed down to her knees. With her arms behind her back there was no way to grab on to anything. She pulled at the bindings wildly, sharp jolts of pain snapping through her shoulders.

She couldn't die like this. Not here in the trash, and not below, in the water, sinking down into the murky blue like her father's still corpse. Too much waited for her beyond this island.

She held Ross's face in her mind. His grim, determined smile. His hair, wild in the wind.

"Pull her up!"

Picker turned toward the voice. Marin fell another foot, her legs swinging in the emptiness below. Sweat mingled with rainwater, throwing a shimmering curtain over her vision. With her fingers, she tried to reach for something behind her, but they slipped off every surface uselessly.

"I said *pull her up!*" It was a woman's voice, low and commanding.

"What are you doing here?"

Marin slid down another few inches. Her waist hung below the landline now, her wrists trapped in the muck. Picker leapt back to clear the sinkhole, and Marin leaned forward, every muscle taut, trying to inch her way back out.

"You sorry, tar-sniffing bastard." The woman was closer now, and even through the rush in her ears, Marin recognized her mother's voice. "Do as I say."

"Can't, Seema," said Picker, though his voice wavered now. "Captain's orders."

"I'm not going to tell you again," her mother said, and even through the chaos, it prickled Marin with fear, and hope, and surprise.

"You don't want to do that," Picker warned.

Marin blinked, and watched as Picker lifted his gun again, this time toward Seema.

"Hey!" Someone from behind snapped her attention away from Picker and her mother. Again, she blinked, and recognized the Shoreling face with the dark, clean-cut hair. He had a few more bruises now, including a split lip, and he lay on his belly, reaching in her direction.

Adam.

A single moment of joy filled her. *Ross,* she thought. *I found what you're looking for.* And then she realized, with a cold, foreboding despair, that it wouldn't matter if she didn't live to tell him.

"I . . . can't . . ." She couldn't turn or stretch out her arms.

"Where'd you come from?" Picker turned back, seeing Adam, just as Marin tried to twist her body toward him in one great heave.

A shot was fired. She lifted her elbows, and pedaled her feet through the empty space. It was too much for the thin surface to hold. The ground gave way and broke off around her, not with a great rumble, or a crack of thunder, but in near silence, drowned out by the pouring rain.

She was sliding backward, sucked into the belly of this cursed place, a silent scream trapped in her throat. Something pinched her shoulder hard, then slid beneath her arm.

"Come on!" shouted Adam.

With a groan, she flexed her body all at once and snaked toward him, chest and face making imprints in the sludge with each desperate movement. Adrenaline coursed through her veins, driving her to climb and free herself from the gateway of death.

Finally, her chest and hips were on solid ground. Then her knees. Her breath came in hard heaves. She turned to see if her mother had survived Picker's shot, and found that Seema had not fallen. She was very much alive, standing tall, and picking her way through the trash toward them. Water dripped from every angle of her small body, and a silver gun extended from her right fist.

She was familiar, and yet different, and looking at her Marin was reminded of the aftermath of the storm, her fists knotted in Ross's drenched shirt as they floated on the wreckage of her precious *Déchet*. Words had formed in her barely conscious mind, and slipped from her lips like a prayer. *Hail Mary, full of grace.* Her mother's words. A chant she didn't even really understand, learned from a woman she'd never really known.

On the ground, an arm's reach away, lay Picker, but Marin only saw him for a moment, because the pit was still swallowing, the mouth closing and opening in strange, hungry bites. It pulled his body into the abyss, and then sealed itself with a fizz of bubbles, as if the hole had never opened in the first place.

"You all right?" Seema asked her.

Marin nodded. She rose, and Seema cut her free with a knife from her pocket. She could feel her mother's hands shaking, and hear the tiny gasps of her breath she tried to hide. Adam didn't seem at all surprised by Seema's presence, though his face was pale as he looked at her gun.

It took a moment for Marin to form the words waiting in her head.

"I need to find Ross," she said finally.

"Ross?" asked Adam. "*My* Ross?"

"Gone," said Seema. "Luc took him in the *Señora*. Just has a few men with him."

Dread pooled in the base of Marin's stomach. What plans had Luc made in her absence? Had he already contacted the mainland for a trade?

She never should have told him who Ross was.

"Where did they go?"

"Same place he goes to meet the terrenos," she said. "Oil rig number four. They haven't been gone long."

Marin rubbed her wrists, feeling as though the bindings had

transferred to her lungs. Luc always traveled with backup in case he ran into trouble, though usually he was the one causing the trouble.

"I need to get on a boat."

The same ripe terror she'd felt when Picker had aimed that gun at her chest slammed the blood through her veins. Every second here was a second wasted, was another moment Ross was with her brother.

"The boat we came on is empty," said Adam. "They docked it out there." He pointed in the opposite direction of Careytown, over the swells of trash that faded in the distance.

"How do you know that?" asked Marin.

"The guys who brought us weren't in the Armament," he said.

She stared at him, glancing down at his leg. He favored it, all his weight clearly on the other side. But though the bandage Hiro had applied was dirty, it looked as though it had held.

Questions whipped through her mind. Had the corsarios taken the ship bearing the prisoners? Had they beaten out the Armament in an attack? If she took a boat the entire Alliance was searching for, it wasn't going to end well.

"Talk fast, Adam," she snapped.

"After I was *arrested*"—his bottom lip twitched at the word— "they put us in these cells somewhere outside the city. We didn't stay there too long—maybe a few hours while more Shorelings were brought in. Before dawn they loaded us up in this ferry, and shuttled us across the bay. I think maybe to the California Islands, or the Armament base . . . it was hard to tell."

"The offshore station," she said. "An old oil rig."

"Maybe."

She motioned with her hand to hurry up.

"They moved us to another boat," he said. "We were kept

below deck, but the guy who came to bring us food and water had a tattoo on his neck. Like yours. He was wearing a uniform, but I've never seen another person with a mark like that."

Marin's fingertips prodded the "86" below her ear. The corsarios were working with the Armament? Did they know that Luc planned on raising an army against them, like Picker had said?

"When we got here, they weren't wearing the uniforms anymore," said Adam. "They tied us together and made us walk across the trash. A few of us were holding up the line so they cut us free." He glanced at Seema. "I followed them this way. Do people *live* here?"

"I found him when I was looking for you," said Seema, ignoring his question. "He's the one who spotted Picker dragging you through the gomi."

Seema touched her wrist gently, and in that touch a lifetime of words were held. For once, Marin wished they had more time.

"I suppose it will do me no good to tell you not to follow your brother."

"No," said Marin.

In an instant, she was eight years old, sitting in her mother's kitchen while fixing a radio. Her stomach grumbled with hunger, but Seema would not let her eat until she was done.

She'd always thought her mother was cruel and her father kind, but now she wasn't so sure it wasn't the opposite.

Seema gave a curt nod. "It will not be long before they wonder what happened to Picker."

"Come with me," Marin told her.

Seema could help—she'd be a valuable crewmember. After, they could go somewhere. Maybe the mainland, if it hadn't been torched to the ground.

Seema offered a half smile.

"Soft to the end," she said, though it didn't feel much like an insult. "Go, and I will make sure no one follows."

It was her goodbye, and it hurt like a punch to the gut, because Marin knew this would be the last one. She would never see her mother again.

"We have to find Ross." Adam looked between them, eyes dipping every few seconds to the gun.

"I've heard that line before," Marin muttered, eyes tilted up to the gray skies.

Seema released Marin's wrist, mouth drawn tight, brows flat.

"It's time for you to go, mouette," she said. "And this time, to stay gone."

CHAPTER 26

LUC'S MEN were not easy on Ross.

As they dragged him through town, they shouted his name, and welcomed those around them to take their shots. He was cursed at, kicked, hit. His hair was pulled. His clothes, stretched and torn. The corsarios threw things at him, cups and cans that splattered against his chest or bounced off his body to splash in the mud. The Shorelings watched from the tavern, afraid.

When he'd hung his head and accepted his sentence, he clung to one final image: a skinny girl with wild curls, driving the boat she'd made with her bare hands into the wide open sea. He thought of Marin, not because she was one of the 86, or because she'd brought him here. Because she was the bravest person he'd ever known, and right now, more than ever, he needed to be brave.

When he woke, he was propped up on the deck of a boat, arms tied to the mast behind him. His whole body felt like one stiff muscle, and when he moved, his bones seemed to creak. Still, nothing appeared to be broken. His mouth tasted like blood, and his face was sticky with it, but apart from smelling foul, he was in one piece.

The sky above was that same perpetual gray, though he was learning to differentiate the intent of the clouds. These were high and wispy, not the wall of black, boiling thunderheads he'd seen coming toward them in the storm. The wind was behind them, and ahead, the ocean met the horizon. It took him a minute to recognize the boat as the one they'd passed in the dock outside Careytown.

This was Luc's ship. The *Señora Muerte*. It was at least twice the size of Marin's, and felt profoundly sturdier as it surfed through the waves. But what it made up in structure, it lacked in comfort, because standing at the helm was Luc, his black shirt billowing around him in bright contrast to the white deck.

Marin.

Where was she? He recalled with gut-wrenching clarity the sight of the other men crowding around her and kicking her on the ground. How badly had she been hurt? Was she still alive?

And where was Adam? Ross hoped he had not been left in the trash fields. The thought of them being close, and then torn apart again, burned a red-hot rage through his veins.

His gaze fixed on the black radio, like the one that he'd seen on the Armament ship, nestled into the steering console beside the GPS. Luc's hand rested on it absently, fingers tapping against the black case.

If Ross could get to it somehow, he might be able to call for help. Luc would probably kill him for trying, but he'd already promised to do that anyway.

"Where are we going?" Ross's jaw ached as he spoke.

Luc had been looking out over the water, but at the sound of Ross's voice spun to face his prisoner.

"He lives!" Luc said victoriously, as if he had played some part in that.

At this, Ross heard movement from behind. Japan was working the ropes, as was Red on his other side. He couldn't see anyone else, though that didn't mean they weren't below deck.

His senses sharpened, and he pulled his knees toward his chest, trying to get his feet beneath him.

"What'd you do with her?" Ross said through his teeth.

"My sister?" Luc laughed, then sobered suddenly. "Have to say, I was surprised at her dedication. To a terreno, no less." He waved his hand in front of his face. "She's dead now."

Ross's stomach plummeted.

"It's a shame," Luc said. "Had she not been so smart, I would have given her to my crew. You've seen Careytown. Pretty girls are few and far between."

The horror ignited within him, and every muscle flexed at once, pulling against the cuffs that bound him to the mast. A terrible growl ripped from his throat, drawing back his lips. There were no thoughts, just a hissing in his ears and a red veil over his eyes.

"You're angry." Luc rounded the steering console, ducked under the boom, and crouched beside Ross. From his hip pocket, he withdrew a small glass cylinder filled with a sloshing black liquid, and uncorked it.

A familiar, heady scent clouded Ross's mind before the salty breeze could clear it away. His body fell slack, as if he could no longer control his own muscles. Blinking, he shook his head, feeling the dizziness resolve into a steady pounding between his temples.

"That's better," Luc said. "Now, there's someone I need you to meet, and I need you to hold yourself together when that happens, can you do that?"

Ross blinked, feeling every inch of his face as it stretched. His mind was fuzzy, but he had the sense to turn away.

He killed Marin.

The thought of it had him pulling at his wrists again, but his arms felt heavy, and his eyelids could barely stay up.

"You look pained, young Mr. Torres," said Luc. "Just a dip of your finger, rubbed along the gums. It'll take all your worries away."

Ross shook his head.

"It's called tar." Luc leaned closer. "I'll tell you a secret if you promise not to share. It's just boiled trash. Boiled and boiled and boiled. The men at home, they swear it's magic, but they're eating the very mierda they step in. I discovered it years ago when I fell into a boca. I landed in a pocket just beneath the surface, hanging from this net anchored aboveground. In this little cave, the sun had baked the trash until the fumes were nearly toxic." His mouth twisted into a grin. "When I finally climbed my way out, I swore I could fly." He cackled. "I've been making it ever since."

"Get back," managed Ross. Vaguely, he recalled Luc emerging from the shack on the edge of the trash field, the one Marin had told him to steer clear of due to the armed guard outside. The thought of people ingesting the things he'd seen in that field made his stomach turn.

Luc corked the bottle, and laughed at Ross's expression.

"I've disgusted you," the pirate said. "Finally we are even."

They sailed into the night, and through it, still moving when dawn bruised the morning sky. Ross drifted in and out, becoming desensitized to the movements of Japan and Red, who worked the boat through the night while Luc slept. At first he thought they would give him trouble, but both men largely ignored him. Twice, they brought him water and food, and when Luc awoke, Ross's arms were freed, and he was permitted to go to the bathroom.

When he was done, Luc presented him with fresh clothes, a bucket of water, and a cloth, and told him to make himself presentable.

The strength he'd found thinking of Marin had been carved from his chest, but as many times as he replayed Luc's words, Ross could not picture her dead. It didn't feel like it had before, after the riots when the despair had hollowed him out. But then, she'd been alive, so maybe this was what her actual death felt like. Like impossibility. Like hope, that she was somewhere, just as Adam was somewhere.

He was brought below deck, past two closed doors, and into a narrow room lined floor to ceiling with three layers of bunk beds. In the glass of the portal window, he caught his reflection. The simple black shirt was a little small, and ripped around the collar, but otherwise dry. The pants were the color of the red-brown mud puddles in Careytown, and came to a frayed end around his exposed calves. He moved closer to the glass, gently prodding his dry, flaking lips, and the salt from the sea that had left white wrinkles from squinting around his eyes. A bruise still stood swollen on one jaw, and his hair was a windblown tangle. Even his shoulders, which had once been permanently drawn back, slumped forward with the weight of these past few days.

He barely recognized himself.

How different he'd once thought he was from the Shorelings, and yet here he was, indistinguishable from them.

He wondered if this was what Adam had felt, coming to the political district. What his life had been like before that move. It seemed impossible that he knew so little about his best friend before they had met. Impossible, and yet unsurprising.

Because Ross had never asked.

If they made it out of this, he would.

The door, which had been left ajar, was pushed open by Japan, who scowled at his new wardrobe. As he stared back, Ross felt his anger burn to wariness.

Luc was standing in the threshold of a room on the opposite side of the hall. Behind him, Ross saw what looked to be an old silver safe with chains crisscrossed on the ground below it. In his hands he held a deep metal tray, and in it he was placing glass jars of the thick, black liquid.

He did not look up at his task, and as Ross watched him, he could feel his time running out.

"I know you want me dead." The words sucked all the air from Ross's lungs. Japan grabbed his shoulder, but he didn't fight.

"I know you hate what the mainlanders have done to your people, and you have every right to. But if you really want justice, you should keep me alive."

Luc finally looked up, a smirk pulling at the stubble on his sharp jaw.

"Killing me is just going to prove what they think about you. That you're the same traitor your grandfather was."

Luc returned to loading his jars into the tray.

"So let them think that," he said. "They wouldn't be wrong."

"No," said Ross. "But that doesn't scare them. Pirates are supposed to murder. Shorelings are supposed to riot. What scares the people above the cliffline is believing that they're just as bad as everyone else—just as bad as you. We've built ourselves up to be better."

"Oh, but you're not," said Luc, pausing again.

"I know," said Ross, thinking of how Tersley had raised his gun in that shop in the docks. How his father had made it all go away. How Ross had gone to the riots in the first place—for fun.

"We'll fix anything so we can sleep at night," he said.

Luc stretched his neck from side to side. "Now that is the truest thing you've said yet, Mr. Torres." He stood, framed in the doorway, his arms crossed. "I assume you have a point."

"Expose Pacifica. Tell the truth about relocation. The entire nation believes it's a tropical island. Tell them where their government is really sending the Shorelings. Tell them about the Eighty-Six."

"Ah, I see." Luc's head tilted back, and he scratched his suntanned neck. "And why would anyone believe me? I'm the same traitor my grandfather was."

"Because I'll stand beside you," said Ross. "I'm the president's son. The whole nation will listen if I'm on your side."

"It would destroy your dear old dad."

Ross nodded. It would, but it would protect the Shorelings, and keep him alive long enough for the authorities to arrest Luc.

"And what of the oil beneath the docks?"

Ross hesitated, unsure of Luc's meaning.

"Come on, terreno," said Luc, the name not nearly as comforting coming from his mouth. "You didn't think it was all about *erosion*, did you? They're moving out the Shorelings for the same reason you clear out the rats. Because they eat your food and get in the way."

The corners of Ross's mouth tightened. No, he had suspected there was more hidden from his view as soon as he'd realized his father was lying about Adam. A part of him had wondered after the attack on the Armament station if the prisoners were being sent away just to stop the violence. Still, if there was oil in the docks, someone would have known. There was no need to relocate the Shorelings; even if they were directly over it, they could have found another way. They could have told them the truth, to start. Those people needed jobs, didn't they? Mining oil could have revitalized the area, just like Noah Baker was always talking about.

He thought of the steward who'd escorted him below deck on the Armament ship. The oil rigs were being converted to bases because the oil was drying up. The Alliance was running out of fuel. *Imminently.* Alternative energies weren't dependable, his father had told the SAF leader that.

"Oil under the docks will just add fuel to the fire," he said, hiding his surprise. "If it's the reason why the Shorelings are being relocated, the people will be furious. They'll look to you as their champion—the one who uncovered all the secrets. You'll be famous."

Luc gave a slow smile.

"I'm impressed, Mr. Torres," said Luc. "My sweet sister must have rubbed off on you. You've got some fire left after all. Sorry to say it won't save you now, but the effort's appreciated all the same."

At the mention of Marin, Ross's resolve broke again, and the terror and fury and panic he'd managed to hold at bay ripped through him. Luc wasn't going to listen—he didn't care about anything but his own greed and vengeance. He spoke only one language, and it involved fists and blood and pain. But before Ross could speak it, something cool and hard pressed against his side, and his eyes lowered to find the barrel of Japan's gun.

"Let's go," said Japan.

"You're making a mistake," Ross shouted as he was ushered up the stairs. "This will destroy your people."

With the sounds of Luc's laughter echoing in his ears, Ross was shoved up the steps, toward the bow of the ship, where his hands were re-bound, this time before him. Red came to assist, but it wasn't necessary. Ross had stopped struggling.

His eyes were locked ahead, on an offshore oil rig like the Armament station where he and Marin had been attacked. As they drew closer, it became apparent that this one was older, or hadn't been attended to in some time. The beams that rose from the water were a twisted mix of black and red rust, and half of the upper deck had fallen into the water, leaving it completely detached in the middle. Sharp arms of metal jutted out in all directions from the wreckage, most of them longer than the *Señora*. The entire thing looked like it might fall at any moment.

Docked against one of the legs was a small ship with navy blue sails. It was neat, clean, and looked like something the Armament might sail. He knew better, though; the military boats had white sails bearing the Alliance's emblem. This was similar, but not quite right.

A tremor of excitement shook through him. Was this his father? Had he been told to meet them here? A second later, his elation came crashing down. If his father were here, Luc would be determined to make good on his promise to Ross in Careytown.

He had limited time left.

"Here we are!" called Luc, coming up from below deck with a patched cloth sack, crossed over one shoulder. The bottles within clicked together as he carefully adjusted the strap. Ross remembered what a single sniff of one had done; he could hardly imagine what consuming that much would do to a person.

Instantly, he became more alert, searching the sailors around him for signs of what might come. They all seemed focused on the ship, and for one dark moment Ross considered what might happen if he jumped overboard and ended this before it began. He could save himself a little pain, maybe, but drowning wouldn't be an easy way to go.

Icy resolve frosted over his fear. He could not jump now. If he ended it this way, there would be no chance to rectify his father's mistakes, no chance to tell anyone that relocation was a myth, and that the Shorelings were about to be betrayed.

It might not matter anyway. Luc could kill him before he could warn anyone. His father might go through with the relocation plans anyway. He even considered that Marin's brother might kill his father, which sent waves of terror cascading through him. Whatever wrongs he had or had not done, George Torres was his dad, the man who'd raised him, and his death would rock the nation.

The boat slowed, and eased beneath the tarnished structure. The two sailors with Luc didn't need direction. While they anchored their ship to the massive metal column, Luc climbed down the ladder hooked around the rear of the boat onto the grated landing, where he was met by two men in suits, not unlike those Tersley or the other security had worn at home.

His father *had* come. And for one foolish moment he was the same boy he'd been in his youth, waiting outside a track meet for a secured car to pull in, so sure this would be the time he would show up.

"Dad!" Ross shouted, before he'd thought it through.

Red hit him hard in the side, and Ross fell to his knees, sputtering out a cough. When he looked up again, all three men had disappeared below deck of the smaller boat.

"Quiet," Red hissed. And then he gagged Ross with a rag Japan handed him.

They waited for long minutes, the only sound the waves against the side of the *Señora*. Time stretched infinitely onward, taunting Ross, holding his very life in its hands. Dusk had come, the orange sky offering little warning of how dark this night would soon become.

Finally, Luc emerged, and waved to the crew onboard.

Without a word, Red and Japan ushered Ross over the ledge and down the ladder to where Luc waited. His hands were sweating, his grip slick on the metal rungs as he lowered to the grate. It bobbed under his feet, but he stayed upright.

His gaze darted to the other boat, then skittered across the gray sea. His throat worked to swallow, but couldn't. He tried to speak the words screaming in his head—*you don't have to do this*—but the gag in his mouth wouldn't allow it.

Luc's head beaded with sweat, his dark hair matted down against his scalp. When Ross jerked away from his hold on his cuffs, he sighed, and patted the knife handle on his belt.

"Let's not be a hero," said Luc.

Ross turned, every single fiber of his body joining for one purpose: to hate the man before him. The sweat slid down between his shoulder blades. If Marin was dead, he wanted Luc to pay for it.

Luc led him toward the boat, and shoved him up the ladder. He moved too slowly, it seemed, because one of the armed men he'd seen earlier leaned over the edge and hauled Ross up.

He searched the man's face for some sign that this was part of a plan. They were trying to get him on the boat, separate him from Luc, and then get as far away from the pirate as possible. It seemed strange, now that he thought about it, that so few people would be here. Was this part of Luc's demands? It made sense that the pirate would arrange for his father to arrive without his usual security entourage, but that didn't mean his father would do it. He was the president of the North American Alliance. Surely there was more security waiting somewhere near. Maybe even in the wreckage of the oil rig overhead.

He might get out of this after all.

But as he was ushered below deck, the men in mainlander suits only acknowledged his presence with a nod. When Luc followed, they didn't arrest him, or even approach him. They cleared the way, so that Ross could pass by, uninterrupted. Telling himself this was all part of a larger plan, he descended the steps below deck, to an open area with plush chairs, topped with pillows, and a U-shaped bar that emerged from the far wall.

A woman wearing simple white pants and a red tunic stood facing the opposite way, one hand resting on the glass jars atop the counter. She was stocky, and short, with auburn hair pulled back in a neat bun at the base of her neck. When Ross's boots touched the plush carpet floor, she turned, and the finger she'd been rubbing along her gums jerked down to her side.

It took less than a second for Ross to recognize her, but it was clear that she did not place him with the same ease. Her gaze traveled down his chest, stopping at his handcuffs, and she gave an impatient sigh.

"Mr. Carey, the tar is quite enough. This is unnecessary and, frankly, inappropriate."

Roan Teller, the leader of the public safety commission, was standing before him, consorting with pirates and trying to conceal the fact that she'd just been taking a taste of boiled garbage.

CHAPTER 27

MARIN HAD never captained a boat bigger than the *Déchet*, but there was a first time for everything. When she'd seen the Armament ship docked alone on the far side of the island she had two thoughts. The first: at least it wasn't an ocean liner—this had sails. The second: she hoped Adam took direction as well as Ross, because there was no way to sail this beast alone.

If she'd wondered why they docked so far away, it became apparent as they picked their way through five miles of trash. There was nothing like facing the filth of the gomi fields to make you realize just what the president thought of you. If Luc wanted his Shoreling army angry at their government, this was the way to do it.

A quick search of the vessel showed that Adam had been right. The boat was empty, apart from the usual emergency supplies, the high-tech GPS, and a radio.

When she'd emerged on deck, she'd found Adam holding a map. Pacifica was not marked, but each of the oil rigs were. A grim smile cut into her cheeks when she saw that the coordinates were marked by a small, black circle, along the same lines as Old San Francisco.

There was no time for delay. Adam seemed to sense this, and silently completed every one of her commands.

Setting her sights on the horizon, she sailed for Ross, and oil rig number four.

They didn't rest. Marin set the coordinates and worked the lines. Adam was sent to search every compartment, above and below deck, and to dump whatever they didn't need overboard. They needed to move fast, and to be fast they needed to be light.

Even with the sails full and the wind behind her, it wasn't fast enough.

She'd willed the sun to stay above the horizon to give her more time, but the day finally gave way to night. She stared into it, hoping for a glimpse of the oil station, but could see nothing.

Adam barely spoke to her. She knew she should reassure him, or tell him something of her plan, but she didn't have a plan, and any reassurances now would have been hollow words. Maybe he knew this. Or maybe he knew that her grip on the wheel was the only thing keeping her from crumbling.

"Hold on," she whispered into the wind.

"He used to run, did you know that?"

She glanced back, seeing little more than the gleam off Adam's eyes and teeth. "He was really good," he added.

I'm fast, Ross had told her. *How about you?*

"He was the captain of the team at school."

"A captain?" He'd never told her that. She imagined him at

the helm of a ship, but it didn't make her laugh as it once might have. He belonged there.

"Yeah. He set all new records. He was probably the fastest runner we've ever had." Adam paused. "He quit. Just like that. Because his teammates didn't like me. Because I was a *trawler*. They'd put together this petition to get me sent to another school. Something about how I was participating in the riots in Lower Noram."

She thought about Luc, sending Picker to shoot her in the trash. Getting rid of her because he'd thought she was a threat.

"He ripped up the petition and told them if they tried it again he'd get them all expelled." Adam gave a humorless laugh. "He didn't know I was close enough to hear. Even if he did, I don't know. No one's ever taken up for me like that. That's the kind of person he is. That's the guy you're rescuing."

"I know," she said after a moment. Maybe she hadn't heard that story, but she already had her own like it. He was a bright spot in a dark sky, and she wasn't going to turn her back on him.

"Are we going to sneak up on them?" Adam asked, changing course.

"No. We're too big. Anyway, Luc's boat has a scanner. They'll see us as soon as we come in range." Ships and bodies of land would register as red dots on the black screen. By the time they hit the mile mark, the *Señora* would know they were coming.

A plan formed in her mind, thin, and risky, but a plan all the same. If they could not avoid being seen, there was no reason for them to hide.

"Then what are we going to do?" asked Adam.

She sized him up, hoping he was indeed the kind of man Ross had sailed across the sea for.

"The only way to beat a pirate is to be a pirate," she said.

CHAPTER 28

"HE'S A present, my love." Luc pulled the door closed behind him.

Roan Teller groaned. "Do *not* call me that."

He smirked, in a way that made Ross think he hadn't meant it anyway. There was no affection between these two.

No affection, but this was definitely not the first time they had met.

"Don't you recognize him?" asked Luc.

"I recognize that I'm going to need to get my floors cleaned . . ."

Roan's smooth pale skin turned a ghastly shade of white as her glossy lips parted. Her brows disappeared beneath her bangs, revealing the tiny red veins in the corners of her bloodshot eyes. She fell back a step, bumping into the bar, and rubbed her bare wrists absently. She was not wearing a comm, and unless this boat had an active tracking device, which Ross doubted based on the party she was meeting, she was as impossible to locate as Ross had been in the riots.

"What is this." Her words were slow, and quaking, but Ross

could still hear the voice-over for the relocation ads within them. His jaw worked over the gag.

The last time they had seen each other they'd been at the museum, dressed for a political celebration. Now they were on a boat in the ocean, and he was the prisoner of a pirate. How much these few days had changed things.

"Never do know what will turn up in the trash," said Luc.

The need to tell someone what was happening, what had *already* happened, had been waiting on the tip of his tongue, but as Roan Teller shook her head in disbelief, he was suddenly sure this proclamation wouldn't matter. The fact that she was here, talking to Luc, made her a part of this.

"How . . ." She shook her head, as if to clear it. "Get him out of here. I never saw him. I don't care what you do with him. Just get him off this boat."

For a moment Ross just stared at her, wondering if he'd mistaken her for someone else even as he knew that wasn't possible. As the shock passed, a dry, humorless laugh filled his lungs. He didn't know what she was doing here, but it was clear she didn't want him to know anything about it.

Luc planted his fists on his hips. "I don't think that's going to work."

"Security!" she shouted.

"That either," said Luc, feigning concern. "Don't worry, my crew is taking good care of your friends while we talk. They'll sail you home if everything goes smoothly."

"That's . . ." Her nostrils flared. She smoothed down her shirt over her ample chest. "That's not very flattering to our established trust, Mr. Carey."

"Oh," he said. "Maybe you forgot. I'm a pirate." His grin was sharp as a knife.

Ross looked between them, listening for any noise overhead, as he assumed Roan was also doing. The only sounds were the waves against the boat.

"You've gotten your money," Roan snapped. "This was supposed to be our last meeting."

"It was," agreed Luc. "But the price for taking your precious Shorelings just went up." He laid a hand on Ross's shoulder, which Ross promptly shook off. "What do you think the president will do when he finds out what I have here?"

Roan's hand, gripping a jar of black liquid, turned white.

His father didn't know she was here. His father didn't know *he* was here. So why was he?

"This wasn't the deal," said Roan.

"The deal's changed."

"No." She sliced her hands through the air. "I give you money, you take the Shorelings. You have no idea the moving parts I had to put in place to make this happen."

"You're right," said Luc. "Tell me, how many terrenos *does* it take to convince an entire nation that Pacifica is real?"

Roan's lips pursed together. "More than you can imagine."

Ross thought of all the pictures in campaigns of the make-believe island. Of the power blackouts and the other "erosion issues" that might not even be real. Hundreds of people had to be involved to make that happen. He couldn't even imagine how much money had traded hands.

"You people will fix anything so that you can sleep at night," said Luc, and ignored Ross's sideways glance at the parroted words. "Now I know folks might not believe a corsario when he says Pacifica is a pile of garbage, but I suspect they'll believe the young Mr. Torres if he stands by my side."

Ross waited, on a knife's edge, for the catch. Luc had denied

his proposal earlier; believing him now felt too much like desperation.

Roan gaped.

Luc laughed, thumbs tucked in his heavy belt. "Take another
dip of tar, love. You look stressed."

"Don't *call* me that," she said angrily, gathering herself to point
an accusing finger in his direction. "You bring *Ross Torres* on my
boat? Do you even know the manpower his father has dedicated
to dredging through the remains of that little showdown at the
Armament station? His advisors are urging him to set a funeral
date. It took everything I had to get him to push it back so it
wouldn't delay tomorrow's launch."

Ross stilled, something breaking inside him at the notion that
his father did really care. That he *was* searching for him. It made
him question if his doubts were misplaced—if there was something bigger going on he didn't understand, and that his father
was doing all of this for a greater good.

But if he was, Ross couldn't see what that might be.

Roan threw her hands in the air.

"If his father finds out he's alive and you have him, this will all
fall apart. He'll bring the entire fleet to your door. He'll destroy
your little island."

"Let them come." Luc glanced at his fingernails, biting the corner of one blackened tip. "I'd kill the boy before he even got close."

"Don't test him, Luc. He's a man who takes action." She laughed,
high and manic. "For God's sake, he sent away a third of his op-
position just before voting season."

Ross's gut sunk through the floor, his suspicions confirmed.
His father knew everything, was responsible for everything. The
man who had raised him, who he'd once idolized, was dictating
the fates of over five hundred innocent people.

He shoved all the dark feelings swirling inside him aside. He couldn't think of those things now. He had to figure out a way to get off this boat. Get back to the mainland before it was too late. He didn't know much about sailing, but he'd watched Marin, and pulled his weight when it had mattered. He might be able to get this boat aimed in the right direction.

His eyes landed on the tar. A whiff of Luc's tiny bottle had made him light-headed and dizzy. If he could break an entire jar, this closed room would be filled with noxious fumes.

Slowly, he inched toward the bar.

"We could make this little hiccup go away," Luc offered.

Ross's blood ran cold. Roan's hand went to smooth down her already smooth hair.

"What do you want?" she asked.

A memory of the first time Ross had met her struck him. How she'd stood across from him at the banquet, forcing her point and insulting his mother. They'd had no idea how dangerous she was.

Luc smiled. "I'm a simple man, with simple wants. The real question is, how much is the young Mr. Torres worth to you?"

Roan cringed, and laughed, and shuddered, all at once, a strange twisting of fear and power. "You think you can play almighty corsario with me, Mr. Carey? Blackmail me into giving you more money, in a world where money will soon be obsolete? In less than a month, the Alliance's oil will run dry, and if phase two doesn't commence, we will be in the dark."

With relocation happening next week, my investors see no need to delay phase two of the project. We could begin as early as next month with your approval.

Ross felt the weight of the giant, rusted steel bridging over them, of the converted Armament station that had recently stopped drilling for oil. He knew, in his bones, that she wasn't lying. What little there was left of the livable world was failing, and that was bringing everyone to desperate action.

"I don't want more money," said Luc. "I'm a pirate. I want boats."

"You have a boat out there," she said. "A very nice boat, which I procured for you."

"More boats," he said. "We lost half of our fleet in the last storm. I need replacements. Something hearty."

This had to be a lie—Ross didn't know how many boats there had been docked outside Careytown before the storm, but he hadn't seen any half-drowned ships. Not that it would have been easy to tell in the trash.

Luc tapped the two guns at his belt with his thumbs, drawing Ross's attention to the tiny silhouette of a black bird on the handle. The image was familiar, though he couldn't place it.

"You're already getting the ocean liner and the ship they used to transfer the riot prisoners," said Roan.

Ross inched closer to the bar.

"More boats," said Luc again. "Six of your warships. For my men."

"Six!" she said. "What do you need warships for?"

"For sailing, love," said Luc. "For making my men feel like kings."

She groaned.

"And in return, the young Mr. Torres will disappear, and your secret will stay safe with me."

He's going to kill me anyway, Ross wanted to shout, but the gag muffled any sound he made.

"Fine," Roan said. "Six warships. Whatever pleases you, Mr. Carey."

The pirate smirked triumphantly, but whatever he was about to say next was interrupted by a shout from outside.

"Luc, we've got trouble!"

If there was anything else that followed, Ross didn't hear it. With both Roan and Luc distracted, he snatched the glass jar from the box Luc had carried, raised it over his head, and slammed it down as hard as he could on the countertop.

It shattered, cutting his hand with a bright slash of pain. Instantly the fumes filled the room, overpowering in the contained space. He held his breath, squinted his eyes, but couldn't fight off the dizzying effects.

With a roar, Luc was on him, forearm locked around Ross's throat. Ross's fingers scraped at the man's wrist, tried to peel back his grip, but it was as solid as forged metal. He bit down on the gag, hard enough to keep his mind sharp. His body fought to inhale, but he couldn't. If he did he would certainly pass out, and any chance of escape would slip away.

"You think a little tar in the air is going to slow me down?" Luc growled in his ear. "I've been making it for years. Breathing it in, bit by bit. I'd have to drink half that jar to feel it."

Near the window, Roan fell with a thump.

Ross thrashed from side to side, hip slamming into one of the stationary stools beside the bar. He kicked back with his heel, and heard a satisfying grunt of pain when he connected with the pirate's knee.

"What was your plan?" Luc's forearm tightened, increasing the pressure in Ross's head. Darkness framed his vision. His body was fighting on its own now, kicking and twisting, just as his mind chanted *no, no, no, no, no.*

"Were you going to knock us out and take this ship as your own, young Torres? Think yourself a corsario, do you?"

"Captain!" called one of the men outside. "Luc, we've got incoming!"

But he was not listening. Ross could feel his fury, his reckless-ness, soaking through the clothes and skin between them. A po-tent, black thing that gripped his bones and squeezed them to the point of breaking. Even in the dim reaches of Ross's mind he understood then why so many had bowed down to Luc Carey. Not because he made the drug they wanted, but because he was more lethal than the storm Ross and Marin had faced on the open sea. He was thunder encased in flesh, and he yearned for death the way Ross yearned for life.

"I wanted your father to see this, but maybe this is better. It feels better, doesn't it?"

Ross was losing the battle. His body was growing heavy. But he had one last bit of fight left in him, and that fight was all for Marin.

Inhaling through his nostrils, he braced one foot against the bar, and then shoved back, hard enough for Luc to loosen his grip. With a roar, he spun, swung hard with his locked wrists, and connected with the side of Luc's head. Luc stumbled to the side, and in that moment, Ross scooped up the black tar and glass shards on the counter in his hands, and threw them in Luc's face.

The man screamed, falling back into a chair, and then top-pling to the floor. He tried to wipe it from his eyes, from his nose and mouth, but his hands were moving slower.

The world tilted, fell out of focus. Ross reached for a second bottle. Missed. Reached again. He finally held it, ready to smash it down on Luc's head, but the pirate didn't rise. He laid on the ground, eyes open, face splattered with black oily liquid, tongue flicking lazily over his lips for one more taste before it dragged him completely under.

Feeling his consciousness slipping away, Ross stumbled for

the door, tripping over Luc on the way. His hands found the knob, and tried to turn it, but his fingers fumbled, thick and slippery and numb.

The world was fading, his vision growing blurry. His lungs burned from holding his breath. He slid to his knees, and his arms, still bound, fell slack before him.

CHAPTER 29

"THIS IS THE ALLIANCE ARMAMENT."

Adam's voice boomed through the dark, magnified by the ship's fancy radio. His smooth, Upper Noram accent sounded just like the other Armament sailors Marin had run up against.

"Was that right?" he asked.

She nodded, gripping the handle of the knife in the sheath at her hip.

The Armament boat careened through the dark, pummeling wave after wave as it made a straight line for the oil rig and the two smaller ships attached to its leg. Through a spyglass she'd taken from the control room, Marin scanned the deck of the smaller boat, but saw no one, so she turned her eyes back to her brother's ship.

Two men onboard were tied to the mast. Two corsarios kept guard over them. Red and Japan, from the looks of it.

"You're sure about this?" Adam asked when she tossed him the spyglass.

"Course I'm sure," she said. What did the truth matter, anyway? They weren't changing their minds now.

Over the surf, she made out voices.

"Incoming!" one of them shouted. "Luc! Get up here!"

They were forty feet away. Thirty. Closing in at a steady pace, a battering ram swinging in slow motion.

Red—she could tell who it was now—ran for the back of the boat and hurdled over the siding. He dropped like a stone, hitting the water with a splash.

"Again," she said to Adam. He pressed the button on the side of the radio.

"THIS IS THE ALLIANCE ARMAMENT," he called.

"Hold on!" she shouted at him.

Her breath came in hard rasps. She hugged the guardrail, the ladder braced against her chest, just as Adam steered the warship straight into the starboard side of the *Señora*. The two ships connected with a crash of plastic and metal, followed by a high whine as they turned, scraping and punching their way down the hull of Luc's boat.

The diversion gave her the window she needed.

She threw the ladder over the side, and swung down onto it. Her hands, wet and slick with sweat, slid on the metal rungs, but her feet held steady. She scrambled down, watching the deck of the *Señora* slide by. If she was going to make it aboard, she'd have to jump.

Using her legs to push off the warship's hull, she flung herself down onto the deck, rolling across the floor planks until she hit the steering console. In a flash, she was on her feet, knife in her hand. She sprinted toward the corsario on her left.

"Who is that?" One of the men in the suits had seen her, but she didn't stop. Before Japan could react, she barreled into him, sending him sprawling onto his back and then leaping onto his chest. He reached for his gun but her knife was faster, and before he could draw breath, she'd pressed the blade to his throat.

He smiled, his one open eye sparkling with approval.

"Marin," he said, voice gritty. The two men tied to the mast wore suits, and grim disappointment settled between her ribs as she realized neither of them was Ross.

"Where's Luc?" Her gaze darted to the portal that led below deck.

Japan kept smiling.

She grabbed his gun from his hand. It looked new, probably one they'd gotten in the trade with the Oilers. With Red's shouts echoing from the water, she pressed the blade even closer to his neck.

In her place, her father would have killed this man. Luc would have killed him. Her mother would have killed him.

She was not them.

She held the gun up, and switched the setting to stun.

"This is going to hurt," she said. And then she pressed the barrel to his shoulder, and pressed the button.

Pop. A tiny sound for such an enormous response. His body went taut as a stretched wire, and before he went slack, she raced past the two men to the stairs that led below the *Señora*'s deck.

The corridor was empty. Each room was empty.

"Ross!" she whispered as loudly as she dared. Outside she could still hear Red calling for help.

She climbed back up on the deck, regarding the two bound men.

"The captain of this boat had a prisoner with him. Where are they?"

"Let us go," said one, a man with a neat beard and skin that had never seen the sun without protection.

She lifted her knife. "Where."

Reluctantly, the closest nodded toward the other ship. Before she left, she did a wide sweep of the deck, cutting every line with her knife. The sail, tacked down, fell in a heap onto the two men tied to the mast.

If Luc got back on this ship, he wasn't going anywhere quickly.

The Armament warship was still coasting into the night, but not quickly. Adam had dropped the sails like she'd taught him. Below, Red had just reached the metal grate at the base of the oil rig's supporting beam. Sliding down the ladder, she launched herself in his direction.

Trying to swing himself out of the water proved fruitless; Red couldn't get his leg over the edge. When he saw her coming, his moves turned wild and desperate, fingers pawing at the grate to find a sturdy hold. The gun slipped from his hand in the effort, and she dove for it, the clumsy bump of her elbow sending it skittering off the other side of the platform. By the time she'd turned back for him, he'd already shoved back into the water, swimming away into the darkness.

She couldn't stun him out there without killing him—he'd sink like a rock. But if she left him, he could come back, find a weapon, cause problems.

Making the decision to move on, she climbed up the back of the other boat and stepped onto the deck. Her boots squeaked on the clean planks, and though she tried to quiet them, she couldn't.

No one was hiding up here that she could see. Her brother and Ross were below, with who knew who else. She came to the closed hatch that would lead down into the belly of the boat.

Her hand, trembling, reached for the silver knob. Until that moment, she hadn't truly prepared herself for what she'd do if she was too late.

The handle turned in her grasp, then released. Turned, and released again, as if someone were preparing to come outside.

It'll be quick, Marin. One breath in, and it'll all be over.

She ripped back the door, causing the person who'd been leaning against the other side to crash into her.

They fell together, a glimpse of Ross's face registering in her mind one second before the weight of his body pinned her down onto the deck. The sweet smell of tar wafted out around him, and she blinked back the sudden mist that fell over her brain.

"Ross?" she whispered, pulling the rag out of his mouth.

"Marin?" Lifting his head, he blinked. His wrists were cuffed, his hands braced on her thigh as she sat up. She examined his face, finding a swollen bruise on his jaw and a cut on the side of his lip, but hardly caring because he was alive, and she had found him, and for once something had finally gone right.

Moved by some force beyond her control, she wrapped her arms around his neck and squeezed until the shaking passed.

"I like your brown hair," he slurred. "And your pretty face. Did you come to rescue me?"

The laugh bubbled out, stretching all the tight places within her ribs with a painful kind of joy. Pulling back, just a bit, she met his eyes, bluer than any sky or sea, and sleepy from what could only be tar. He was close enough that she could feel his breath on her lips, and smell the salt in his hair. He tilted his head, and his nose brushed against hers, and she felt her hard exterior crack as warm, soft feelings she couldn't even name came rushing to the surface of her skin.

"You're not dead, right?" he asked slowly.

"No," she whispered.

"Oh, good," he said. "That would make this awkward."

He kissed her then, sweetly, and gently, and more than a little drunkenly. His lips curved into a smile against her mouth, and even though her heart had stopped beating altogether, she smiled too, because in all the times she'd imagined kissing someone, she never thought she'd feel as happy as she was right now.

She didn't want to stop.

But then she blinked, and looked beyond him, into the room, and saw the outstretched legs of a woman half hidden behind a couch, and her brother's still form on the floor beside the exit.

She pulled back.

"Ross, did you . . ."

He followed her gaze, head bobbling. "Your brother's a real cabrón, you know that?"

The word didn't exactly sound right when he said it. She forgave him, because he was right.

"We need to go."

"Whoa. That's a big boat."

She turned to follow Ross's gaze over her shoulder, to the Armament boat still drifting away.

"Did it hit us?"

"Yeah," she said, realizing there may have been damage to the other ship as well. The warship could be taking water. They needed to get to Adam soon.

She gripped her knife. "One of Luc's men is in the water. Keep an eye out."

He gave her a wrists-bound salute, which made her think he probably couldn't be trusted just yet.

While Ross kept watch, she climbed out the hatch, weapon braced before her.

The scent of tar still filled the room, and she pulled her shirt over her nose and mouth as she rolled her feet across the plush carpet. Sensing that the worse threat was her brother, she made her way to him first, and found his face covered by his precious tar, and his eyes rolled back. She knelt beside him, searching for wounds but finding none.

"I broke the bottle," said Ross, weaving near the door. He was tall enough he had to duck to fit into the doorway. "Tried to think of what you'd do."

She pressed her fingers against her brother's neck where his pulse beat slow but steady. Ross hadn't killed him, and it weighed on her that this was somehow less of a relief than thinking he was actually dead.

She glanced back at Ross, watching as he screwed his thumb between his brows, and felt her throat grow tight. Not because of the tar. Because of him. Because he had done this, and it felt like he knew now that sometimes you had to be a pirate in order to survive.

He was looking straight at her, just like the first time when they'd met in the riots. When she'd felt exposed, like no one had ever really seen her before.

It had unnerved her then. Now, it made her heart feel too big for her own chest.

"I'm glad you're here, Marin."

She smiled, and maybe it wasn't big on the outside, but inside she was glowing.

"You breathed in too much tar, I think."

He looked down, and gave an awkward laugh. "I've never been high before. Add that one to the list."

She snorted.

"I'm still glad," he said.

322 — KRISTEN SIMMONS

She was too.

Her gaze turned to the woman across the room, eyes widening as she recognized her face.

"I know her," she said.

"Roan Teller," said Ross. "Head of relocation."

"She used to buy drugs from me," Marin said, remembering the riots, and the jars of black liquid in her pack that she'd been trying to take above the cliffline.

The night she'd met Ross.

Ross nodded. "I'm not sure which part of that is more disturbing."

She laughed. And then he laughed too, even though none of it was funny. Roan Teller, the head of relocation, was making deals with her brother.

Ross pushed the door open wider with his bound hands. "Can you take me to the mainland? I need to speak to my father."

And just like that she felt something snap inside of her. Whatever connected them, they were still from different worlds. Even with the bruises and the sun on his skin, even with the clothes that looked like hers, he would always be better.

"Let's get your cuffs on him," she said, nodding down to her brother. "And tie her up too. I've got something to show you."

CHAPTER 30

IT DIDN'T take as long to find the right key to the cuffs this time. The ring was in Luc's pocket, and once they'd fastened him to one of the immobile barstools, they turned to Roan, who had roused, and was giggling about taking a bath in oil as they tied her to a table leg on the opposite side of the room.

Part of Ross had wondered if they should have left her behind; kidnapping a federal official didn't seem like the smartest plan. Regardless, he told himself she would have certainly been killed if they'd left her at the oil rig. The City Patrol could sort her out once they reached the mainland.

"What about your brother's boat?" Ross had asked Marin as they finished.

"Leave it," she had said. And he knew she didn't just mean the boat, but the people on it, and maybe even more based on the way her voice cracked at the end.

He hadn't realized until that moment how much he hoped

she'd never go back to Careytown. She deserved more than an island made of trash.

While he locked the hatch below deck, she sailed them to the Armament warship, where she'd told him her crew was waiting. The guy who'd helped her must have been injured, because Marin had to climb halfway up the collapsible ladder to help him down onto the deck of Roan's boat. As he gripped the silver rail running the perimeter of the deck, Ross wondered how he'd fared as a pirate when the waves pitched him back and forth so easily.

"Ross?"

The stranger straightened, and in the glow of the deck lights, Ross caught the mess of his hair, and the dull glow of a dirt-streaked undershirt, and nearly buckled.

He didn't remember walking forward, or swinging himself up onto the siding, but the next thing he knew, Adam was before him, closer than he'd been since the riots. His mouth quirked up at the side, and Ross was overcome by a hundred different thoughts, all bouncing around within his skull:

You're here.

I'm sorry.

How did this happen?

He saw the hardness in Adam's expression, and the way he favored one leg, and couldn't help but notice how different his friend looked, and how different *he* must have looked, and that this wasn't just because they were beaten and bruised. It was because they were changed. It was like seeing an old friend after years apart.

Ross reached out his hand, just as Adam opened his arms to embrace. Ross laughed, and went in for a hug as Adam immediately dropped his hands. They both stopped and grinned.

"Crazy terrenos," Marin muttered. She shook her head and walked toward the helm of Roan's ship.

"We're crazy?" Adam asked. "She just took on two grown men with her bare hands."

Ross's grin widened as he glanced after her. "You know what they say. It's not the size of the boat, it's the wind in the sails."

Adam gave him a strange look.

"Did they hit you in the head?" he asked. "I guess so. Look at your face." He reached for Ross's jaw. Until then, Ross hadn't realized how swollen it was, and when Adam's fingers grazed it, he winced.

"Do I look tough?" Ross asked.

"You look like you walked in front of a city bus."

That was unfortunate.

Ross wasn't sure what to say then. There was too much to cover, and nowhere to start.

"I'm sorry I fell out of the car." Adam stuffed his hands in his pockets. His head bowed forward, and as if he couldn't hold it together any longer, his shoulders started to shake.

Ross wrapped his arms around his friend, and kissed the side of his head, and let every drop of relief and happiness pour through him. There would be time for more words, but now, only one came to mind.

"Brother," he said.

Adam nodded against his shoulder. "Yeah."

They sailed into the night, keeping just one light on the door to the hatch. There was no sound from within, which Marin told them was to be expected, and while Adam kept guard, Ross helped Marin work the sails.

She'd been quiet over the last hours, even for her, and the way she gave him space whenever he passed, and avoided meeting his eyes, was making him edgy. He wondered if it had to do with the fact that he'd kissed her earlier. Maybe he'd overstepped. Maybe she thought he was too drunk to remember.

He wasn't.

He remembered every one of all three seconds it had lasted. He remembered the soft feel of her mouth, and the salt on her lips, and the way her big brown eyes had closed.

He wanted to do it again.

"How far away are we?" he asked.

Her gaze flicked his way, then back forward. "We should be there by morning."

Relocation happened in the morning. The ocean liner was to meet the first wave of Shorelings bound for Pacifica in Noram Harbor. There was going to be music and fanfare—his mother had been in charge of the party committee.

Time was running out.

He moved closer to Marin. "Everything all right?"

It was a weak question and he knew it. How could she be all right? Her brother, who'd tried to kill him, was currently tied up and passed out below deck. The island she'd called home was about to be filled with unwilling Shorelings, and because she'd helped him, she'd now have nowhere to go.

No. She'd have somewhere to go. He'd make certain of it.

She shifted away, and he felt his brows draw together.

"When you talk to your father, you should tell him that Luc's been getting weapons from the Oilers," she said.

He stilled, absorbing her unexpected response. Remembering the small bird on the handles of Luc's guns. He *had* seen that image before. The leader of the Oil Nation—Píero—had worn the same pendant around his neck when he'd spoken to Ross's father.

"Tell him," said Marin, "my brother was building an army to attack the Armament. Picker told me before he fell in a boca."

Her lips twitched in a way that made Ross think that had not been a pleasant conversation.

Adam slowly made his way toward them, never letting go of something stationary. His face was a pale shade of green.

"An army of pirates?" he asked.

"Of Shorelings," she said. "Five hundred, give or take a few."

Her words lanced every muscle in Ross's body, making him sag against the bench. He thought of Luc's speech to the prisoners his pirates had dragged, bound in lines, through the trash field. *We mean you no harm. In the coming days there will be much to talk about.* He urged their boat to fly faster, to reach the mainland before dawn.

"He asked for Armament ships in his meeting with Roan Teller," said Ross.

"Roan Teller? The safety woman?" asked Adam.

Ross nodded.

"The tar junky," said Marin.

"She helped my father create Pacifica. What we thought was Pacifica, anyway."

Adam and Marin stared at him.

"I need to talk to my dad," he said. "But I don't know if I can trust him."

"Why?" asked Adam. Marin gave him a look like he might be an idiot.

"We're running out of fuel," Ross told them. "And there's oil beneath Lower Noram. To clear the way, she and my father, maybe others too, invented Pacifica. All the ads, the pictures, it's all made up. Maybe the erosion problems are too, I don't know. They'd planned to send the Shorelings to that island—to Careytown—the whole time. She paid Luc to take them."

Adam's eyes widened. "Your dad did this?"

Ross couldn't look directly at him. "I think so. Yeah."

Adam's hand squeezed his shoulder, and he'd never been so grateful for such a small gesture.

"When we came here, I was next to a guy from above the cliff-line," Adam said. "He had information that had gotten him in trouble, that's why he'd been arrested."

Ross remembered a man with the Shoreling prisoners who had been wearing a suit. He'd told Ross that Adam had been left behind in the trash.

"What kind of trouble?" Ross asked.

"He said he was supposed to doctor satellite images of an island. Make it look like something tropical. He thought it might be about Pacifica, and when he started asking around, he ended up in a cell."

They'd fallen into deep, murky water, learning things none of them had been intended to know. Part of Ross still held out hope of his father's innocence. The bigger part of him knew better. It was like all the walls in his life had suddenly been made into windows, and he couldn't close his eyes or turn away.

Adam continued. "He said there was a whole team in the department of safety working on it. Fixing pictures, making ads. Making *Pacifica*."

Ross grit his teeth. When Roan Teller had brought up phase two at the dinner, his father had acted reluctant, not confused. Was that because he'd wanted to ensure the Shorelings would be gone by then? What was his plan for the future, when they wanted to contact family back home, when they wanted to visit the mainland again? Adam had been gone a day and Ross had gone looking for him. If he'd been sent away to a mysterious island, never again to be heard of, Ross would definitely be asking questions.

He thought of what Roan had said to Luc—that the president would blow up the island. Maybe his father's plan had been to pretend the first five hundred were dead—that the ship had sunk in a storm on the way to the island.

"I keep thinking this is a dream," Adam said. "I just need to wake up."

Ross knew the feeling.

"Did that guy say anything else?" he asked.

"No." Adam shook his head. "But . . . people talked about a lot of stuff. They said they'd seen boats leaving with construction supplies for Pacifica that came back empty, and whole apartment buildings in the docks that had been cleared by arrests." He pulled at the collar of his shirt.

"The construction supplies could have been dumped in the ocean," said Marin.

"How many people know about this?" asked Adam. He glanced around him, as if someone might be listening.

"Probably the same number who know the Eighty-Six were dumped with the trash," said Marin.

"We need to tell my dad," Adam said, wrapping his arms around his chest. "He's known something's been wrong the entire time. He can stop this."

Ross considered this, feeling like he was betraying his own father for even considering it. Noah Baker had been true to his convictions throughout his time in office. He'd never agreed with the relocation initiatives, even when they made him unpopular in the political district.

"Does this ship have a radio?" he asked. Marin nodded toward the steering column, where a black box sat above a circular scanner, marking their coordinates.

"We didn't have the radio's access codes on the last boat to call out," said Adam. "It was locked when I tried to let them know where I was." Marin nodded in confirmation.

Frustration pressed down on Ross's hope.

"Could always check with your friend down below," Marin said.

"They're still out," said Adam, checking through the circular window of the hatch.

Ross glanced at Marin, and found her face scrunched in concentration.

"What is it?" he asked.

"Nothing." She frowned. "Just . . . why would the Oilers give weapons to Luc so that he could attack the Armament? I guess if the Shorelings overpowered the patrol in the riots, there'd be no one to contain the mess. But why don't *they* just attack the Armament? Why pay a middleman?"

She had a point. If the Shoreling riots escalated, the City Patrol would not be able to contain them. Without the threat of the Armament intervening, the chaos could easily travel above the cliffline, and civil war, his father's fear, would become a very real possibility. But the SAF didn't need pirates to make that happen; they had the manpower.

"Because they're trying to arrange a trade," said Ross. "Oil for food . . ."

He stopped. Stared at Marin.

"Uh-oh," said Marin. "He's thinking."

"Luc wanted the warships to attack the Armament station," Ross said. "Or maybe just get them out of the way . . ."

"For what?" asked Adam.

"For *who*." Ross scratched absently at his neck, and the stubble that had grown in the last few days.

He was back in the meeting room with his father, facing the screen where the leader of the SAF was asking for a trade. Oil for food. His father had come back with a proposal for an aid package, which had been taken like a slap to the face. At one point his father had mentioned knowledge of the SAF troops, mobilizing near their western border.

Ross had asked if they were going to war, and his father had told him they were on the verge.

Was this what the SAF was waiting for? A distraction, so that they could slip past the Armament and into Noram, just as they had eighty years ago in the last war? Surely if his father knew about this, he would be preparing the military to fight. If Roan was right, he'd sent his people away in order to drill for oil, but may have had no idea of the ripple effect caused by supporting relocation.

"Ross?" Marin's voice broke through the haze of his thoughts. He looked toward the hatch door, wanting to go below and shake Roan Teller and Luc until they both woke up and confessed the truth.

But it would never happen. Even sober, they wouldn't tell him what he wanted to know.

"We have to hurry," said Ross. "If we can't call home, we have to get home. Fast."

CHAPTER 31

THEY SAILED with the wind, galloping blindly through the darkness. Roan Teller's boat was faster than the *Déchet* or even the Armament warship, and glided over the water like the hull had just been greased.

Her crew was quiet. Adam had fallen asleep, curled into a ball in the back of the cockpit. Ross sat on the deck in front of the sails, perched on the slick fiberglass as if he'd never stumbled around a boat. He faced away from Marin, his shirt stretched against his broad back, arms hugging his knees. She stared at him for a long while, memorizing the shape of his shoulders and the taper of his waist, and knew that even if he left, he would not disappear as suddenly as he'd entered into her life. His presence would linger.

Better to get it over with now than later, when she may not have the chance.

After checking their coordinates, she hoisted herself up onto the deck, and took a seat beside him. He made room for her to sit closer, but she stayed an arm's length away, needing the strength of distance.

"What are you thinking about?" she asked.

He kept looking forward, and this made it safer to steal glances in his direction. His hair stretched back in the wind. His thumbs tapped against his knees.

"Nothing," he said. "Everything." Another beat passed. "You."

A strange thrill shivered through her. She waited, like she was standing on the edge of the world, toes off the ledge.

"What about me?" she asked.

"I don't know," he said, looking out into the dark. "I wish we met someplace else, I guess. I wish we could go somewhere we wouldn't get shot or abducted."

"What fun is that, terreno?"

He laughed quietly.

Corsarios didn't date really, though they did marry. There was nowhere to go on the island except the Blue Lady or out on the sea. She'd seen it in her time on the mainland, though. Shorelings going for walks together. Making each other meals. Laughing. Kissing.

She would have liked to kiss him again.

"If we hadn't met this way, you wouldn't have talked to me," she said. It was the truth, though not one she liked the feel of. Soon enough he'd be back above the cliffline, and this time they had together would be only a memory.

"You wouldn't have talked to me either."

That was probably true too.

"You wouldn't have gotten shot," he said, straightening one leg and dropping his chin. "You wouldn't have gotten picked up by the Armament, or lost your boat in the storm, or had to go back to Careytown."

He wasn't lying. But those things didn't seem so grim in hindsight. Not when he'd been beside her.

"It wasn't all bad, was it?" she asked, thinking of his arms around her, and his lips against hers, and of right now, sitting beside him on the deck of a stolen boat.

"No," he said. "That's the worst part about it."

She buried her chin in the crook of her elbow, resting on her knees.

"My mom used to tell this story about a gull and a moonfish," she said, cheeks warming. "They used to meet every day at the shoreline and talk about running away together."

"Did they?" he asked.

"Where could they go?" she responded.

Her mother used to tell that story when she asked why they couldn't go back to the mainland, live as Shorelings like her grandfather. *We are too different*, Maman would say. *A fish might love the land, and a bird might love the sea, but where would they live?*

Right now it felt like that story had always been about Ross.

"You think you can fix this?" she asked.

"I don't know. I have to try."

She breathed in the salty air, feeling the breeze dance across her skin. Of course he had to stop it. It was what made him *him*. Important. The kind of person she was willing to sail across the ocean for.

"All my life, I've been a corsario," she said. "I wanted to be my father, even after all the things he did. I wanted to sit at the captain's table, and have my own crew. Even when I left, I wanted to go back. I thought if enough time passed, they might forgive what I'd done. They might want me again."

He looked her way.

"But now I'm not sure I want them anymore."

She blew out a breath, thinking of her father as they'd fought on that last day. How he'd tried to force her to push a bunch of kids overboard. How he'd pointed his knife at her.

If she'd gone back, she would have become Luc.

"My people are who they are because of that island," she said, imagining for a moment what her life would have been like if she wasn't trash-born, if she wasn't raised to cook drugs, and rob people to stay alive. "If someone had stopped what had happened to the Original Eighty-Six, you and I might have been neighbors. I might have gone to your fancy school. *You* might have been the one taking *me* out on a fancy boat."

It made her feel better to think that even if history had re-played a different way, she and Ross could still be here, right now, listening to the waves and the luff of the sails.

But it hadn't been that way. And soon, there would be too much happening for a proper goodbye. She'd never said one before to her mother, or gotten the chance with her father. For once, she wanted to do this right.

"Ross, I—"

"Where will you go?" he interrupted.

She wasn't sure. It wouldn't be as simple as dropping him off and sailing away. She was in a stolen boat, holding a government official and a corsario captive beneath. If she were able to get away, she'd have to hide, maybe for the rest of her life. Even if she went back to the library, she wasn't sure she could make and sell tar for Gloria again. That was what corsarios did, and she wasn't a corsario anymore.

At some point she'd need to find work, a place to stay. A home, and a family, like her mother had said.

An unfamiliar longing pulled at her ribs, slumping her shoulders. There were things she wanted, but they seemed too delicate for her callused hands to hold. *I must believe there's something better out there*, Hiro had said.

"I don't know," she said. "I don't know where I fit in anymore."

His hand rose around the back of his neck, and he gave a small laugh. "I know what you mean."

You fit in with me, she thought, but she didn't dare say it. She wasn't a Shoreling. He wasn't kanshu. They were both stuck somewhere in between.

He reached for her hand, threading his fingers between hers as they'd done on the *Déchet* before the storm. It was still new for her, and she wasn't sure if you were supposed to feel tied up in knots, right in the center of your chest, but she did.

"Let's go see that peacock," he said.

He pulled her closer, so that their legs touched. His thumb moved over her wrist and it sent whispers of heat across her nerves. She held her breath until he spoke again.

"I'll take you," he said. "We'll go to the nature preserve, and then we'll eat oranges, and reminisce about the time I got kidnapped by pirates."

She laughed, but it was watery and hiccupy, and felt a lot like crying. He turned a little, so that they faced each other, and touched her cheek with his thumb, and the pads of his fingers. Her heart was racing as she leaned into his touch, and let herself have this good thing, for just a little longer.

"And the time we sailed through a storm," she said.

"And how you found Adam."

Her gaze dropped to his mouth, and his fading grin.

"And when you kissed a pirate," she said.

He leaned closer, and she mirrored the move, watching his thick lashes dip as his gaze lowered to her mouth. She lifted her fingertips to his lips, feeling how soft they were. Feeling the black, starless sky like a blanket around them.

He was a breath away. His fingertip circled her ear.

She leaned in first, brushing her lips against his, and then tilting her head to kiss him. At first he barely moved, just smiled against her mouth, and she smiled back, but only for a moment before his hands cupped her cheeks and drew her closer. Her breath caught. Her eyes drifted closed. There was only the feel of him, the perfect mix of soft and firm, reassuring and kind, everything she never thought she'd deserved. Slowly, he pulled her into his world, carefully peeling back the already cracked shell around her heart, until there was nothing but her throbbing pulse, and the rasp of his breath, and the scrape of their teeth. His fingertip circling her knee. Her hand spreading over his back. The grip of his shirt in her hand, and the spark inside her chest that burned bright enough to read the truth by.

If only for right now, he was hers.

"Marin," he whispered roughly, and the change in his voice brought an ache deep inside her.

"Marin," he said again, this time more urgently.

Her eyes fluttered open. Turning, she followed his gaze over her shoulder into the night, where she saw the spray of water, like a fountain, barely visible in the stretch of the deck light.

In an instant her heart was pounding in a different way. She jolted up, slipping on the deck before catching herself on her hands and knees. They should have left the lights off. She should have paid more attention.

Another spray of water, and then a slap against the surface. It was unlike any ship she'd seen, but that didn't mean . . .

"*Marin,*" said Ross, and there wasn't fear, but wonder in his voice. He grabbed her elbow and pulled her up. She stood, though everything within her screamed to fight.

"I think . . . Is that . . ."

She saw it then. The giant curve of a wet, petal-shaped fin, rising in the air, gleaming black in the dark night. Even at a distance of a hundred yards she could tell the entire length of it was taller than she was. The fountain of water hadn't been the spray of a ship, it had come from a *whale*.

Her hands covered her mouth. She hadn't even realized Ross's arm was around her shoulders until he squeezed, and laughed like she had never heard him laugh before. Like he had never seen anything so amazing.

She didn't blame him.

Adam roused at the sound, but didn't see what they had. It was a secret. Just like all the other secrets they'd shared.

Tears filled her eyes, and this time neither of them bothered to wipe them away. She stared at that spot long after the lost animal disappeared, laughing, and crying, and silently telling her dad that she'd seen one too.

CHAPTER 32

THE SUN rose before they reached the California Islands. It burned through the clouds, a white orb in a haunted, gray sky. In preparation for relocation, security was on high alert. The Armament was stationed just outside the islands, in great white ships bearing the Alliance flag on its sails.

"I think I'll swim from here," Adam joked, but Marin didn't slow. She stared straight ahead, gritting her teeth and gripping the wheel as she had in those moments before they'd sailed into the storm.

Ross couldn't help but wonder if this might have a similar outcome.

"They think we're Roan Teller," he told the others, feeling her presence below deck though she was still delirious. "We'll just proceed as though we are." *Until we can't any longer.*

The line of ships stayed at their regular intervals as they came within hailing distance. Ross's gaze switched between their looming presence before him, and their position on the small black scanner beside the steering wheel. The red dots did not gather or come to meet them.

He blew out a shaky breath, the lines gripped in his fists. As he had twenty times in the last hour, he stared at the radio on the steering console, wishing he knew the access codes so that he could call Noah Baker, or his mom or dad—despite everything, his father wouldn't leave him out here. Adam was scanning the public frequencies, listening for any signal that they'd been spotted, but had yet to find anything but static. Even if he did, even if the Armament hailed them directly, they would not be able to respond without the proper contact codes.

It was probably for the best. Chances were the Armament wouldn't believe their story anyway, especially once they found the two below deck.

They didn't have time for a delay; he had to get to the president before the ocean liner launched.

Ross held his breath as they coasted through the line of ships. Without pause, they slipped into a waterway between two islands, and entered the trash-filled Sacramento Bay.

"I can't believe this is actually work—"

Before Adam had finished the thought, the scanner began to beep, a high-pitched sound that gripped Ross's spine. A quick glance at the circular black screen revealed twin red dots on the far left side of the screen.

"We've got two on the port side coming fast," Marin said.

Ross scanned the horizon, but had yet to see any sails.

"The Armament?" he asked.

"Fast enough to be," she said. "Another coming from the south, but farther off."

His stomach climbed into his throat. The radio beeped again.

"They're not going to listen," he said to Adam, whose face was set in a grimace.

"I know," Adam said. "We have to turn back. We don't have a choice."

Desperation pitted out Ross's stomach. They couldn't turn back. If they did, the Armament would know something suspicious was going on. He remembered too well the chase that had sent them barreling through these islands the first time.

"We can make it," said Marin.

He glanced over at her, her lifted chin and determined gaze sharpening his confidence.

"We can't," said Adam. "Those ships are blocking our path to Donner Cove."

"We'll go straight to Noram Harbor," said Marin.

"You're not serious," said Adam. "Everyone will be at the park. There's no way we'll get by without being noticed."

The celebration to launch the first passenger-bound ship to Pacifica was taking place there. The president and vice president would surely be in attendance.

Ross pictured it in his mind. The harbor was industrial, once the fishing industry's main port, but now primarily used for the Armament. Ross had been there once when his father had given a speech about military recruitment. The "park," as they had called it, was scarcely more than a dirt field between the car lot and the pier, and the shops that had once lined the waterfront had been since dedicated to mainland offices for the military.

He might have been safe there, but Marin wouldn't be, and after all that had happened, Adam might not be either.

All at once, he felt the weight his father had once described. His friends' lives versus the fate of more than five hundred innocent people.

"The Armament's going to know something's wrong when we don't answer the radio," Adam insisted. "We plow through them, they'll treat us as hostile."

He was right. Roan Teller's staff would answer the call, or stop for the Armament, but that wasn't an option. The delay, once the Armament figured out their cargo, would cost them too much time. Their only chance was to outrun them, and hope that this government official's boat would offer some protection.

"We can't stop," he told Adam.

After a moment, Adam nodded. But Marin just stared straight ahead, eyes on the water before her. She'd already made up her mind.

Part of him loved her just then.

"You'll stay with me when we dock," he told her.

She glanced up at him, and gave a quick nod.

"Get on the lines," she ordered. "It's time to move."

He did as she said, taking the starboard while she covered the port side. Ross didn't have to be told what to do—they moved as a team now, cutting across the bay with the wind filling their deep blue sails. Finally, it registered that the beeping of the scanner had stopped, and when Ross looked down, he saw that Adam was holding the entire contraption in his hands. Severed wires dangled from the back of the black screen.

"Kind of annoying, right?" he asked.

Ross grinned.

The coastline rose like a mirage from a trash-filled bay, white stone and rust, dancing on the horizon. From the haze emerged two white sails, scaling the water, outstretched and filled with the breeze. They grew larger with each passing moment, until the Alliance flag waved clearly above them.

Warships.

"Faster," Ross muttered, praying for stronger wind.

Muffled over the distance, he could hear the magnified call of the first ship. It was probably announcing who they were, and requesting that Marin stop at once. She ignored them, barreling on, leaving a spray of water and white foam in their wake.

They didn't take that well, and pursued at full speed.

"They won't shoot at us," Ross called to the others. He hoped it was true.

Finally, they entered the harbor, just as the two ships closed in behind. He could see the ocean liner in the deepest part of the cavity, the red and blue banners hanging in stark contrast to the fat, white hull.

They'd made it in time. Cool relief doused through his veins, just as his stomach twisted in preparation for what would happen next. Beside the ocean liner were two more Armament warships, and the patrol presence on land would surely be enormous.

"There!" Marin pointed ahead to the farthest pier to her right, where the docking stations at the end of the floating walkway were empty. She steered in that direction, and as they drew closer, Ross could see the crowd that gathered on the field just beyond, pressing against a chain-link fence that blocked access into the park in front of the relocation ship.

Rioters.

He could hear them shouting now, over the waves, over the water. Over Marin's orders and the boom of the voice from the warships ordering their surrender. Over the music at the park, where the band his mother had booked was playing.

They were going to dock the boat right in front of the riots.

"We're going to land hard," Marin shouted. "Brace yourselves, boys!"

For a few long moments, it felt as though the land were racing toward them, not the opposite. The concrete pylons anchoring the ends of each finger grew larger as they neared, and though Marin tried to steer around the closest support, they were moving too fast to cut away without capsizing. Holding tight to the lines, Ross grit his teeth, and counted the seconds to impact.

One. Two. Three. Four.

They slammed into the closest pylon, rotating hard into the pier, which shattered with a groan and a series of snaps and cracks. Ross was thrown forward, toppling onto his knees, his grip on the rope the only thing preventing him from going over-board.

Before they'd fully stopped, he jolted to his feet, and leapt down to the cockpit. Skidding on the shattered glass that covered the floorboards, he lunged toward Marin, who'd been thrown to her back in the collision. The steering console had fallen over her, the wheel pinning her to the ground. Blood beaded from a gash on her bottom lip, but there was fire in her eyes as he heaved the heavy wooden circle off her chest.

"Quit playing around," he said, the side of his mouth tilting up.

Muttering a curse under her breath, she reached for his hand. When he pulled her up, she braced herself on his waist, fingers twisting his shirt in her grasp for one moment before they stumbled toward the side of the boat where Adam was waiting.

"We'll have to jump," Adam said, anxiously peering over the edge.

It was ten feet down to the rickety boards, now free-floating, unattached to the pylon they'd crashed into. Ross glanced behind them; the warships were approaching.

"Go," Ross told Adam. "*Now.*"

Sweat dripped down Adam's temples. "I can't. My leg."

"It'll be fine," Ross assured him, though he had no way of knowing.

Adam hesitated. Ross shoved him over.

His friend landed with a cry of pain, and crumpled onto his knees. He meant for Marin to go next, but when he turned, she was facing the opposite way, toward the cockpit, where the hatch door leading below deck had swung open. The handle hung, broken, having popped free from the lock in the impact.

Standing in the doorway was Marin's brother.

Luc staggered out, crimson streaks gleaming on his dark forehead. His wrists were still encased in shackles, though the chain between them had somehow been severed. His gaze, glassy and wild, turned in their direction, and a small smile twisted his lips.

Ross didn't realize he'd reached for Marin until his hand twisted in the shoulder strap of her shirt. He didn't know what he would do, what he might say. A white-hot rage raked through him, burning away all thoughts but one.

Get away from her.

"Guess you'll have to go be a hero without me, terreno," said Marin quietly, breaking the icy stillness of this new nightmare.

She placed her hand on his, and patted it twice. Then reached for the knife at her belt.

"No," said Ross. Through the pounding in his ears, he heard Adam shouting his name from the pier below.

"Don't worry." Marin rose to a stand. "My brother and I have a few things we need to work out. Family business, isn't that right, Luc?"

Luc inhaled the fresh air above deck, nostrils flaring.

"Ross!" shouted Adam again.

There was no good choice. He had to get to the Shorelings now, before the boat left, before the Armament reached them.

But Luc was dangerous, and free. Who knew what had happened below deck. He might have killed Roan. Now, he might kill others.

They could deal with this pirate, or they could stop more from becoming like him.

"Come with me," said Ross. "Leave him. He's weak. He won't get far."

She hesitated.

"Come with me," Ross said again.

If she stayed to fight, he would stay to fight, despite the consequences. He would not leave her to face her brother alone. But on the mainland, she could change things. Make things better. There were bigger, more important battles they could face together, the kind that ensured that no one would ever be thrown out in the trash again.

Air hissed through her teeth.

"All right," she said.

A breath huffed from his lungs. It felt like they had beaten Luc, without even touching him.

She turned away from her brother, and stepped to the ledge. He didn't question if the decision to leave Luc was the right one. Time was against them, and when she lowered her stance to jump, Ross leapt.

He hit the ground beside Adam a second later, tumbling to his knees. Jolting upright.

Marin was not beside him.

He looked up, and in her sad smile he saw that she hadn't intended to come with him. That she would take care of Luc alone.

"Goodbye," she mouthed.

And then she was gone.

Gone.

Like Adam had been gone.

"Marin!" he shouted, banging his fists against the hull of the boat. The boards, unanchored, slipped back, a foot of water between the dock and the siding. He looked for the ladder, for a line, something to get back on that ship. His ribs felt like they were caving in on his chest, crushing his lungs. He knew what Luc could do—what she would do, if given the chance.

Marin saw her brother as her responsibility, just as he saw his father as his.

She was strong, but Ross feared that strength now, because if she killed him, here, on the mainland in full view of the Armament, there would be no going back. She would be a pirate forever.

A sharp *crack* filled the air. The boards beside him splintered to pieces in a tiny explosion that threw him to the side. The warships were here, and were shooting at them. Ross should have called out, but they couldn't hear him. Didn't know who he was. Wouldn't believe him anyway.

"We have to go," said Adam in his ear. "We have to move, Ross!"

"Marin!" Ross shouted again, but he knew she was out of his reach.

He would find her. He'd found Adam; he could find her.

He pushed Adam toward the riots, just as another shot fired beside them. When Adam sidestepped, his leg buckled, and he fell to the dock. Ross pulled him back up, slinging his friend's arm over his shoulders.

"Leave me," Adam said. "I'll tell them . . ."

"No," said Ross, blood running cold. He would never leave Adam again.

He charged toward the crowd, dragging Adam as best he could.

They made it to the riot. To the thrashing, crushing mass of bodies. Though taller than most, Ross couldn't see beyond their raised hands and waving signs to the fence, or beyond it, where his father would soon be giving a speech.

He pushed aside his thoughts of Marin, or how they should have been together now. Instead, he gripped Adam's arm over his shoulders, holding on to his friend like a lifeline, doing his best to protect him from the jabbing elbows and shoving hands of those around them.

A woman screamed. And then another. It was just like the riots then, everyone moving in different directions, pushing, trampling each other to get away.

"FACEDOWN ON THE GROUND," boomed a male voice over a loudspeaker. In the background, dancing music still played. Relocation's celebration continued.

He shoved forward.

"FACEDOWN ON THE GROUND."

A woman in front of him looked back, just before a soldier in a black uniform and face mask burst through the center of the crowd and knocked her down with a body-length shield.

"Stop!" Ross shouted.

She cried out in pain, and then crawled away through the legs and mud, hidden by the flashes of clothing and swinging weapons of the soldiers.

Steeling himself, Ross turned and rushed toward the fence. He carried Adam's weight, straining and sweating and focusing on one singular goal. To find someone who could bring them to their fathers.

There were more uniforms around him now, everywhere, filling the spaces between the Shorelings, who shouted in pain and cried, and lay on the ground, their hands behind their heads, their clothes splattered with mud.

And then Adam was ripped from his side. Ross tried to hold him, but his shirt stretched and slipped from his fumbling fingers.

The fence was ten feet away, but he wouldn't make it. Not without his brother. He raised his hands and stood, as tall as he could, surrounded by the black uniforms bearing the city's emblem. *His* city's emblem. The crest on his Center uniform. That hung in the house he'd lived in for seven years.

"Get on your knees!" one barked through his mask.

They didn't recognize him. They thought he was a Shoreling. That he was dangerous. They didn't even look at his face, or his hands, outstretched and empty.

"My name is Ross Torres!" he said. "I'm the son of the president. I'm unarmed."

"Get down or I'll shoot you!" said another.

"My name is Ross Torres!" he repeated. Again and again.

They knocked him to his knees.

"My name is Ross Torres. I'm unarmed."

He wove his fingers behind his head, as they shoved him to the ground.

CHAPTER 33

MARIN TRAINED the knife on her brother's chest, ignoring the calls of the Armament approaching from behind. As much as she'd wanted to go with Ross, to believe there was another life for her out there, a part of her had always known it would come down to this. The blood of the Original 86 ran through her veins, and it was time for her to face the captain's table for judgment.

"Looks like you finally gnawed through those chains," she said. "Hope they broke every last one of your good teeth."

His lips pulled back, revealing the same yellowed grin.

"Pried a screw free when you crashed us," he said. "Lucky the links were already rusted."

A shot fired, hitting the pier somewhere below them. She listened for a cry of pain, but heard none. If Ross was hurt . . . if he'd come this far just to take a bullet . . . It took everything she had not to look back over the side of the boat.

Marin nodded to the open hatch. "The woman. You kill her?"

"Not yet. She still owes me."

"Warships, you mean." That was what Ross had heard—that Luc had asked Roan Teller for warships to fight in his battle.

Luc rolled his shoulders back, watching her knife. They were only ten feet apart and the weapon felt heavy in her grasp.

"The younger Torres told you," Luc realized with a nod. "Got that one by the throat, don't you?"

The Armament was still calling their threats over the loud-speakers. Luc didn't bother glancing in their direction, nor did he look particularly flustered. Maybe he still thought he was under Teller's protection.

He would not be for long. Not once Ross reached his father.

"How'd you find us? I'm a little fuzzy on the details," Luc asked.

"You sent Picker to have me killed," she said, ignoring his question.

He gave a small wince. "You tried to let my prisoner go."

"He wasn't yours."

"Sure he was," said Luc. "You tithed him. He became property of Careytown."

She flinched. Took a step closer. Her brother wasn't wrong. She *had* given Ross over, but only to keep him alive. She was not the corsario her father had always wanted her to be. She never would be.

"I made a mistake," she said.

He only sneered, then took one step back, and another. It was then that she saw what he intended to do—jump over the edge, swim under the cover of plastic, probably to the riot where he could blend in and disappear.

She wasn't going to let him leave this boat. Not when he'd hurt Ross, and not when Ross still had work to do.

This was her job now, she realized with startling clarity. To help Ross protect the Shorelings. To stop them from going to Careytown, and coming back like Luc. She couldn't do the things Ross could, but she could keep him safe.

Another shot pierced the air and implanted in the fallen wheel on the cockpit floor between them. It threw Marin back a step, and forced her to listen to the call from the larger boat slowing fifty yards behind the stern.

"PUT DOWN YOUR WEAPONS."

Her body trembled with the volume of the voice, her muscles twitching with adrenaline. She knew what waited for her if they took her alive. A terreno prison. A life of walls and barred doors. Maybe she deserved it for the things she'd done to her father, and even stupid Picker, but Luc deserved it more.

Knowing the Armament would shoot her if she killed him, she threw the knife over the side of the boat. Luc shook his head, then turned and ducked under the boom, making for the opposite side.

Launching toward him, she threw her body forward into the cockpit. One step on the fallen steering console gave her the height she needed to leap toward her brother, and with outstretched arms, she landed against his back, throwing him to the gleaming, glass-covered floorboards.

They fell in a heap, rage pounding in Marin's head, forcing her hands into fists. The shards of glass cut her elbows and pricked through the knees of her pants, but she didn't hesitate. She clambered over him, wrapped her forearm around his throat, and pulled back.

He snuck a hand in just in time to keep his windpipe open, but she had the leverage, and groaned as she attempted to choke him out. Still, he was bigger, all wiry muscles, and in a surge of power, he flipped them both onto their sides.

"Stupid little girl," he growled. "I'm doing this for *us*, for *our people*. Finally, the terrenos will pay for what they did."

"You're no better than they are," she said, throwing herself back to avoid his swinging fist. Her back slammed against the hard side compartments. "Taking free people. Throwing them in the gomi fields. Making them fight to stay alive."

His eyes widened, black pupils nearly overtaking the rings around them. "You want to die? Is that what you want? They won't take mercy on you, soeur. They'll break you, and then feed you to the moonfish."

His spit peppered her cheeks. The pungent smell of sweat and tar made her eyes water as he rose on his knees and twisted toward her. His elbow connected hard with her jaw, and sent her reeling back, vision tilting sideways.

"You think that boy is going to help you?" He fell toward her, throwing a punch into her stomach. Her organs jammed upward, forcing the air from her lungs. Weakly, she coughed, protecting her middle with her trembling forearms.

"He's already forgotten you," Luc hissed. "He's back in his castle, and you're still nothing but trash."

It hurt, worse than any blow, because she knew he might be right. The chances she would ever see Ross again were slim. But that changed nothing. She would fight for him as he'd fought for Adam—to the very end.

Swinging hard, she hit him square in the cheek. Her hand stung, but she hit him again. His lip cracked, spilling blood down his chin.

A great shadow fell over him, and then she heard the voice of the Armament, booming in her ears.

"SURRENDER AND PREPARE TO BE BOARDED."

Distracted, Luc flinched, and in that moment, she tackled

him, knees on his shoulders, pinning down his arms. Her hands went around his throat, pressing down, and she watched as his eyes again went wide, this time not in fury, but in fear.

Her blood buzzed. Her body trembled with power.

She could end his reign forever. Stop others from hurting because of him, from being like him, from ever tasting his precious tar.

Her father's face appeared before her, like a mask over Luc's features.

There are two kinds of people in this world: ones that stab you in the chest, and ones that stab you in the back.

And then there were those like Ross, who didn't have to hurt anyone at all.

She released her brother at once, leaving him sputtering, blinking.

"I'm not trash," she said, through heavy breaths.

Behind her, she heard the heavy boots of the Armament. Without looking, she raised her hands in surrender. Roughly, she was dragged back, then thrown onto her stomach and told to weave her fingers behind her head. She did so without a fight, eyes on Luc the whole time.

They asked her name, and where she was from, and how she'd gotten the boat. She said nothing, because no answer would help her.

Marin turned as two men in blue uniforms escorted Roan Teller from below deck. Her eyes were wild, her hair disheveled. She wobbled between the soldiers, claiming she'd been drugged.

"Pirates," she huffed. "I was abducted by pirates."

"Me too!" Luc straightened, wiping the blood from his nose and mouth with the back of his hand. "We're lucky to be alive, aren't we, love?"

"Don't *call* me that!" she screeched. "He's one of them." Roan pointed an accusing finger in his direction, as if this weren't the most obvious thing in the world.

"That's no way to treat a friend," he said, offended. "Especially not one you've paid so handsomely."

The Armament soldiers looked from Luc to Roan. Marin had to hand it to her brother; he didn't go down easily.

"I would never!" She backed away from him as if she were afraid she might catch a disease. "I've never seen this man in my life before today."

Luc's expression hardened.

"And her." Roan blinked at Marin. "I have no idea where she came from. Probably one of his lackeys or something. Goodness. I'm lucky to be alive."

The Armament tried to help her sit down, but she shook them off.

"I have to see the president," she said. "Take me to him, right away. I have important information he needs to hear. Matters of national security. Information regarding his *son*."

"Why don't you take it easy," offered one of the soldiers.

"He's a threat to national security!" she bellowed. "Roosevelt Torres has been making deals with pirates!"

"Ross had nothing to do with it," Marin said, her first words spoken since the arrival of the Armament.

The officer at Roan's arm gave her a strange, wilting look that made Marin realize she probably should have continued on in silence. He crouched to where she lay, and pulled back her hair, revealing the black ink tattoo just below her ear.

"Eighty-Six," he said grimly. And then, "Inform the president we have a situation."

CHAPTER 34

Ross was lined up, facedown in the mud with the other Shoreling rioters. Though they told him to shut up, he kept talking, kept telling them his name, until finally he was removed from the group and given an eye scan.

The officer who ID'd him was a woman with raven black hair and tired, worried eyes. She apologized profusely for the confusion, and said that she would bring him to his father immediately.

He refused to leave the scene without Adam. And when Adam was lifted off the ground, he refused to leave at all.

"Bring my father here," Ross insisted. "And Noah Baker as well, please."

"What is going on?" Barreling through the crowd was a security officer, dressed in a familiar navy suit. His bald head gleamed with perspiration as he shoved through the patrolmen who had gathered around Ross and Adam.

"Tersley?" Ross felt something well up in his chest in his old bodyguard's presence. The feeling was so powerful, he nearly forgot how they'd parted ways.

"*Ross.*" Tersley hooked a hand behind Ross's neck and smashed him into an embrace. Tears burned in Ross's eyes. There were things he wanted to tell him, about Marin, and the boats, and how he'd fought a pirate, just like Tersley had shown him so long ago. Instead, he patted the big man's back.

As if remembering his station, Tersley whipped away, arms dropping to his sides. Beside them, Adam was helping one of the rioters, a woman whose head was bleeding.

"How'd you know I was here?" Ross asked.

"I was just over at the ceremony," said Tersley. "Your eye scan registered on my comm."

It could have been standard procedure, or something he'd been ordered to do, but Ross felt a well of gratitude that he'd been looking.

As always, he was here before Ross's father.

"You look like hell, kid," said Tersley, resting a tentative hand on his shoulder. "Are you hurt?"

Ross shook his head. Tersley turned to Adam, the scar on his jaw pulled tight, relief in his eyes.

"You?"

"I'm fine." Adam straightened his hurt leg, as if to hide the injury.

"Good," said Tersley. His cheeks grew pink. "Good. I'm glad."

Ross glanced back to Roan Teller's boat, now closed in on both sides by Armament warships. The dark uniforms of the sailors flashed over the siding. He couldn't see Marin from where they stood, or her brother, and the fear of what had happened since he'd run toward the riots cut deep into his bones.

"Tersley, I need a favor," said Ross.

"Let's talk favors later," said his old bodyguard. "If I don't get you to your folks, I'm dead. I've outlived all my second chances."

Ross planted his feet. "It has to be now."

Tersley's brows lifted.

Quickly, Ross explained what was happening on the boat, and how they'd come to be in the riots.

"The girl from that shop in the docks?" Tersley asked, leaning close. "The one I . . ."

Ross nodded.

Tersley exhaled roughly, one hand splayed over his chest.

"Help her," Ross said. "For me. She's the only one on that boat who isn't lying."

After a brief hesitation, Tersley grabbed the nearest patrolman and spouted off a quick list of orders, then turned back to Ross. "The two of you better be here when I get back, understand?"

"Yes, sir," said Ross. Adam snorted.

As he jogged away, Adam nudged him with his elbow.

"It's going to be all right," he said, staring toward Roan Teller's boat. "Marin's tougher than anyone there."

"I know," said Ross. But that didn't make him feel any better.

Noah Baker was the first family member to arrive. Wearing casual pants, and a shirt that wasn't even buttoned straight, he burst from the back of the government car and ran toward the park bench where they waited. Ross rose immediately, but Adam, struggling with his leg, grimaced, and pulled himself up by the armrest.

"Adam?" Noah threw his arms around his son, nearly knocking both of them over. Tears streaked his dark face, and though it felt like a ratchet tightening in Ross's chest to watch, he did not look away.

"You're both all right." Noah grasped Ross's shoulder and pulled him close as well. They'd never embraced before. They'd barely even shaken hands. But crushed against Noah's chest he felt a strange sense of comfort.

Their mothers had arrived by the time Noah finally let them go. Mrs. Baker was already bawling by the time she reached them, and kissed Adam so many times he turned a deep shade of red and sat back in his seat to get a little breathing room.

Ross's mother took his hand, pulling him toward the cars. She was shaking, blinking back the tears so as not to make a scene. She wasn't wearing her usual makeup, and her hair was flat, like in the mornings just after she woke up. He remembered she'd thought he might be dead, and felt awful.

She informed him his father would meet them in private.

Ross's feet rooted to the ground. Beside him, on the bench, Adam's dad was examining his son's leg and calling for a medic. Ross doubted the concept of gossip or privacy had even crossed Noah Baker's mind.

"Dad needs to meet us here." Ross knew what he was asking. His father was a public figure. *The* public figure. Showing up on this side of the relocation activities, with his son dressed this way, would be more of a story than the Pacifica launch.

His mother's lip quivered, her gaze returning again and again to the Shoreling rioters just beyond in the grass, but to her credit, she stepped aside to grasp her assistant's arm.

The call was made, and less than five minutes later, George Torres arrived.

The team of security surrounded the president like a moving wall, hiding his father from view until they broke rank to surround the two families. The suit he'd chosen for relocation day was as dark blue as the sails on Roan's boat, but the bruised half circles beneath his eyes spoke of sleepless nights and worry.

George Torres did not rush toward his son the way Noah had Adam. He walked carefully over the dirt, chin held high. It was only when they were standing a foot apart that he spoke.

"Son." His voice cracked over the word.

Waves of emotion pelted Ross, making it difficult to stay standing. Making it difficult to speak at all. He'd trusted this man his entire life, looked up to him, believed in him. He'd wanted nothing more than for his dad to show up at a track meet, but instead he'd been working, always working, and Ross had justified it, told himself that it was okay because his dad was important, and the country was important, and Ross was just a kid who could barely read his own name.

He'd never considered that he had the right to feel disappointed.

"We need to talk," said Ross.

Set aside from the others, Ross told his father how he'd gone for Adam, and how Marin and he had been intercepted by the Armament and ambushed at the station on the old oil rig. How they'd escaped, and survived a storm, and that she'd brought him to Careytown, where he'd learned about the 86, and the old war with the SAF, and been brought as a hostage to meet Roan Teller.

"Ross." His father's eyes widened. He moved closer. "This is not the place."

"She's in the boat behind us," said Ross. "The one with the blue sails." He lifted his chin. "I know about Pacifica. I know that

Roan's been making deals with the pirates to take the first five hundred to an island of trash."

George Torres looked in horror at the boat, still in the harbor, blocked in by the two larger warships.

"That's a very serious accusation," he said slowly.

Tell me it's not true, Ross thought. But his father did not.

"The pirate's there too." Ross's words came faster now, trying to fit it all in before he was forced to stop. "The one accepting the money. He tried to kill me, but I escaped. Marin sailed us back here."

"Marin," said his father blankly. "Another pirate."

"She's not a pirate anymore," Ross said.

While his father turned gradual shades of white, Ross detailed the things they had figured out sailing toward the harbor—how the SAF was supplying the 86 with weapons, and how Luc planned to attack the Armament.

His father told him to stop. A whisper at first, and then louder, and louder, until his voice broke through the other conversations around them.

"I will not stop," said Ross, squaring his shoulders. "You know the SAF is moving their troops and that they're supplying weapons to those the Alliance has kicked out. You have to do something."

"Do something?" The president's hands opened before him. "I'm still trying to figure out how you abducted a government official."

Hot fury bit at the base of Ross's neck. "You should be more concerned with sending hundreds of Alliance citizens out to an island of trash."

It was clear in his father's face that of all the things he had said, this was the least expected. Concern warped into anger, then to panic, every emotion playing across his face filling Ross with a validation he didn't want to have. His father had known what was happening all along. He had agreed to condemn over five hundred innocent people. Even if it hadn't happened yet, he was still guilty of terrible things, and Ross was disgusted.

His father grabbed his shoulder, speaking in a low, pressured voice.

"You can't tell anyone this, understand? It's important you understand."

Ross shook free, tired of the secrets and games.

"Do you remember what you told me when the Bakers moved to the South Wing?" Shock had his father's mouth gaping open, though if it was because of the information, or Ross's defiance, he didn't know.

"You told me that it wasn't going to be easy, but that it was my job to make sure Adam fit in here."

"Ross."

"It's the only thing you'd ever asked me to do."

Ross had taken the job seriously because he'd wanted his dad to be proud of him. He'd stuck up for Adam when the others had picked on him. They'd traveled to school together in the same car, and sat together, even when Ross's friends had gone to another table. And then there'd been the incident in the locker room, when the other guys had wanted Adam expelled, had expected him to go along with it just like every other rich, spoiled kanshu. It had been that moment he'd realized he wasn't, and that he didn't want to be, and that this "job" of looking out for the Shoreling kid had turned into something he was willing to stand up for.

"Now I'm asking you to do something for me," said Ross. "Be the kind of person I always thought you were."

George Torres hung his head, hiding his thoughts but not his strife.

"Mr. President." It was Noah who was speaking, calling from the opposite side of the bench, where a team of soldiers was approaching. Roan Teller was near the front, stalking toward them, and the sight of her made Ross's stomach feel like he'd swallowed nails.

Behind her was Luc, wrists in cuffs.

And off to the side was Marin, walking a full body's length away from Tersley, and eyeing him as if he might spontaneously combust.

She was alive. He hoped that someday he'd stop being surprised by that simple fact.

Ross turned his attention back to his father, though everything within him screamed to join Marin.

"Choose better friends, Dad. Pretty soon we're going to run out of fuel, and handing people over to pirates cannot be the only solution."

"I . . ." George rubbed at his chin, looking as if he'd gained ten years of age in the last ten minutes. "I know."

Ross wasn't sure what he'd expected, but this simple affirmation made him feel a little better.

"Mr. President," started Roan. "I don't know what your son's been telling you, but he has crossed the line. Consorting with pirates? Kidnapping innocent people? I—"

George Torres held up his hand, a hush falling over the team of security officers, patrolmen, and Armament.

"Take her into custody. I'll be in touch soon."

"Take me into custody? *Me?* Who do you think signs my paychecks, Mr. President?"

George Torres's head tilted forward.

"I know who signs mine, Captain." Luc raised his hands,

bound together before him. Even with a bloodied face he maintained a pirate's smile.

"And if you kindly remove these cuffs," he added. "I'll tell you all about it."

"Do not . . ." started Ross.

"I won't," muttered the president.

"Sir . . ." Roan began one more time, but Ross's father had already turned toward the nearest security officer.

"Keep her quiet," said the president. "I need twenty-four hours."

With a "yes, sir," the security officer spoke to the Armament, and soon Roan's demands for her lawyer were punctuating the still air.

Ross's father stared after her.

"Dad."

George Torres's shoulder caved forward at Ross's hand on his shoulder, as if the small move held the power to wither him.

"In case it matters, I want you to know that this wasn't an easy decision. I thought it was the only way. I thought . . . the sacrifice would save so many more." He shook his head. "None of that makes it better. I let Roan convince me it was right."

The weight of what Ross had done settled between them. Soon there would be investigations. Maybe even jail. Their lives would never be the same.

"I'm sorry," Ross said.

His father's assistant was calling for him. It was time for the speech.

For the first time in Ross's life, the president raised his hand to hold off the rest of the world.

He looked to Ross, and straightened.

"Never be sorry for doing the right thing," he said, and then called for the vice president.

CHAPTER 35

Ross HAD asked her to come back with him above the cliffline. He'd find a place for her to stay, make sure she had food and anything else she needed, but she'd said no. Not because those things didn't sound nice—they'd sounded *more* than nice—but because it was time to start over. She didn't know where she'd go yet, but she knew she had to make her own way; otherwise this new land would never feel like home.

Besides, Ross was facing a new storm—one she couldn't help him through. His father and Adam's were going to delay the launch until they could formally announce the failure of the Relocation Act. Roan and Luc would be kept in custody until they could be safely and discreetly questioned. The Armament would be sent to the oil rig, where they'd left the *Señora* and the other ship, to investigate, while another team would make way for Careytown and the Shoreling prisoners. She'd already heard whispers of the questions the president would face, and how the next weeks would be the hardest. She didn't tell Ross, but she sort of hoped his dad had some time to think about things in prison.

After Ross's father made the announcement that there would be delays in the launching of the ocean liner, Ross had walked Marin to the back of the park, away from the crowds who gathered around the podium.

"I owe you some money," he said.

She'd forgotten about that. The idea that he'd pay her for what they went through tainted it somehow.

"Send some food down to the library in the docks," she said. "We'll call it even."

He nodded.

She knew he'd make good on it.

"You sure you'll be all right?" he asked.

It was cute that he asked, even when he knew better. It occurred to her, when he squeezed her hand, that he might be letting her go for her own protection, to keep her out of the spotlight that would surely fall upon his family. It wouldn't have surprised her.

But as they stood there facing each other, she wasn't sure how to walk away.

"So," she said. "I guess this is it."

"I guess so."

A dozen memories crashed through her mind—eating moonfish in the dark, a game of *I've never*, his hand on her cheek in a storm. She'd sailed across the ocean for him, faced death with him, seen things she'd never thought she'd ever see—whales, and riots, and freedom from a life she'd only thought she wanted. Her course had changed since she'd met him, maybe *because* she had met him. Nothing would ever be the same.

She swallowed a breath, the pressure building in her chest. It felt like drowning on land. It felt like saying goodbye.

So she took a step forward, and rested her forehead against his chest, fisting his shirt in her hands. He was warm, and smelled like the sea, achingly familiar.

He kissed her—once on the head, once on the cheek—and said, "I'll find you, terreno."

She gave a quiet chuckle; she may have been trash-born, but she was one of his people now.

He walked away standing tall, with the kind of strength she'd envied, right from the beginning.

"Goodbye, Ross," she whispered.

EPILOGUE

"I'LL BE back in three weeks to check in." Marin refolded the towels on the shelf over the sink in the tiny one-room clinic. "You have enough food to make it to next weekend, but Seema said she'd be around in case you need something." Her mother was down the street working in the kitchen at the motel, a job she'd taken as part of President Baker's Reintegration Bill after being brought to the mainland with the other corsarios six months ago. Marin had reminded her three times to look out for Hiro when they'd said their goodbyes this morning.

"I did manage to survive before you," Hiro mused, pushing his glasses up his nose. He sat at the table, reading something on his tablet. "I know it must seem impossible."

She smiled to herself. No, it did not seem impossible. It was she who'd needed him more than the opposite. Though it had been almost a year, she still remembered, clear as a cloudless sky, the night she'd returned to his shop after leaving Ross at the harbor. How the old man had set up a blanket for her in the corner of his back room, and told her that if she was around in the morning, she could pay him back by cleaning up the shop.

She'd stayed, telling herself it would only be one night. But soon it was two, and then a week. Though she'd visited Gloria, she'd come back every day, first fixing up things that had broken around the shop, then his screen on the wall, then his generator.

One day he'd asked her if she thought she could fix people the way she fixed other things. That night, she'd begun assisting with the patients he brought behind the curtain.

As the days passed, Hiro taught her to dress wounds and check a person's pulse and blood pressure. She had strong, nimble fingers, and soon was suturing by herself, and knew what to give someone for a sour stomach or a migraine. People were not like machines—they were much more difficult to figure out—but she liked that. Each case became a puzzle she needed to figure out.

But she never forgot who she'd been, or the boy she'd taken across the sea.

Reaching for the envelope sitting atop the counter, she traced the scratchy letters of her name, knowing it had taken him time and care to get each letter right. She thought of him as she always did, with the wind in his hair, laughing and whooping into the night like they were the only people left in the world.

The envelope had shown up last week, filled with a ticket for the nature preservation. The back talked about a new exhibit opening next month—an animal called a lionfish was going to be out on display. She wasn't sure how that had come about, but she doubted it was pretty.

Tucking the envelope into her pocket, she stifled the urge to check the contents of her bag one final time. For someone who'd spent so long blowing with the wind, it felt nearly impossible to remove herself from this tiny room.

"I'm leaving a blade under the counter out front," she told Hiro. "And another beneath the mattress."

"Ack." He groaned, and waved a hand. "This is a safe place. I do not need *blades*."

"This is the docks," she said, her meaning clear enough.

"It's better than it used to be."

Yes. That was true. One of President Baker's various missions had been to appoint a Shoreling patrol chief, and since then, the faces of the officers on the streets had changed. They weren't all kanshu now, they were Shorelings, too, and though it didn't stop all the violence, it helped that la limpieza was gone.

"Marin, you'll miss your train if you don't leave soon."

Brows pinched, she pulled the strap of her bag over her head.

He stood, and when he beamed and rested his hands on her shoulders, she felt something loosen in her chest.

"You will be a fine doctor," he said.

"I have a long way to go before then." It was true. Through night classes and the help of a public education bill, she'd been accepted to a school on the northern coast, one with a refugee program where she could attend college classes as soon as she tested into them. They partnered with the same medical school Hiro had attended.

It would take a lot of work, but one day she would return a doctor.

"I'm very *orgulloso*," he said. "Very, very proud."

She turned before he could see the way her eyes turned glassy with tears. Maybe it was a lie, but she told herself her father would have said the same thing.

"Ah, Vancouver," he said. "I hope you enjoy the nature preserve. It was my favorite place to think."

She narrowed her eyes, but a shiver of nerves worked through her chest. It had been a long time since she'd seen Ross Torres, but somehow the feelings she'd had for him had grown stronger, solidified in her bones, a permanent part of her body.

"You've been going through my stuff," she said.

"Well," he said with a guilty shrug. "It *is* a wonderful place."

Rolling her eyes, she kissed Hiro on the cheek, and said goodbye.

One week later, Marin stood outside the twisting silver trellis marking the entrance to the nature preservation. It was on the eastern side of Vancouver, away from the waterfront and her school, and it had taken half a day to get there by train.

The first week of classes had been easier than she'd suspected—Hiro had prepared her well—but she still had homework. She'd tried to do it on the trip, but she found herself reading the same lines over and over again, able to focus on nothing but the beating wings of the butterflies in her stomach.

For several minutes she waited, wondering if Ross was near. It occurred to her then that they'd never set a time to meet. He'd never even said he would come. This could have been just a gift for her, with no intent to reconnect.

Disappointed, she fixed her long curls over the tattoo on her neck, presented her ticket to the clerk, and edged past the crowds. Vancouver was smaller than Noram, but you wouldn't have been able to tell inside the preservation walls. People were packed in, bumping into each other as they talked or chased after children. They gathered around a glass enclosure, filled with water—a marine exhibit of some kind. Marin couldn't see anything around the people in front of her, but from the sounds of it, the lionfish wasn't a giant cat with gills, it was just a pretty fish.

She searched every face, but there was no sign of Ross.

Finally, she got past the throng of people oohing and ahhing over the mystical lionfish, and found the stone path before her much clearer. It cut between trees—real trees, she realized as she touched the leaves of a low-hanging branch and found them soft and supple. Plaques embedded in the ground beside each trunk detailed the name of each. *White ash (Fraxinus americana)* and *Paper birch (Betula papyrifera).* Those that followed held fruit. Oranges and lemons.

The breeze ruffled the hem of her flowing top, and she smoothed it down over her flat belly, feeling, as always, the scar on the right side of her ribs. It had been a long time since she'd thought of the night she'd gotten it, but when she did now, it didn't hurt like it once had. The past stayed in the past, a stone in her foundation, nothing more.

Not all things stayed behind her, though. More than one night she'd stared out her window, and let her mind drift back to the sea, and her patchwork boat, and the broad-shouldered boy who'd made her skin grow thin with the way he'd looked at her, and her hands warm when he'd held them.

The trees cleared and gave way to another exhibit, where an animal like a horse with black and white stripes grazed from a bucket of hay in the center of a dirt paddock.

She blinked. And rubbed her eyes.

"Zebra," she read aloud from the description on the sign against the enclosure's fence. She laughed so hard at how absurd the animal looked, the people on the other side of the exhibit lifted their chins to stare at her.

She thought of the night Ross and she had seen a whale, and missed him even more.

Moving to the next exhibit, she found an African elephant, and then an animal she'd thought was extinct—a long-necked, horselike animal called a "giraffe."

Laughing, she moved from exhibit to exhibit, jogging to get to the next section as fast as she could. Finally, she came to an oval-shaped pen, covered with a thin black web of netting. It was easy enough to see through, and when she came closer, her heart stuttered at the sight before her.

Two large birds stood on rocks beside a small watering hole. Their faces were black as oil, their necks a shimmering blue like the water in her dreams. Long tails stretched out behind them, draping over the rocks like a cloak, a mirage of silky green and gold and blue.

She moved closer to the fence, mesmerized, feeling her throat grow tight. Her fingers traced over the letters on the sign. INDIAN PEACOCK.

"I've waited a long time to see you," she said out loud.

"I was going to say the same thing."

She turned sharply, finding someone sitting on a bench behind her. In her rush, she hadn't seen him, but now she wondered how that was even possible. He was not subtle, his presence not quiet. He was the kind of person people noticed; long-legged, and wide across the chest, with a mess of dark curls that hung over the tips of his ears, and eyes as brilliant blue as the feathers of the birds behind her.

She went absolutely still, the world around them falling out of focus as he unfolded himself from the bench and strode toward her. Her heart struck her ribs with hard, bruising strokes.

This moment had played out a hundred different ways in her mind, and as much as she'd longed to see him again, she'd known it would hurt too. He had woven himself into the fibers of her history, linked to the girl she used to be, the one she'd forced herself to let go. When he appeared, so did the corsario she'd once been.

"You're here," she said, a little breathlessly.

He smirked down at his feet.

"I live in the city now."

She was reminded how much she'd had to tilt her head to look up at him, and how deep the dimple was in his cheek when he smiled. His skin was darker than it had been when they'd first met. Bronzed, like he'd built a slow tolerance to the sun.

He rolled his shoulders back, hands resting in the strap of his bag that crossed his chest. He was bigger than he'd been before, more defined, and she found herself staring at the cut lines of his forearms, and the swell of muscle in his biceps that peeked out beneath the sleeves of his shirt. It was hot out, and his neck was covered with a thin sheen of sweat.

She'd forgotten what he'd said until he added, "It took a while to find you. I came by a few times." He smashed his lips to one side. "Hiro is very protective. He said if you wanted to find me, you would."

She wasn't sure if she was more happy or shocked, but looking up at him, she felt the lines between the pirate and the girl she'd become blur. He'd been thinking of her while she'd been thinking of him.

"I heard about everything with the Eighty-Six," he said. "That's incredible."

Her cheeks stretched with the smile. After the people from

Careytown had been brought to the mainland, she'd found herself as a bridge between the terrenos and the corsarios—an ambassador of sorts, explaining to the government workers in the old hospital that pirates couldn't be expected to live in interior apartments, that they needed a view of the sky or else they'd go crazy, and that they worked best with clear leadership as they had for captains. Many of them joined the other Shorelings in the oil field in the lower quadrant of the docks that President Baker had had cleared as part of his Revitalization Project, and found apartments he'd had refurnished just above the cliffline. The transition had not been easy for any of them, but they looked to her for guidance, and when her mother set the table for dinner, Marin sat at the head of it.

All at once she was overcome with the need to tell him *everything* she'd done in the last ten months. How she'd started taking classes, and working as Hiro's assistant. What it had felt like the first time she'd set a broken leg and the boy she'd worked on had thanked her. How she was here, going to school to become a doctor.

She wanted him to know the woman she'd become, in part, because of him.

But before she could start, he reached into his bag, and pulled out an orange, and the words were replaced by laughter.

"If that's not for me, you'd better hide it before I rip it from your hands, terreno."

She paused at the name, glancing up to make sure it was still okay after all this time.

But he was beaming, and when he placed it in her hand, a smooth, orange globe, she bit her lip in anticipation.

"Wait. You live here?" It had comforted her in Hiro's shop, thinking of him just a few miles away.

It struck her now that *she* lived here too.

"I do," he said. "My mom and I moved here after . . . well, after everything."

His words took her back to Hiro's, just days after she'd said goodbye to Ross, when the news had broadcasted images of Pacifica as it had appeared in the relocation ads, side by side with what looked like satellite pictures of her island. She'd recognized the gomi fields, and the port, and yet couldn't even differentiate between the trash and the houses that lined the streets of Careytown.

Pacifica: NOT REAL, the headlines had read. But it had been real. It had been home.

"It was meant with the purest intent," President Torres had said in a press conference. He'd looked like he'd spent the last month living in a holding cell at the bottom of a ship, so much worse off than when she'd seen him at the harbor. *"I am deeply shocked and saddened by the reality of this matter. I can only say that I am grateful for our vice president, Noah Baker, and his diligent efforts to uncover the truth before it was too late."*

Ross had stood behind him, nearly out of the picture. His suit was clean and pressed, his hair trimmed. But the sun had not faded from his skin, nor had the depth from his eyes, and that made her proud even while she'd hurt for him.

The elder Torres had apologized for the work of Roan Teller, someone he had placed in charge of the government's safety division. He declined to comment more on the Pacifica scandal, but assured that reparations would be made to those who had suffered, including the descendants of the Original 86. Then he resigned, and agreed to a public inquiry on his role in the matter—one that was still going on, the last she'd heard.

That night, the riots were replaced by a candlelight vigil. It was the first night no one was hurt or arrested. She'd gone to the roof of Hiro's building and stayed there until dawn, staring at the haze that blocked the cliffline, wishing Ross knew she was still with him even if they weren't in the same place.

The next morning Noah Baker had been sworn into office, and his first course of action was to sign a peace treaty with the SAF. They would begin to trade soon, fuel for food, and though this was met with resistance from those above the cliffline, she believed him when he said that in this desperate time, they had no choice but to think on a global scale.

"Adam and I are working with a refugee program," Ross said. "Interning, anyway. He's in the Noram branch, I'm here." He looked like he wanted to tell her more about it, but was uncertain. "I have a boat. There's a pier on the south side of the harbor where I keep it docked. It's not much, but if you ever want to go out on it . . ." He was talking fast. "I don't even know how long you're in town."

"*You* have a boat?"

He smirked at the ground. "That's right."

"What kind? I bet it's a yacht, isn't it. Something with big plush seats and a padded wheel."

"No." He shook his head. "I built it myself with scraps from the marina. It barely floats." He laughed.

She stood on her tiptoes, grabbed his collar, and pulled him down to her. She hadn't done anything so reckless or wild in a long time, but when his lips crushed against hers, she didn't think about whether it was the wrong thing to do. She thought of the salt in the breeze, and the wind in their hair, and his gentle mouth, curling into a smile.

His hands came around her waist, and pulled her close, and she closed her eyes, feeling strong and important. The months between them melted away, and, with them, the burden that he was the son of the president, and she was a lowly pirate.

They were not so different now. Maybe they never had been. Pulling back, she braced herself against his chest.

"I demand to see your barely floating ship," she said, but before he could answer, she kissed him again, and again, and one more time, just because she could.

ACKNOWLEDGMENTS

I'M NOT going to lie, this was a difficult story. From the moment it was conceived, I knew it would hit close to home, and it did, every step of the way. From incorporating my great-grandmother's internment in WWII, to the loss of my grandma during revisions, I was constantly torn between inspiration and loss, imagination and grief. I wanted to write the kind of story that empowered, that helped me process all the things we face each day while honoring my history, and as I learned, that's an incredibly challenging task. I hope I have served my family and my characters well.

Because this was such a big book in many ways, I have many people to thank. First, my family, who shared this great big history with me, and encouraged me to sort through it in my own way. My mom, who taught me from a young age what it means to be a Japanese-American woman, and my dad, who taught me to be brave like Ross and Marin. My great-grandmother, who lived through things I will never fully understand, and my grandma, who was kind and wonderful, and who I miss very much.

A very special thank-you to Rahul Madhusudanan with Trash-Free Waters at the U.S. Environmental Protection Agency for his thoughtful discussions about the future of our world, the state of the ocean, and the melting of the polar ice caps. Thank you also to Elizabeth and Steve for every article you sent on the Pacific Gyre, and the trash accumulation there, and for basically just being the best family ever.

Thank you to Luke Murdock for your help with the Spanish in this book, and to Nobuko and Krutula for double-checking my Japanese. I am grateful for your time and responses!

I owe a great debt of gratitude to Carrie Greene and Terry Holcombe of Tampa, Florida, for giving me a crash course on sailing—it is SO much harder than I could have imagined! Thank you for teaching me the language, letting me take a zillion pictures, and putting up with my questions about pirates and what exactly has to happen for a boat to capsize. (I see now how these things are bad luck to bring up while on an actual sailing vessel.)

Thank you, as always, to my agent, Joanna, for pushing through with me on this one (you are the best), and my editor, Melissa Frain, who, as always, makes me a better, more thoughtful writer. To Amy Stapp, who is the best editorial assistant ever; Alexis Saarela and Wiley Saichek, who are publicists of the century; Seth Lerner, who always gives me the best covers; Chris Gibbs—my stories are always honored to host your artwork; and of course, Kathleen Doherty, the publisher at Tor, who makes it possible for me to do the things I love.

Thank you to Katie McGarry, who always reads my work early and knows just what to say to get me back on track when I'm stuck, and Sara Raasch, who helped me plot myself back from the gates of Mordor. To Mindee Arnett and Kendare Blake, who are the best cheerleaders; Rachel Strolle for knowing everything YA;

Caitlin Fletcher and Cori Smith, who are amazing booksellers; and Meg, Kass, Jaime, and Erin, who I now carry around in my head, hoping they giggle (and okay, cry sometimes, too) at the words I put down.

A special thank-you to the aforementioned Erin Arkin, as well as Emily Roycroft-Stone and Amber Hendricks, who have supported my books for a long time, and who were particularly excellent in helping me spread the word about *Metaltown*. You guys. I tell ya. You're the best.

And finally, thank you to my boys. Jason and Ren, you make this world better, and not just for me. I love you.